SLITHER

Melody Steiner

DMP

SL|THER

Melody Steiner

I dedicate this book to my daughters, my mother, and my sisters. Strong individuals, each, who daily teach me what it means to be a woman. Also to Ryan Steiner, who (fortunately) didn't have to imprison me on a dragon island to get and keep my attention.

A special thank you to my writing and critiquing friends, Sonja Hutchinson and Erin Fitzgerald, for your thoughts and feedback on the book.

ONE

R<small>AT</small>

MUUTH SWEARS THERE ARE still peckerheads living in Trana who believe the dragons disappeared after the stone soldiers came alive and conquered them. They see the distant, silvery forms slash the azure sky and say, "Look at those birds!" They find molten patches of scorched farmland and, frowning, think to themselves, *The sun is merciless, and the straw caught flame.* They see the tiny speck of our emerald island from their ships across the crystal sea, study archaic maps, and decide the red skull icon means the water is poisonous or the plants have teeth and will bite. They will never see the dragons, even if the fat beasts squat on their beloved ships.

I can't afford such a delusion. For me, dragons are as real as the prison they've locked me in: an icy black mountain in the center of the wild, malevolent Onyx Island. My home isn't remarkable, even by the grand standard of dragons. Brown rags hang over the entrance and provide coveted privacy. The room boasts little more than a brass chamber pot in a corner, a hole dug in the ground for hot embers, a clay bowl, an ivory comb, and a doll.

Twelve years ago, the worst of them snatched me in his steel talons and hid me away like a useless bit of gold. I was only nine winters old. My parents, murdered that day, called me Elanor. I was Elanor Landis, the daughter of a farmer who lived on the outskirts of Foghum City. Now, at twenty-one years of age, I'm "Rat," slave to the dragons.

From my perch on the side of the great mountain, I can see the ship. It floats like gossamer on the seafoam horizon.

However, the sight doesn't quicken my blood the way it used to. I pause and study the billowing sails on my way back to my room. The ship won't dock here, even if I send a smoke signal. If I want an end to my imprisonment to the dragons, I will have to do it myself. The ships do not carry heroes. *I* am my only savior.

On quiet days like today, I spend free moments tucked in my room, scratching chalk impressions on the wall. Adom is the only dragon who could fit into my hovel, and he doesn't bother me here. Still, I keep a strip of gray linen over the drawings. If anyone ever looked closely at them, they'd see violent plans unfolding, growing more organized by the day. Better safe than a scorch mark on the floor.

Light from a wax candle sputters, and a bent, spidery body creeps into view. "Fine day for killing dragons." Muuth rubs a bony hand over a hairless, pointed head.

I let the curtain drop over my drawings and transfer powder from my hands onto my sleeves. Muuth knows my secret thoughts and plots—he's the only one I trust. "Have you eaten yet, old man, or do you want me to cut up a nectarine from my stash?"

"Does earwax count?"

My mouth curves, and I am at once amused and a little concerned. I've caught him eating earwax once, so it isn't out of the realm of possibility. "I'll go get that nectarine." After I give him the fruit, help him settle on the straw pallet and ask, "What's the vile one up to?"

Muuth cranes his neck to meet my gaze. His joints pop, the sound echoes along the sides of my cold little home. "Adom is leaving, judging by the way the females fawn over him. I suppose he's headed for Trana again. He's developed a fondness for it, I think."

I suck in stale air. He always chooses Trana. Not Eppax. Not Corva. He makes mysterious trips every dozen nights, sometimes more, and returns with spoils from the raid. "If it was my country, I'd wake the stone soldiers to slay him."

"That's not how…" The old codger taps his knobby chin and sighs. "Ah. Never mind. With Adom gone, chances of escape are better."

I note the patchy spots on his beard. He's at least a hundred winters now. And yet, despite a deteriorating body and mind, Muuth can hoist great brass vats of dragon food and not flinch. He can push a boulder for a mile up a mountain. But he can't live forever.

"If I escaped, where would I go?" I ask.

His wrinkled face splits into a pained smile. "Back to Trana, of course."

Sometimes I stand at the edge of the mountain: my wild, nut-colored hair tossing in all directions while I overlook the island. Ocean breezes, salty and sour, float to the mountain. When the sun lands just right across the tossing tide, I catch a hint of that familiar spicy smell: autumn leaves crackling over an open flame. Trana.

"Maybe I can knock sense into King Siles?" I say, daring to allow a speck of excitement sneak into my voice. "March right into the palace and demand an audience?"

Muuth's smile slips away. His bloodshot eyes dilate, pupils widening. He cocks his misshapen head to one side and holds a crooked finger to my gasping mouth. A moment passes, then two. He breathes. "I heard one of them passing through the windpipe cave." He waggles his head. "You should be quieter, El. They might've heard you."

My heart warms a little at his use of my nickname. Muuth won't call me Rat like the dragons do, but he doesn't call me Elanor, either. That was the name of my past. To Muuth, I'm simply "El."

"So what if they heard?" I ask. "I'm tired of cozying up to them."

The moment Muuth and I settle in for a cup of fresh-brewed peppermint tea, the walls vibrate and the sound of an immense metal gong throbs in the air around us. Muuth and I both cover our ears. The sound rattles my teeth and wobbles my bones before it subsides. When I was ten, Adom told me that if the gong ever rang, I must come immediately. He used to sound it daily, but the noise has come more infrequently because of all his trips.

At last I lower my arms.

"Does he want me deaf? Fool dragon."

"What?" Muuth still hasn't removed his hands from his ears.

"I have to go," I shout.

He nods, sheet-white.

Years before, I clung to cave walls until they became so familiar by touch I could judge distance by number of footsteps and the unique wall imprints at my fingertips. Over time, my eyes adjusted to the darkness out of necessity. My bare toes patter against the cold, uneven ground, following the familiar route to Adom's private chambers. None of the other dragons have the privilege of a private room, or a gong with which to call their favorite servant. But Adom is a changeling and according to whatever arcane logic guides the dragons it also entitles him to a certain degree of privacy.

He's a deceiver, I think as I pass through the mountain core, *who lures humans to doom.*

~ * ~

An elegant statue now stands in one corner where before were only spider webs: a nude woman holding an elegant pitcher. Three glistening broadswords stretch out across his long table, their hilts tinged with blood and ash. Where does he find such things? They aren't items he can have scrounged from a peasant's house. Farmers don't own such spoils.

It frightens me to survey the vast bounty littering Adom's room, a constant reminder of his sinister activities. He stores his collection in a cave no other dragons can access, as if he mistrusts even his own kind. A dragon's greed, as Muuth says, is his crowning glory.

I glance at my reflection in an antique mirror, pleased to present myself to the changeling Adom in such state. Scratched face, dirty arms, and ratty ankle-length mud-colored braid stare back at me. My clothes are tattered and shabby. Sometimes, Adom finds me women's clothing to wear. I almost never accept his *generous* offers.

The moving reflection behind mine catches my attention. Adom's straight hair falls loose around a pale, pointed face. Like black shadows. He watches me with unnatural, unblinking violet eyes, from a wooden chair. My heart pounds. Slowly, I pivot.

Only Adom's eyes betray amusement. Everything else about him is poised and perfect. Like a stone soldier, every hair is in place, his cream tunic falls just right, not even the wind could ever ruffle him. "Squeamish today, Rat?"

My resistance fills the silence. I'm not the first human he brought here. Once in a while, frightened children turn up. None of them survive past morning. They all disappear during the night. I don't dare ask Adom what happens to them.

As he rises in one fluid motion and covers the distance between us in two steps, I back into the corner of the cave, where silver tapestries and paintings adorn the tiled walls, images of faraway places and people I've never seen, now long gone. If Adom has their crafts, they probably met with a bloody, undeserved demise.

He lifts a band of leather. Never breaking the gaze, he ties his hair back, revealing the sharp arch of his eyebrows and powerful, broad shoulders. "How are your lessons with Muuth? Do you like the Tranar textbooks I found for you to read?"

I nod curtly, because the books are the one privilege I don't want to lose. Three winters ago, Adom suddenly announced that Muuth could teach me Tranar history if I wanted him to. I'd already learned my letters and mathematics, thanks to Muuth, but of course I jumped at the chance to study more about my homeland. Muuth said he thought Adom felt sorry for me, being so wild and ignorant about my own background. But I think it's more to torture me, to remind me of all the places I'll never go to, and the people I'll never know.

"Do you have any questions for me about the material? Anything you want to know?" His lips quirk to the right. "I've been there, remember."

There's the taunt. His generosity has a sort of perversity to it. He may think it is kind of him to leave me with wardrobes full of clothes, textbooks, even paintings. But I remember what he did to my parents. I'm keenly aware that I'm his prisoner. I turn my head and refuse to answer.

"I'm leaving tomorrow." That wry curve of his lips indicates mockery. "Come with me. Unless you don't think you're ready to face your past?"

I snort and roll my eyes. I won't let him bait me only to see my hopes crushed again.

"I'm not teasing this time."

His steady gaze fills me with uncertainty. I often wonder if Adom's eyes possess hypnotic powers. Those eyes make me weak, make me want to trust him even when I know he can rip me in half. "Why?" Adom never let me go with him before. Not that I want to under his conditions—witnessing a scorching doesn't appeal to me.

He smiles. "Ah. So nice to hear your voice again."

My pulse returns to a normal rhythm. He's just trying to get a reaction out of me. He isn't really offering to take me back to Trana. *Or is he?*

He takes a step closer to the desk and picks up a quill, dips the end in a glass container of ink, and scribbles something I can't see onto a piece of parchment. "Ona wants to eliminate you." He doesn't look at me. "You're not as young as you used to be, and you cause more trouble these days. You know how they feel about humans. I'm worried Ona will kill you while I'm away."

Ona? The dotty old dragon with the clipped ear hasn't said two words to me in years. Why would he want to kill me now? "You? Worried about me? How kind you are." I can't resist a little dig. "If only all Tranars were so lucky."

A frown deepens on Adom's face. Every time I mention his murderous proclivities, he looks this way. "On this journey I have no plans of..." he waves a dismissive hand, "that sort. If that is your concern."

That sort? As if the fiery destruction of a country is as light as a walk in the forest. My fingers tingle standing so close to those shiny new broadswords. How satisfying would it be to thrust one into his midsection? How good would it feel to see the look of surprise?

"What are your plans?" I try, but he shakes his head. Sullenly, I say, "I don't trust you."

The frown slips away. His eyes, ever flickering, glow like diamonds. "Good. Then you'll have a fighting chance in Trana." Nodding at an inner thought that seems to please him, he leans in. "I want you to see your home."

Somehow, I manage not to pull away. "Why not Muuth?"

He considers a thought for a moment, "And I don't want to find you dead when I return. Aren't those satisfactory reasons? Think of it as an opportunity to show me what Muuth is teaching you. I'm keen to test your knowledge."

Tell me why you really want me with you.

Out loud, I ask, "Do I have a choice?"

His eyes, fixated on my hair, seem to grow softer. "If you wish to remain here and die then, yes, you have a choice. Do as I ask, however, and you will live."

Why the cryptic responses? And why in the world should I do as he says if I don't trust him? Didn't he just applaud my distrust? Now he expects loyalty?

Adom's face becomes a granite slab. When he speaks, his voice affects the bored edginess of an aristocrat. "Silva's also angry with you," he says with indifference. "You're neglecting the younglings."

I don't bother to tell him I stopped cleaning their cave a week ago. I'm certain he already knows. "Maybe Silva should spend more time with them herself." Why mask my feelings now when I know exactly what will come next? He'll punish me by making me climb the hazardous part of the mountain to find roots at the top. Or I'll have to run barefoot in the piranha pit. Or he'll order the young dragons to chase me through the ever-changing forest for sport.

"Where does this negativity come from?" he asks. "You were such a happy child once. You even used to like me a little. What happened?"

"I realized my life wasn't worth faking niceties to the man who murdered my parents." My panic subsides and cold resignation sets in. "What are you playing at?" I say through a sigh.

"Forgive me," he says. "But when I say the word, you really should scream."

That's all the warning I need. If Adom wants me to scream, he wants the others to think he's hurting me. He wants to send fear shuddering down their monstrous, twisted spines, to dry their mouths and shrivel the pits of their cavernous stomachs. He wants to show them that *he* is the king, the master of this mountain, the master of *me*.

Adom averts his gaze. "Scream."

In the seconds it takes him to morph from human to dragon, his chest expanding, scales popping out of his skin like boils, I'm already at the door. I scream, just as he asks me to.

The full blast of flame doesn't hit me, but it's enough heat to sting my lower back. Good thing I tied my hair this morning—he misses singeing it off by a few inches. The monstrous roar he releases bursts a decanter on the table. The mirror cracks. But the fire inside me has nothing to do with Adom's monster, and everything to do with my own. Only mine burns for revenge.

~ * ~

I lay on a pallet in Muuth's spacious cave, his own "laboratory." Unlike my sparsely furnished room, homey effects litter every spare inch of his cave. "Damn that dragon."

"At least he didn't really hurt you," says Muuth. Then he lowers his eyes.

"Are you siding with him?" I ask, propping myself up by an elbow.

"No." Muuth coughs. "Never. He's still your captor and a fire breathing beast."

Then he focuses his attention on connecting two wheels in a wooden box using a nail and a mallet. In spite of his dementia, Muuth can whittle clever gadgets to provide us with hours of entertainment. Once, he created pipes and stuffed them with leaves to smoke. He made a lantern of four stone slabs fastened to the cave wall. In the corner is a chair made from tree branches, a burlap sack, and sheep's wool. Seashells; daggers made of wood and stone; and small, colorful glass beads all sit cozily on a shelf affixed to the wall. He even built a loft in a high crevice using flat planks of driftwood, where he keeps useful things he discovers on the beach. Netting. Glass. Things that wash ashore from distant shipwrecks.

None of his weapons or inventions could kill a dragon, though. Muuth has already tried everything, and all he gained from his efforts was a gauged out eye and a burn across the back.

Along the adjacent wall, a repurposed tree trunk displays Muuth's most prized things, things he couldn't have found along the beach, the things he must have had with him when he first arrived here as an unfortunate explorer. A wooden sphere with lines and numbers and a map of lands carved into it, on a spinning axel and surrounded by metal rings. Several beakers of colorful liquid that sometimes bubbled and burped and changed colors inexplicably. A large, oak, conical tube about eight feet in length mounted to a platform with wheels. While he sometimes took the latter outside and peered through an eyehole at the night sky, he never let me handle the device. He calls it a *telescope*.

I wince. "Why doesn't he ever pick on you?"

"I'm so old he's afraid I'll die." He wheezes with laughter. Then his smile sags. "And they can't afford to kill me. Not yet, at least."

Ona wants to kill me. Silva burns with rage because she thinks I'm neglecting the younglings. If Adom hadn't roughed me up, Ona might think he'd grown soft. And a soft dragon is akin to mold on a cave wall to the dragon herd. Worse than useless. A nuisance. According to Muuth, before Adom overtook the others in a battle of strength, Ona was the herd leader. It's Adom's ability to inspire fear in the rest that keep them all in line.

My position in this fragile ecosystem isn't secure. It's an odd paradox. The dragons need slaves like Muuth and I. We cook and clean, affording them a certain luxury. Yet I'll forever be haunted by the lullaby of my first nights here, the screams of others like me who didn't please their masters quickly enough. Child slaves howling in the night.

Gingerly pushing myself off the ground, I half turn to a sitting position and give my friend a long, thoughtful look.

"What are you thinking, child?" he asks.

Deep wrinkles on his withered face remind me of the bark of an ancient elm tree. Muuth taught me how to survive both in this world and in the world outside. He taught me how to read, taught me arithmetic, and how to please the dragons. I love him dearly for all he's done for me. So I can't help but feel a twinge of guilt when I say, "Adom asked me to go with him."

His eyes dim and Muuth picks up a stick from the ground and draws a deep line in the sand. There is a heaviness between us for a moment while he digests the news. "Well?"

I swallow, hard. "Do you think I'll pass it up?" I sniff. "Maybe I won't come back."

His face grows thoughtful. "I hope you don't, lass." Then he drops the stick, rubs his face, and makes a small sighing sound. "We'd best stop dawdling. You'll be asking for another taste of fire-breath if the food's not ready by suppertime." He pats my head.

"Maybe I could poison them tonight?" I suggest, as he hoists me up.

Muuth strokes the pockmarks on his leathery skin, dimpled bits of extra flesh that remind me of the fungus growing along an old tree trunk. "There's only one poison that can kill a dragon. You're lucky if you never hear it mentioned again."

I flash him my best conspiratorial look. "Don't keep it from me."

"Sun's acid." His gray gum houses few teeth, a spotted tongue peeking between the spaces. He cackles and points to his one bad orb. "At first, you can't even see it with a naked eye."

"Compared to a well-dressed one?" I joke.

He points to his collection of mysterious odds and ends. "Girl, before you and before this god awful place, I had a life. I had a wife, a daughter, and my inventions. The dragons lived among us, infiltrating us, and there were more like *him* who..." he spat, and continued. "Then one day I saw it, sun's acid." He looks far away, like he had opened his mind and peered directly into the past. "And I don't like to think about what came after. The acid fell, a cloud of black that came from the sun and blotted out the whole valley. The soldiers turned to stone. Most of the dragons on that battlefield perished."

This is a story I've never heard before. "Can you make it?"

"No, I can't make it." His voice comes out snappy and

annoyed. "It comes from the sun."

Why does he look so cross? "But you said you couldn't see it with just your eye. How did you find out about it? Was it in your laboratory?"

His forehead crinkles. "I was in my laboratory, tinkering with one of my devices." His eyes stray to the telescope. "I saw the black dots on the sun. Didn't know what it was then. Not three days later, the acid fell."

"And it summoned the stone soldiers?"

"Now you're just hurting my head," Muuth groans. "I'm a scientist, El. Not a magician."

I recall my studies. "But the history textbooks say a witch summoned the stone soldiers, and that they battled the dragons and killed them all. Maybe she summoned the sun's acid?"

"Don't believe everything you read in those books," Muuth grumbles.

Sun's acid, I repeat to myself. It'd be nice to be able to forecast the end of a few dragons.

Adjusting the front of my tunic, I follow him to the cave where we keep the animals. Inside, great masses of emaciated sheep, cows, and pigs pack the area, secured by wooden fences and ropes wrapped with thorny vines to keep the animals inside. We check each stall to make sure there is plenty of water and food for the creatures. Muuth cleans the stalls and feeds the animals each morning, so there isn't much work to do now.

We open the gates and allow twenty grungy sheep to waddle out of the encampment. Muuth opens another gate so two of the cows wander out with affected dignity. Then six wiry pigs join our motley, macabre crew. We lead the creatures, eager for freedom, to a space in the cave meant for butchering and hanging the meat. There is ice from the top of a mountain lake packed along the walls, and a stream of water not far from here for washing up after the deed is done.

I shiver, but it isn't the cold that unsettles me. Animals bleat and squeal. Muuth unhooks the tarnished cleavers from the wall. He hands one to me. We make fast work of it, expertly slitting throats and skinning the animals. Muuth has a special invention that speeds the work, pulling the meat from the bones and sinew by turning a crank with a wooden wheel.

I'm good at this. Muuth and I function smoothly, like the clock Muuth put together using dozens of carved wooden pieces made to fit exactly. Everywhere I look, there is blood in frosty piles, magnified by ice blocks. I can smell it in the air. My fingers and arms are coated in it. And yet, it doesn't frighten or faze me. The dragons made me a butcher, like them, and like them I don't even think twice about it when I kill. It has become almost second nature to me.

Ona used to watch us work. As a child, I always vomited afterward, and he used to rumble with glee as he heard me retch. Someday, I'll take the cleavers and cut through Ona's neck flesh, and then show him the same courtesy he shows me as he gags on his own black blood.

~ * ~

Hours later, in another cave with an open view of the forest, I stir stew over a cauldron while Muuth pours more water into the bubbling broth. It's a sign of prestige in the herd to consume meaty stews and roasted chops. The others envy the herd leaders for the luxury of having food brought to them. The rest hunt on their own, capable of finding meals to scorch. The island has a host of wildlife: fish, birds, and beasts in the forest. We have wild cattle and horses that graze on the other side of the mountain. Occasionally, the dragons will leave the island to hunt, but it is only under Adom's direction. They avoid cities and places where wealthy Tranars live. No one listens to simple farmers and peasants, so they can plunder with discretion on those lands. And if they're seen, one blast of fire takes care of the witnesses.

The gong rings. *Dinnertime.* I wipe condensation from my brow.

Muuth steers the wagon to me. Seven horses pull it. He helps me hoist one of the cauldrons off the ground. We carry it to the wagon. Ten more cauldrons follow, each one heavier than the last. This routine, at least, has made me strong.

I hop onto the front of the wagon while Muuth steers the horses to the central cave. Dragons eat, sleep, reproduce, and give birth there. They use it as their conference hall, the only place large enough to support all eighty-five of them. The open roof of the mountain provides ample sunlight and a convenient exit. As the wagon creaks into the cave, horse hooves clicking against the stone path, dragons watch us with green and gold eyes.

Muuth pulls back on the horses' reins, and the wagon slows to a stop. Sharp talons scratch against the ground. Other dragons breathe more heavily, sucking in the scent of the food with massive nostrils. Ignoring the sounds, I spring off the wagon and move to the back. Muuth rolls out of the driver's seat and shuffles to my aide. We maneuver the first cauldron, careful to touch only the wooden handles and to cover our hands with the gloves Muuth made for us.

We serve Adom first. He glares at me silently in his dragon form, flecks of violet glowing in his eyes. I hope his cauldron is the one I spat in.

"Over here," Ona rasps in dragon tongue. He points his claw down. Speckled brown, yellow, and red, Ona's scales seem to match his impetuous and unpredictable personality. I can't find a pattern in his scaly form, almost as if he'd found a vat of colored paints and splashed them on his body with no regard for aesthetics. He has a lean tusk that protrudes from one side of his mouth, but nothing on the other. His tail is deformed at the end, twisted into a stump the size of the trunk of an elm tree.

Muuth and I struggle to roll the cauldron to him. I recall

what Adom said earlier. Ona wants to kill me. I take careful pains not to spill his food. His clipped ear twitches.

After Ona, we lay cauldrons by the four breeding dragon females. They're the fattest of the herd, and I can tell them apart by their varying shades of gray. They are unremarkable except for their considerable girth. They can barely fly, and almost never leave the mountain.

Next we dole out cauldrons to three other males. Two of them, Neller and Greego, have wings that also function as fins. They often skulk in the water around the island and emerge for meals in the mountain as it suits them. Neller is a sea green with a lovely comb on the top of his head that looks like kelp. Greego is sandy white, and the scales on his broadside glisten like diamonds. They both can travel deep to the bottom of the ocean floor, and sometimes they do not emerge for days or even weeks. Muuth tells me that even sailors from Trana recognize the existence of sea monsters, and their maps contain dire warnings about which parts of the ocean to avoid in order to keep from meeting a horrible, watery, serpentine fate.

Canna and Nerama, the youngest of the dragon leaders, come after the first eight. Canna isn't a breeder yet, but she soon will be.

The dragons ignore us while they slurp their meal. They converse in the clucking dragon tongue I've come to comprehend. It isn't a fluid sound, but scratchy and guttural.

Dragons of lesser status occasionally meander into the central cave to sniff the cauldrons of the dragon leaders. The rest of the herd can come and go through the central cave as they please, but they are not welcome to partake of the food or participate in the conversation.

"You could slit their bellies when they collapse from overeating," suggests Muuth while we sit in the shadow of the hulking beasts and wait for them to finish their food.

I struggle to maintain a straight face. "Only if you roll over their claws with the wagon."

He scratches a bald spot. "I've got the cleavers."

Our dark jokes give us fragments of levity in an otherwise pallid life, but there's real longing behind the banter. Freedom. I haven't tasted it since I was nine. Only glimpses here and there, when running from the mountain. When was Muuth's last free moment?

Then Silva's words catch my ear. "I think they're talking about me."

Muuth shrugs. "She's complaining you haven't cleaned the younglings' cave." I'm used to Muuth translating for me even though I can understand most of what they say by now.

My back burns, sensitive from this morning's treatment.

As if he can read my thoughts, Adom speaks up in lilting dragon tongue.

Muuth leans in. "If he catches you neglecting the younglings again, he'll kill you."

Adom said earlier that he wants me to survive. That he plans to take me away from Onyx Island tomorrow. Then again, Adom always tells half-truths. My stomach sinks. He'll kill me, someday. Even though he dangles Trana in front of me, I'll never let my guard down.

Let him try. He'll fail, and I'll kill him, instead. I won't suffer my parents' fate.

TWO

THE GONG JOLTS ME awake. Bounding out of a bed of dry, crackly leaves, I scramble for last minute artifacts to fill a partially packed, moth-eaten bag. I pick up a lopsided candle, a small bit of frayed rope, and an ivory comb I stole from Adom several years back. I also pack the leather water skin Muuth made for my name day.

With the satchel ready, I dart through the caves. Interminable blackness hardly inhibits my flight. I round several corners and hop a couple of dangerous pitfalls, and yet my calloused feet know the path so well I run it by memory. My heels thud against the ground.

Adom waits for me in his private quarters, wearing only a black robe tied securely with a velvet waistband. "Leave the satchel," he orders, tapping his foot in increased agitation. He glances over his shoulder as if he expects to find someone there at any moment.

I rock back and dig my heels into the ground. "I need it."

He pulls the leather bag from my hands. "What's in it?"

"Why do you want to know?" My cheeks warm when he pulls out Fifi.

"What *is* this?" He holds Fifi out with his thumb and index finger, eyes glittering. He stares, this time with an open expression of disapproval, like he questions my state of mind.

"My doll," I whisper. My body braces for a fight. I cradled Fifi in trembling arms the day my parents died. The day he took them. She's not a very pretty doll, missing half her hair, one eye permanently closed, and with a crack between her brows where I dropped her once.

A perplexed crease deepens on his forehead. He scowls at the porcelain moppet with such fierce confusion I worry he'll drop it. My stomach sinks. He doesn't remember.

"Why do you have a doll?"

"It's all I have left." Even though I will myself not to reveal emotion, my voice cracks as I speak. I hate showing weakness, especially to Adom.

The answer seems to shock him to silence. He swallows and stares at the doll's cracked face, dirty clothes, and bald head. He can crush her in one swift motion with his fingers, and she'd be nothing more than fine, white powder gathering at his boot-clad feet. Sick with the fear of losing my most prized possession, my heart thuds heavily with dread.

He roughly pushes Fifi back into the satchel and thrusts the worn bag at me. "Take it with you, then. But don't let anyone see it. It could threaten our mission."

How could a chipped bit of porcelain in a worn rag dress endanger a dragon? I'm numb at his inexplicable mercy, but not too euphoric that I fail to take in what he just revealed. A mission?

"Come with me," Adom instructs, his voice gruff. He reaches for the piece of parchment with the writing he penned last night. He folds it, melts wax, and seals the back of the paper. He blows on it until it dries, and then he tucks it into his waistband and marches out of the cave.

I follow in strained silence. There is a part of me that does not believe he'll really do this, take me with him to Trana. He said he thought it would be good for me. If that's really the reason, why hasn't he taken me before? He says Ona wants to kill me. But this isn't the first time I've fallen out of his favor. What's changed? Why does Adom want me to go with him now?

He mentioned a mission. Maybe he thinks I'll be useful. I'm not blind—I watched him write a letter even though I haven't had a chance to read it. What kind of purpose can a girl like me serve on a mission *Adom* wants to undertake? Whatever it is, it can't be a good.

I stub a toe on a rock that shouldn't be there. *Clunk*. Pain lances through my leg and settles in the spot between my eyes. Lightning makes circles across my vision.

Adom swirls in the blink of an eye and catches me before I fall.

For two seconds I am in his arms and every nerve in my body *zings* with shock and awareness and the unsettling feeling that I am not just any woman to him, not just a slave, and not just a Rat. I can't breathe beyond our close proximity, and he seems equally as startled.

"Get off me, Snake."

He pulls away and resumes his trek without a word. My ankle throbs, but if I expect him to ask if I am injured, I'll be waiting for the rest of my life. Adom clears his throat. The sound tosses me back into the real world where he is a creature of the earth, and I am El. Why did he bother to sully his hands catching a clumsy slave?

As soon as the question comes, the breathlessness disintegrates. He's a monster, I'm his prisoner, he killed my parents, and someday I'll kill him. The world is simple, and I need only worry about placing one foot in front of the other. I breathe and push through the pain.

We approach the central cave. A few lazy beasts curl around each other, sleeping soundly. Snores rock the cavern. It vibrates my bones. The cave floor glistens with molted scales, hard as diamonds and every bit as precious. Dragons don't shed skin, like snakes and other reptiles. When they scratch, the scales pop off like dandelion heads. Muuth told me once that the scales are considered rare gems in Trana. People think they come from the ground, and yet they call these "rock formations" *dragon scales*. They whittle them, and purify them, and string them up in fancy necklaces or set them in rings.

"Stand back," Adom commands.

He doesn't raise his voice. Dragons scatter at his order. I pivot slightly so I only see him out of the corner of my eye. He disrobes and hands me the garment. I stuff it carelessly into my satchel. Then he crouches. His body swells, turning green and blue and gray. His neck stretches to grotesque proportions while his lower back flares up to accommodate the crushing weight of a hideous monster the size of a redwood tree. Harsh ridges burst from his spine in dramatic accents of blacks and grays. His skin becomes thick like limestone and scaly. Spidery wings sprout from his cracking back. His face distorts, elongates, and forms a narrow snout. A flowing mane of inky black hair pours over his shoulders, wild and full, like a river spilling over his neck.

Reptilian haunches explode from human arm and leg muscles. Teeth gleam in the smoky light. It all reminds me of the first time we met, when I thought he was one of us: a naked, lone human wandering the scorched fields in search of survivors. Like me. What a fool.

In the seconds it takes him to *change*, my hands move almost without permission, and I grab hold of three nearby dragon scales piled on a stalagmite. They are the size of seashells, but polished and heavy, like marble, and perfectly symmetrical. I shove them into the satchel.

When I look up again, I peer into glittering green and violet gemstones—Adom's eyes—watching me keenly. His long neck bends until hot breath tickles my face as he says in dragon tongue, "Get on."

My feet move quickly, toes catching a groove in his scaly neck and using the horns and ridges to propel myself forward. My bare feet are adept at grappling with the slick scales, and I take advantage of friction and balance to clamber up his back. Once I reach the broadest spot between his neck and shoulders, I split my legs, collapse against his twitching body, and cling tight to his mane and neck. It's been a long time since I last left the mountain. On occasion, one of the other dragons takes me out for fresh sky because I'm becoming wilder and smellier than Muuth. But not Adom. Not since the first time.

"My parents are gone. Who will watch over me?"

"I will."

"You will?"

"But you'll come to hate me for it."

Adom was right. I do hate him. He tricked me in the worst way, took advantage of my innocence and trust. He did not try to make it right, after. He never apologized. I have no memories of kindness, of humanity, from him. He's a blank, cold slab of emotionless granite.

This is the closest we have been to one another, physically, since that time. If I'd grabbed a knife from his room, I could take it out of the satchel and plunge it into his neck. But he checked the satchel. Now I have the scales, which, if Muuth's words count for anything, could prove useful as long as I survive the trip to Trana.

Adom takes one great leap and settles on the yawning summit. His tail totters over the edge of the gaping hole. Below, the central cave looks like a black pit. I lean closer, squeezing legs around his neck, wrapping fingers and wrists around the loose folds of his mane. If I fall now, I'll tumble into the farthest recesses of the mountain.

His wings expand. *Whoosh.* Sound batters my eardrums. The ascent sends my head spinning out of control, and I lose all sense of direction. The next leap causes us to spiral out to the base of the mountain. My weight pitches forward, only stopped from rolling off and slamming into the tree growth ahead of us by the vertical angle of his neck. My stomach shoots to my throat, and I have the strongest urge to vomit. The ascent is always the worst part for me.

Sunlight burns the top of my head while cool wind beats against my body.

I lived in that hole for twelve years.

Adom's wings open, broad webs of silver as fine as any art a spider could craft, and we soar through the sky. The forest blossoms in the showy beauty of spring.

Acres of green and brown cover the island, a land fertile with life. Now the beach stretches out below us, a long white line snaking the forest and the mountain. Adom roars the sound thunder makes, and I hear the echoing response of the herd where they lie, indistinguishable from the rocks, along the shoreline. We sail over the deep blue expanse. I cling to Adom, unease replacing my fascination.

Vibrant blue-green color invades my vision. From this distance, I see the spray of foamy sea waves and massive creatures moving along the shadowy depths. Maybe it is Neller and Greego traveling deep below the waves.

A huge creature emerges, flat tail shooting sprays in our direction. It spurts a stream of water, and Adom dips lower, so that we are flying perpendicular to it. I have a moment of terror as he tilts sideways and I feel myself slipping, certain I will fall into the deep only feet away from the creature's massive mouth. "Adom…" I start, then bite my lower lip. I'm off balance, my body sliding forward. I cling to Adom's neck and my legs lock together at the ankles. For one exhilarating second, the hungry eye of the creature follows me before it dives, swimming away.

Adom's body rights itself. We sail upward and alongside a flock of birds. Adom roars a gentle rumble, sending the flock off in every direction. He slides into a cloud, and my eyes perceive nothing but fog. Adom's scales dampen, slick as a fish, and my skin slips against them.

Then he is gone from under me, and my body is weightless for one breath. My heart shoots to my throat. I drop, scream, and he is beneath me again, his wings sweeping over me like a protective casing. "Damn you, Adom," I curse, smacking the back of his neck with my palm in one quick rap before I clutch him tight again. Beneath me, his body rumbles—he's laughing. He thinks me funny. I fume.

By the time the ocean ends and land begins, I have barely regained my ability to breathe. Adom flies lower, until we skim the tops of trees. Leaves scatter and rise around us, a blanket of colorful foliage. *Home.* He lets out a soft growl and with a rough thump he digs his claws into the ground, locking us into a secure position. My body jerks back with the force of the landing. Muscles in my shoulders and neck take the brunt of the motion and keep me from tumbling back.

"Get off," he commands in raspy dragon tongue.

I slide from his back as quickly as I'm able. The world rocks beneath me. I tumble to the ground and clutch my gut to stop the spinning sensation.

Adom shrinks into his human form, once again naked. "Land sickness."

"I know that!" With shaking hands, I pull out the black robe and toss it to him. My stomach lurches. I shut my eyes and swallow until my gorge settles. Then I crack an eye open.

Adom ties the robe together and approaches me. He bends carefully—as though his body aches, too—and touches my damp temple with cool, firm fingers. "Are you hurt?"

Both eyes are fully open now, and I stare at him with silent defiance.

Shadows obscure his face. "I didn't intend to frighten you."

"You didn't," I insist, batting his fingers away from my sweat-beaded forehead.

His eyes are serious and probing. "You screamed."

"You were showing off," I accuse. "I could have died."

He touches my shoulder lightly, as if he expects me to push him away again. "I swear you're safe when you travel me. I won't let anything happen to you, Rat. You don't need to be frightened." His legs straighten, and he extends a hand. "Do you need help standing?"

I don't need his help or his pity. I stare straight into those familiar green and violet eyes, throw back my head, and bark out a laugh. Dew trapped in the moss beneath me soaks through my backside, but I enjoy the damp because it reminds me I am alive and *this* much closer to freedom.

His concern dissipates. "Get up."

Shaking, I place my palms flat on the moist soil and push off the ground. He reaches to help me and I take a firm, deliberate step away. "How can I assist you, *master*?"

He rubs a spot between his eyebrows where there is an angry vein reacting like a cat caught in a burlap sack. "Walk three paces to the right and lift the shrubbery."

I give him an exaggerated curtsy and prance away. Underneath the brambly bushes, I find a pair of clean trousers and a snow-white tunic. The fabric sticks to long thorns as I pull the clothes away from the needling shrub. I hand the pile to him and look away.

"I don't normally bring a robe with me," he murmurs.

"Oh?" While he is dressing, I consider my escape route.

"I did so for your benefit. To make you feel more comfortable." The tunic over his head muffles his voice. Now is my chance. I should run while he's distracted.

But where can I go? From above I saw nothing but grass and trees and fields. I could be lost in this wilderness for days before I find civilization. *You want to be free, don't you?*

In a split-second decision, the muscles in my legs spring into action, almost as if they planned this all along. Then I am gone, away from the copse, away from Adom, charging through the tangled forest. I don't dare turn around for fear that he is there, right behind me.

I duck around an enormous tree and continue in a different

direction. My feet are well accustomed to an uneven landscape, to rocks and roots and squishy mud between my toes. My lungs are used to climbing at high altitudes. I'm capable of running long distances if I have to. On the island, I used to run through the forest all the way to the beach, navigating all manner of terrain. And though I lost my balance in the caves this morning, my ankle feels fine now.

A shadow blots out the sun.

My stomach jolts and my heart suspends out of time. Does he see me? Do the trees shield me from his merciless, dragon eyes? Shivers of fear trail down my spine. *Lodin's ashes, what am I doing?* Hairs rise on the back of my neck. One blast of heat, and I'm gone.

I round another tree and suddenly I am standing in another copse, exposed, completely visible to the bird-like shadow looming above. Wind presses me down, stirring up dirt and branches and pebbles. I retreat into the forest, arms shielding my face.

Adom lands in front of me, crushing saplings, blocking my path of escape. Bark splinters and cedar cracks beneath his uncompromising weight. He *changes* in seconds and grabs my shoulder with iron-tight fingers. "Don't move." Irritation coats his steely voice.

Every muscle in my body stiffens, alarmed.

He speaks again, low and threatening. "Try it again and I'll send you back to the island."

"By boat—with an armed escort?"

A muscle moves in his jaw. "Don't test me."

I keep my eyes firmly on his face, aware he isn't dressed. "I'm sorry, Adom. I won't do it again." Of course, this is a promise I fully intend to break sooner rather than later.

Heat cools in his eyes. His mouth twitches. "I expect you won't."

"Where are your clothes?"

"Ruined, thanks to your failed getaway attempt."

He needn't sound so smug about it. "You don't have a plan for everything?"

"Yes," he says with a flicker of a smile. "Come with me."

He pushes me in front of him, watching with the eyes of a hawk. I am sure he expects me to try to escape again. I'll have to lay low for a while, wait until his guard is down, and try later. At least the other dragons aren't here. If they were, I wouldn't have gotten away with merely a stern word from Adom. They would have hung me upside down from a stalactite until I saw stars, or made me catch a wild boar without a weapon, or crawl through beached jellyfish.

We walk for a short while and reemerge in yet another copse where I find a horse tied to a tree. The dappled creature doesn't start when it catches sight of us, but continues grazing peacefully. Adom whistles, and the ears of the creature respond with a twitch. Adom reaches for the satchel tied to the creature's back. He undoes the strings and pulls out another set of clothes complete with a pair of sturdy black riding boots. He changes facing me. While I keep my gaze fixed on the sky, I sense his sharp, suspicious eyes on me.

"Finished," he announces.

"That's a nice horse," I comment drily. "Who'd you steal it from?"

He grins. "Did your father ever teach you to ride?"

I jerk my head, unhappy with the reminder of my family.

"Then you'll ride behind me."

I want to ask why the horse is conveniently tied up when and where we need him, but I doubt he'll answer. "Where are you taking me, Snake?"

Adom shows perfect white teeth. "To a village." He takes hold of the horse and mounts with ease and precision. Then he holds out a hand. "Let's go, Rat."

Hesitantly, I take his hand.

He swings me onto the back of the horse. "You might need

to hold onto me."

Because I'm already beginning to slip off the broad creature's sweaty backside, I comply with a strange combination of revulsion and alarm. This is different from holding on to Adom the dragon. His slim waist is warm and solid beneath my touch. Human.

Anger curls in the pit of my belly.

"Tighter. I don't want you to fall off."

Frowning, I hold him tighter, making sure a knuckle finds the underside of a rib for good measure. "Better?"

He speaks to the horse instead. The animal jolts, kicking dust as it moves, and I lose my grip. My satchel slips low on my waist. I adjust it and hold Adom more firmly.

We ride past small brown cottages and quilted farmlands. A small girl plays outside. My mind crashes. That was me, once.

Run away, I warn her. *Run, before he kills your family!*

The landscape stretches all the way to the horizon. Flat, green moors fill my vision. Even in my early memories, Trana never appeared this vast. A sea of grassy plains sways in the breeze, only broken up by the occasional tree. Before this, no one could have convinced me Trana looked any color but black. In my imaginings, Adom scorched the whole countryside.

When we reach the outskirts of a village, Adom slows the snorting horse to a trot. Cottages lining the road are quaint and well-kept, with rose bushes and petunias adorning walkways and lovely young shrubs shaped into animal forms. Chimney stacks spout smoke above lumber or clay houses, hinting at warm fires inside the cozy abodes. Cows graze behind fences, not in caves. The sheep are full and fluffy, not scrawny and wild like the desiccated critters that scurry around the dragon warren. A young boy tends them, sitting watch on a fence post.

I had brothers once. The tip of my tongue retraces friendly banter around the dinner table. Sammy, shy and self-conscious, often smuggled extra portions of sweet pies to me when Mama wasn't looking. Strong Nathan hoisted me over his shoulder and carried me round the barn. Musical Collum sometimes played the violin after dinner. We got along quite well, and when we didn't there was always another person around. Now, it's only Muuth.

"What are you thinking, Rat?"

"I'm thinking of everything you stole."

Adom's whole body tenses beneath my fingers.

His reaction makes me think I've struck a chord. I smile serenely.

Nearing the village, I spot a group of people gathered around a small tower of wood and stone. I point at them. "What are they doing?"

"Pulling water from the well." He sounds distant.

Have I offended him? Adom never cared about my opinions before.

Made of gray, crumbling rock, the well seems to be the focal point of the peasants' attention. A wooden overhang shelters it from passing birds. Three buckets lay overturned on the ground beside the structure, and the women surrounding the well vie for these precious vessels. Everywhere I look, there are people dressed in colorful skirts and laced tunics. Studying the front of my worn attire, I realize how out of place and time I look. How old is this piece of faded, brown cloth? I don't look anything like the villagers.

In contrast, the red and black outfit Adom has donned fits in all the right places, accenting his broad shoulders and slender figure. Buttons on his carmine vest are made of brass, and there is gold embroidery along his neckline and sleeves.

"Headed to the inn?" croaks an old woman who stands no taller than four feet.

Adom bobs his head. "Will the scorching make it hard to get a room?"

"Naw. They're taking in more survivors these days, but

from what I hear, most of the rooms are open. Make yourself at home." The old woman slaps her palms together. "They're always thrilled to see you there."

Her accent catches my attention. It takes a moment to realize I've grown accustomed to both Muuth's hideous slurs and Adom's meticulous enunciations, and can no longer remember my own native dialect. How could I let that happen – does that make me a kind of traitor? I correct certain pronunciations in my head. Then I focus on her words: *they're always thrilled to see you there*. What's that supposed to mean?

Adom kicks the flanks of his horse. The beast trots in the direction of the inn. Only a few buildings make up the village, with the largest in the center of the square. A wooden sign hangs above the front that reads "Havensworth Tavern and Inn." Then, in little words, it declares itself to be the "Finest in Town." Probably the *only* inn and tavern in town.

Children scramble underneath the sign, poking at squawking chickens with sticks and playing an unusual form of "catch me." The game consists of a dragon side and a human side. The human group is currently winning. Adom doesn't seem nearly as amused about this as I am.

"Stay here." He slides off the horse. Stalking past the shrieking children, he enters the building. I watch him through the window. He's speaking to a younger man at the counter.

I contemplate riding away on the horse. I'm not sure quite how to make the thing move, let alone how I'll stay on the creature's back with nothing to hold. My thighs ache, chafed by the horse's hot, hairy hide. I am not certain I like traveling by horseback; it is too much like traveling by dragon. But, if I leave now, Adom might never catch me. Or maybe he'll return and find me gone, change into a dragon, and scorch the entire village to punish me. I wouldn't put it past him. There is no freedom in guilt.

Adom emerges not long after. The inn proprietor, a stubbly

man with a sniveling set to his features, follows him. "I'll have this horse taken to our stable right away, m'lord," the man says, rubbing his fingers together like matchsticks.

A young woman with vibrant red hair and a freckled, pink complexion bursts from the building, blinking at the sun. She wears a bright blue frock, and her necklace encircles a blazing red stone that reminds me of the dragon scales in my satchel.

"Raina," the inn proprietor says to her. "Show the lord and his... girl... to their room."

Some hot, uncomfortable emotion sprouts up inside. *His?* I want to spit, but hold my tongue.

"Sure thing, boss man," she replies in a singsong voice, practically skipping up to Adom.

Adom helps me dismount. I avoid touching him more than is necessary, and my feet land in what I hope is only a mud puddle. Raina takes us up a long flight of uneven stairs and through narrow and stuffy hallways. The scent of roasted partridge and whiskey coats the walls, and as we thump through the corridors, doors open and curious eyes peek out at us, watching our procession toward the room at the end of the hall. Raina unlocks the door and swings it open with a flourish.

"Here's your room, my lord," she gushes, fingering the necklace.

Adom takes the jangling key from her other hand. "Thank you."

A scarlet flush creeps into her cheeks. "If you need me, your wench can come and fetch me. There are fresh linens on the bed, and Hanson's making hot cinnamon tarts tomorrow morning."

Wench? I bare my teeth and make a low hissing sound at Raina.

Adom pinches me until I quit the sound. "It all sounds wonderful." He bows.

Raina, apparently oblivious to our tussle, slides past me and ambles into the hall, all smiles and hair flips. I glare at her back.

He enters the room. I follow, sulking, and tug my satchel tighter around my shoulder. The room is smaller than my cave, but there are cozy accents covering the walls. Candles. Artwork. Decorative paper. A plush chair squats in a corner opposite a small table.

Then I freeze. In the middle of the room sits a solid oak, four-poster bed. It isn't large, and the thought of having to share it makes my legs go wobbly.

"What are you gawking at?" Adom asks.

I tear my eyes away from the bed. "I haven't slept in a bed for twelve years."

Adom's visage clouds with shades of regret and pity. Why? The Adom I know always has a perfectly schooled face. "You're sleeping on the floor," he says quietly.

I ball my fists. "I'm not surprised, Snake—" Before he can open his mouth to question this, I continue. "*Don't* think I don't know what that word meant!"

"What word?"

"Wench."

"I didn't realize you were so world-wise, Rat." His eyes shine, more with amusement at my outrage than apology. "I can't call you my wife or my sister." He scans my form, revulsion marring his aristocratic profile when his eyes settle on my mud-caked toes. "You need a bath."

"I hate baths," I hiss. "They make me cold."

He dips his forehead. "They make you clean."

"They make me sick."

"You'll take a bath."

"I hate you."

His eyes flash gold —a sign of anger. "Good." But he sounds bleak. "I'll have Raina bring up water." He backs away, looking as though he wants to…to what? To *apologize*? Surely not!

When he leaves the room, I race to the door. The *click* that comes from the other side doesn't sound promising. Grasping the handle roughly, I twist it clockwise. It doesn't budge.

An hour later, Adom returns with the inn-keeper, who is carrying a warped metal basin filled midway with sloshing, opaque water. He sets it down on the center of the room and quickly leaves. A few moments later Raina enters the room with moony eyes, carting buckets of scalding water in each hand. She adds water to the half-full basin. What the hell is she doing?

"I'm supposed to bathe in *that*?" I ask, pointing to the basin.

Raina chuckles. "Of course you are. Where did you think you would bathe?"

"In a creek?" I squeak, then feel my face heat up when they both burst out laughing. Raina has tears in her eyes, but Adom's laugh actually sounds forced. Back in Onyx, I had a watery lake inside one of the caves to bathe in and before I was a prisoner my parents had a creek next to the house where we would wash up.

I almost make a comment about the hot water they're putting into the basin—isn't hot water for soup not bathing?—but I decide against it. Don't want to be laughed at again.

Adom chats with her in an easy manner, teasing her for spilling water and complimenting the elegance of her fingers until she trembles and turns pink. It's a fascinating interplay of subtle banter and deliberate touches. I've never watched Adom interact with a human female. With female dragons, he's aloof and disinterested. Is this his usual way with Tranar women?

Raina scowls at me as if I'm a mangy cat. "Your girl needs a good scrub."

"My thoughts exactly," he says.

I catch the subtle look in his eyes—if I rise to the bait and argue with him in front of Raina, he'll eat me alive—and I boil on the inside.

Then he winks. Before I fully register the behavior, he returns to Raina. "I found her wandering in a scorched cornfield. She's the only survivor. A dragon slaughtered her family."

How can he bring that up? Doesn't he know it still hurts. We don't talk about that day, but I remember it clearly. Every scream of my family. Finding their charred bodies one after another. Cradling my dying brother in my arms as he breathed the word "dragon" over and over again. Stumbling over burning logs and broken dishes until Adom appeared.

Her putty-eyes tempt me to blurt out the reality. "So she isn't your…"

"She's my ward," Adom replies, avoiding my sharp gaze.

Raina looks me over again. "Someone needs to stand up to them dragons." She raises eyes to Adom with hope and admiration. "Someone like *you*, my lord."

I sigh, loudly.

"Poor girl. Probably lost her wits, too." She finishes pouring the water, drapes a washrag on the bed, and stands. "Don't forget, Lord Malandre." She squeezes his shoulder, leans close to his ear and mouths, "Anything you need." Her backside sways as she slinks out of the room.

Adom's eyes follow her exit. "A voluptuous little thing, isn't she?"

"She waddles like a pig and she's twenty times as stupid."

His eyes widen. "Rat, you astound me."

"You disgust me," I snarl.

To my surprise, he laughs. "I never noticed your short temper before."

"You don't know anything about me," I reply. "We only interact if I'm in trouble, and I'm not especially talkative during those moments." Normally, he'd tell me what to do, then ignore me. I almost prefer the rough, unkind Adom to this new breed of the man.

Adom rests a hand on his forehead. "The others would think me soft if I didn't show some backbone," he says, subdued. "I have to act indifferent."

"You don't have to *do* anything. You're the herd leader."

He crooks his head. "When I reintegrated into the herd, my changeling ability was viewed as a sign of weakness. They treated me the way they treat you."

Reintegrated? I thought Adom always lived with the herd. The dragons enslaved him? But I thought the other dragons appreciated his ability to *change*. "Then why did you stay?"

"I bore it, unflinchingly, to show them my dragon side was stronger than my human side. When I defeated the herd leader, I convinced the herd of my worth as a changeling."

"But why do all of that? Why bother reintegrating in the first place?"

He doesn't answer. I watch him get up and pace the length of the room. After a moment, he returns to the bed. "Take your bath, Rat," he instructs, turning his back.

It bothers me that he uses the name I go by on Onyx. Perhaps it's because this is a new place, a chance at a new identity. "My name is Elanor," I growl.

He stands and stalks to the door. "Take your bath, Elanor."

The door swings open on creaking hinges. Then it slams shut. In his absence, a strange disquiet blossoms in my chest. Why didn't he answer my question? Why didn't he yell at me?

I peel off my clothes, confusion muddling my mind almost as much as my desire to bathe. I cherish the liberty of choosing when to wash myself. It seems like one of the few things the dragons do *not* force me to do. Until now. Steam cools off the basin of water, so I dip in my foot, biting my lower lip as dirt ripples away from my toes. It's not too hot. With ginger motions, I slip both feet in. Sighing, I collapse against the sides of the basin.

Raina left a bar of lavender-scented soap. I pick up the purple bar and build a lather. It works wonders. Much more than the oily soap Muuth taught me to make out of pig's fat. Dirt foams off me. I dunk my head in the water. Scrub my flat hair with the bar.

I rinse out my matted tresses. Foamy suds become black with sooty dirt, the mark of Onyx that has stained my body for far too long. There now. Adom can't say I stink anymore. I stand and squeeze water out of my hair, dwelling on Raina's short, curly red locks. No wonder Adom calls me 'Rat.' My dark hair looks long enough to be my tail.

Someone knocks on the door.

I climb out of the basin in a hurry, then slip and fall in again. Water sloshes over the sides. I nibble my lower lip. Adom wouldn't knock without speaking up. It must be someone from the inn come to check on me. "I'm in the bath!" I call out, suddenly embarrassed. I don't want some stranger to see my scrawny, naked body bruised from hard labor.

Raina pokes her head into the room. "Your lord had me bring these up to you," she announces, handing me a towel and some folded clothes.

I stand and wrap the towel around my body, step out of the basin, and back into a corner.

Raina snatches my old clothes from the bed. "These oughta be burned." She busies herself around the room, seeming oblivious to the emotional anguish she puts me through. Muuth always respects my privacy, taking care to sing and stamp on the ground so I have plenty of forewarning when he comes to visit my cave. And though Adom often summons me to his quarters, he never once invaded my room. I take solace in privacy; alone I have time and space to collect my thoughts. In the silence of my room, I find peace in the midst of captivity.

But Raina knows nothing about it and hums merrily. Meanwhile, I face the wall and cover my front as best I can while discreetly pulling up the knickers and skirt.

"Oh dear!"

I whirl around.

Raina gawks as though wings have sprouted from my

shoulders. "Are you...?" I can see her eyes flicker as she considers finishing the question.

She's seen my scars. There aren't many old ones left, but I gained a few new ones in my last attempt at escape. After my soak, they probably appear raw and brutal. I'm used to the throb and sting of slavery, but with Raina watching and after the warm bath, every ache feels like a knife slashing my skin. At least the heated water dulled the pain of my twisted ankle.

Telling Raina the truth about my injuries will only put her life in jeopardy. Adom might be fond of his little "pet," but I doubt he'd let her live if she knew his secret. My mouth moves before I have time to think of a response. "Not to worry," I take control before she makes up her mind, "I cut myself on the brambles by my house while escaping the dragons." It isn't exactly a lie. For now, I'll take a lesson from Adom's book and tell a stretched truth.

Raina draws near, her pretty face marred with concern. Her eyes trail to the door, and I realize she's contemplating additional ways to loosen the ties on Adom's money purse. "Is there something I can get for you? Some salve, perhaps?"

After washing, the wounds are especially tender. "Salve. Yes. That will do nice."

She pivots to leave, her eyes revealing a mind already distracted by another thought. "Right away then." Her hair bobs lightly as she makes her way to the door. A ray of sunlight catches the red-gold sheen, and a sudden bolt of envy fills me.

"Raina," I breathe. "Do you have a pair of cutters?"

The maid faces me again, nodding with vigor. "Why, of course I do." Her eyes grow sharp and her smile knowing. "You want to cut your hair, don't you?"

When I admit it, she bursts into laughter.

"Well, that's a relief." She studies my hair as one might stare at a dirty mop I insist on wearing on my head. Flouncing out of the room, she closes the door behind her.

I change into the new set of clothes, hoping she won't come in to ogle at my back again before I finish. Doesn't a person have a right to change in peace? And what about this funny attire Adom bade her bring me? The waist hugs tighter than what I like, causing my bosom and bottom to protrude. I have to shimmy into the dress instead of dropping it over my head!

My solitude lasts for only a few brief moments.

Raina returns with some salve and cutters. "This oughta do." She pauses to survey me. "You clean up well." When I don't respond, she asks, "Need anything else?"

I think of a polite, *human* way to dismiss her. When have I ever heard the dragons say a single kind word in all the years I served them? "No, thank you," I manage, though it takes an ounce of energy to squeeze the words from my prideful lips.

After cutting my hair and applying the salve, I sink into the infinitely soft mattress. Strange. The salve jar looks similar to the jar Muuth always produces whenever I'm hurt. For the first time, I wonder how Muuth obtains his medicine. I always thought he made it.

My thoughts don't keep me awake for long.

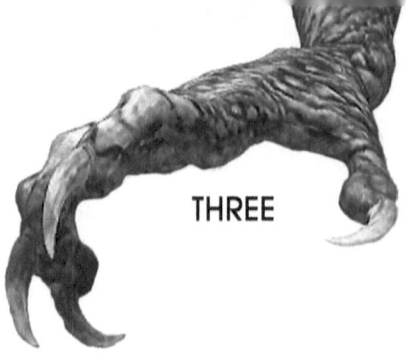

THREE

IN THE MIDDLE OF night, the moon peers in through the foggy window. Laughter peals from outside. I peek outside and see stable hands chattering by the horses. The glass won't budge. I stand and try the doorknob again. Locked. Did Adom creep in while I was sleeping? Or did Raina lock it? I can't do much now. I resettle into the warm blankets, inhaling the scent of lavender soap in my hair and amber incense from the room next door. He'll return soon.

Morning comes. I open my eyes and stretch my back. It makes popping sounds in a million different places. I feel like I slept three nights in a row, and if I'm honest I could probably sleep another two nights in this bed without complaint. Groaning, I roll over. Adom sits sideways on the bed. In his hands, he holds Fifi. Immediately awake, I swipe at the doll.

"Give me that!"

He holds it up high, just out of my reach. "You left her lying out for anyone to see." He studies the doll's visage. After a moment, he frowns. Does Fifi unnerve him? Of course she does. She's a hideous, broken doll. Any normal person would be frightened by her ragged form, her pale, cracked body, and her glassy eyes.

I stretch my hand out and wait. "She's my doll. Give her back."

He ignores my hand, and instead reaches out to take a strand of my hair. Now shoulder-length, it glides silky against the back of my neck after the bath. "Why did you cut it?"

"It was too long," I answer, uncomfortable with the gentle touch. So he hasn't reverted back to his old self? "Besides, I don't know when I'll see the cutters again." Maybe my words are an exaggeration—he's never withheld resources from me if I needed it—but Adom is acting so strange at the moment ,and I want to remind him of the situation he's put me in.

Adom runs his fingers through it like a pile of thread, eyes transfixed. "I liked it long."

"All the more reason for me to cut it."

He lets the strands slide. "Tavern maids and wenches wear their hair this short."

I grab Fifi and roll across the bed, victory warming my insides like a hot drink. My stomach grumbles, but I have no intentions of complaining to *him* about my hunger. He's probably eaten already. "Good. Now your story about my being your wench is more believable."

But Adom seems to lose interest in bantering. His face clears, and he leans against the headboard, arms crossed, watching me. "I never had things as a child."

"Seems like you overcame that deficit," I retort, referring to his bounty room. He could feed an army for a month with all the *things* he has stashed away on Onyx.

His nostrils flare, but instead of arguing, he pats my hand. "I don't blame you for wanting to keep your doll. If I had anything to remember my parents by, I'd treasure it, too."

There's a tray of food sitting by the door. I get up and help myself to a piece of fruit—I can't recall the name although I know I've eaten it before—and a small plate with what looks like a breakfast pie. It's been so long since someone else has cooked for me, since I've had food made with whole grains and cane sugar. I bite into the crust and let out a little moan.

We never talk about our pasts. I figure it's only right to preserve what little part of me isn't owned by him. But now he offers to tell me about his life, and even though I hate him I never could resist a good story. I brush crumbs from my lips. "What happened to your parents?"

"Ona killed them." He says it curtly, matter-of-fact, but he isn't quick enough to hide the flicker of regret in his eyes. It affects him, even while he pretends it does not.

A swift pain stabs at my gut. "I didn't know that." Was that when he left the herd? After Ona murdered his family? Then why did he return, when he *knew* it would be rough-going?

"There's a lot you don't know about me." He's using my words from earlier.

"Do you hate him?" I sit down on the bed and finish off the pie, then begin peeling the fruit. In moments, that is gone, too. My stomach is full and my mouth is content.

"Hate is a waste of energy. Life is what it is. People die."

"Dragons die, too," I add, with as much relish as I can muster.

"That's true. Especially the weak ones." Adom screws his eyes shut for a moment and bows his head until a ray of sunlight kisses his profile. He breathes in deep, throwing his head back as if inhaling the light. Then his eyes open and meet mine. "I'm not the only one."

"What?"

His fingers play along the end of the magenta quilt. Silence wraps us and stills the moment. He isn't about to hurt me and I'm not about to escape. "There are other changelings."

I cross scratched legs and scoot a little bit closer. I leave Fifi at the edge of the bed. Her crack is beginning to widen, and I have fears that soon her head will split in two. And Adom's words are making my heart go wild like a rabid rat. "Are they living on Onyx or in Trana?"

He stares at the ceiling, studying a beetle moving across the room. His chest swells and then deflates. It is difficult for him to speak so honestly, I guess. "I'm the only one on Onyx."

"Where are the others?"

"Here." His eyes follow the bug until it reaches a corner of the room. Then he wets his lips and sweeps hair away from his face. "I'm tracking them."

I sit up straight, shoulders perpendicular with the ceiling. "Don't you have some kind of dragon sense? Can't you recognize your own kind?"

"Can you?" He glances at me and smiles. There is sadness in the look, a weary vulnerability I have never seen before. "They're living among the humans. They smell just like you and I."

My mind absorbs this new information. If there are other changelings living in Trana, it means the dragons didn't all leave like the legends say. Why would Adom track them except to make them join the herd? "The Battle of the Sky Rock is a myth?"

"You learned about the stone soldiers?"

Avoiding his eyes, I say, "Muuth taught me a little bit of history." I don't want to give too much of my knowledge away. He might reconsider keeping me with him in Trana if he thinks I know enough to get by without him. Besides, I don't want to put Muuth in danger.

If he's angry at this, he doesn't reveal it. "Muuth was there the last time the stone soldiers appeared. The day the sun went black and many of my kind died."

"But if it's true, why are there still dragons?"

He shrugs. "Because the story is distorted, and Muuth has a touch of the theatrical."

"He's got a touch of *something*, that's certain."

Adom's eyebrows crinkle. "It isn't his fault. He's bound to the mountain. Muuth lived there before the dragons came. He considers himself the guardian of the island."

I always thought the dragons kidnapped Muuth the way they kidnapped me. "Maybe you don't know Muuth as well as you think. He hates it there."

He hesitates. "If he hates it, why doesn't he leave? Last time I checked, his boat was still tied to the underground dock. Nothing is stopping him from leaving. *He's* always had a choice."

"What do you mean? What boat?" *And why did Adom emphasize* he?

"It's hidden in the cave used for bathing. I'm surprised he never told you about it." He can't seem to meet my eyes anymore. "You couldn't have used it in any case," he mutters. "The water dragons would have overturned it and drowned you for sport."

I'm angry that Adom has me stumped. I can't ask Muuth whether or not it's true unless I go back to Onyx. And I don't plan on going back to the island. *He's just toying with me. Muuth wouldn't have hidden a boat all these years.* Adom wants to drive a wedge between us, to make me question my loyalties. I won't waste my energy on his lies.

"So we're here to track down the changelings?"

The corners of his eyes tighten. "That's right. We're here to find them."

My stomach contracts. "And what will we do once we've found them?"

"That depends on how...*compliant* they are."

"You're trying to move them to Onyx? To reintegrate them into the herd?"

He turns and gazes out the window, grim shadows haunting his visage. Sunlight glints in his eyes, making them glow like violet gems. "That might be ideal in some cases." Then he looks at me with hollow eyes. "In other cases, we may need to resort to drastic measures."

My breath catches. "You expect to kill some of them, don't you?"

"I already have—"

Someone raps on the door. I bound across the room, dread coursing through my veins. A changeling? A nosy neighbor listening in on our conversation? I press a hand to my collarbone.

Adom doesn't look perturbed. "Here," he thrusts a pile of

ruffly clothes at me.

Heartbeat slowing to a relatively normal rhythm, I let my hand fall to my side. "I've already got clothes on." I stare at my white attire. I've only worn it one day.

He snorts. "Those are night garments."

Night garments? "Very well." I snatch the clothes from his hands. "But turn around." Fabric slips out of my hands as I fumble to undo all the buttons and ties.

The knocking grows more urgent.

"Hurry," he urges.

I throw the clothes on over my head and pull them over my waist. "I'm ready," I declare, proud about how fast I managed to finagle the thing on me. Why in the world do women wear such excessive folderol? To look like a cake? I'll take my airy and simple shifts any day!

Adom turns around and lets out a curse. "It's on backward."

I right the outfit. "Now?"

His eyes light with approval. Then he pivots to the door and calls, "Come in."

"Brought something for the we—" Raina stops midsentence, her rosy cheeks puffing in exertion. "Oh. Sorry to bother you, my lord. I just brought up a blue ribbon for your ward." She flutters in, right hand on her buxom chest. "Would you like me to put it in her hair?"

He catches my eye. "It's *her* hair."

"Just put it on the bed." I back away from Raina's eager hands.

She lets out a tireless sigh, places the ribbon gently on the bed and then turns to Adom. Curls bounce like springs against her shoulders. "Lord Faigen's having a celebration in an hour." Color deepens in her cheeks, underscoring cornflower eyes.

Adom surveys the maid with a flat, unimpressed lip line. "Faigen's hosting a party? Why?" He glances at me and for a moment we share matching expressions of disgust.

"He's leaving to become a soldier," Raina croons. "He

wants to battle the dragons." She spares me a look so full of sympathy I want to pull out her curls strand by strand. I can't tell her the truth with Adom in the room, but why can't she see through his guise? Isn't it obvious?

Then I realize the significance of her words. So people in Trana *do* believe in the fight against the dragons? I wish I'd known there were efforts of that sort. I'd have sent messages in bottles or by pigeon, if I could have trained them. I glance at Adom to read his reaction.

He's turned white. "Tell Lord Faigen we'll have to decline."

Raina's forehead creases; her enthusiasm dims. "But why? The good lord wants to see you before he travels to the city. It's been such a long while since you've visited!"

Adom visited here before? He knows this town? He knows Raina? And he's a *friend* of this Lord Faigen? Adom never told me he had human friends. How does he scorch the fields of people he knows? How does he do it and possess a shred of humanity?

But it explains the doe-eyed glances Raina keeps giving him.

"We're also on our way to the city," Adom says. "The king wants to see me tonight."

The king? How can he lie so boldly? And yet I can't contain the thrill of excitement that flows through me when I hear him mention the city. It's the perfect place to lose him.

Raina looks like she wants to persuade him otherwise. The maid's eyes mist, but before she bursts into huge crocodile tears, Adom changes the subject. "How soon can the footman ready a carriage? I'd like to leave before dark, if possible."

I've never ridden in a carriage before. Papa used to say they belong only to fancy people. An icy chill goes through me. How does Adom have the money to pay for an inn, much less a carriage? I think of simple farmers like my father. Heat surges through my veins.

Raina's smile returns as his eyes caress her. "Do you have to leave tonight?"

"Unfortunately, yes," Adom says reaching for her hand.

She giggles when he presses lips to her skin. "Our driver raved about you all morning, though he'll be disappointed when he hears you won't attend Lord Faigen's—"

Adom pauses mid-kiss. He elevates his chin, dark black hair falling over his left eye, and relinquishes her hand. "The king said no one should know of my comings and goings. Hire someone from out of town. Someone who doesn't know who I am."

She looks like she wants to cry again. *What the hell is wrong with the woman?* "I'll tell Simon," she sniffs. "We'll see what we can do." She lets out a small sob and flees.

I straighten the neckline of my pinching dress, and then tuck hair behind my ear. There's a reason he wants me here, and why he expects me to play the part of his *ward*. In the startled silence of Raina's departure, I give him a measured look. "Why am I here, Adom?"

"I need to you help me locate the changelings and convince them to leave Trana, to leave all they know, and come with me to Onyx. It's the only way to strengthen the herd."

"Why me? Why would you suppose *I* would be a good candidate for this?"

"Because it benefits you. With other humans on Onyx, life won't be so horrible. You'll make friends. You'll have helpers. Things will reform as the changelings begin to integrate."

It does no good to remind him that life will *always* be horrible, purely because I lack basic freedom. How could he think I'd wish that curse, enslavement, on anyone else, changeling or no? "What if they don't wish to come with you?"

"You want to kill dragons, don't you?"

"No. I want to kill *you.*"

He winces. "Put aside your desire for revenge for a short while longer, Rat. If they choose not to come, the changelings risk endangering all of us. You know the stories. You know how it ended the last time the stone disease afflicted them."

Stone disease? He assumes I know more than I do, but I don't plan on revealing my ignorance. "So you want me to spy for you, to tell you if I discover one of these changelings?"

He nods. "I need someone who can go places I can't and be my eyes and ears."

I consider this for several seconds. "Then I need more autonomy."

Adom's eyes linger a moment too long on my face. He swallows and lifts the bit of blue ribbon Raina left behind. "You heard me tell Raina I have a meeting tonight. That isn't a lie. I'm not leaving without you." The set of his brow softens as he studies the bit of silk in his hands.

The ribbon looks like the kind of flouncy thing Raina would wear, and I would not. Ever. Watching Adom with Raina is unsettling, because he isn't the man I know and it makes me doubt myself. If Adom is attached to a silly, giggly Tranar human, he can't be the monster I've labeled him. That would change everything. But he can't feel genuine affection for her, can he?

I worry the inside of my cheek. "How far away is the meeting spot?"

"Two hours by carriage. A few minutes flying." Adom's eyes intensify. "But I don't plan to fly so close to the city. It isn't a safe place for dragons."

My eyes settle on the window. It's not yet noon. "What time is your meeting?"

"Midnight."

"It's only mid-morning. Whatever will we do to pass the time?" Maybe I can ply him with alcohol at this extravaganza Raina was telling us about and confuse his wits. Or maybe the other human females, like Raina, could distract him all evening so he later sleeps soundly and I could make an escape. I cross my legs, expectantly.

He avoids my merciless gaze. "I'm not interested in the party."

I tap my foot impatiently against the floor. "You're interested in keeping up this Lord Malandre ruse," I guess. "You think playing a lord will help you uncover changelings."

"I have other priorities."

"But you wouldn't want to insult Lord Faigen."

He releases an exasperated sigh. "It sounds to me like *you* want to go to the party."

I shrug. "I've never been to a party. How should I know whether or not I want to go?"

His eyes fix on mine, suddenly intense. A crooked smile crosses his visage, now shades brighter than a moment ago. "It would overwhelm you."

I fake a confidence I don't feel. "Then I'll stay here and see if I can uncover changelings at the inn," I promise, patting my hand on the bed. "You go. Have fun."

Adom nods to himself, almost as if he fully expected this response. He tugs me off the bed. "I know precisely how your mind works. If I go, you must come with me."

I spread my hands apart. "But I have nothing to wear."

"I'll buy you a dress," he replies too quickly, as if he's already considered this.

I have the strangest feeling he tricked me somehow. My objective was to send *him* off to this party, to keep *him* distracted so I could slip away. I don't have any interest in parties or people, for that matter. "You said I would be overwhelmed."

He flashes a wolfish grin. "I'll protect you."

Adom now seems so eager. Suddenly, I'm not sure this event is the wisest idea. "I don't need your protection." I put as much space between us as possible without being too obvious.

"Fine." He grins. "But there are rules. Stay close beside me. Don't ask questions. Say nothing about dragons. And tell no one my real identity," he warns. "If you do, I'll have to resolve it in possibly bloody and probably violent ways. It could get messy."

My eyes trail to the closed door. "You're heartless, Adom."

"I am," he agrees. "But this is as much for your protection as it is for mine. Some people want to see both of us dead." He says this with such a composed look I almost miss his meaning.

"Why would anyone want me dead?" I reconsider my question. "Not counting Ona."

"My enemies are your enemies."

"Who are your enemies, Adom?"

"Never mind that now." He clamps his mouth shut.

I try reading his thoughts. Why can't he be transparent *now*? Only moments ago, he poured out his motivations in uncomfortable abundance. Now my life hangs in the balance of some unknown aggressor? Why the secrecy?

*

Raina rejoices when she learns we've changed our mind. "I'll send for the seamstress to fit your ward into a lace dress for the party. She'll do wonderful as a swan, and I think you'd make a fine garden snake if you don't mind my saying so."

"A swan and a snake? Whatever for?" Adom asks.

"Oh, didn't I mention? Lord Faigen's party is a costume ball. You're meant to dress as the animal you think best represents you."

If that's the case, I should go as a rat. I'm as small, and as ugly, and as resilient.

Adom glances at me. "A swan," he murmurs. "Yes. I see it now."

I bare my teeth and then look out the window. He wants me to be a swan for the party? To preen and smile and play the part of an elegant, giggly companion such as Raina? Fine. I'll go as a swan. I once saw one of those lovely creatures peck out the eyes of a squirrel.

*

As soon as we enter Lord Faigen's assembly hall, my heart begins to race. Open-mouthed, I slide the swan mask away from my eyes until it rests above my forehead.

Animal heads and furs hang along the gray-green walls, gory symbols of the conquering warrior. Loud music, sharp scents, and bright paintings contrast starkly with the dark wall color and lurid animal pelts. Already, I can tell Adom is right—this party will overwhelm me if I'm not careful. The stench of sweaty, human bodies weaving around each other on a dance floor, gyrating and swaying to the beat of a hide drum.

A woman standing next to the drummer plays a smaller stringed instrument that looks similar to my brother Collum's worn old violin, but the strings sound like a horsehair bow dragged across a wobbly saw. Then there is another man, seated on a pincushion pillow, strumming on an oval sitar. The man and the woman playing the spellbinding instruments also sing with raw conviction while the percussionist whoops and groans in the background.

Neither Adom nor I are dressed as elaborately as some of the individuals before me now. I'm wearing a white dress with ivory feathers Raina stitched on along with small, glittering glass gemstones, and a slender, silver-colored mask secured to my face with a bit of string. Adom is wearing a garden-snake green jacket paired with a black velvet mask, leather gloves, a gold vest, and matching boots over black trousers.

"Welcome, welcome," says a glittery tiger climbing down a grand staircase in the colorful foyer. He gestures to the red buffet table. "Lord Faigen has already gone, but in his honor you are welcome to imbibe exotic wines and feast on musty cheeses."

Adom lets out a curse as a servant passes by with a tray full of yummy niblets and glasses of wine. "You see?" He turns to me and spreads his hands wide, as if this is somehow my fault. "Of course Faigen would abandon his own party. That man is as fickle and as useless as—"

"Mold on a cave?"

"How did you know I was going to say that?"

I cock an eyebrow, raise a fan over my mouth, and whisper,

"Dragonisms."

He bends until his nose aligns with mine. We are hidden behind my lacy black fan. Adom reaches for a glass of wine from a passing tray. The thudding beat of the music shakes the red liquid as it exchanges hands. Noise rises from the ground beneath me, a steady *thump thump*.

Adom sways an inch closer. "I can see I'll have to keep a closer eye on you."

I snap the fan shut and take a deliberate step away. "You'd have to find me to do that." The air is too tight in this room. And what is that horrible smell? It smells like sandalwood, only there is a human odor to it, like these people haven't left the room in a week. Who is this Lord Faigen and what does he do for a living? Why doesn't Adom like him?

He straightens and folds his hands together. "I have a gong."

"I won't always be around to respond to that horrid thing." A newcomer pushes past me in his enthusiasm to join the raging pile of humanity in the room beyond ours. I bare my teeth and hiss the way a dragon would. He can't hear me because of the noise of the music.

"No, I suppose not." Adom studies his wineglass. "You're nearly of age now."

"Yes?" *What does that mean?*

He swallows. "Something will have to be done about you."

My heart beats into a rhythm that is faster than the tempo of the music. I find my hips pivoting to one side, then the other. My toes tap inside the awful shoes Adom and Raina insisted that I wear. "You mean you have plans to let me go?"

He polishes off the wine and sets down the glass. "I have... plans." He begins to veer in the direction of the dancing bodies—curse him—leaving me with too many questions in my head.

Without thinking, I reach out and weave my arm around his. He stops and looks over his shoulder at me, his eyes drowsy slits of fire that come alive and expressive in an instant. The question is plain on his face. *Why are you touching me, Rat?*

"Why don't you let me go now? Today?"

He removes his arm from mine. "It isn't sensible to free you." He points at the beheaded animals along the wall. "Not unless I want to end up like them."

"Tell the others you ate me. I won't return to Onyx for revenge. I just want freedom."

"If you impress me on this mission, I'll remember your contribution." Adom stares at the moving bodies, and then his eyes fix on mine. "Lord Faigen is gone, so there's no point in staying any longer." His eyebrows rise. "Unless, of course, you wish to learn how to dance."

I swallow, my tongue suddenly thick and my brain foggy. It's the damn heat in this room and all the swaying bodies. And I'm hungry.

My mind refocuses. Adom is teasing me, is all. "You said you're looking for other changelings." I gesture to the full room. "Have all these people been cleared?"

The glint in his eyes fades. He studies the room. "No, I suppose they haven't. My current investigations have been a bit more targeted."

"Let me walk around the room, Adom. Please? I've spent my whole life lurking in the shadows, overhearing things I shouldn't hear. I'll bet I can learn something useful to you." The sounds and noises of the place are, as predicted, a sensory overload, but I'm determined not to let Adom catch on to this fact. How am I ever going to get away from him if I don't learn to navigate the human world?

His chin tilts, eyebrows pressed together. His lips begin to form a "no."

"Excuse me," says a sweet-spoken gentleman dressed flagrantly like a black and gold speckled dragon. He extends a hand to me, but his eyes are on Adom. "I should like to dance with the swan if her snake guardian would unravel himself from around her neck."

I stare at his extended hand with dismay. Who is this strange person and why is he asking Adom's permission to dance with me? I give Adom a horrified look, hoping he correctly interprets my stony silence. I'm not dancing with Adom *or* this prancing dragon-fellow who won't even look me in the eye. I didn't come here to dance. I came to do what I do best, to blend in, gather secrets, and make my exit as uneventful and anonymous as humanly possible. I take a hard look at the man, at his widely curly blond hair, his sapphire eyes, and the stretched smile on his too-friendly, too-symmetrical face.

The corners of Adom's mouth curve up, and the mischievous glint returns. "She's a recent debutante." He yawns. "Her parents asked me to look after her tonight. She hasn't yet learned to dance, so you may want to move along."

Oh, so now I'm a *debutante*? I'm moving up in the world, I see. Only now, the fool dragon-man thinks we're on equal footing. I catch the determined gleam in his eyes and clench my fists together. Is this Adom's way of trying to discourage the man? If so, I'm not impressed.

"I'll teach her," the man volunteers. His hand is still extended toward me. "Welcome to society, my dear. Would you like to learn to dance?"

Adom looks completely disinterested. Clearly, I will have to shoo the man away myself.

"I don't know you," I say flatly.

"Lady Elanor," Adom helpfully gestures to the unwanted dragon. "May I introduce you to Lord Rhydian Berrel? He's quite an ingenious man, with a razor mind in the mining business. He's contributed millions to the king's army for the campaign against the dragons." The words sound hollow, like an obligatory introduction. I get the sense that Adom isn't particularly impressed with Lord Berrel's business savvy—or his money for that matter.

"Really?" Adom might not realize it, but even with the tepid introduction he's selling Lord Berrel as a potential ally. I don't want to dance with the man, but if my blockhead captor makes himself scarce I could pick Lord Berrel's mind like a carrion bird enjoying a bloody feast. I glance at him again. He's not bad looking.

Berrel gestures toward the dance floor. "This way, my lady."

"But I'm not sure..." I pat Berrel's hand, growing more and more flustered, all the while glaring at Adom. He's fidgeting with his pocket handkerchief, not even bothering to look up.

The lord misreads the intentions of my pacifying hand and grasps hold of it, then tugs me away from Adom and meets my gaze for the first time. At the center of his eyes, a jealous spark catches me off balance. Suddenly, I have the suspicion that this is all a power show and I'm caught in the middle, an unintentional casualty of a secret feud. It reminds me of one very unfortunate game of *dragon slap* I was baited into playing three years ago. The rules were simple enough: tie a rope to your midsection and hang from a cave ceiling, playing dead, while two dragons bat you back and forth like a couple of cats pawing at a mouse.

I'd be damned if I let these two imbeciles treat me like a dead mouse. If Berrel wants to dance with me, it probably has to do with plying me for information. If Adom seems disinterested, it's because he wants Berrel to think I'm irrelevant. Time to stir the waters a bit.

I escaped the grisly game of *dragon slap* by clinging to one of the dragon's talons. When it tried to shake me off, it pulled the rope from the ceiling, freeing me. Then I ran. I smile, my strategy forming. I shift willingly toward Lord Berrel and curtsey. "There's no need to pull. I'll gladly dance with you, my lord."

Adom's reaction is as startling as a clay wall turning to feathers. His back is stiff and straight, and his eyes are suddenly attentive and sharp. "Elanor?" His voice lilts in surprise. "You don't have to go if you'd rather not. It's getting late."

So now he shows concern? Ah. He was counting on my bullish manners and my lack of social skills to drive Berrel away. "Don't be silly, *Count Malandre*." I grit my teeth. "This clever young dragon wants to teach me how to dance. Isn't it wonderful?"

He reaches for my arm, and there is an awkward tug-of-war between myself and the two men. "Remember we have responsibilities to attend to?" Adom says with a tight jaw. "We have to leave. It wouldn't do to be caught up dancing."

If that's all the fight the man has, I might as well elope with Lord Berrel here and now. Adom can't steal me away or kill me if someone expects me home in time for supper.

"Nonsense." My voice drips with syrupy sweetness while I push him away. "Isn't that why you brought me here? To learn about society? My parents would be so disappointed if they heard you wouldn't even let me dance at my first event."

Adom gives me a warning look before stalking to one of the serving tables. He's not happy with my performance, but how can he expect a flawless act when I never pretended around him before? Besides, doesn't he want me to mingle and learn more about the dragon changelings? Or is everything he told me this morning a lie?

Berrel seems immensely pleased with himself for acquiring me, as if I had nothing to do with the arrangement whatsoever. He grins hard at Adom's retreating back, smug, as if he won a joust or cut off a dragon's head. In fact, I'm a tinge more impressed with Adom for showing an extraordinary amount of will power by not *changing* and swallowing Berrel whole. Adom the human is a yawning house-cat compared to his rip-you-in-half counterpart. He's bound by all the same rules and niceties as everybody else in Trana.

At last, my would-be dancing partner seems to recall my

presence. He crooks his head and smiles at me. "Where do you hail from, Elanor?" he asks, all traces of pomp and pretense gone. Now his voice sounds benign and conversational, the heat and urgency from before mysteriously purged from it. "You seem older than the usual debutante."

"I'm from an island not far off the coast of Trana. I'm twenty-one. It's the normal age to go into society where I'm from." I hope he doesn't catch the slight breathlessness in my voice and detect the lie. It's not, technically, dishonest but I'm certainly not a debutante.

"Meriddow," he guesses. "Or Cornoc."

"Close," I say. "South of Cornoc."

"And what are you doing here with the Count?" He glances toward Adom and sneers. "The man has quite the reputation with the ladies. He's been known to leave decimation and mayhem in his path. I hope you have your guard up."

How in the world do I answer? Decimation and mayhem? Maybe not in the way Berrel is thinking, but Adom *definitely* leaves both in his wake. "As he informed you earlier, he's my guardian this evening. He's accompanying me to the city." I avoid addressing his last statement, although I feel like the twitching muscle near my eye is giving away my discomfort.

"I see." He intertwines my fingers into his. "Let's waste no more time on pleasantries. Allow me to show you how this is done." He winds my free arm around his waist and rests his hand gently on my hip. "Follow my lead. One, two, three. One, two three. Move with the music."

For several focused minutes, I tune out the sound of glasses tinkling and people laughing. My eyes fix on the glowing pinpoints of Berrel's blue irises and my ears latch onto his voice as he counts out the rhythm. My body vibrates to the beat of the percussion. The lord moves with precision, each step a thoughtful and deliberate placement. After a time, my eyes screw shut. I pretend I'm walking through black caves, the delicate balance of toe and heel essential for safe passage, for survival. Berrel's fingers tighten around my hip and he draws me closer. He smells pleasant, like the bark of a Black Jack pine on a sunny day. And his palm against mine is dry and firm, neither coarse like Muuth's nor insistent like Adom's.

"You are quite agile for a young woman with no tutelage in dance," Berrel comments, his voice warm with unexpected emotion. "You're a natural on your feet."

"Thank you." I peer up at him with drowsy eyes.

"So you aren't lovers, then?"

All fuzzy feelings disintegrate. "Excuse me?"

"You and Count Malandre?"

I step on his foot. Hard. The mask slides down the bridge of my nose, and I have to pause for a moment to push it up. When I can see again, I realize I've done real damage.

"Ow." His eyes slide shut and his foot shifts away from mine.

"So sorry," I say without a hint of remorse.

He flashes a brittle smile. "I'll pretend that was an accident."

"So will I."

Berrel gives me a measuring stare. "I can see why he likes you."

"Why do people always assume—"

"It's the way he looks at you."

It takes me several seconds to recover from this. Whose business is it what Adom is to me? I have no interest in chit-chat with strangers about non-existent relationships with individuals I happen to loathe. Maybe this is how strangers talk to each other in Trana? I think hard about a polite way to tell Berrel to mind his own business. "You're mistaken."

"I think you're new to affection, madam."

Ugh. Could this 'gentleman' be any more condescending? "Berrel, was it?"

The corners of his eyes crinkle. "That's my name."

"I'm a bit fatigued."

"Would you like to dance closer to the punchbowl?"

"That would be appreciated."

The moment we reach the table, I pull away and fill my hands with a glass so I have an excuse to discontinue the activity. I drink it slowly, counting the seconds in the hopes that he will become bored and wander away. On the whole, dancing is not entirely unpleasant. On the other hand, when dancing with Lord Berrel each and every step seems like a calculated move to ensnare me in some way. Adom is right to distrust him.

"Where do you come from?" I ask, because he isn't going anywhere. Furthermore, it's uncomfortable just standing here staring at him, and about time I reverse the tables.

"North of this country," he answers vaguely.

I motion to his excessive costume. "Do you have dragons in your land?"

He blinks. "Don't tell me you believe in all this dragon gossip?"

"You don't?"

"I supposed you were smarter than that," he admonishes. "Where I come from, there's a theory about what's happening here. Trana is angled closer to the sun than the rest of the land. There's a drought. The land is scorched by dry air, lack of rainfall, and the parched farmlands."

"You don't think dragons could do it?"

"The stone soldiers killed them all, didn't they? It's just fear and superstition talking."

Maybe it's because I'm used to quibbling with Adom by now, or maybe it's because I can't seem to forget ships sailing to avoid Onyx Island, but I find myself on the defensive. "You believe in a mythical stone army, but won't entertain the possibility of dragons in spite of the eyewitness accounts? Lord Berrel, surely *you* are smarter than that," I repeat his own words. "What if the stone soldiers didn't kill them all?" Hadn't Muuth implied this, after all? He'd said *many* dragons had died in the battle, not *all* of them.

"We wouldn't be celebrating Jetarna Day next week if it hadn't happened."

I feel my face going long and blank. "Jetarna Day?"

"I forgot you aren't from here. There was a woman, Jetarna, who went to all the nations and prophesied that the stone soldiers would come and defeat the dragons. Three days later, the soldiers appeared. They came from the mountains, from the farmlands, from the ground itself. They drove back the dragons, their simple touch changing the fiery beasts to stone."

"So the dragons turned to stone? They didn't die?" Is that what Adom meant by the *stone disease*? I'm dying to ask, but what if I'm wrong and it catches Berrel's attention?

"That's what killed them. People gathered the stone dragons after the battle and ground them to dust. They spread the dust across the country so no one would ever be able to put them back together again. And guess what they did to Jetarna?"

"What?"

He grins. "They hung her."

While strong horror and even disgust surges, provoked by his frank insensitivity, there's a dark part of me that connects on a very base level with his transparency. It's the same part that connects me to Muuth, as twisted and confused as my cave-dwelling friend might be at times.

"Why did they hang her?"

"How could she predict the dragon's downfall? Obviously, she must have been a witch."

"Then why is there a Jetarna Day?"

"The threat's gone. There are no witches, and there are no dragons. People love to believe in the unseen, they love a martyr, and they love the excuse to drink and revel. The dragons haven't returned, Lady Elanor. Superstition and wild imaginations have."

I think of the bit of scale around Raina's neck, and of the two scales in my satchel. "And what do you make of the dragon scales? Where do you suppose they come from?"

His eyes narrow wickedly. "I deal in dragon scales. It's how I made my fortune."

"You don't believe in dragons, but you sell the scales and make money off of *superstition* and *wild imagination*? Why do you contribute money to the king's army?"

"It's my civic duty to support the king in his endeavors no matter how the funds are used. I own a mine where the 'scales' are found in abundance. Believe me, madam, they don't come from dragons. They're rocks with pretty designs that can be purified, shaped, melted and fashioned into exquisite jewelry." His chest puffs up. "Why, if you go to the city, you'll see every person of influence wearing one of my pieces. It's quite the thing, now."

Berrel thrusts a hand in his pocket and pulls out what looks at first like a gold bit of thread. He holds it up to the lamplight, revealing a flat, glossy bead the size of a coin at the end of the delicate length. "You can have one, if you'd like."

I stare at the pretty trinket, then back at Lord Berrel's bearded visage. "No, thank you." I think about the millions of scales I left on Onyx. "It's kind of you, but I don't wear jewelry."

Berrel nods, his eyes narrowing as he puts the necklace away. He combs a hand through thick, curly hair. "You're absolutely right. I wouldn't wear one of these gaudy baubles, either."

Instead of flattered, I feel vaguely uneasy. It's almost as if Lord Berrel means to insult me, only I can't figure out how. "I think our time is at an end, sir. The dance is over."

"Forgive me." He folds at the waist and dips his head low. "I didn't mean to offend you."

Adom manifests in front of me. "I take it you're ready to go?"

I gaze from Adom's profile to Lord Berrel's. For all I know, one is a cooking pan and the other is a hornet's nest. But chatting with Lord Berrel gave me some useful food for thought. Muuth is right: some Tranars don't believe the dragons exist, and yet dragon scales are still a valuable commodity. Berrel might prove useful if I ever need to trade those scales in my satchel for money. Nothing is more reliable than a person's greed, and something tells me that Berrel has plenty of that to fund my interests. He also told me a little more about the local superstitions about the stone soldiers and the woman who supposedly predicted the dragon's demise, Jetarna.

I take Adom's proffered arm and give Lord Berrel a tight nod. "Thank you for teaching me how to dance. It was a welcome distraction. Enjoy the rest of your evening."

"You as well." He smiles knowingly. "I hope we meet again, Lady Elanor. Our chat was... enlightening." He nods at Adom and turns his back.

Adom leads me away from Lord Berrel, to a corner of the room closest to the door. He shoves a baguette into my hands. "We should have left without indulging you.."

I tuck the baguette into the dress pockets. "I learned valuable information."

Alarm creases Adom's forehead. His eyes linger on Lord Berrel for a brief moment, then he returns his gaze to me. He strokes his chin thoughtfully. "Somehow, I suspect the information you're uncovering isn't the information I need to know."

I play with the ends of my newly cut hair. "You might be right about that."

The pupils of his eyes shrink. He guides me from the dance hall and signals for a driver. As soon as we're alone in the carriage, Adom swivels in the seat and puts an arm across my chair so the palm of his hand rests against the coach wall by the window, cornering me.

"Tell me what you and Lord Berrel discussed."

Casually and calmly as ever, I pull out the baguette and rip into the tough crust while he waits. "He told me about his dragon scale business, and about Jetarna Day next week," I inform him between bites. If he thinks he can intimidate me with the aggressive human act, he'll be sorely disappointed. I'm already annoyed with him for failing to smuggle some of the meat ground into a dip and those crunchy, twirly snacks in a napkin. A piece of bread? Really?

"Did he ask any questions?"

I finish the bread and wipe crumbs away. "He asked where I come from and how I knew you. I told him I come from an island south of Cornoc and you were my guardian as you said."

"What did he try to give you?"

So he spied on me? Of course he did. Adom trusts me about as much as a rickety bridge. I raise my eyes to his in silent rage. "He offered me a cheap necklace made from a stinking dragon scale, but I declined. I also told him to quit complimenting me. *Again.*"

Adom lowers his arm and nods. "Did you talk about anything else?"

My dancing? Superstitious Tranars? Adom's reputation with women? I have a mouthful of things I can share with him, but somehow I suspect he's after more specific information. "We didn't talk about our mutual hatred of you, if that's what you're after."

"You suppose Lord Berrel hates me?"

I smile brightly. "I thought that was obvious?"

Adom's nostrils flare. "What gave it away?"

I press my index finger to the lower right corner of my lips, feigning concerted thought. "Hm. I think it was around the moment you two almost ripped me in half."

He grunts. "Now you sound like Muuth. Sarcastic and imaginative."

"Why does Berrel hate you?"

"I thought I was interrogating you, not the other way around."

I straighten. "If you want my help in finding changelings, I need honesty from you. You told me before that you had enemies. That *we* had enemies. If Berrel is an enemy, you have to tell me why. It isn't fair for you to withhold the truth when my life is at stake."

He ducks his head. "There was a woman."

"A *human* woman?"

"Yes." Adom can't seem to look me in the eye. "She died, and Berrel never forgave me."

"You took away someone he loved?" *Why does this story sound so familiar?*

"His sister. I didn't kill her, if that's what you're implying."

"How did she die?"

He puts a hand on the foggy glass of the carriage window. Glass squeaks as he drags his hand down, wiping away the condensation. "A fever took her. Before she died, she asked to see me. I was on Onyx and the message didn't reach me in time. When I returned, she was gone."

"Did you love her?"

"It was a long time ago," he answers abruptly, without thought.

"You didn't answer my question."

"It isn't relevant."

"Did you love her?" I ask again.

He meets my eyes at last. "You of all humans should know I'm incapable of love," he growls. "Rat, I can guess what your end game is, but if you try escaping again I'll have to kill you." His visage grows solemn and severe. "I'll burn half the country to keep my sights on you."

"So why don't you just kill me now and be done with it?"

"Don't tempt me," he warns.

I dig my feet into the floor of the carriage and rock forward, fists clenched. "I'm tired of hollow threats, Adom. If you don't trust me to keep your secrets, why am I here?"

"It isn't just about me. The future of the herd depends your discretion and obedience."

The future of the herd? What about *my* future? As long as I'm with Adom, I have no future. As he said, my life is as good as worthless unless I continue to serve him without question. Earlier he said he'd consider letting me go—now I'm certain he won't.

~ * ~

We return to the inn, and Raina announces to Adom that they fixed up our carriage and have already loaded our supplies. He kisses her, then takes hold of my hand and pulls me to the door without a word. My gut sinks—if I enter the black carriage, it will seal my fate. I'll become his partner in crime, his accomplice.

He guides me into the coach. All hopes of an alliance with Berrel fade.

"My position in Trana is as Count Malandre," he instructs, once we are situated.

"I know." I look out the window. "How'd you manage that?"

"The real Count Malandre was a recluse. He...died. Unexpectedly. I took his place."

Died unexpectedly? Does he think I'm an idiot? I scoot as far from his side of the carriage as I can without making a scene. The last thing I want is for him to lose his temper now, while we drive through the isolated Tranar plains.

Adom grabs the seat beside my knee. "Please, El. Look at me."

I comply. Not for long.

"We're going to Foghum City," he informs me softly.

My father went to Foghum a handful of times in my youth. The city of King Siles. *What are you plotting? Why the king's city?* Questions I don't dare ask.

"I need you to be my ears," he says. "I can't be everywhere at once."

You mean you have scorchings.

He seems to sense my cynicism. "Why are you sulking?"

I straighten. "You just told me you'd kill me if I sought freedom. Earlier you promised to free me if I proved myself.

You think your lies and threats should make me happy?"

Adom sits back in his seat. I frown, confused, as he runs a hand through raven hair. "I'm sorry, Rat," he says. "Sometimes I can be too rough. We were discussing a sensitive subject and I live in two worlds; a world of physicality and a world of illusion. On occasion, my reactions are disproportionate to my environment." He lowers his eyelids. "I'm still trying to adjust."

I can't speak for a moment. Adom is apologizing? A day ago, I'd never have believed it. Why now? What does he stand to gain by making amends?

"My name is Elanor," I murmur. "You want me to call you Count Malandre in public? Quit calling me Rat."

His lids snap up but he doesn't protest. "Done."

"Quit threatening to kill me."

The curve of his mouth softens. "I might *have* to kill you, someday."

"And I might have to kill you first," I bark. "Let's not discuss it anymore."

"I'll...try."

I study him, anger mounting. He can't be sincere. He wants us to get along, to keep me passive and lure me into a false sense of safety. Just like before. I press my forehead to the glass.

After a few tense moments, I open my mouth again. But Adom's head is bent against the window and his eyes are closed. He looks so peaceful. Younger, too. Not at all how he looks awake. How old is Adom, anyway? Too young to be a herd leader *and* live a second life as a fake nobleman in Trana. Too young to be both hunted and hunter. I think back to our first encounter. He seemed so grown-up, but he can't have been that old. Maybe seventeen? Dragons don't age like humans, do they? Another question I'll never have a chance to ask Muuth.

The carriage jostles me as it rolls down the rickety path.

The driver only stops once to let the horses cool off. Soon, cottages line nearly every street. *We must be nearing Foghum.*

Adom rubs his eyes. "I shouldn't have slept," he murmurs, but he looks much better. Then he smiles. It is a curious, unguarded look of pleasure. "You didn't split my guts?"

"I thought about it."

"You didn't escape, either. I'm impressed at your self-restraint."

"We're almost at Foghum," I inform him.

He glances out the window. "So we are."

"What are your plans?"

"I'll get us rooms at the best inn in the city." He leans across me and flicks up the shade between us and the driver's box. "Driver, take us to the Volcourt Inn."

In a short while, the carriage stops. I gaze out the window. Everywhere there is madness. People shuffle past wearing bright turbans and tartans, ruffles of lace, hats of all shapes and sizes, and great clunking shoes that keep long silk dresses from trailing in mud. Colors swirl dizzyingly, a thousand peacocks *whooshing* around the carriage with wide mouths and angry chatter.

I hone in on one of the individuals, because trying to take them all in makes me nauseous. A young woman pushes a cart holding a clay jug of what looks like fresh milk against her hips. Her visage is fresh and smooth with clear brown eyes sparkling under a red scarf. She stops to talk to at least three people as she makes her way onward. Three people. Strangers, not family. She is confident, smiling and happy. I can't tell if she's close to my age or not—it's been too long to discern those differences, but she closer to my age than Muuth for sure. Except for Raina, I haven't seen anyone young, like me, since I was kidnapped at nine years old.

Adom glances at me. "You might want to hold my hand when we disembark."

It would be easy to lose him in a crowd like this. I savor

the thought for a moment, but as he opens the door and steps out, all ideas of escape shatter. The disorienting noise reaches my ears. Talk over talk. Feet clomping. Over there, someone shouting. Over here, someone crying.

He reaches out a hand. I take it in an instant, numbed by the chaos. He squeezes and gently helps me out of the carriage. Noise spins and follows us, inescapable.

Adom shelters me under the wing of his warm arm and points to a building looming over us like a mountain. "This is the Volcourt Inn." he breathes into my ear, a welcome, familiar whisper in the wake of alien sound. "It isn't far. Just a few steps further."

I tilt my head to observe the great architecture. Awe overtakes me as I stare at its magnificent height. Clinging to Adom, I move up the steps until we approach the broad door.

Two finely dressed young men pull the massive door handle, and the hinges groan as it opens. We enter the foyer, where sparkling candelabras shine like stars overhead. I've seen pictures of such finery in the books Muuth showed me, as well as in Adom's chambers. An elaborate desk rests along the wall beside a grand curving staircase. The staircase winds across the entire room revealing another, equally dazzling level. Scribbling on some parchment with a long feather quill, the host of the establishment glances up from his work and beckons for us to approach.

"Are you all right?" Adom asks me.

"I'm fine." In this mountain of architecture, my voice sounds shriveled. Diminished. Not powerful and echoing like on Onyx.

Adom releases my hand and strolls to the proprietor's desk. After a few moments of hushed dialogue, the man rises from his work and gestures for us to follow him. Gilded paintings hang on the walls above colorful furniture. We follow along through a vaulted corridor.

The proprietor jingles a long train of metal keys, chooses one, and unlocks the glass doorknob. This door doesn't creak open like one at the main entrance. It glides discreetly to a standstill against the wall. We are ushered into a sitting area with tables and chairs. A set of sliding doors drawn aside reveal the bedchamber. Lamps are already lit. The walls boast decorative paper and books in a glass case.

Again, there is only one bed in the suite. Where does Adom intend for me to sleep?

"My sister and I will require meal services only once a day," he says.

"We have the usual complimentary tray to help you recover from your journey. I can have a dinner prepared and brought up immediately. Let me know if you need anything, Count Malandre, and I will personally see to it." The proprietor closes the door behind him.

Adom settles on a chaise with an eagle pattern stitched into it. He grins. "You look as nervous as a rat confronting a cat." He crosses his legs, perfectly at ease.

I sit cross-legged on the floor. "I'm not used to having things in my room. Anyway, you said you would get us *rooms* earlier. Why are we sharing again?"

"I reconsidered. It's better for you to stay close to me. The city might seem like a safe place to hide, but I can track you anywhere, Elanor." He touches his nose. "Your scent."

I glare, certain he means it as an insult. Shifting positions, I lean against the leg of a broad armchair. "I'm not your sister any more than I am your wench."

"You objected to the other word. I didn't want to make you uncomfortable. Besides, it won't look natural if we don't have some reason to share a room," he explains.

"I wonder what human society would think about the dragon den." All those unmarried males and females, piled on top of each other. The chair leg begins to dig into my back. I squirm to find a less awkward brace.

"They probably wouldn't approve," he agrees, and frowns. "You could have borrowed things from my chambers at any time on Onyx. You never had to make do with so little."

With the blandest look I can muster, in spite of emotions boiling beneath the surface, I say, "Did you think I'd accept charity from my family's murderer?"

Adom's cheeks bloom into a nasty shade of magenta. For a moment, I worry he'll *change*. Then he takes a deep breath. His coloring returns to normal. "Never mind."

My stomach growls, reminding me we have more important matters to focus on. "I'm hungry," I complain. "A roll isn't exactly a full meal, you realize."

Adom arches an eyebrow. "We'll have to remedy your current state." Then he shoots me a leveling look. "If you're willing to accept charity from your family's murderer?"

"I prefer to think of this as stealing."

He doesn't look pleased. Without rising, he points to a tray in the corner with an accusing finger, the curve of his lips thin. "The tray is there."

The silver dish displays slices of bread, cheeses, and dried meats. I rise and pour a glass of dark red liquid. It tickles my nose and burns in my throat.

"Wine," Adom says as he watches me.

"I hate it," I growl, coughing. "It doesn't taste like water."

"Most things don't."

I bite into the bread. "It's bland."

"You're impossible to please." Adom advances, wearing a lopsided smile. He picks up a small knife and coats it with a yellow substance on the side of the tray. Then he smears it on the bread. Next, he dips the knife in an amber syrup. "You should recognize this."

"Honey?" I ask. "But how did he get all this honey away without the bees stinging him?" Wincing, I think of my few experiences with the coveted sweet stuff. I tried stealing from the bees in the Forest of Four… and failed miserably.

"They have experts trained in that profession." He smears honey over the bread. "Try this. It's bread with butter and honey and a pinch of cinnamon."

I take a bite. Then another. It tastes like being reunited with a long-lost friend. I can't get enough of the stuff. Soon, I finish off the entire tray.

Someone knocks on the door. Adom calls for the person to enter.

"Sorry to bother you, my lord," says the proprietor. "Someone left you a letter at the front registry." The man produces a parchment sealed with wax.

"Thank you." He takes the parchment, shuts the door. I see Adom frown as he paces forward and examines the wax blob. The seal is an orange flame. I remember a notice my Papa once received at the farm, sealed with the mark of a local lord. Whose sign is that?

Adom catches me staring. He shifts away and tears open the letter in haste. I watch emotions flicker across his countenance as he reads its contents.

"What is it?"

He shakes his head. "Another time."

"So much for honesty."

He doesn't bother to respond.

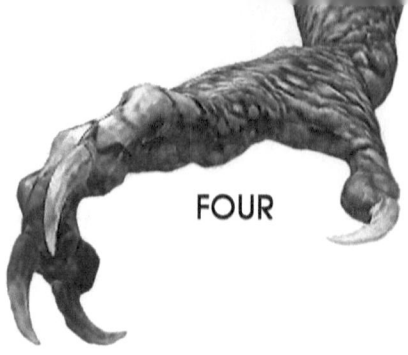

FOUR

WHEN I AWAKEN, THE sun's dying rays visit the room in a last, failing effort. Adom is sprawled across the chaise, softly snoring. I extend my cramped legs and creep closer. *He must be exhausted.* Aside from the brief nap in the carriage, Adom hadn't slept since we reached Trana. He stayed away from the room all last night. And where had he gone? To entertain Raina?

The letter hangs from his hand, its seal now broken, parchment crinkled.

I lean close, not daring to breathe, and grasp the mysterious document. Inch by inch, I ease it out of his grip. He doesn't stir. After several moments of watching his ribs expand and contract, I move into a corner, and open the letter.

Slayer, it reads. *Claron is gone. Decimated by dragon scorchings. I made contact with Leviathan and Cinderrider, and a third, a purple-speckled hunter. – Fire Breather*

Seconds tick by as I study the letter. Whoever wrote this meant to inform Adom about a recent scorching. I don't recognize the name, *Fire Breather*, and I don't recognize any of the other names in the letter. It could mean that all the names are coded in order to protect dragon sympathizers who are human. Or, more likely, it means that Adom has made a connection with the dragon changelings and they are all working from within Trana to…

…to do what?

A hand grabs my arm in an iron-tight grasp.

Gasping, I drop the letter.

The fury in his eyes is plain as dawn. "Did you read it?" He picks up the parchment.

"Just the first word," I lie. "Just 'Slayer.' What does it mean, Adom?" The shaking overtakes my whole body now. *Claron is gone. Decimated by dragon scorchings.*

When he answers, his voice rings dark with malice. His eyes, cold and severe, peruse me. "It means I'm a murderer. I earned the name slaughtering enemies of the herd in cold blood."

Horror branches out from the core of my chest into my extremities. It crawls up my throat and out my lips in a panic-ridden scream. He stifles my outcry with an uncompromising hand. I sob hot waves of molten tears. *Who will you murder tonight, Adom?*

He pushes me against the chaise. "Stay here, El. I need to go. I'll deal with you later."

The moment he releases me, I scramble away. "Curse you to the Abyss, Snake. If you hurt someone, I'll kill you. I'll stab you with the honey knife if you come near me again."

Emotions stretch taut and thin on his visage, mouth contorting as if holding in vomit he longs to spew out. His internal struggle becomes clear, and I hold my tongue, waiting, hoping for an explanation. He lets out a breath. "You're in too far, Rat. You can't go back."

I bare my teeth at him and hiss.

And then he's gone.

Of course he locked the door. I have to find some other means of escape. I packed some rope away in my satchel, but it doesn't stretch long enough. Our room is several stories above the street. Has Adom anticipated my thoughts? If so, he drastically underestimates my ingenuity. Does he think I'll get discouraged by the sheer height alone? Why, I live in a hollowed-out mountain! I have climbed heights far beyond the vastness of this building.

I run to the window and peer down. How many years

have I invented makeshift soaps, ropes, beds, rags, bowls and other various oddments out of nothing? My eyes wander to the bed. Layers of fine silk covers and satin sheets pile high. They will do nicely. Pulling the sheets off the bed, I rip them with abandon, experiencing some primitive pleasure in the destruction of such finery. I braid the long pieces into one thick cord, tying them end to end. Then I tie one end of my rope to the elaborate foot of the bed. My pulse escalates.

Opening the window, I throw the length of my sheets out into the cold night air. The resounding *thud* startles me. I hold my breath and wait to see if anyone emerges from the inn. My eyes scan the deserted streets. The last thing I need is a townsperson running to get the innkeeper assuming I mean to rob the place. The side of the building is dark.

Grateful for the cover, I face the room. Fifi rests against a pillow, staring longingly. It will be difficult to take her with me, even if I hide her in a bag. My eyes fall on the dirty satchel.

Just as I contemplate going back to grab those few necessities, a knock on the door drives all such thoughts away. I take hold of the makeshift cord and crawl out the window. As my body sinks below the windowsill, I lower my eyes and swallow a pang of guilt.

It doesn't take long to shimmy to the ground. When my feet touch solid earth, I release the bed sheets and look around. I suck in my first breath of air as a liberated person. My heart surges against my ribs. Drunk with the blood of a quickened pulse, I race down a dusty street.

But when I careen onto a large road, a chill tingles through me and gooseflesh rises across damp skin. No women are out. I spot two men fighting, and it occurs to me that during these hours the city is no place for a lone woman.

I spot a well-lit building. Creeping closer, I hear laughter and singing coming from within. It seems a safe place to rest for a while. I reach the door and hesitate only a moment before pulling the handle. Light pools onto the street.

A stocky man steps aside and lets me through. "Good evening, lass,"

I greet him, inexplicably rocked: the first time in twelve years I am able to speak to a person without Adom or any of the other dragons hovering close by.

My stomach growls.

"Are you hungry?" the broad-shouldered man questions.

"A little."

He presses me underneath his sweaty arm and ushers me into the noisy chamber the same way my father used to. He shelters me from the prying stares of the more drunken customers. Once we move past the initial tables where the drinks flow in abundance, he lets his arm fall.

"Let me take care of you." The man tosses a coin at a barmaid wearing a dress with a neckline that displays all her prized assets. "Food and ale for the young lady, here."

The serving maid brings two mugs of ale and slaps a platter of rice and beans in front of me. I thank the kind man and find us a seat in the corner of the tavern. Within moments, the man sloshes down his mug, wipes foam from his furry beard with the back of his hairy arm, and lumbers away from my table to greet other friends and consume more alcohol.

My tense muscles begin to uncoil. In the back corner of the room, a couple dance with bawdy enthusiasm. He stomps her foot and she elbows him while twirling. The dance looks nothing like the formal movements Lord Berrel and I attempted together at the party earlier today. Explosions of laughter ripple through the tavern, echoing my own.

A young man with cropped auburn hair and skin dark like a milk stout sits beside me. He strokes a trimmed beard. His emerald stare bores into me. "You don't belong here."

"Why do you say so?"

I catch a glimpse of straight white teeth.

"You're dressed too well for this place."

I compare our attire. My dress looks no different from his frilly tunic. The collar plunges, and the skirt flows to my ankles, but we're both wearing silk inundated with over-the-top embroidery. I survey the room. Others wear neutral garb in thick, starchy fabric with no additional flourishes. My mauve and his navy stand out next to dull browns and faded whites.

"I suppose I am." My eyes narrow on his fine outfit.

The man holds out a hand. "I'm Theodore Faigen."

"Elanor." I jiggle the hand thoughtfully. Why does his name tickle my memory? "What are you doing in a place like this, Theodore?"

"I seek entertainment." His eyes glitter. "Naturally."

A thin woman wearing a crocheted brown shawl enters the tavern. Like myself and Faigen, she doesn't fit with the local scene. Though disheveled, her hair is swept up in an elaborate coif peaking at the top of her head. Other women in the tavern wear loose hair and even looser clothes. This newcomer has fringes of lace decorating her multi-layered dress.

I glance over at the dancing couple bumbling around the room.

"Ah, yes," Theodore grins. "Drunks are especially engaging." His gaze pinches me like a set of sharp dragon canines. "But I'm here for the poetry hour."

I mouth, "Poetry?"

Theodore stands and bangs a mug on the wooden table. All eyes fix on him. "My dear friends." He brandishes the mug as though it's a sword. "It is my delight to grace you with another one of my creations." The audience blinks drunkenly. "My *vision* comes from the mere observance of common man gobbling up earthly needs and sating the fire of lust."

From the look of his audience, I'm not the only bewildered party. I slide away from the seat. The lord catches my hand, trapping me.

"Tonight I met a muse. She took hold of my imagination,

and from our passionate union birthed a masterpiece." He bows and grips me with uncanny strength. "I share it in the greatest humility." Then, clearing his throat, he recites:

"Sweet tragedy, how I long for thee,
my lover, my comfort, my best of friends.
The spirit that whispers across the sea:
O life-giver, mother and seer of ends.
The bride of my art by divine inspiration,
the shadow that lurks beneath all belonging,
and may your sweet throbbing fill me with elation
so moved by the waves of my transient longing."

The poem earns a few whistles and cheers from the tables closest to the door. The woman standing at the door claps, the tips of her fingers peeking out between holes in off-white gloves.

Theodore bows a second time, plunks into the seat, and throws hands to his hairline. "I haven't done it justice." Music starts again, and dancers take their places. "Unappreciative hogs!"

"They cheered for you, didn't they?"

"Bless you, beautiful creature." He dares another breathtaking smile. Then the smile wobbles and his head hangs below his shoulders. "But they didn't request a second exhibition."

"You have other poems?"

He waves a dismissive hand. "Oh, hundreds. Thousands."

This is a comfortable line of conversation for me. Muuth often recites rhymes. It was one of the ways we used to pass the time. He'd make up a riddle about his lantern, or the cows, or Adom, and I'd have to guess the meaning. Little word games that filled our days with meaning and kept our minds sharp.

Oh, Muuth. I have a strong urge to see him again. Guilt burns my esophagus, and I take another swig of the ale to numb away the pang. "What else do you write about?"

"Tragic events." He taps his chin. "The dragon scorchings."

This strikes a chord. Something Raina said... the memory

returns. "A Lord Faigen lives in the village we went through today." Blood rushes from my head.

Theodore's smile broadens. He hasn't noticed my discomfort. "Salcom village?" His eyes light up. "Were you accompanying Count Malandre this morning?"

Alcohol stirs in my stomach with unpleasant foreboding. What if Faigen tells Adom he's seen me? Adom will hunt me down and—and what? Will he kill me? I clutch my abdomen.

"Theodore?" a timid voice calls out.

Theodore finally meets the eye of the woman standing at the door. "Harminy?"

She plods nearer to us. "I wouldn't come here if I didn't need your help."

I seize the moment of distraction and push myself to a stand.

The lord's eyes flicker from my toes to my face, searching. "I'm sorry if I've been too familiar," he gushes, reaching for me. "Lord Malandre is a dear friend."

I stand. "You have the wrong person, sir."

Theodore frowns. "Did I disturb you in some way?"

"Please," the woman interrupts, creeping closer. "Faigen, it's an emergency."

I ease around her and push her in front of Faigen, blocking myself from view. "I don't know any Count Malandre," I call over my shoulder. Once outside, I don't stop to breathe. I run as far from the tavern as I can, taking careful pains to ensure he can't follow me.

Rough hands grab me from behind. "Look here, Signot. Look what I found!"

Warm, foul breath tickles my ear as the captor presses my arms together. I quiver; the ill effects of the alcohol haven't worn off, and my body hasn't regained full control of its capacities. The man in front swivels. His face is a misshapen lump, as though a dragon spat acid-bile on him. Catching my chin in greasy hands, he leers. "She's a fine one. She'll fetch a pretty price."

Confusion creeps into my intoxicated mind. How dare they manhandle me this way? No one, not even Adom, has permission to grab me like this. What have I gotten myself into now? A lump grows in my throat, making it hard to breathe. I want to break down and cry. Instead, I bite into the fleshy, salty arm nearest to my face. Hard.

A crooked nose prods my cheek like a hen's pecking beak.

"Let me go," I shout.

The hideous man backs away, startled, but the person behind me clutches tighter. I scream until my lungs completely deflate. Louder and louder I cry, begging for someone to come and save me. Sound bounces off the walls and floats into the midnight air. Surely no one can sleep with that ear-piercing shriek crawling in through the windows.

The man behind me lets out a sharp, visceral curse. Spit lands on my neck. He hits me with a hard object. "That's enough out of you, missy."

White spots swarm in my vision. "Count Malandre," I whisper. "He'll kill you."

One of the kidnappers laughs. "She knows someone," he says. "Even better."

An icy chill shoots through me. Adom will never pay ransom. He'll leave me to be sold by these dogs! I struggle, but the blow to my head throbs. The man shoves me toward a building. I topple, unable to maintain my balance. He kicks until I hobble where he directs. Nausea ripples through me like the tides, threatening to push me into unconsciousness.

"Let's keep her in old Takma's cellar until this lord gives us the money."

The cellar?

A voice from another lifetime calls to me in memory. *"Elanor! Get in the cellar!"*

Panic takes over. I renew screaming until they hit me again.

It doesn't matter anymore. I'd rather be unconscious than go down there.

"Elanor! Get in the cellar."

The men open a door leading into blackness. A dirty rag slides across my mouth.

"Get in the cellar."

They gag me, tie my hands behind my back and bind my feet together. "Down ya go," one of the men hiccups. They push me in.

"Get in the cellar."

I tumble to the ground. The door slams above me, the room encompassed by darkness so thick it clings to my skin. Silence alters my mind. I hear things, and then I grow confused about which cellar I'm in. *"Sammy, no!"* It happens again and again, each time the anguish and horror of Papa's last words grow more and more real to my ear until I choke on tears. I hear the howl of the dogs, the flurry of thick dragon wings bounding from the ground.

Hours pass in this way, paving a way to madness. If I don't take action, I'll go insane. Fighting past terror, I rally courage. *You're stronger than this,* I remind myself. *You've been through worse before.*

Sitting still never suited me. Not then and not now. In spite of the rag muffling my noise, I scream and grunt in anger, demanding to be let out. My fingers twist and writhe against damp ground for an object to cut my bonds. I palm a smooth rock behind my back. Maybe I can use it.

I lean against the wall and inch to my feet. My eyes adjust quickly to the blackness. Darkness served as my shield before. Now, I make out rows of wooden shelves covered with clay jugs. Mixed among these are sealed jars of food. I won't starve if they forget about me.

The jugs spark an idea. I pivot with a decisive hop, bend, pointing my bound hands to the ceiling, pull back, and fling the rock. The unimpressive *thud* tells me my tool misses its target. Cursing, I squint to see where the rock fell. No luck.

I bounce to the shelves, then lose my balance and slam against them. My head cracks against wood. Dizzy, fire sears my neck and tingles in my abdomen. Something smashes and pinpoints prick my legs and arms. The scent of beets saturates the air. Wet climbs up the hems of my skirt. I broke a jar! My fingers close around a bit of broken glass.

I squeeze it and begin desperately cutting at the rope around my wrist. It's a sloppy knot, so it falls apart in twenty-six heartbeats. I thank Muuth for teaching me all about tying and untying knots. Some tricks I never imagined using in civilized society. My hand aches from the damage the glass caused, so I drop the shard and yank the rag from my mouth. Then I untie the ropes from my ankles and push myself to stand.

Door hinges creak. My body tenses, my head protests and painful flashes of light dart across my vision. Someone pulls the door open. I squint to make out the form that enters. But the figure can't be the tall, misshapen figure of the first kidnapper. The silhouette doesn't match. Maybe the kidnapper who lurked behind me? I haven't gotten a good look at him. My hands tighten into fists behind my back. I will fight until I kill them. I will not go quietly.

The man descends the stairs and approaches me.

"Oh, Elanor," he breathes.

Adom. Why, oh why, did it have to be him? My relief gives way to shame then doubt. Will he kill me now that he saved me? Can't I find *any* place to hide from him? I collapse, my legs cramping under hours of crunched abuse. I'm tired and angry and certain I'm going to die tonight, anyway. What's the point of fighting? I can't escape him.

He lifts me. The scent of pine and rainfall lingers on his tunic. Adom's dragon eyes enable him to see without light. "You're covered in blood," he says, and utters a foul word.

I fist the front of his tunic desperately. "Not blood," I

whisper. "Beets."

"But your hand is bleeding."

"It doesn't hurt."

Long ago, shortly after Adom brought me to Onyx, I tried to escape. I was just a frightened child, crying by a stream, sure I'd die alone. Who would care if this little 'Rat' died? Then Adom appeared in human form and scooped me into his strong arms.

"Why are you crying, Rat?"

"I thought I was lost forever!"

"You aren't lost. I've found you, haven't I?"

I almost liked Adom then. I almost like him now, as he carries me to his horse through narrow streets where only drunkards loiter.

"What happened to them?" I ask.

He stares straight ahead, but a muscle twitches along his jawline. "What do you think? The same thing that happens to anyone who harms what's mine."

Such stoic words for such horrible deeds.

My heart drops. Adom sets me down and wraps his cloak around me. He rips the hem of his cloak and ties it around my bleeding hand. His words keep me frozen to the spot.

He thinks I'm his property. I should run before he destroys me the way he destroyed those men. How many innocents did he kill, all for the sake of the herd? I should flee before I become his next nameless victim. But my knees are quaking like jelly, and I'm terrified of things I do not understand. I do not belong here. I do not have a home here. Nobody cares about me in this cold, dark place. He drags me onto the horse, positioned in front of him.

"Are you going to kill me, too?"

Adom's eyes glitter as he gazes at me. "You've been more of a burden than a help. We're going back to Onyx."

I draw a sharp intake of breath. "But what about Ona?

Won't he try to kill me?"

Adom's shoulder muscles flex against my forehead. "You had a chance to live."

"Oh, why don't you just kill me now and get it over with?" I murmur, too tired to argue.

He doesn't reply.

Adom tugs at the horse's reins when we reach the steps leading to the entrance of the Volcourt Inn. The animal stops abruptly, quick to respond, almost as though it senses its rider's dark mood. Footmen scramble to help me dismount and before I know it, the stable hand is already leading the steed away. I steal a glance at Adom, but he is all brimstone and fire.

"I'll only be a minute," he informs the stable hand. To me, he says, "Go get your things."

I obey, frightened by the tight tone of his voice. I lift my skirts and run through fine corridors, Adom looming darkly behind me, until at last I burst into the well-lit room. It takes a moment to reorient myself. I have been up most of the night, cramped and suffering the after effects of too much alcohol. Now my head pounds and my legs and ankles throb from ill use.

Perusing the room, I swallow regret rising in my throat like vomit. I take in all my eyes can hold of the finest establishment I will ever see again. Even Fifi, who rests in the exact place I left her, looks perfectly at ease on the plush pillow covering the otherwise bare bed. I stuff her in my ragged satchel with finality. On the floor next to the window sits a pile of shredded linens, my escape ladder. I can just imagine Adom storming into the room, discovering my absence, and flying to the window to find the trail of damaged bedsheets. I can see him pulling the rope up slowly, eyes blackening with every angry tug, muttering curses into the cold night air.

Hair on the back of my neck pricks with sudden awareness. Two round, bright orbs peek over the edge of the dresser. Large brown eyes, full of some haunted memory. They blink, and I spot one glistening tear trickle onto a pale, translucent cheek.

"Who's there?"

"Me. Nathaniel." A little boy creeps from his hiding place. His cheeks are wan, and his body thin from malnourishment. "You're not another dragon, are you?"

My heart stops short. "No," I reply. "I'm just a woman."

"Good." The boy rubs his ashen visage with sooty hands, and his lower lip trembles.

Years of hardened self-absorption crumble away. I hug him close.

"Dragons," he sniffles. "Mama and Papa..." Sobs wrack his entire body.

"I'm so... sorry," I whisper.

As I stroke hair away from his forehead, guilt demolishes me. My fault. I helped the dragons. All these years. I cooked and cleaned for Adom. But it isn't just Muuth and I who suffered. He destroyed whole families because I never had the spine to show him we humans are more than rats. This poor boy is another product of Adom's destruction, because no one dared to stand up to him. Adom killed *children*. I have no excuse for my years of self-preservation.

The door opens. A chill trickles into the room as the beast himself enters in his lurking human form. Does he mean to consume us both? Me for dinner and the child for dessert?

His eyes narrow when he sees my arms tucked around Nathaniel. "Leave the boy."

I hold fast. My knuckles turn white with exertion. "No. You're no better than those monsters who wanted to sell me to the highest bidder. You leave him, leave *us* alone."

Adom springs across the room and takes hold of my shoulders. "Let him go."

With an easy step, I slide between the child and the changeling.

Adom drops to one knee. "I'm not going to hurt you," he

whispers to the boy. "I'm leaving with this woman, and I'll be back in the morning. Just try to get some sleep." Then he rises, grabs my arm, and pulls me out of the room without giving me a chance to say goodbye. The boy gazes mournfully after us. Adom pauses only to lock the door behind us.

"You'd left the door unlocked before. Why imprison him now?" I mutter.

If his expression could poison, I'd be dead in an instant. "I'm only locking the door now because you've managed to terrify him the way no dragon scorching could have."

His words take me aback. "If you hurt him, I'll kill you."

Adom doesn't speak. Instead he storms out of the inn, breezing past serving maids and proprietor alike with the air of a pompous, irritated lord. Outside, the horse whinnies. The stable hand hurries to remove the feeding bag. Adom produces a carrot and allows the creature a moment to enjoy the small luxury before he places his foot in the stirrup to gracefully swing up over the animal's back. I climb behind him without any assistance, clutching my satchel.

With two precise kicks to the animal's flank, Adom's horse gallops fast through the city. Buildings whirl by. Just above them, the sun creeps up in vibrant hues of reds and gold. People begin emerging from little stone houses, and signs appear on store windows announcing the business day. Market vendors stock their stalls with goods preparing for the busy day ahead. No one seems to sense the coming danger I grasp so tangibly in my arms.

At last we reach the gate. A line has already formed in front of us.

"There wasn't a line here earlier," I whisper, shivering. I'm still wearing his cloak to hide the blood and beet stains that will surely attract attention, but the long fabric has slipped off my legs and I'm too cold to move my arms away from the radiating warm of my chest to fix it.

Adom adjusts the cloak so it covers my legs, probably

because he notices the stains on my dress and doesn't want any questions. "We arrived before curfew."

Soon our turn comes to greet the gatekeeper. "Next."

"Count Malandre and his ward. We're on urgent business for the king."

Again, the lie. I wince as the gatekeeper comes nearer. He wears a blue uniform and seems exceedingly proud of all his many badges. "Show me your document," the man demands strutting closer to get a better look at our faces.

Adom produces the letter I glimpsed earlier. I gape. Is he mad? He can't give it to the gatekeeper! That letter contains incriminating evidence. I almost speak out. But if the man discovers Adom's plot right now, I'll be sent to prison for aiding him. That is, if Adom doesn't *change* and murder us all. I say nothing, and pray the man won't discover our terrible secret. The guard takes the document and studies the orange seal. He seems to recognize it, but doesn't open or read the letter. After a moment, he seems satisfied.

"All right, then." He nods. "Go on through."

Adom accepts the letter and nudges the horse's flanks. We surge forward.

How did he know the seal would let us through? It must be someone important. That explains why he insists on the pretense of a lord. I shudder as the horse clips through the gate.

Adom doesn't seem to notice my anxiety. Once outside, he urges the horse to gallop again. We ride over several large hills. The city of Foghum fades into the distance. Was it all just a glorious memory? I squint at the distance, hoping for one last glimpse of my freedom.

He slows the horse to a trot. I stiffen. We're in the middle of nowhere. Why here?

At last we stop. He dismounts and pulls me roughly down with him. "Let's go."

We move toward a grove of trees. Dread sits in my stomach

like a cold, hard stone. It weighs me to such a degree my legs become heavy boulders. In an effort to regain feeling in my body, I struggle against him. "I can walk by myself."

Adom releases me so abruptly I fall backward and tumble onto the ground. "Fine." He balls his fingers into a fist then stares at his hand. He spins away and proceeds toward the trees.

I fix my eyes on his back, horrified. So this is it? He'll kill me here, in the middle of the country where no one will ever find my remains? I always envisioned dying on Onyx. At least there Muuth can bury me. "Adom, wait!"

"There's no time," he insists, his voice cold and steely.

A breeze blows through the valley, gently tossing his hair so he doesn't look so wild or frightening anymore. The warmth of the breeze also seems to have a calming effect on his soul. Sad eyes gaze at the horizon, blocked from my view in part by intense, furrowing eyebrows.

"I never properly thanked you for helping me escape from those men," I offer.

His eyes soften. "They left a message for me at the Volcourt Inn, so I followed the instructions and made them suffer. I knew you would be in the midst of saving yourself, and thought only to keep them occupied. You didn't need me there." Adom exhales loudly and returns to me. He extends a hand. "Do you think I *want* to see you dead, Elanor?"

"You've said as much," I point out, refusing his help as I rise. "You killed those men. You killed my family. Hundreds of people have perished by your scorchings." I can't control the shaking that takes hold of my body. It frustrates me to show him my weakness.

Adom says nothing at first. Then, "You wouldn't believe me if I told you that what you thought you saw that day was a lie. I had nothing do so with those villages that burned."

"If that's the truth, why haven't you said it before? You say you have nothing to do with the scorchings, but—" I stop myself before I blurt out *your letter tells me otherwise*. "—But there is a mountain of treasure in your cave that belongs to someone else. Where did it come from?"

"There's an explanation for that."

"And what's the explanation for the little boy crying about his murdered parents at the Volcourt Inn? And why were *you* the first dragon I laid eyes on after my parents died? *And why the hell did you keep me as your prisoner on Onyx for twelve years?*"

"I can't answer all your questions, Elanor. But I do care about your well-being."

"Hogwash," I say. "You say you care? Then free me."

"I can't." His voice sounds hollow. "I still need you."

"Ah. I see it now. *You* need me. Not the dragons. You could free me if you wanted to. But you won't because you think I have a part to play. You think I am relevant somehow."

"You *are* relevant," he answers.

"And you care."

"I do care. More than you know."

"How sweet. Then I suppose I must forgive you."

"Elanor, be serious."

"I'll tell the truth, Adom, even though you never do me the same courtesy. I don't respect you. I don't like you. I don't care about you, and I certainly don't believe you. I despise you, and someday soon I am going to kill you. Is that serious enough for you?"

His eyes darken to shimmering bolts of red. "I suppose it is for the best." He turns. "Now come with me."

FIVE

THE MOUNTAIN

I FOLLOW HIM TO the nearby forest. Neither of us speak; Adom because of the dark mood encompassing him, and myself because nothing I say will help my position. The forest thickens around us, huge trunks twisting from the ground as if to suffocate us. It puts me in mind of the two kidnappers whose massive hands roughed me up only hours ago.

When we find ourselves behind a dense copse of trees, Adom strips, folds his clothes and places them beneath a bush. He crouches on all fours. His body contorts, his back arches, and his face elongates into a snout. When he has fully changed, I climb onto his back, hiking ample skirts to my thighs.

He leaps into the dawn sky and spreads his wings wide, the morning sun shining through the translucent skin. With one flap of those membranous limbs, we fly beyond the city of Foghum, with another we sail past more cottages and houses. Now we pass new hills and valleys.

My heart pounds, an intoxication that renews with every powerful pump of Adom's massive wings. Wind lifts hair away from my neck. I raise a hand away from Adom's mane, careful to clutch him tighter with the other. Air flows between outspread fingers. I laugh aloud. Then a song—a soulful tune Mama once sang—comes to me:

"*Beauty never looks as sweet as when I dance on merry feet*
And run t'ward where the Falls divide to douse myself of
  years of pride.
Oh tell a tale, my rosy maid, of dragons and the games
  they played

And I will hear with all my ear and not the half I used to hear.
All knowing, I alone may stand, to guard the mystery of
  thy land,
And on the Skylark Mount I dive, a Dragon Woman
  come alive."

As I sing, my mother's voice rings out loud amidst the roar of the wind, the first time I've heard it since my capture. A strange twist of fate it should be on a dragon's back. The words of my mother's lullaby seem to speak of happier days, when man and beast understood one another. Days before Kainan, and the war that took place between humanity and the stone soldiers.

A low hum resonates beneath me. Adom sings, too, a deep rumble. Muuth told me dragons only sang in the sky so no one else can hear their wretched voices. He's wrong about this one thing. Adom's voice is dark and haunting and his song, mournful. My gooseflesh rises.

"Adom," I whisper so he can't hear. "Your song is beautiful."

In another moment, we sail over the Forest of Four. Adom flaps his wings once more and we descend into the mountain, the central cave below us now. My fingers slip, and I lose grip on his mane. Heart dropping, we plummet uncontrollably to the ground.

My whole body shifts forward, swinging helpless against the momentum Adom's body creates as he spirals downward. Dragons shuffle aside as we land.

Somehow, Adom's solid form catches my fall as ground rises to meet us. We're no longer moving, but the cave swims in circles above my head. My ears throb with the cold chill of the night sky. I can hear the grumblings of the other dragons as they creep back to their spots, surrounding us. They don't look happy to see me. Adom tilts his head toward me.

"Go to a safe place," he says. "I need to speak with Ona."

There remains no trace of the pensive concern from before. I bristle at the commanding tone, but decide now isn't the time to start an argument. Instead, I slide down his side and hurry out of the cave careful to avoid eye contact with the other dragons. Ona's sharp nails scratch the ground as I pass. *Don't let them hurt me, Adom.* As the thought passes, I curse myself. When had I come to depend on Adom's good will for my survival?

I race to my cave and settle on a bed of crunchy leaves in misery, certain I missed my one chance of escape. Adom will probably return to the mainland right away. Part of me wants to believe the things he told me in Trana. I can guess which bits ring true. Other changeling dragons are out there. But in spite of his protests, he killed my family. He murdered and lied about it, just like he lied about having nothing to do with the dragon scorchings.

Claron is gone. Decimated by the dragon scorchings. I made contact with Leviathan and Cinderrider... That's what the letter said. He wanted to "strengthen the herd." What better way than to take out as many Tranar towns as possible?

Down the hall, someone chants an obscure rhyme in a singsong voice I know all too well. Muuth hobbles to his usual spot, a wide grin on his mottled visage. "Back already, are you?" he asks obviously pleased with this development.

I throw my arms around him. "I missed you too much to stay away for long."

"He cut your hair." He tilts his head and laughs. "Adom didn't kill you, at least." He wipes excess moisture from his eyes and peers at me, studying the changes in my appearance. "Although it sounds like *someone* is dying in the Central Cave right now."

My heart quickens. I tilt my ears to listen. Fire and howls bounce off the walls. Ona? Or is it a challenge? Adom is challenged by one of the younger males from time to time. I shouldn't care. It shouldn't bother me. Except I can't shake the dark suspicion that it all has to do with me.

"Adom didn't kill me," I say slowly. "But I wish he had. Then I wouldn't have to bear the burden."

The sounds subside, and I breathe a little bit easier.

Muuth sobers, searching my face. He finally asks the obvious: "What burden?"

I exhale, lowering my voice so the echo will not carry through to the other caves. "Muuth, I think Adom plans to start a war with the king's army. I think he's building the herd to that end. He intends to bring more changelings to Onyx to strengthen his numbers."

His brow furrows and he scratches his patch of hair so aggressively pieces of scalp begin flaking off, revealing more diseased skin underneath. "I don't think Adom would do that."

After all he ever said about Adom, his doubt shocks me. "I've found evidence."

He looks uncertain. "I've watched the lad grow. Scorchings are one thing. There's good plunder to be had from scorching. But what would he stand to gain with war?"

"The respect of the herd," I respond in an instant. "Adom confessed his one weakness to me—his humanity. The herd scorned him for it. What better way to prove his strength?"

Muuth's eyes widen. "And what if you're right, lass? What will you do?"

I frown. "Adom brought me back because I tried to escape when I suspected the truth. But before I could find my way through the city to warn King Siles, men captured me, and then Adom found me again." I frown. "There's something I need to ask you."

"Anything, El."

"Adom said you had a boat hidden away somewhere. He's lying, isn't he? You wouldn't keep something like that from me when you know I've dreamed of escaping for years."

"I *had* a boat, the one I used to sail here, but it was damaged in a storm. That was long before you. I would have told you about it if it would've helped you escape."

"Where is it now?"

"It's in the bathing cave, hidden behind a rock. All that's left of it is one of two rotted wooden planks with a handful of barnacles growing on it."

"Why didn't you ever try to fix it?"

"There wasn't much left to fix after the storm, and the water dragons keep a close eye on boats in their territory. I've seen them swallow a fishing boat in one vicious chomp. It's why sailors avoid these waters. They believe in sea monsters, but won't recognize them as dragons."

Even though Muuth's response makes perfect sense, I can't help but feel disappointment. Adom had been right about the boat, after all. Why hadn't Muuth ever mentioned it before? He had always led me to believe he had come here as a prisoner, like me.

The gleam in his eyes causes me to break our shared gaze. "Why are you staring?"

Muuth wags his head. "I'm sorry. I'm growing so old. I need to pass on my stories."

I'm practically his daughter. If he wants to tell me more tales or recite more rhymes, I'll sit and listen. So why does it seem like he wants something else? "Well, go ahead then."

His expression slackens. Intensity fades from his eyes. He puts a hand to his forehead. "I can't live forever." He straightens and shudders, shaking his head as though coming out of a trance.

Pulling away, I pat him gently on the back. "You can come with me. Let's run."

"My place is with the dragons and the stones." His voice sounds firm, his tone, resigned.

Why he wants to die with these foul serpents is anybody's guess—I have no inclination to delve any deeper into his insanity than proximity allows. Chills creep up my back as

I study his veined, heavy-lidded eyes. Have they changed colors? Or is the darkness playing tricks on my imagination?

"The next time Adom goes to Trana, I'm going with him," I murmur.

"Why did he want to take you with him in the first place?"

"I suppose he thought my humanity would validate his claim as Count Malandre."

"Count Malandre?" Muuth breathes, eyes widening.

"It's what he calls himself." It's been a long day and a longer night. "I need sleep."

The old man rises. His bones groan painfully. Hobbling around the room, Muuth careens at the entrance and jiggles his foot. "I'll see you when you wake up, then."

When he leaves, I hug my knees to my chest for warmth. Those Tranar beds were so soft. I miss them already. And the tarts and the honey and the warm baths! Salvaging a few old leaves for a nest, I curl into a tight ball and force myself to sleep.

~ * ~

I awaken as the afternoon heat breaks. Head groggy and aching from an uncomfortable few hours of sleep, I stumble straightaway into Adom's chambers. No hypnotic fire flickers from the stone furnace. The room is still and cold. Too late. He's already returned to Trana.

I pick out one or two of the dresses he stored away for my use. My new plan is to check out the bathing cave to verify Muuth's story. Of course I believe him—Muuth has never lied to me before, and I trust him completely—but I want to see the old boat with my own eyes. Besides, I need a bucket of water to clean the younglings' cave afterward.

The bathing cave is a lake near the mountain's base. Its only opening is blocked by vines and trees so the filtered light creeps in with greens and purples. The lake is a mystic blue, stalagmites lurching up from the bed of coral. Moss decorates the walls of the cave, the most homey wall decor I have yet to see, even with all the finery I saw in Trana.

Muuth said what's left of the boat is hidden behind a rock. I stalk past a pile of moldy old ropes and dingy burlap sacks, strip out of my clothes, and leave the folded pile on a rock. The lake water slips over my skin, raising gooseflesh as I wade out toward the middle of the lake where there is a large rock. The 'sugarloaf' as Muuth calls it, is far enough away from the shore that I don't often go there. He refers to it as his sunbathing rock, so I've let it be his territory, same as his room. It's an easy guess where he's hidden the boat.

I reach the rock and drag myself out of the water, shivering. Sharp stones scratch against my skin, drawing pink and white lines across my knees, legs, and forearms. Uneven pebbles bruise my palms. A few days in Trana, and I am becoming soft. I crawl around the rock island, searching for the pieces, but I don't see any boat wreckage. Mud sticks to my fingernails. Maybe I have the wrong rock. Or maybe Muuth dismantled it last night after I confronted him about it.

Or maybe he moved it, a nagging voice says at the back of my head. I shake away the ridiculous idea. Muuth would never... *Well, where is it, then?* Why would he hide the wreckage? I think about Adom's words. Maybe it isn't wreckage. Maybe it's really a boat. And for some reason, Muuth doesn't want me to have it.

"This is crazy," I say. "He wouldn't do that to me. Adom is getting under my skin."

I swim back to the shore, dry off, and change into the plain dress I borrowed from Adom. I tie my short hair back using a fresh rag. The scent of fire and grease fills the cave. Muuth is cooking breakfast. He's always taken care of me. If he says the boat is wrecked I will believe him. I wet my lips and move toward the cave entrance.

~ * ~

Nerama and Canna are sleeping in the central cave when I enter. They uncurl their long tails and bat sleepy eyelids. The pungent scent of dragon dung permeates the air. When Nerama sees me laying a plank of wood on the floor to serve as a dustpan, he hisses.

"What are you doing here, Rat?"

I hold the broom in my right hand and force a smile. "I'm sweeping scales."

Canna snorts and farts at the same time. "You must be in a good mood today."

My arm slows as I notice mysterious splotches on the floor. "What happened here?"

Nerama yawns, his tongue lolling out over his teeth. "Ona nearly killed Adom last night. He smelled like stinking human food. Your scent was all over him." He taps one of the spots with a talon. "Don't worry. The blood will wash out when we have another rainfall."

The broom slips from my hands. *Thud*. "Is he all right?"

"Ona? He's salting his wounds on the beach, but he'll be fine."

I bend over to retrieve the rolling broom. "I meant Adom."

Canna's eyes narrow. "It isn't your business, slave."

"Please tell me."

Nerama and Canna exchange glances.

"She thinks she can mate with him," Nerama taunts.

"Have some decency," I scold. "Your herd leader is injured."

"In his dragon form, Adom may be strong enough that he can't be defeated," says Canna. "But that doesn't make him one of us. One day, a stronger dragon will rip his head off and when that day comes, you're welcome to have him all to your lonely self. Until then, stay away from him. Silva has her claws deep under his scales, so you have no claim on him."

Taking a step back, I spit to show my disgust. "I never said I wanted to claim him."

"Then why does he slither to your defense every time the

Head Dragons vote to kill you? When you forget to feed the cattle, or fail to clean the younglings' cave, we're reminded how useless you are to us. We don't need you here, but Adom disagrees. When the Head Dragons vote against him, he must fight to win his way. To win your life. Every time he takes your punishment, he enrages the herd. The next time you climb to the top of the mountain or wade through the leech bog, think about how you were supposed to burn for your failures. How Adom is burning in your stead."

My stomach hardens up until it feels like the dense pit of a peach. Adom is taking punishments *for me*? But why would he do that? If he felt sorry for me, why keep me here like a prisoner?

I boost the plank and carry it outside, sickened and confused by their words. I separate the scales from dust and pocket them in my satchel. If I return to Trana, I need to be able to pay my way to Foghum City. I'll collect as many scales as I can while I'm here.

The island is summery today. Scattering dust to the warm wind, I study the sky. Dragons cut the perfect blue like fish through sea. Their bodies glisten in the sun, great floating gems.

Does Adom really take the punishment for me whenever I overstep? Why would he do it? We aren't friends, and we never talked before the Trana trip. I've never had any indication...

Scream, he told me the day before the trip. Then he blew fire at me and let me escape. He didn't ask me to do it because he derived pleasure from my shrieks of pain. He asked me to do it so I could spare *him* the pain the herd would cause him if they knew he let me off soft.

I do care, he told me yesterday. *More than you know.*

I double over and hug my knees. The balmy wind turns chill, and the bite feels deserved. What if Adom wanted the changelings to come to Onyx so *he* wouldn't be alone? So he wouldn't have to face the dragons by himself. So others could stand beside him and fight.

We fly to fight.

"Why wouldn't you tell me?" I whisper. "If this is true, why wouldn't you trust me?"

A soft glow of light bounces across the walls of Muuth's den when I enter it later in the day. "Does Adom take punishments for me?" The question bubbles up without any forewarning.

Muuth sits crouching like an old toad, staring bug-eyed at small inscriptions on stone slabs. "Where is this coming from?" He fingers the slabs like some of his little creations.

"There was blood in the central cave. Nerama said—" my voice cracks.

"Ona and Adom fought yesterday, but not over you," Muuth says quietly.

I draw circles in the dirt with my fingernail. Does Muuth know I went to the bathing cave this morning? Does he know I checked on his story? "Why did they fight?"

"Ona wants to control the herd, and he's using Adom's human side to make him look soft. It has nothing to do with you. He has to fight to keep his place, even without you around."

I stare at the gadgets along the walls of his den. "Then why does he put up with it?"

He jabs one of the slabs into the ground. "With what? Their aggression? You know what they are, El. You've seen them fight each other on the beach and in the air. They're creatures made of flame, and have you ever seen flame sit still and be at peace? No. It is greedy, and all-consuming, and ever-changing. That is what dragons are. Adom knows this. Adom *is* this."

I wet my lip, thoughtful. "How old is he?"

He wobbles to his feet with his stones weighing down his sagging forearms. He carries them to the wall and places them in slots around his lantern. "Twenty-eight."

Dragons live for hundreds of years. Dragon younglings don't reach adolescence for thirty years. Why did Adom age so rapidly? "How can he be so young?"

Muuth shrugs. "All part of the changeling curse, I suppose."

There's more to it. I force him to meet my gaze. "Who cursed him?"

He scratches his head and goes wide-eyed. When the ploy doesn't soften me, he speaks reluctantly. "A woman named Jetarna. You know about the stone soldiers?"

The words of the man from the ball—Lord Berrel, was it?—return to me. "The Tranars believe she was a witch because she predicted they would come."

Muuth studies the patterns on the ceiling with great interest, all the while steepling his hands. "She wasn't a witch. And she didn't make any prophecy. Remember the invention I told you about? The one that allowed me to glimpse the sun's acid?"

My eyes fall on him. "The gadget you said summoned the stone soldiers?"

"I never said that." He shakes his head. "It wasn't only mine. Jetarna and I built the telescope together. She'd been experimenting with dragon blood and observed a strange effect when the blood was exposed to sunlight. It turned into dust."

As my mouth drops open, I take in a soft breath. "I didn't realize you knew Jetarna."

"Of course I knew her. She was my wife."

My eyelids flip open. "Jetarna? *The* Jetarna?"

"Yes, *the* Jetarna. She studied things. I built things. Once in a while, we collaborated and discovered together. We documented everything, but it was all destroyed during the war."

The thoughts won't settle into a coherent sentence. "So the sun's acid—"

Muuth bows his head. "We wanted to see what the sun looked like up close. Jetarna hypothesized that the coagulation effect she observed in the dragon blood corresponded to changes on the sun's surface. The sun's acid proved her theory. Then she confessed to me that for decades, she'd been using stores of dragon blood to test the healing properties on humans. In particular, pregnant women. The women who came to her were desperate, and the dragon blood seemed to solve complex issues during pregnancy and labor. But there was a side effect."

"She experimented on pregnant women?" the words wheeze out.

"I know. The horror in your voice matches what I felt when she told me. And when she told me she suspected that the dragon blood *changed* the infants born after treatment, I knew we had to destroy them. All of them." His voice grows husky. "I don't hate the dragons, El, not like you do. But I do hate the changelings. They're an abomination, a failed experiment. And they're stronger than normal dragons, and they have unheard of abilities. Things no living thing should be able to do. I once saw a changeling control a human with his mind." Muuth scrubs his face.

"Do you understand? We couldn't let them live. Not when we already had full-blooded dragons scorching the land. Some changelings came from high-ranking families, even. They had power, strength, and money. Can you imagine what would happen if they came together?"

Yes, I can *imagine.* I'm living proof that a herd of dragons means nothing good for Tranars. "You're telling me you were responsible for ending the war with the dragons?"

His eyebrows scrunch. "I'm telling you we were responsible for the changelings. We tried to track them all, but we couldn't. There were about forty originally. Jetarna treated that many women with the dragon blood over four winters. And by the time she told me, thirty winters had gone by. They were living among us, grown by then and had children of their own."

I rub the spot between my eyes as a headache builds slowly. "Did they pass it on to their children? The forty original changelings?"

He nods, his head bent low. "They did. It's in the blood of forty families now. Some had twelve children, some had only one. And then, by chance, we saw what happened when…" He closes his eyes as if the memory pains him, "when one of the changelings was exposed to sun's acid. When the fog came, it burned and seemed to disorient her. She tried to *change*, but in the process, her blood coagulated. The dragons call it the *stone disease*."

The stone disease. That's what Adom said would weaken the herd. So the young man—Berrel—his story about the dragons all turning to stone was true. The Tranars didn't have words for the transformation, didn't know why it happened. So, they called it a prophecy.

Muuth's lower lip trembles and his eyes turn dewy. "Jetarna and I never agreed on the changelings. She wanted to help them. I thought we should terminate them. Using the telescope to read the sun's surface, I was able to predict when the next sun's acid would fall. I'd already discovered that by measuring the black spots as they grow, you can estimate when the fog will fall. From my measurements, I calculated that the next event would happen in twenty-two days."

My eyes shift to the white structure in the corner of the room. I'd seen Muuth peering through it at the starry sky on occasion, but had no idea he was seeing anything meaningful. What was he looking for? The next sun's acid fog? "What did you do?"

He swallows loudly. "I went behind Jetarna's back to convince the king to attack the dragons on that day and draw them out. That was the last battle between the king's army and the dragons. There were changelings in the army, too. Soldiers. As they writhed, suffered and *changed*, the dragons tried to save them. But they, too, were exposed. Some had fresh wounds from the fight, and their blood reacted to the fog. They turned to stone on the battlefield."

Thinking of battle, of blood and suffering, brings back memories of my family's murder. Of the animals I slaughter for the dragons. I can't control the grimace that those thoughts put on my face. "But they didn't all die like the Tranar legend claims."

Muuth's frown deepens. "We've always known that, El."

Confusion makes my head throb more intensely. "So why did the war end?"

He lays on his pallet, his hands interwoven across his chest. "The youngest ones didn't fight that day. They hid in a cave in Trana. That protected them during the battle. Dragon scales became a symbol of wealth and position. Those dragons eventually retreated to Onyx Island because they were outnumbered by human enemies and poachers seeking their scales."

We are silent for several moments while I process the story. Why hadn't Muuth shared any of this with me before? And how did he get here after all of that. "So they didn't kidnap you then, like you led me to believe? You came here on your own?"

His eyes, dewy and sad, stream tears. "I have no other place to belong, Elanor. My daughter, Jamie, is dead and they murdered my wife. I packed my things and roamed the country for a long while before I landed here, on this godforsaken island that I've come to call home."

"You roamed the country of Trana before coming to Onyx?" I can't imagine anyone coming to this place willingly. I think of all the ships that sailed past here, none daring to stop. Even though I've only glimpsed it from afar one or two times on the back of a dragon, I know the island looks like a fortress on the water, and even the forest looks black and dangerous.

He nods. "I heard rumors that dragons still scorched the lands, but they stopped coming in a herd that blotted out the sun, burning everything in its path. I realized the ones scorching were acting on their own, outside of the herd. That some were the changelings Jetarna created. So, I hunted them. I slaughtered them. One after another." He nods again, several times.

I slide away from him, shivering. "You *killed* innocent children?"

His eyes widen. "Not children. Changelings. Mistakes. Sometimes I had to kill an entire family, because without sun's acid there was no way to know which ones were infected by the blood passed down from the original victim. I know I've told you that sun's acid is the only way to kill a dragon. But a changeling—even though they are stronger and heal more quickly than a human— you can kill by severing the head when they are in their human form. I did it while they slept, so there was no chance of them changing. It was a messy, gruesome process."

Bile rises in my throat, and I can't help but look away from Muuth. *He couldn't help it*, I told myself. *He had to fix Jetarna's mistake.* But when my eyes return to his, I see a savageness there that defies anything remotely human. He murdered, and it changed him into *this*.

He sees my reaction and blinks. "One day, years later, I could not kill anymore. I spared a child. A boy whose family thought he was cursed by a devil. I took him in. I cared for him. And then I brought him here. The dragon pair, Eni and Furo, claimed him as their youngling. Years later, Ona tried to kill the boy and Furo challenged him. Eni and Furo both died that day."

"You're telling me Adom's story." I always thought Adom had come from the dragon herd. That somehow he was born to the dragons. Learning he's actually a Tranar, like me, does little to settle my nerves. Despised by his human parents and also by the dragon herd. What a horrible, lonely life he must lead. No wonder he can't stay in one place or the other for long.

"He is the cleverest and the worst of them." Muuth takes in a breath. "I'm sorry, El. I knew telling you would change everything. Adom brought you here. But it's all my fault. I'm responsible for him and for everything he's ever done to you."

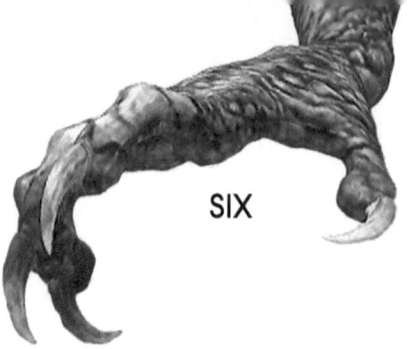

SIX

THE NEXT FEW DAYS, I plant lettuce seeds, hang herbs out to dry, scour the caves, cook, and feed the younglings. I haven't given up hope of escape, but when I go Muuth will stay and he'll need the garden and herbs to survive. While I was in Trana, mountain goats ate the turnips and nibbled the herbs that ripened in my neglected Onyx garden. So, on a gloomy day, I venture into the Forest of Four to restock my store of seeds. A smug goat bleats in my cave when I return, chewing the leaves of my bed. I count it among the supplies for the evening meal.

Muuth helps me gather buckets of water for the cauldrons. Even though I don't blame him, after what he told me I still find it difficult to look him in the eye. It isn't his fault his wife experimented on people using dragon blood. It isn't his fault he spared a child who would later destroy my life. But I can't help but feel a little doubtful about him now. He didn't tell me about the boat. He didn't tell me about Adom. He didn't tell me he had killed as many children as Adom had, that he could be a more violent murderer than all the dragons combined. He was my friend, the person I trusted the most. We spent years together, and he could have told me things that might have changed my thinking about the dragons, about Adom. About him. He chose not to.

We light the fires and boil water with the herbs. After distributing animal meats among the cauldrons, I throw in several beetroots I dug up in the forest. I also deposit multitudes of wild mushrooms and tomatoes in the mix.

The meal takes a greater time to prepare, for the roots have to soften. The gong resounds two times before the dinner simmers to completion. But the meat shreds tenderly, and the stew tastes more textured than usual. It brings to mind the food I ate at the tavern. Thick, and meaty, and full of flavor.

Once Muuth and I place the last cauldron by Ona's feet, we slide into the shadows of the cave to enjoy our own meal. Dragons slurp the meal in silence. I wait with baited breath.

Red juices pour over the sides of the cauldrons, oozing to the ground while thick steam curls up. Root gore drips off slippery snouts. Scaly eyelids sink. At last, Ona's head bobs. He speaks in dragon tongue. Silva studies the soup and heaves a sigh that buffets the cavern walls.

"Well done, girl." Muuth slaps me on the back. "If you are trying to buy their affection, you may be succeeding. They are singing your praises." He hunches over and eats the stew straight from the bowl, face to food, same as the dragons.

"I don't want them to sing my praises," I say, keeping my eyes trained on the masticating dragons. They are a parade of colors, light bouncing off their scales, illuminating the darkness of the cavern. "I want them to decide, of their own volition, to set me free."

Muuth gargles and gulps. "You think making delicious food will make that happen?"

"No. But proving to them that I'm strong might."

He stares. "The dragons won't defy Adom's order."

"Because they're fearful of the changeling curse." I slide my wooden spoon in the bowl. "What if I can make them believe I am stronger than he is? That I could cause the curse the same way Jetarna did? They would have to listen to me."

"Jetarna never caused the curse, El." He wipes his mouth with the back of his hand. "It doesn't work like that. Sun's acid isn't something you can make happen. It happens on its own."

"But she used dragon blood to make the changelings. And

during a sun's acid event, the changelings can infect the full blooded dragons with a single touch, correct? So, what if I used changeling blood on the dragons during a sun's acid event? Would that turn them into stone?" My heart quickens. For the first time, we have a plan. A real way to kill the dragons of Onyx.

"I've thought of that," he mutters. "But you can't get them all at the same time. The event doesn't last long—last time it was under an hour. Dragons fly. We don't. So how do you get all of them at once with the blood before they figure out what you're doing and kill you?"

"Cover yourself in the blood."

"That's crazy. The blood reacts to the sun's acid. I mean fizzles and coagulates and turns solid. I don't know what it'd do to a human who was wearing it like battle armor."

I savor a mouthful of hot stew. Potatoes melt in my mouth as the broth settles in my stomach. "Okay, so actual changeling blood won't work for us, probably."

"Not to mention there isn't a sun's acid event anytime soon."

I perk my head up. "Do you know when the next one will be?"

His eyes go blank. "No, I do not."

And here again, I have a wave of distrust about Muuth. I want to believe him, but doubt is itching inside me. "So, no sun's acid. How about poison? I know you said before that poison won't kill a dragon, but could it put them to sleep?"

"Nightshade *could* work on the younglings. But won't last long."

"How about an elixir to put the younglings to sleep for several hours?"

Muuth pokes at moss growing along the sides of the cave. He sets his bowl down on the ground and sighs. "I'd need to run some calculations. Can you bring me five bushels of nightshade? There is some growing on the south end of the island. Use gloves and a mask."

I take another thoughtful bite. "I'll do it tomorrow. But to be clear, I don't want to hurt them. They may not be humans, but they're still babies. Make sure the calculations are accurate."

He nods. "I hope you know what you're doing, El. One wrong move..."

He leaves the thought unfinished.

~ * ~

Muuth equips me with leather gloves so I can collect the bushels of nightshade without exposing myself. I take the rickety wooden wagon and hand shovel and scoop chunks of decomposed granite clay from a muddy rock bed on the south side of the mountain. In two hours, I reach the spot Muuth showed me on the map. When I get there, all I want to do is take a nap. There's no time for sleep, though, I've got younglings to feed and a meal to cook. I withdraw the axe tucked into my belt and hack at the woody stems of the shrub, careful to preserve as much foliage and plump berries as possible.

"What took you so long?" Muuth asks when I stumble into his cave hours later.

I move to brush a twig from my hair, but his hands fly to stop me.

"Fool," he growls. "You still have your gloves on. Take them off and wash your hands."

I do as he instructs, tossing the gloves in his cleaning bin and scrubbing my hands thoroughly in a soapy bucket on the floor. "How long will this take?"

"The rest of the evening," he answers tersely. "You'll have to make the dinner yourself."

Sighing, I leave him to the work and go out to the bathing cave to wash and gather some water and leaves to keep the clay and sediment moist overnight, before going about the strenuous evening duties so the dragons don't notice anything awry.

The following morning, I hear a whisper in my cave. "El,"

the voice hisses. I jolt awake, brushing leaves off my shift and pad through my cave on curled toes. Then I dart around the corner to discover Muuth sitting by the entrance, holding a green vial of sloshing brown, distilled liquid.

I wipe the sleep from my eyes. "What is it?"

He grins. "Six drops will knock out the entire litter of younglings for one day."

"And you're sure it won't hurt them?"

"They're little, but they're dragons. It would cause a more serious reaction if you gave it to Adom or one of the other changelings. I reinforced it with a dash of rosary peas and poppy."

"And what if I put it on their food?"

"Double the dosage." He hands the vial to me. "Now tell me your plan."

"Not yet," I say. "But when Ona takes me to Trana, I need you to sneak into the younglings cave and give them each a bath. Can you do that for me?"

"Ona? Why would—?"

"Can you do that for me?" I plead.

He nods. "El, if this works, do you plan to return to Onyx?"

"You know that was never what I wanted."

"So, I might never see you again?"

I hug him. "If you want to see me again, all you'd have to do is apply some of your secret brilliance toward building a boat and outwitting the dragons. That shouldn't be too hard for someone as clever as you, Muuth." It's a slight jab, but I say it with a smile.

He dips his chin, but his eyes look hollow and lonely.

I take Muuth's vial and the bucket of clay. Immediately, I dash to the meat cave to collect slabs of chuck for the younglings to consume. I divide the carrion into even pieces so each youngling will consume a poisoned portion. Sprinkle twelve drops evenly on the cuts, careful not to touch any of it without a glove. Then I collect it all in my wagon and roll the squeaky carrier to the younglings cave to move to the next part of my plan.

The younglings are as rambunctious as ever when I first begin cleaning their cave, but throwing raw beef in their trough distracts them enough for me to finish my work without the usual scratches and burns. A few days ago, one opened its mouth and said, "dragon." Silva corrected the youngling—making it speak in dragon tongue instead. Thankfully, Silva is not here to oversee my work today. As soon as it sees me, the little one spouts the word. I toss out the meat and let the younglings go to work on it.

Halfway through their revelry, I begin to worry. Is Muuth *certain* the poison won't kill them? Has he ever *tested* it on them before? How can he know? What if he's wrong? Then I will have the blood of innocents on my hands. The dragons will kill me. Or I'll become like Muuth, wild and unremorseful and half-crazed.

After a short while, they begin dropping like sleepy pups, midflight or between sloppy steps. I gather the still creatures into a line and check their pulses to ensure they are still alive. So far, so good. Then I lift each youngling carefully and place them—one by one—into the wagon. I have to make several trips outside, but finally I have all thirteen of them sprawled out in an open area where a tunnel opens onto a ledge that is small enough the adult dragons won't notice right away. The sun is shining down on us.

I pull out the clay, whip my hand in, and begin "painting" the younglings with the sediment. It is wet and chunky and obviously slapped on them. I hope that when it dries, the effect becomes more frightening. I am careful to give a wide berth around their eyes, and their snouts so they won't have a difficult time breathing. At last, I reach the end of the line and clean my hands with a wet rag. The first few of them have already dried.

They appear to be stone.

Now, all that's left to do is wait until Silva discovers them. The dragons won't dare get too close to examine them—one touch could turn them to stone. They'll believe a sun's acid event is occurring and will not want to risk getting infected. I will have to convince them that I know of a cure. They'll have to trust me if they want the younglings restored to normal.

I set about my normal tasks, humming the lullaby my mother used to sing. Wash and hang my clothes out to dry on the clothesline. Dig up mushrooms and wild berries and store them in containers. Pack my bag and fill it with dresses and shoes from Adom's chambers. Oh, and all the dragon scales I'd collected the past few weeks. The next time I'm in Trana, I won't be reliant on Adom to feed, clothe and house me. My eyes fall on Fifi. My hands waver over her head. Should I? An image of Muuth's lonely profile fills my head. No. I love Fifi for what she represents, but she is only a doll. Muuth will suffer in my absence. He needs her more, now.

Withdrawing my hand, I spare a sigh. *Goodbye, Fifi.* I throw the satchel onto my back packed and prepared to flee. But first I must go to prep the food for dinner.

A bellowing shriek arrests me in the middle of my trek.

A gloomy smile splits my face.

~ * ~

The sun creeps up in vibrant shades of pink and orange. Ona descends. Before I can register our bearings, he lands. My body whips forward. I lose my footing and tumble, landing on the ground in a heap of bushes. Ona nuzzles me. Warm slime covers my forehead. Black breath curls my toes. Gagging, I wipe insidious dragon saliva off of me. Fearing another accidental bout of drool, I spring to my feet and face the Head Dragon.

"I did as you asked, human. We are in Trana. Get what you need."

It was easy to convince the dragons that the younglings were infected by the stone disease. No problems there. The harder part was convincing them that I knew of a cure, but I'd need resources on Trana to make it. Ona wanted to stomp my head off with his huge claw. Silva threatened to skin me alive. Nerama wanted to drown me. The threats grew increasingly more violent until Muuth vouched for me. He claimed he gave me the list of ingredients for the cure, and that he'd be able to make it if I brought back the right things. So the dragons listened, like they always seem to do with Muuth.

"Muuth has been collecting samples of their scales for the antidote," I say. "Trana is still new to me, so I need to find Adom to help me get herbs for the cure. You should go back to the mountain and wait for him." Muuth is bathing the younglings now. They should awaken while Ona is in flight, and all will be restored to normal by the time he arrives on the island.

"Someday, I'll kill you for poisoning the younglings," Ona growls. "I can tell the wild one I let you go. He will not know."

Another lie to save my skin. "Yes, he will. Adom has changeling abilities. You don't. He has a heightened sense of smell. He'd know in a second if you killed me."

"And how are you going to find him?" Ona demands.

I touch my nose and grin. "Lucky for you, he has a soft spot for me."

Ona examines the sky. "How much time do we have? Before it is irreversible?"

"Not long. Two days, maybe? You'd better hurry back so I can find Adom."

"And you will accompany him to Onyx with the supplies needed for the antidote?"

I grin. "I'm not an idiot, Ona. You'll never see me again. Adom will bring you all the supplies you need, and Muuth will make the cure." *And you'll look like a complete fool when the younglings wake up and the dragon herd realizes I tricked you,* I think. I would never have tried something like this in the past because I would have been too afraid of what they'd do to Muuth. But now that I know they need him to observe the sun with his telescope.

Ona's eyes darken, like he's reading my thoughts. "Thanks to you, we know now there is a cure for the stone disease. Quite the useful piece of information. We don't need Muuth to tell us when to protect ourselves from the sun's acid event anymore. We'll torture him and force him to tell us how to brew the elixir. That old man will make a nice bit of gristle at our next meal."

Horror sticks in my throat. There's no elixir to brew because what I did to the younglings isn't really the stone disease. But when Ona realizes I tricked him, he might still retaliate. Muuth could hide from them, but once Adom finds out about our trick we'll both be in trouble.

My breath catches. The dragons might not be able to manage Muuth's laboratory equipment, but Adom could. A chill sinks into my bones. If the herd was angry enough, could they make Adom assume Muuth's role so that they could eliminate Muuth? I swallow past a hard lump in my throat. "You'd still need someone to distill the elixir. You need him." It can't hurt to remind Ona that Muuth has other scientific talents, too, not just his ability to use the telescope.

"We still have the changeling. The others will blame him for allowing you on the island, for putting our younglings at risk." He raises powerful wings. "It's finally time for a new Alpha."

I throw hands over my head as a shower of wind and dirt blows against me. Sand scatters. Ona's form fades to a pinpoint in the sky. My eyes water to clear themselves of grit. What have I done? Muuth protected me from the dragons, helped me escape, and this is how I repay him? I cross my fingers, hoping that once Ona sees the younglings—alive, awake and well—he'll forget all about hurting Muuth. Or challenging Adom again out of anger toward me.

Foghum is a minuscule oasis buried in a field of dry grass. I peel off my satchel and search for a pair of sturdy mossacs. After donning the boots, I begin the long trek. The sun peers above the trees. I estimate I'll reach the city by nightfall. I need to stay out of Adom's sight—at least for the time being. If he discovers me, he'll try to take me back to Onyx again. To my death, and very likely to his own as well. I can't let that happen.

By noon I stumble across a small stream. The water is icy, perfect for a cool drink. It's a good place to stop and rest. I take out the container of shriveled brown mushrooms and the jar of bruised berries I gathered the day before. Fall-apart blackberries stain my fingers red, and juice drips down my chin. Kicking off my mossacs, I dig bare toes into the cool, sandy ground.

After the meal, I strip off my clothes and plunge into the stream. I swim, moving my legs to stave off frost. The sun bears high overhead. An easterly wind blows pinecones off a nearby tree. I dip under the water. Chilly. I toss out my hair. Short, wet strands slap across my face.

A horse trots to the stream. Another icy shiver attacks me. I crouch low in the water.

"Lady Malandre. What a surprise." Lord Faigen dismounts. "I'm giving Tonga a rest."

I have an instinct to be shy. But then I realize it is Faigen who should be embarrassed, not me. He saw me, recognized that I'm bathing, and still he's standing there with a crooked crack on his amused face. Pervert.

"Good morning, Lord Faigen." I rise, dripping, and remove myself from the stream. Gooseflesh dimples my skin. I grab a garment from my satchel and step calmly behind a tree. My lip quivers. Then I curse, realizing I grabbed a "nightdress." I pat myself dry, barely, and throw on the outfit. By the time I finish tying the sash, Lord Faigen has mounted his horse again.

"What brings you here?" he asks.

"I'm talking a walk," I manage, grimacing inwardly at his surprise.

His jaw drops. "Foghum is a half day's walk from here."

"So? I got here in half a day. I can return in half a day."

"A walk?" Lord Faigen repeats dumbfounded, staring at my attire. "In a nightdress?"

His shock does not bode well for me. I have no more explanations for him. Instead of attempting another watery excuse, I try another tactic. "What brings you here?"

Faigen's visage brightens. "Glad you asked." He tosses a hand to his forehead. "About week ago, I left Foghum to visit my mother." A modest blush creeps into his cheeks. "She's ill and not faring well. I'm only just returning from the visit." He eyes the deserted plains. "Those horrible creatures," he murmurs. "They ruined my hometown, Salcom. You were there once, yes?" His pupils dilate and the horse whinnies.

"Did dragons scorch it?" I picture Raina and the children playing in front of the inn. My heart stops. Are they all *gone*?

"They demolished it. All to get back at me for joining the king's army."

"Did anybody..." I choke on morbid images. "Did anybody survive?"

Faigen nods. "Half the village was saved. Count Malandre arrived in time to usher people to an underground safe place. But my mother breathed too much ash and her lungs haven't recovered yet. She's staying in a neighboring town at an inn run by another scorch victim, Sam Collum. The inn's overrun with all the refugees." Curiosity creeps onto his handsome features. "Do you want a ride back?" he asks then he holds up his hands. "Please, don't run away again."

My heart quickens. It's too late now to shield my identity. Lord Faigen already knows me, and it will seem suspicious for me to ask him not to tell the Count of our encounter. Adom will probably learn of my presence because of this meeting, but as long as I avoid revealing my whereabouts, he can't do anything without risking his identity and position.

"I won't run. Just give me a moment to change."

Lord Faigen smirks. "I like what you have on."

"Then I suppose you can wear it." I grab my bag and hurry to the nearby oak. Sorting through the garments in my satchel, I select a simple one. I step out from behind the trunk wearing my new attire—a magenta linen dress with pockets on the sides and a pleated skirt.

"About our first encounter," I begin. "Thank you for not asking questions. We just married, you see, and I was homesick when I saw you that first time at the tavern. He didn't know where I'd gone. When you mentioned his name, I thought you might tell him."

Lord Faigen's face softens. "Ah. High society life stifled you, and so you went searching for some deeper communion with humanity in a more... rustic setting."

I shrug and don't answer. It can't hurt to let him think we're kindred souls.

"He went looking for you," Theodore mutters as he reaches down to hoist me into the seat behind him. My legs dangle on one side of the horse, and I grasp Faigen with both hands to keep from falling off. This isn't how Adom positioned me, but it seems more dignified than hiking up my skirt and facing forward. "He came into the tavern in search of you."

"He did?" That surprises me. I never questioned how Adom found me. He said the kidnappers left instructions that he followed. Did he search for me *before* they left the message?

Lord Faigen nods. "He was terrified for your safety, distraught."

"Really?" My heart thunders. Why is my breath shortening so abruptly? It's just nerves. Adom said he can track me by my scent. He followed his nose and found Lord Faigen at the tavern. Then he had to put on a concerned husband act for Faigen's benefit.

"I told him you'd visited earlier, and a burly man by the door said he saw you run down an alley," the young lord explains as the horse trots obediently.

"Well, we found each other and that night is long gone," I murmur, shuddering.

The trip to Foghum doesn't take nearly as long riding on the back of Faigen's able horse, Tonga, as it would have had I chosen to walk the whole way. As we approach the city gates, I plot my next move. If Adom is still staying at Volcourt, I have to avoid that area. Where can I go that will draw me closer to Adom yet keep me safe from his sharp eyes and his keen sense of smell? It has to be some place I can figure out what he's planning with the changeling recruits, and do something about it if he's up to no good.

Why don't you just run? a voice in the back of my head asks me. *You've wanted freedom all this time. What business is it of yours what Adom is doing now?*

But if Adom is building a changeling army to strengthen the herd, what does he plan to do next? Adom says there's no point in revenge, but Ona killed the pair of dragons Adom considers his parents. Ona challenges Adom and tortures him routinely. Sometimes, it's to protect me, but sometimes it's just because Ona is an ass. For one moment, my mouth curves into a frown as I think again of the blood marks on the floor of the central cave. Then I shake it off. If Adom's smart—and I know he is— he'll use his changeling army to get rid of Ona and all the dragons who oppose him. Maybe it isn't revenge. Maybe it's strategic.

But then there's still the threat of the king's army. Unless his changelings can infiltrate the courts, as Adom has done. They could overthrow the king of Trana. They could rule Onyx and

Trana. If that's his plan, there would be nowhere I could go to escape him. And Adom has always said that if I run, he'll find me and kill me.

"Where's Count Malandre now?" I ask, masking my concern.

"I spoke with my associates at the Volcourt Inn this morning. They reported Count Malandre would be hunting with the king all day today," Faigen responds.

Hunting *with* the king, or *for* the king? He'd have the perfect alibi. "Take me to the castle," I tell Theodore. "I intend to meet him there."

Lord Faigen shrugs. "I'm at your service."

My *service*? I like him more and more.

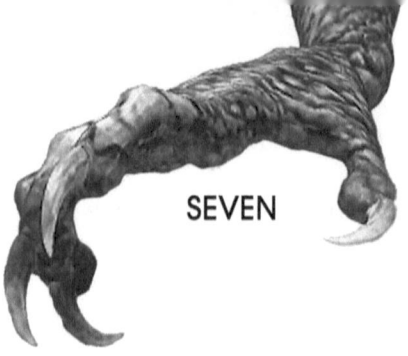

SEVEN

LORD FAIGEN'S METAL GAUNTLET clicks and clanks as he leans into me. He doesn't have a scratch or a stain on his armor, which makes me doubt his story about fighting the dragons in Salcom village. "I hope the sun isn't burning your complexion. You're used to carriages."

He thinks carriages made my skin so light? Perhaps he should try living in a cave for the rest of his life. My amusement fades as we ride past the Volcourt Inn. The same window I crawled through to escape is now drawn with thick, navy curtains

"Do you want me to stop here, instead?" Faigen asks.

"No, thank you." I grip him tighter. Adom isn't there, so I shouldn't be frightened. And yet, the bones in my back align one after another until I am stick stiff.

The first time I met Theodore, he was reveling in poetry at a tavern filled with drunks, completely unaware of the dark plans unfolding a block away from the place. I can't help but wonder what ever happened to little Nathaniel.

Theodore kicks his horse's flanks. "We're nearing the castle." He needn't have spoken. In a moment it appears between buildings, a colossal, multi-tower vision of grandeur. It gleams in the sunlight with ivory-gold beams reflecting off walls for miles.

We clop through brick streets until at last we reach the gates of the castle. Guards cluster by the door, swords at their backs, a veneer of hard planes. Weathered creases curl around black, wary eyes. They are tanned men, seasoned by nature and hours of physical exertion.

"Who goes there?" the guard asks.

Theodore removes his helmet and lowers it to his waist. "Lord Faigen, servant of the king." He gestures to me. "And this is the wife of one of the visiting lords."

The leader seems to recognize Lord Faigen. "Another one?"

Faigen straightens, his chin reared in pride. "Another what?"

"Conquest," responds the bold guard his lip curling. The men surrounding him tense.

"I'll take your name." Faigen draws to mighty proportions, his shadow casting darkness over the guards. "Count Malandre's wife doesn't deserve your ill treatment." His voice lowers until it becomes a dangerous whisper. "She'll have your heads served on a silver platter for this."

Whatever bravery the guards exhibited only a moment before seems to vanish. Does invoking Count Malandre's name cause that response everywhere? Is he *that* influential? It chills my bones to see these mighty warriors cowed by the mere mention of Adom.

The leader, realizing at once that he overstepped his bounds, raises a hand. "Forgive me, Lord Faigen. I meant no disrespect to the lady." At last, he gestures for his men to move. "All clear, my lord. Come right through."

Guards hurry to open the gate.

Faigen passes them and escorts me through the outer courtyard.

As we move forward, I rotate and witness the friendly smiles slip off their faces. Hard stares replace the admiring eyes. A couple of guards glare at Lord Faigen's back, whispering hateful remarks that bounce off the walls of the gate and enter my ears. They don't like him. In fact, it seems like they can barely tolerate him. I can't help but wonder why.

The troubling moment vanishes the instant I see the splendor of the wonderland before me. Bushes trimmed to look like animals. Rainbow-colored flowers whose peachy aroma hits me like a solid force. Dyed parchment pinwheels whirl as wind blows.

While the rest of Trana burns, the castle grounds flourish. No wonder the guards have a dislike for someone like Lord Faigen, a hedonist who treats the dragon scorchings and poverty as something like a sport. For all his talk of work with the king's army and the suffering he's endured, he doesn't strike me as the kind of man who would fearlessly dive into a battle.

We follow a wide, cobblestone road until we come to the front entrance of the castle. The outer courtyard stretches on for miles with orchards filled with every fruit imaginable—kumquats and huge gardens of exotic blooms. Beastly statues and marble fountains decorate the walkways.

The front entrance stirs in a flurry of action as servants dart in and out of an open door constructed of immense wooden planks and broad iron bars. I marvel at the size and girth of the door, boggled by the idea that mere men open and close it. But then I see thick iron chains wrapped around a wheel, and realize the castle doors are held open using complex contraptions. Brilliant! Has Muuth ever seen anything like this?

Beside our horse, twelve glistening black carriages line the cobblestone street. A man in black uniform steps forward as we slow. He's a squat man, with graying hair, blue eyes and large jowls. "Welcome, Lord Faigen. May I take your armor? The footman will be here shortly to take your horse to the stables."

"No need," Faigen begins his speech, flourishing colored handkerchiefs. "I'm only here to deliver this lovely Lady to her family. You will take care of her, won't you Ryrick?"

"Of course I will." He extends a hand to help me dismount. "What's your name?"

I ignore him and glance up at Theodore. "Thank you for bringing me here."

"The pleasure is all mine." He takes my hand. "Take care,

fair lady. I will see you again shortly, I hope." Lord Faigen bows low from the saddle and brushes his lips over my fingers before nudging the flanks of his steed.

As soon as he leaves, the servant spins toward the giant door and reaches for my satchel. "My name is Ryrick Siron, Butler of Callihan Hall. I apologize for the confusion; I can't imagine what happened to our footmen, but I can show you to the drawing room to wait for your family."

I stop mid-step and snatch the satchel. "I need to speak with the Head Housekeeper."

He hesitates. "Is something the matter?"

"I'm no lady, just a simple serving woman." My voice rises an octave. Now they will either stone me for my deceit or hire me for my courage. So long as they don't send me away.

"I don't understand. I thought you were here to see your family? I'll need your name—"

"No, there's been a misunderstanding. I don't have family here. I'm from the country." Guilt gnaws at my throat. "I was traveling to Foghum on foot when Lord Faigen found me. He brought me into the city to find work. I'm one of the scorch victims, you see."

Ryrick's eyes flicker with compassion. "I see. Did you...lose anyone?"

"I did. My entire family."

"I'm so sorry for your loss. Was it the Salcom village incident?"

It makes the most sense to name the most recent scorching. It also explains why Faigen was with me and brought me here. I nod. "Lord Faigen thought maybe I could start again here."

"We don't have any positions open," Ryrick replies. He sounds apologetic. "Cydra hires the chambermaids, and only those on high recommendations from the Houses. I'm sorry."

"I have work experience. I worked for Count Malandre once."

"Count Malandre?" The man's brows furrow. "What job

did you do for him?"

"I was his housekeeper."

"You managed staff?"

"I managed assets."

"Which house did you keep?"

"His country house."

"*Which* country house?"

I swallow. Adom has more than one house in the country? "He took me from one house to the other. I also served as his personal assistant." Even *I* think this explanation sounds feeble. Cursing myself for poor preparation, I prepare for the inevitable rejection.

"You were his estate manager?" The man seems paralyzed in disbelief. "Wait right here."

I watch as he strides through the entrance. Now and then, servants stop to observe me. The pins-and-needles feeling grows. Impersonating a noble, and then impersonating a housekeeper? And using the names of important lords? The servants will find me out, and I'll be killed. I break into a sweat. The heat of the summer day doesn't help much.

Everything in me is telling me to run the opposite direction, but Adom said he has a plan for the changelings and I want to know what that plan is. Besides, even if I run, he'll find me eventually. I'm not about to let him hunt me down like a fleeing prey.

A harsh *clopping* bounces off the marble staircase. My eyes follow the slimmest ankles I've ever seen to the angular torso of a tall woman in front of me, her gray hair tied back in a stingy, no-nonsense bun. The male servant from before is two heads shorter than the woman.

"I'm Cydra," she barks. "You wanted to see me?"

My gut sinks. "I'm here to ask for a job," I tell her. "Lord Faigen suggested I see you."

"Lord Faigen doesn't hold much weight around here."

The male servant stands on tip-toe to whisper loudly in Cydra's ear. "She says she used to be Count Malandre's Head Housekeeper. And his estate manager."

Cydra crooks her head at me. "Where are your documents?" she challenges. When she sees I have none, her smile grows. "You must have documents. Else you cannot work here."

My heart slams against my ribcage. Where can I get documents? Do they hand them out on the streets? I straighten, preparing to leave and spare myself any further humiliation.

A woman glides through the garden arch, translucent skin shimmering in the sunlight. An ivory, lace dress spilled over her decanter-shaped waist, a fragrant bit of baby's breath woven through her golden braid. Her hand flutters to her mouth. "Oh dear."

Cydra eyes grow large, and she quickly bends her head. "I did not see you there, Lady Celeste." Her cheeks turn pink. "Ryrick wasn't paying attention."

"Forgive me, Lady Celeste," Ryrick answers. "Can we help you?"

"I'm lost," Lady Celeste replies, her voice soft as a cat's purr. "I took a wrong turn, and somehow ended up at the main entrance. How do I get to the gazebo from here?"

I remember glimpsing a gazebo on our way through the gardens. "Around the corner past the dragon statue and to the right of that bush shaped like a bear," I say without thinking.

Celeste's eyes brighten to a sea blue. "A new hire, Cydra? She's quite sharp."

"I was just sending her away."

"I'm looking for a job," I explain to Lady Celeste.

She pulls her braid in front of her shoulder and plays with the end. "Can you cook?"

"Yes. And I can clean, and brew beer, and feed livestock, too."

Her face splits into a smile. "Well, aren't you talented?"

"I can read as well, milady."

She pauses and looks me over with curious eyes. "Cydra,

why are you sending her away? Didn't you recently mention you needed a between maid to share with Longley and Ryrick?"

"She isn't suited," Cydra says. "She doesn't have papers."

Celeste reaches for a parchment in Cydra's hands. "Can you read this, girl?"

I take the parchment and look at the small black scrawl. *Three pieces of toffee. Twelve small cucumber sandwiches. One bottle of wine.* I read the words aloud.

"Quite right, my lady. Quite right," Cydra manages, fidgeting with a blue rag she holds in her hand. I can't help but stare as she proceeds to unravel the cloth in silent rage.

"Hire her," Celeste urges. She waves her hand in a sweet farewell gesture. Then she glides away in a flurry of white silk, drifting like an apparition back into the garden.

"Well," Cydra says after a long moment of silence passes. "Her Highness has interceded for you. You'd best come along." She casts me a sidelong look and frowns.

Cydra takes me into the castle using a servants' door along the side of the stone wall. We meander through several long corridors until reaching an open area. As we walk, I can't help but notice peculiar similarities between the castle structure and the mountain on Onyx. Many of the hallways lack windows, and torches hang on the walls to provide light. The winding staircases and narrow back halls remind me of home.

"These are the servants' quarters," Cydra says once we reach our destination gesturing to the rooms on each side of the wall. She takes me inside one of the empty rooms, the first down the hallway to my left. A neat bed hugs the wall with a pine desk close by. "This will be your room." She shows me how to use the space underneath the bed for clothes. "Don't even think you're welcome to any of the castle's goods. We've had a rash of stolen items recently, and the thieves will find their hands cut off. We check rooms every week to ensure all is tidy and in order. If you can't maintain our standard of cleanliness, you'll be fired."

The housekeeper's word of warning about thievery sends goosebumps up and down my arm. I secretly vow to never touch an item I'm not asked to clean or move. As to the room, I can manage the upkeep. Fortunately, I never owned many possessions, and so never deemed myself disorderly. My eyes fasten to the desk. Dull scratches mar the surface. My heart quickens when I imagine the letters I can trace onto parchment on that desk. And the bed! At long last, I have my very own, feather-stuffed bed. One that I don't have to "share" with Adom. Anticipation of long, blissful nights on that cozy albeit yellow-stained mattress warms me.

Cydra orders me to follow her once again. She leaves the servants' quarters and trails along the back rooms until she reaches the kitchen. "You may be given assignments here. Because of your… unusual circumstances, we're not sure what your area of expertise is."

I shrink under the scrutiny of her towering presence. "I can clean," I offer. "Scrub floors, feed animals, wash laundry. I'm good at those duties."

"We'll see about that," comes her ominous reply.

~ * ~

Cydra puts me to work in the laundry room that very evening. The uniform she hands me is two sizes too large. The laundress is kind enough to lend me some thread and cutters to modify it so it fits better. Every morning after the first evening, I'm awakened by a rough rap at the door and I'm expected to dress within a half hour and line up outside with the other servants for morning orders. My duties are spread, as I'm shared by three territorial servants; Cydra, the head housekeeper, Ryrick the butler, and Longley the cook.

For several weeks, I take careful pains to avoid the main halls and keep my head down. I glimpse Adom a time or two in the feast hall or parlor, always talking with other nobles and aristocrats. One time he surprises me around the corner ,and I have to duck behind a row of curtains. Peering at him between the folds of cloth, I watch him pause, mid-step, and tilt his nose to the air. My heart almost explodes. But then another nobleman, a Lord Darton, comes around the corner and greets Adom, and the two of them walk off together.

Maybe his nose isn't as sharp when there are so many scents in the castle to mask mine. Or maybe *I* am changing, and he doesn't recognize my smell anymore. I *do* bathe every day and add rose oil to the water. Perhaps it is working in my favor.

One morning, Cydra sends me to clean the windows in the library. I'm normally with one of the other girls, Donja or Belin, but today no one is sent along to help me. It isn't a problem. I'm accustomed to working alone. Besides, the library is quiet and often abandoned, so if I finish the windows early I can sneak a peek at one of the tomes of modern literature and learn more about the fashions and interests of Tranar people. I have basic information thanks to Muuth and the textbooks Adom provided me with on Onyx, but I'm thirsty to learn more about my new home.

A man sits by the fire in a gray wingback chair when I enter the library carrying full buckets of soapy water and freshly wet rags. A casual glance at the stranger's profile assures me he isn't Adom, so I am not overly concerned as I move near the windows. I set the bucket of water in front of the wall and begin to draw back the navy and gold curtains.

"Lady Elanor?" asks a familiar voice.

My hand flies to my throat. "I didn't expect to find you in here, Lord Berrel."

"Nor I you." Lord Berrel rises from the wingback armchair. His curly blond hair has grown a bit longer since the last time I saw him. It's battling the ends of his ears now, trying to swallow them whole. His beard, too, has some length to it. "I arrived yesterday."

How did he recognize me? I was in a swan costume, Raina had decorated my face around the eyes, and my hair was done up so nicely. Did I really make that much of an impression? I survey him again, debating whether or not to run.

Run, I decide. I pivot and quickly take a step away from him. "I didn't realize you were a visitor at court. If you'll excuse me, I didn't mean to disturb your reading—"

"I'm a frequent visitor." He shows his teeth. "My sister lives at court."

"You have another sister?" I forget my maid's outfit, the millions of questions Berrel must have, and the fact that I don't completely trust the man.

"I do. She's really all I have." He grins, his eyes scanning my outfit like he finds our position amusing. "I'm estranged from the rest of my family." The words don't match the twinkle in his sapphire eyes. "My father cut me out of his inheritance and denounced my title. My younger sister is the only one who will see me."

"Estranged?" I repeat the foreign word, realizing the weight of its full meaning.

"Don't look so troubled, my dear." Berrel takes my hand in a paternal, friendly sort of way. He pats it with a light touch. "I have plenty of money, thanks to the lucrative mining business. You remember that from our dance together, don't you?"

"How could a father cut off his own son?" I ask, disbelieving.

Berrel's eyes sadden. "You recall what I told you about Tranar superstitions?"

I nod curtly.

"This insistence they have about believing in things that no longer exist?" He makes a face. "My father was—is—convinced that his...*seed* was tainted by such a curse."

"How can a *seed* be tainted by dragons?"

Berrel squeezes my hand. "You are untrained in the verbal

subtleties of Tranar court life." He peers at me. "It must be your refreshingly sheltered upbringing."

"Must be," I grumble.

He breaks eye contact and stares at a point behind my shoulder, suddenly lost in his own thoughts. After a while, he shrugs. "I'm telling you all my secrets, but you haven't offered me an explanation for *your* little charade. Why are you dressed like a castle maid?"

Ah, so here is the price for Berrel's moment of honesty. He expects the same of me.

"Do I owe you an explanation?"

He blinks. "Of course not. But if we're going to be friends…"

"Whoever said we were friends?"

He drops my hand and takes a step back. "I apologize. I misunderstood the nature of our relationship." Then he picks up the book he had set down on the end table. "I'll excuse myself from your presence so you can finish cleaning the windows as you clearly intended to do." Berrel pauses a moment, his foot ticking against the floor as though he can't quite make up his mind whether to stay or to go. "I need to warn you, though. I'm especially picky about smudges on the glass. I'm afraid it's the curse of my class to be particular about such things."

"I'll try not to disappoint," I mutter, without much enthusiasm.

"Since we are not friends, I'm sure you won't mind if I inspect your work later and offer my critique to your superior? Who should I speak to first about it? The housekeeper?" His eyes grow wicked. "Or Count Malandre?"

It sinks in. My jaw drops. "Are you threatening me?"

A dimple appears to the left of his mouth. He taps the book against his palm. "I believe in a job well done. I'll be sure to pass on compliments if they are earned."

My options are limited. I could feed him a line, give him

just enough to satiate his curiosity and keep him quiet. Or I could refuse and risk him exposing me to Adom. I'm not ready for the latter as yet. Adom might return me to Onyx and Ona will kill me for sure this time. I'm here to watch, to learn, and to keep Adom from hurting anybody else. Berrel could ruin all of that, unless I go along with him. For now.

"Malandre sent me away after we left the village. I'm supposed to be safely ensconced in the miserable place I call home. But I don't want to be there."

Berrel tilts his head. "You were quite sheltered on your island, weren't you?"

I watch the flames flickering in the fireplace. "I was alone."

"So you disguised yourself as a maid to experience castle life? Does Malandre know you're here?" When I shake my head, he asks, "You think he won't discover you?"

"Not if I'm careful."

His mouth quirks up. "I can see you're being careful."

A sour taste tingles on my tongue. My lips pucker. "Is that sarcasm?"

"You're catching on to our modern way of talking. Congratulations."

I scowl. "I don't especially like you, Lord Berrel."

He beams. "You don't have to like me. But I can help you... for a price."

"Do you intend to tell Malandre if I don't pay you?" I mentally calculate the number of scales I have in my stock. I haven't used any yet. Would Berrel take them as payment?

"What's bad for Malandre is good for me. I'll work with you. You may need a nobleman to cover for your absences or ensure you aren't scolded for poor work. I'm sure you're used to living a slightly different lifestyle. I'll help cover for you if you need anything."

"I have dragon scales I can give you for payment."

He grins. "Let's not discuss payment just now."

"To be perfectly clear, I don't trust you at all."

"You don't have to trust me, either. Just call me Rhydian."

~ * ~

Even though I'm still an outsider, I do hear the servants gossip, which is a benefit. Lady Celeste, the woman who interceded for me on the first day, is betrothed to the King. Lord Faigen has a reputation as a rogue, and will seduce anything with legs if given the opportunity. That's the primary reason the reason the guards don't like him—he's blatantly cuckolded more than a few of them. Because of his reputation, Ryrick always waters down Faigen's ale and wine whenever he attends any of the lavish castle parties, to avoid scandal.

I'm not worried about Theodore catching me dressed as a maid. Since I don't serve at the parties, and that is the time Faigen emerges, I only ever catch glimpses of him from a window in the servants' quarters. Adom, however, is becoming more difficult to elude. There's a rumor that he's left the Volcourt Inn and is now staying in one of the guest rooms in the castle. Something about him traveling less due to a complication with one of his island ventures. A shudder runs down my spine when I hear this. While I don't want Adom to catch me here, I also don't want him to pay the consequences for my deceit with the dragons.

The emergence of Lord Berrel means I now have to spend three times the effort avoiding the noble folk. Berrel, Faigen, and Malandre all frequent the dining hall, the courtroom, the ballroom, and the gardens. Berrel thinks his offer to help is worth something to me. But I just don't trust him. If he catches sight of me, he'll try to help. It will only attract Adom's attention. No matter how I look at it, I can't see how Berrel's alliance will benefit me unless I need a quick escape. I do what I do best—stay out of his way at all costs.

Fortunately, Cydra's suspicion keeps me out of sight on

most occasions. I'm good at lurking, ducking, and making myself invisible in a mountain. What fails to come naturally to me is staying out of places Cydra forbids me to go.

"I need to restock our supply of witch hazel cream for the staff," Ryrick says one day.

"I can do it. How much do you need and where are the physician's quarters?"

"I thought Cydra said you weren't to go to the east tower," he replies. "Too many noblemen drop by that place with ailments and Cydra is concerned about your reputation. She doesn't want you conversing with any of the noblemen after the rumors she heard about you arriving here on Lord Faigen's horse." At my look, he flushes. "Well, don't look at me. I didn't say anything to her about how you arrived that first day."

"Since I now know it's in the east tower, I should think it's your tongue Cydra should be concerned about," I say to him, smiling.

He wrinkles his nose. "You're a cheeky one."

"Let me do this, Ryrick."

Finally, he sighs. "I need six jars of the cream." Ryrick's head ducks. "Please give her this note from me. And thank her for the headache remedy."

I raise an eyebrow and then pocket the letter.

The east tower is beyond the stables, before the walkway to the king's forest. I veer a slight right, under the archway, and climb the stairs. How in the world do they get the sick and the lame up these stairs, I wonder. Then I remember how many times I've heard the words "send for the physician" since I started here and I realize that the truly sick and lame probably don't come here much, anyway. By the time I reach the top, I am breathing incrementally faster. Mountain climbing, I can do. Running long distances in the forest, I can do. Manmade stairs? Apparently not. And here I thought I was in peak physical condition.

The door to the physician's chamber looms before me. I gulp air and knock.

"Come in," a woman's voice speaks softly, a delicate, wavy sound.

I open the door and peek my head in. "Are you the physician?"

The young woman smiles. Her auburn hair is tied in a pink sash. "I am."

She's a younger, rosier version of Ryrick. She has his same shade of deeply olive skin, hazel irises, and almond-shaped eyes. "I see."

"What do you see?"

"You must be Ryrick's daughter."

"That's right." She timidly holds out a hand. "I'm Patience Siron."

"My name is Elanor." I pass her the note. "Ryrick wanted me to thank you for the headache remedy. He asked me to pick up six jars of witch hazel cream."

She quickly tucks away the note. "It'll be a moment. I need to mix the cream."

"It isn't a problem. Do you want me to come back?"

Patience smiles. "If you don't mind, I welcome the company."

Conversation doesn't come naturally to me, but Patience is an unusually focused and quiet individual. I find her personality calming, much like her father's. We don't say much to each other, but I watch as she melts beeswax and oil in a small pot suspended over a candle. She adds water and lets the mixture simmer over the low flame, stirring constantly.

"My father's mentioned you, Elanor. He says Cydra gives you a hard time?"

I bare my teeth. "She's a nasty old dragon."

Patience unties a cloth sack, revealing witch hazel bark as well as the leaves of the plant, both dried. She pours the entire sack into a mortar and pestle. Then she begins grinding. "Don't mind her. She lost a son a while back and never recovered. She's always been a hard woman, but the loss turned off her empathy. Now all she has is work. It's really very sad."

"Have you known her long?"

When there is nothing but dust left in the mortar and pestle, she looks up. "All my life."

"Did you grow up in the castle?"

"I did," she says, pouring the contents of the container into the small pot. She uncorks a vial of amber liquid and adds in several droppers-full. "Father let me apprentice with the previous physician until he passed away last year. The king chose me as his replacement."

"So you've always lived here at Callihan Hall?"

"I have. I've never even left Foghum."

The air burns my face like an astringent. I take in a breath—it smells of rosemary and marjoram. This reminds me of Muuth in his lab. "Doesn't it feel like a prison to you?"

"Why should it? Everybody I love and all the happy memories I ever made are here."

"But don't you ever wonder what life is like out there?"

"Sometimes. But this is my home. I couldn't leave it."

"What if something were to happen to it? What if the dragons burned it down?"

She turns startled eyes onto my own. "Then they would pay for doing it."

Patience opens a cabinet and removes four empty glass jars. She sets them on the table and reaches for a rag to grab the handle of the small pot. She gently spoons the warm, thickening cream into the jars and screws the lids shut. In another cabinet, she pulls out another two jars, these already full. The jars look familiar, like the kind of salve Muuth would give me for a dragon burn or skin irritation. I open one to look inside. It even smells the same. Then I recall that those same jars were at Raina's inn, too. How—? But in the next moment, I put the pieces together. Adom comes here for medicine. Raina has it, so he must give it to her, maybe to help with the survivors who end up at their inns. And he gives it to Muuth, too. But why?

For me? My cheeks burn, and I suddenly feel a rush of shame.

"Do you know why Ryrick needs so much witch hazel cream?" I ask.

"It's good for a variety of skin issues, like burns and insect bites," Patience says.

"Burns?"

"Minor burns, like the kind you'd get over an open flame when trying to toast bread." Her eyes widen. "Not dragon burns, if that's what you're thinking. Ryrick keeps an emergency stock of medical supplies in the cupboard near the kitchen. Servants can take what they need."

Not me. With my luck, Cydra'd catch me with a jar and accuse me of stealing it. Still, it'd be useful to have some on hand. Muuth won't always be around, and I need to learn how to survive on my own. "Could you teach me how to make it sometime?"

"Of course. Just not tomorrow. My father has a hunting trip planned, and I usually go with him. One of the benefits of working at the castle is that the servants can hunt in the king's forest for sport. It's one of my father's favorite pastimes." She smooths Ryrick's note. "The message you delivered is an invitation for me to join him tomorrow."

"What about the day after tomorrow?"

"That will work. Can you come by around noon?"

I nod and fill a sack with the clanking jars of cream, say goodbye to Patience, and follow the spiral staircase to the ground entry. At the bottom, I turn toward the servants' quarters but stop just as Lord Berrel's bushy blond head comes into view. He's carrying a bow, and at his side is a tall gentleman with a massive red beard that droops to his stomach.

Berrel's eyes scan me as he passes, but I don't see any recognition in them. "Lord Darton," he says. "I understand your alliance with Count Malandre, but it doesn't hurt to hedge bets, does it? Why, even King Siles has a mine just north of the forest that he allows me to run for him. Malandre may have the cornerstone on agricultural revenue, but he doesn't own all the land. What we need are investors to purchase and front costs for more processing factories."

"But if I build a factory on my land, how do we make up the losses in food production and export income? If Malandre knew I was even considering your proposal, he'd drop me from his list of feed suppliers in a heartbeat. Or worse." Darton shudders.

"With the money you make from processing raw minerals like the dragon scales, you can more than make up those anticipated losses. You could afford to import food from the neighboring farms, even as far away as Newaka. People want the dragon scales, Lord Darton. They are no longer just opulence for the upper classes. They are a talisman. A sign of hope."

"You're slick talking, Lord Berrel, but you forget one thing. Not all of us believe dragon scales are merely pretty rocks. I see what those beasts do to my countryside. If I invest my inheritance, my life's work, to a factory and a dragon burns it down, I have nothing left."

Their words fade as they move toward the forest, and I hurry back to Ryrick.

~ * ~

"King Siles is holding a banquet next week," Ryrick announces as I help him move barrels of wine from the king's wine cellar.

"What did you say?" It takes mighty power to hoist the wooden barrels and drag them upstairs for the cook. My eyelids droop.

Ryrick has trouble carrying his burden, and he eyes me when I insist on carrying my own. "There's a banquet next week. We'll need twice the help on the floor that day."

"I'll help in the kitchen," I volunteer. What better way to meet the king? Nobles never look twice at the servants. I can blend in perfectly. Granted, Adom might see me if he comes. But with so many people in the hall, the odds are in my favor.

Ryrick pauses in his work. "Are you sure about this, lass? You're fresh here. We can't afford mistakes on an occasion of this magnitude."

"I'll do my best." I hoist another wine barrel—the third in ten minutes.

My actions seem to please the old butler. He frowns. "Cydra works you like a dog," he grumbles, clearly troubled. "Maybe you ought to take a break that night—"

"Please, Ryrick," I beg, sensing I'm losing him. "I need the work. I need... the money."

Ryrick's visage softens. "I don't know what trouble you've gotten yourself into, lass. But I'll let you work that night if you promise to do your best."

"I promise!" I almost drop the barrel of wine in my excitement, and catch it mid-fall.

Ryrick shakes his head.

"Sorry." Embarrassment tinges my cheeks.

Cydra descends the cellar steps, each footfall creaking – like a willow tree groaning against the ground with every forceful gust of wind. "What's keeping you?" she gripes. "Longley needs wine to cook the meat, and the lords are complaining in the parlor room because we haven't refilled their glasses. Could you move more slowly, you lazy beasts?"

My fingertips are snow-white, straining to keep traction around the barrel's rim. I adjust my hold and pull myself up the steps. Cydra stands in the middle of the staircase, barricading my way, tapping her toes in impatience. I attempt to squeeze past her.

And miss a step. My foot falls on air and my body rocks forward. The barrel flies out of my hands. It lands on Cydra's extended foot, bounces, and rolls down the stairs. Her mouth forms a perfect 'O' and her eyes widen in shock and pain.

Crrrack. Wood splits. Blood-red liquid trickles across the ground.

"Your very best, eh?" Ryrick groans at the bottom of the stairs.

Cydra's veneer is mottled, like a beet about to burst. "Upstairs," she gasps. "Now."

"Do you need help?" I frown at her bruising toes. Are they broken? Nausea overtakes me. Have I permanently damaged her? Will she dismiss me for this? *Can* she dismiss me? I curse my clumsiness. Why hadn't I asked her to move from the stairs?

She grips my tunic. "Get upstairs."

Ryrick makes a soft *hemm*ing sound. "Leave her be," he breathes. "Just take it out of her pay." His voice sounds soft and sympathetic, inciting my further distress. I failed Ryrick.

"I'll make her pay," Cydra promises. She looks like a dragon. Except uglier.

I climb the rest of the stairs, preparing myself for a beating. She limps after me.

When we reach the surface, she grabs my hand and drags me to an isolated corner of the courtyard. "Look what you've done." She points to her feet. Light illuminates her red, swollen limb clearly. She forces my chin up. "You're a stupid, stupid girl. If Lady Celeste hadn't intervened, we'd have called the guards to take you away. You're common, lying riffraff."

"I'm sorry, Cydra. I'll pay for the damage."

Cydra's countenance, if possible, grows redder. "Of course you'll pay. You'll pay for the wine and you'll pay for my foot. Nobody, not even a dog, would want you working for them."

A surge of rage boils my blood. "If you don't want me working for you, release me to Ryrick and Longley. They don't seem to think I'm *lying riffraff.* I'll pay for the damages, but I won't stand here and let you abuse me just so you can feel better about yourself."

Cydra's shrill laugh pierces. "Don't be an idiot, girl. I know you never worked for Count Malandre. I checked in with him, and he never had a girl who managed his estates. The man who's been doing it has been in the position for forty years."

My mouth opens, but I can't seem to form any intelligible words. I'm caught. She *knows*. It's only a matter of time before she rats me out to Count Malandre.

The victorious glint in her eyes burns brighter. "Count Malandre wouldn't associate with the likes of you. You're a liar, and only wenchers like Lord Faigen would ever pay you mind." Cydra steps closer to me. "I want you out. *Tonight*." She pinches my ear until I think it will bleed, then, after I let out a small, mewling cry, she releases me and hobbles away.

I try breathing, but it only aggravates the lump in my throat. Instead, I settle for wheezing. Slowly, I become aware of curious eyes watching me. The servants witnessed the display. I walk slowly, shakily into the servants' quarters, only to find Ryrick blocking my path.

"Elanor," he croaks, eyes soft and sad. "Let me talk to her. She'll change her mind."

Emotions are useless. Like mold on a cave wall. They'll call me weak if I show my feelings. So I take a deep breath, shove it all down, and push past him.

When I enter my own, private sanctuary, I close the door, stretch out on the bed, and cry.

EIGHT

MY SECOND MONTH ON Onyx, Adom punished me for killing a youngling dragon. I had just turned ten, and in my mind, the younglings were scary little beasts who wanted to eat me but unlike the grown dragons exhibited no signs of self-control. Every morning, I'd fling animal carcasses into their caves and leave the surly creatures to fight for the bits by themselves.

Younglings must be monitored when they are fed; if they are not, the strong will eventually starve out the weak. One of the younglings failed to thrive, and the dragons caught on to my neglect. That day, the discussion was so intense the walls of the mountain shook. Hot dragon breath poured like lava smoke from the summit top. In the central cave, cold dragon meals lay forgotten in the heat of the moment. And I kept myself hidden away.

Irna thought they should eat me for my insolence. Ona agreed. Silva wanted revenge for the vicious atrocities committed against her litter. Others fell in line until only Adom was left.

"They're angry with you, El. They want you dead," Muuth translated for me.

"Tell them I'll do what they want!" I begged. "Tell them I'm sorry."

Muuth curled next to me behind a rock. "Don't fret," he said. "Adom will protect you."

I started to cry.

"He's pleading for you," Muuth whispered in my ear.

I stared at my dragon-intercessor with hope, his speech nothing but unintelligible gibberish to my ears. Ona silenced him with one sharp word. The other dragons howled.

"What did they say?"

Muuth smacked a wrinkled hand to his aging forehead. He seemed tired. "They're calling him soft. They say he must pay the price."

Adom spoke again. At last, they all made sounds of agreement.

"Did he win out?"

"He compromised," Muuth says. "He didn't win, and he didn't lose." Then he observed my stricken countenance. "You're not dead, lass. You'll be punished, but you're not dead."

That night, Adom made me sleep in the cave with the bloodthirsty dragon younglings. I couldn't close an eye for even a second, because the beasts wanted to feast on me. They slithered like snakes and came at me from the air like bats. I had no weapon. I knew I'd be killed if I hurt them, so I spent the night running circles around the cave. When Adom came to get me the next morning, he walked with a limp and his skin around his neckline was healing from fresh burns. He told me it was a game the dragons sometimes played with him. Afterward, he went away for weeks. And I grew to hate him for leaving me behind.

~ * ~

Maybe I'd suppressed the memory after years of racing through pitch black caves with scaly tails winding around my legs and gnashing teeth at my arms. Maybe cowering in corners avoiding the mad flutter of wings pushed it all into my subconscious. I don't know why I'd forgotten about that night, about Adom's injuries. Why I'd never made the connection between his wounds and the argument he'd gotten into with the other dragons the day before.

So maybe it was true, after all. He felt sorry for me, in his own way. Did that make him a decent person? Was he more human than Cydra?

No. He wasn't better than Cydra. Because unlike Cydra, Adom had total power over me. She could pinch my ear and call me names, but she couldn't hurt me. Not really. I could leave this place at any time. I've never been Cydra's slave. Thinking this puts me into my right self. If I can survive burns and talons, Cydra was nothing.

No use crying. It wastes time, and does nothing but give me a headache when what I really need to do is come up with a plan. What do I do now? Find the king? Expose Adom? Somehow, I'm convinced that if Cydra could be so cruel and unforgiving, just because of my lowly position, then the king could be worse. He could have me thrown in prison for lying. Or worse. Adom would still be free, and I couldn't do anything to protect the people of Trana from a cell. So what? Go to Lord Berrel? Tell him I need his protection after all?

I lift my head from the tear-soaked pillow.

The door creaks open. "Elanor? Are you there?" Patience stands on the other side, eyes wet with worry. She carries a wooden tray of food, a bowl of white potato soup and a bit of flaxen bread. "Ryrick said you dropped a wine barrel on old Battleax. How are you?"

"How am I? Shouldn't you be more concerned about Cydra?"

Patience shrugs. "Cydra will recover. He said she screamed at you. She can be such a—"

"She fired me," I whisper, propping myself up on elbows.

"I'm so sorry," Patience says. "Can you talk to someone? Your previous employer?"

"There might be someone I can talk to." Suddenly, I think about the scales I have stashed away. Berrel said they were worth money. Maybe I could sell them to someone?

"Good," she says. "Let me know if you need my help to get

things sorted out." She makes no move to leave. After a quiet moment, she crosses the room and sets the tray on my desk. Patience reaches into a satchel and pulls out a glass jar of pale pink cream. "Ryrick thought you might need this." She sets the jar down beside the tray with a *clunk*. "I can make more, if you need it. I'm always giving them out by the dozens to the nobles. Just today, I filled an order for four dozen for Count Malandre. He likes to give them as gifts to an inn he stays at."

"Are you still hunting with your father today?"

She plops onto my bed and swings one leg over the other. "Yes, I am. Do you want me to bring you back a rabbit or a quail? We usually collect more than enough for the both of us."

"No, thank you." Since she is making herself at home, I settle next to her with the tray. The soup is hot and dumplings add comforting fullness to my innards. "Be careful in the forest."

Her eyes, usually wide across like eggs, shrink to the size of peanuts. "Are you concerned about other hunters or about dragons? You don't believe there are any hiding in the forest?"

"There are all manner of terrifying things that live there." I shudder, thinking of the Forest of Four in Onyx. It isn't a place I would casually take a stroll. I'm not afraid of bugs or cobwebs or even slithering things. It's the things lurking in the shadows, waiting to pounce and claw at your guts until you are nothing but entrails and gooey blood that fill me with unease.

"I know the king's forest like the back of my hand," Patience assures me. "It's where I go to extract herbs for my medicines. Did you know belladonna grows by the west trail?"

"Belladonna? Isn't that nightshade?"

"Yes, but in the smallest doses it can be useful for certain conditions."

"Remind me to keep you around if I am forced into a life of poverty and have to resort to roaming the forest. You would be a useful companion."

She giggles. After a moment, the laughter fades and she's

somber again. "Don't you have a family who could take you in? At least until you get back on your feet?"

"No family."

"None whatsoever?" She stands. "Then Ryrick and I will be your family."

"That's kind of you, but I can't exactly stay with you after I leave here."

"Why not? We have family visit us often. I'll say you're a cousin."

"Cydra will know you're lying. Ryrick didn't claim to know me when I arrived."

"Ryrick's a blind old bat, and Cydra doesn't employ me."

Maybe I won't have to rely on Berrel's "good will" or selling scales after all. Hope radiates in my chest. "I'll consider it," I tell her. "And thank you."

After she leaves, I poke my head into the hallway to make sure Cydra isn't lurking in the immediate vicinity. All clear. I creep through the servant's quarters, stepping lightly so I can dart out of sight. Two slumbering mongrels guard the door to the courtyard. The beasts' ears twitch as I pass, but they do not awaken. Sunlight pours over my profile as I bend the creaking hinges of the wooden door. A lush floral aroma sweeps over me; I pause to breathe in the scent. Then I cross the courtyard. Reaching the wall closest to the forest, I hesitate. A nearby well often attracts attention; servants use it for bathwater. I peek around the corner. No one in sight.

This strikes me as unusual. The past two weeks have been a constant flurry of activity. Solitude in the courtyard, the absence of servants, baffles me. They must have all gone to the kitchen on the opposite end of the courtyard to get ready for lunch.

I'm just clearing the doorway toward the courtyard when Ryrick bursts through the green labyrinth. "Quickly," he shouts. "Lady Celeste twisted her ankle in the forest and needs help. Find Patience and then report this to Lord Berrel immediately."

"Lord Berrel? Why?" *Shouldn't I report it to the king?*

"She's his sister. I'll see to it that the king is informed."

Lord Berrel's sister? I frown, reverse my direction and quicken my pace. Why didn't Rhydian mention that Lady Celeste was his sister? She intervened on my behalf the day I arrived at the castle looking for work. *And she's the future queen.* I've avoided Rhydian for enough time that of course I know which room is his. And Adom's, too, by this point. You can't actively avoid someone without digging into their personal habits and routines a little. And because of my ability to quickly memorize winding routes even in pure darkness, I'm able to figure out the fastest way of reaching the room without having ever been there before. At the door, I take a deep breath, straighten my shoulders, and knock.

The door squeaks open. Berrel is shirtless, a drowsy smile imprinted on a sleepy face. "I've been expecting you," he says. "Come in." He widens the door and waits expectantly.

"Sir, I'm only here to report that your sister hurt herself walking in the forest. Ryrick found her, and he and the physician are transporting her back to her chambers now."

"Celeste hurt herself?" He yawns.

"It's just a twisted ankle. Nothing serious."

He nods. "Thank you for the report. She's remarkably resilient. I'm sure she'll be fine." He stands at the door and continues to stare. I begin to make up something about having duties to attend to, but then I realize I don't. Cydra fired me. So where do I go now?

Berrel gestures to my uniform. "Are you really working or just dressing like a maid?"

"I was hired to work, so I'm working." Or rather, I *had* been working until this morning.

"So they pay you?" He doesn't wait for my response. "What

do you plan to do with the money you're earning? Are you keeping it safe somewhere?"

"What do I—?" I glare. "You want the money in exchange for your silence."

His eyes dart back and forth down the hallway. "Don't be ridiculous." He grabs my arm and tugs me into the room. "We should discuss this discreetly." Berrel closes the door before me. "You wouldn't want anybody to overhear us, would you?"

Adom's room is on a different floor, but I suppose Berrel is right. "Why would you ask about my money? And why have you been expecting me to come to you?"

He puts his hands between us and backs up several steps. "I wondered about your work, and I wanted to find out if you needed anything. And to report a few things that I've learned. Things I think you'd appreciate knowing. That's all."

I glance around the room. It's a suite, similar to the room arrangement at the Volcourt Inn. The front room is a sitting room, and sliding doors lead to the bedroom. The bedsheets are chaotically splayed. Somehow, it brings me relief. Berrel is not a placid sleeper. He has a flaw. He's not always a smug, slick businessman. "You said you would help me."

"That's what I'm trying to do." He grimaces. "Badly, so it would seem."

"I need an audience with the king, and I need to ensure that Lord Malandre is not there."

Berrel digests this. "Why? That isn't a simple task."

"Can you help or not?"

He stares at me for a long moment. "I might be able to arrange something for tomorrow night. The king is hosting a small banquet, just a few intimate friends. I could invite you as my guest." He looks at the floor for a moment, and the tips of his ears turn red. "Celeste was supposed to attend, of course, but I'm not sure if she'll be able to after what you said about her ankle. I'll check on her today. Rumor has it

Count Malandre's leaving this afternoon to finalize business contracts with partners in the south. He should be gone for several weeks, at least."

My heart chills. Adom is leaving? What are the chances that he's actually going to Onyx Island to check in on the dragons? And if he does...Ona's threats rings in my head.

There's a knock on the door. Berrel and I glance at each other, sharing mutual terror for a fraction of a second before he composes himself, grabs hold of my arm, and guides me into a linen closet. "My deepest apologies," he says, and shoves me inside.

"Who is it?" he calls.

"Count Malandre," replies the voice from the other side of the door.

My stomach drops to my feet. I can just see Berrel's expression from between the slats of the closet doors. The friendly countenance drops. I push open the door and motion for him to come within range.

He moves my direction and shouts at the main door. "I'm busy. Come back later."

"This can't wait," Adom's turgid voice answers.

"You have to warn him. Tell him not to go back to the island," I whisper.

Berrel's eyes widen. "What?"

"Tell him I've run away from home and if he goes back, my parents will attempt him bodily harm." I swallow, hard. "Please. I'll give you all my scales if you do this one thing."

"And if he asks where you are now?"

"You saw me several weeks ago, but I'm long gone now," I respond, concealing myself in the closet again as the Adom raps at the door more insistently.

Berrel sighs, loudly. "Very well. Come in." He swings the door open.

Adom stands on the other side. "Lord Berrel. I trust you are finding the accommodations comfortable?" His eyes zoom beyond Berrel's shoulders and for an instant they hone in on the linen closet. The corner of his mouth crinkles slightly.

My heart leaps to my throat as I peer through the slats. *He knows!*

Berrel gestures to his bare chest. "As you can see, I'm not quite ready to greet the world."

"I'll be brief. I'm leaving this afternoon," Adom says. "But I wanted to speak with you before I left. Lord Darton mentioned you've been hawking your wares to the other nobles."

"Hawking?" Berrel expels an irritated breath. "I'm expanding my business ventures. There's no crime in that, and now is the perfect opportunity to meet with potential partners."

"It isn't the 'perfect opportunity' at all. Your sister is about to be married. Many of the people staying at the castle now are here for the celebration. It's inappropriate for you to approaching the guests with your scheme."

"Somehow I doubt you care much about my sister's marriage, and frankly, I suspect this has more to do with the fact that I've been approaching *your* people." Berrel folds his arms.

Adom's eyes drift toward the linen closet once more. "Darton's lands are agricultural. Building a factory there would ruin the quality of the harvest, and would damage the livelihood and health of the people in the neighboring towns. Is that really what you want?"

"My goal is to make those people prosperous. To raise them out of their circumstances the same way I was raised out of mine. There's nothing wrong with that."

"And I suppose it is even more incentive for you that this would also wound me financially? You know I provide the seeds, equipment, and transportation. And you know a percentage of the harvest goes to me at deep discount."

Berrel smirks. "Yes. It is incentive."

Adom steps closer. "I am fully aware of your plans against me, Rhydian. I've been lenient because of my fondness for your family, and for our shared history."

"*We* don't have a shared history, Malandre—"

"Lady Elanor told me all about your obsession with me. She noticed when she met you."

"And just where is Lady Elanor right now?"

Adom clamps his mouth shut.

"You should know. Isn't she your ward?"

Adom's hands become fists, and his face blanches. Then he takes a breath and after a beat he is calm again. "That's irrelevant to the conversation." He slides backwards into the hallway. "As for Darton, you already heard from him about your scheme. Don't approach him again."

Adom melts into the darkness of the hallway, and Berrel slams the door behind him. He whirls around and thunders toward the linen closet. I open it before he reaches me.

"Why didn't you warn him?"

"There's more to your story that you told me, isn't there?" Berrel growls. "I'm not a fool, Elanor. Tell me what's really going on."

"My business is my own. I told you I'd give you my scales if you warned him about my parents. You said you'd help."

"You. Not him. And I don't want your money."

"You're a businessman, aren't you?"

"I have more than enough money. It's not the kind of payment I'm interested in."

"If you're implying—"

"I'm not." His eyes dig into mine. "If I was a lesser man, I might, but I prefer to take my payment in secrets. Obviously, I'm not at court for innocent reasons, either. I'm here for my sister, yes, but I have plans to act out a revenge on the man who destroyed my family."

There's a moment of silence between us. "Lord Malandre."

He doesn't blink. "Does that offend you?"

I have to think about the question for a moment. Berrel wants revenge. So do I. Even though Adom might have protected me in his own way all these years, there are things I can't forgive. He held me prisoner when he could have let me go. For twelve years. Maybe I don't want him to be torn apart by Ona, but he deserves *some* punishment for what he did to me. While I sat huddled in darkness, he clicked glasses of wine with snooty noblemen and women wearing fake hair just because. "No," I say, finally. "He told me about your sister."

Berrel's eyes widen. His breathing quickens slightly. "He mentioned Siren? I would have thought he'd forgotten her by now. Did he tell you why she was ill? That my father imagined he saw her with a monster and poisoned her food to cleanse his bloodline?"

I can't help but wince at that. How could a parent kill his own child? Then I think of Muuth and a shudder starts up my back. "Malandre said she had a fever."

He sneers, shakes his head, and glares at the wall to his left. "He won't admit his part in it." His eyes seek out mine. "Siren was our middle sister. The favorite. Celeste adored her. Malandre courted her for political gain, and when he had what he needed from the Berrel family, he abandoned her." He dips his head, his shoulders hanging slightly. "Siren was never the same. My father killed her because of his radical superstitions. That's why I can't go back."

I touch the corner of my mouth with my index finger, thinking. After a moment, I ask, "Why take your vengeance out on Malandre? Why not your father?"

"Because Malandre distorted his mind. Has the man not talked to you about his changelings?" His eyes scan mine. "Ah, but I see he has. He had Siren convinced she was one of them. She wanted to leave home and live on an island with wild dragons. My father, he overheard them plotting to elope and put an end to it. But the seed of doubt grew in his mind. He became convinced that all of his children were changelings. After he killed Siren, my father tried to hurt

Celeste and me. For her protection, I brought her to court. That's how she met the king."

I'm lost in my own thoughts. Adom must have believed that Siren was really a changeling. He would never have told her about Onyx Island and the dragon herd unless he was convinced. Was he wrong about her? I can't imagine Adom making so massive a mistake. "Why tell me this?"

Berrel flattens the blond curls at the top of his head with his palm, but when he moves his hand the curls just bounce back into shape again. "Because I suspect you and I are working to the same end. I could tell at the party that you seemed an unwilling companion to Malandre. I can also tell that he has a greater interest in you than you realize." His blue eyes flicker with indecision.

"You mentioned something like that already," I respond.

"We can use that to our advantage." His voice is soft now, almost a whisper.

"There is no *we* in this game," I remind him.

"There could be if you would trust me."

"I don't. Rhydian, I'm not used to trusting people. I work better on my own."

He smiles.

It unsettles me. "What?"

"You used my first name." There is warmth behind the words. "So?"

"That's the first step in learning how to trust."

I sigh impatiently. Berrel might want a friend he can connect with and bare his soul to, but I don't need the mess and distraction of people. It will only get me in trouble, the way working for Cydra only caused problems. I think about the scales and remember that I no longer have a place to live. Then I remember Patience's offer. I can't burden her. I have to take care of myself, like I always have. "You said you wanted to help me before," I say. "Well, I need your help."

"Anything," Rhydian says with conviction.

"I have a bag of dragon scales. I need you to buy them from me."

He squints. "Where did you get dragon scales from?"

"It's not important. Will you buy them or not?" I can't quite look him in the eye.

"Will it help you financially?"

"Yes. And you can turn around and sell them for a profit."

"I don't normally buy the scales. I mine them. So I won't make as much of a profit from yours as I would selling my own." He studies me, a frown growing on his face. "What's happened? Why do you need the money so urgently now? Aren't you still working?"

"I have to leave the castle and I don't have anywhere else to go. If you buy the scales, I'll have money to pay for an inn."

"And what about meeting with the king? You asked about that, earlier."

I raise my chin a fraction. "I have inside information for him that could benefit his army of dragon slayers. I have an acquaintance, Lord Faigen, who joined the army to help prevent dragon scorchings. Then his village burned. I think my information could have helped."

Rhydian frowns at me for a moment. "You want me to arrange a meeting between yourself and my sister's fiancé..." he shakes his head, "...the *king*, to talk to him about dragons? Did I mention they don't really exist?"

I offer him a thin smile. "Does King Siles believe dragons are scorching his farmlands?"

"Yes, but—"

"Doesn't he have an army of knights dedicated to battling the dragons?"

"They're called Scalers. They don't actually battle dragons. Probably because dragons aren't real," he digs. "They do, however, bring food and aid to people whose villages have burned. The sun is especially hot in the summer and fields spark and catch fire quickly."

Laughter bubbles up out of my throat. "Count Malandre believes in dragons, too."

His eyes narrow. "But you don't want him there when you speak to the king. Why?"

My lips press shut. "I have information it's best if only the king hears." *I know things about Count Malandre that would turn your blood to ice,* I could add, but I choose not to tell Rhydian this. If he thinks his father is mad for believing in the existence of changelings, my words will not convince him.

He steps away from me and sags against the wall, his muscular arms crossed. "I'm confused. You obviously don't want to hurt Malandre, or you wouldn't have asked me to warn him about your parents. But you don't trust him, even though you both entertain the idea that dragons are wreaking havoc on our land. And you don't want him to know you are here in the castle. Why?"

You obviously don't want to hurt Malandre. The words burn in my ears. I do, don't I? Didn't Adom kill my parents? Didn't he keep me as a slave for twelve years? For some twisted reason, he protected me from the worst of the violence at Onyx. But he didn't protect me from it all. There were plenty of horrors I had to face on my own. He could have freed me at any point—but he didn't. So yes, I do want to hurt him for everything he's done to me. I just don't want Ona to do it. I swallow before responding, hoping the intensity of my emotion doesn't come through.

"You said before that Malandre believes people can be dragons. That he tried to convince your sister that she was one, too," I reply. "Stop and think a minute. If I have information on this subject, do you really think sharing it with Malandre in the room is safe?"

"No, I suppose not," Rhydian answers after a moment.

Then his eyes widen. "Wait. You aren't saying that the scorchings… are somehow connected to Count Malandre? That he's so delusional he's burning whole villages to keep up this ruse that he's a dragon?"

I back away, shaking my head. "I'm not saying that."

"But you *are* saying he's not trustworthy. And implying that your information could help King Siles and his Scaler army and therefore hurt Count Malandre's personal agenda."

"I…I think you're reading into things," I stammer.

"Well, I suppose I'll find out tomorrow night." His smile returned, Rhydian says, "Meet me here at five o'clock. You can go to the king's banquet as my guest. I'll provide the clothes and wig, all you need to do is bring whatever evidence you've collected and those scales you want to sell me."

~ * ~

There's only one problem with Berrel's plan. I don't have any place to go before tomorrow night. When I return to my small, cozy room, the tears begin to prick my eyes again. I pack my bag slowly and then the emotions overwhelm me. I lay out on the mattress.

What if King Siles doesn't believe me? What if none of it matters anyway, because Adom has gone off to Onyx where the dragons are waiting to pounce on him? Where will I go if everything unravels? Where will I go even if the king believes my story?

I sit up and hoist the bag over my shoulder. I can do this. I can sleep in the forest if I have to. I know how to make myself a bed of leaves, and I know what plants are edible at least on Onyx. I can't use a fire, because it would draw too much attention.

I open the door, and move out into the hallway. Ryrick stands in the middle of the path, blocking my way. His eyes are soft and contemplative.

"Come with me," he says, and turns.

I follow him outside, away from the courtyard, to the east tower.

"Patience already has a bed made up. There's soup on the hearth."

"Ryrick, no," I protest weakly. "I don't need help. I have a cousin—"

"Don't lie to me, El," Ryrick says. "I know you have no one. I'd be a heartless monster if I let you sleep in the forest with the boars, elk, and the murderous dragons."

My blood runs cold. He and Patience both said there were dragons in the king's forest. Were changelings really hiding out so close to the castle?

No, I decide. If there were changelings in the forest. Adom would have found them by now. It must just be an expression.

"I don't want to be a burden," I mumble.

"You aren't one," he assures me as he knocks on the door to the physician's chambers.

"I thought you and Patience went hunting today?"

"We had to cancel. Patience was needed at Lady Celeste's bedside."

"Oh. Right."

Patience opens the door and smiles widely when she sees us. "I hoped Ryrick would be able to convince you to join us."

"I'll only trouble you for supper, then I'll be on my way."

Patience gives her father a knowing look, and then places a gentle hand on my arm. "Stay as long as you feel comfortable." She takes Ryrick's elbow and drags him to the cooking cauldron and the two of them fuss about the color of the stew and how it doesn't taste salty enough.

I set my pack down and close the door, gratefully breathing in the scent of rosemary, sage, and beef simmering in a delicious medley. When I straighten, I notice that Ryrick was telling the truth: Patience has a second bed made up in her laboratory.

Then food is served, and the three of us sit down and eat. I laugh more this entire evening than I can remember laughing the whole of my life.

When I wake up the next morning, Patience is in the next room, humming, her delicate hands working over what looks like a great mass of dragon scales. I shoot out of the pallet immediately and peek around the corner to get a better look at what she's doing.

"You can just ask me," says Patience, without turning around.

My cheeks heat up, but I slip smoothly around the corner and sit next to her. "What are you doing with all those dragon scales? Where did you find them?"

"Some of my visitors pay me in dragon scales." She peers at me and then her eyes go quickly back to her work. "I've also found some in the forest. Not a lot. But enough to make me suspect there was once one living there." She threads a needle and begins to sew. "I'm making a new kind of armor. Dragons are impervious to blades and arrows, yes? And they can withstand an intense amount of fire. It seems more sensible to use the dragon scales to make armor for when Ryrick and I go hunting than to string them into jewelry and sell them for things I don't need, doesn't it?"

I notice many of the scales are purple and speckled. It reminds me of the note Adom received at the Volcourt Inn. The note said Fire Breather found another changeling, a purple speckled dragon. Maybe this new dragon was living in the forest now. If that's the case, Ryrick and Patience weren't safe hunting. The dragon-scale armor could protect her from a blast, maybe, but it would be no match for the fierce chomp of dragon incisors.

Patience sets aside the project. "But this can wait. You're here to learn about salves. Want to go to start in the forest? The best way to learn is to start with the healing plants."

Soon, Patience and I are on our way, she dressed in deer hide and sturdy boots, a bow and arrows slung over her shoulder, while I'm dressed in what was a breezy yellow dress that Patience modified with rope to turn it into baggy yet practical harem pants.

"Do you like it?" she asks, while I skip over a rock.

"Can you turn all my dresses into pants?" I ask. "It makes movement much easier."

She laughs. "It was a fast job because I didn't want you tripping over your hem while we walked. If you want it to be a permanent change, I'll get out my sewing basket tonight."

I'm amazed. Patience is an apothecary, physician, hunter, and seamstress. I think about her stew from last night and smile. At least she's not perfect at *everything*. I stare at her, grinning, and she blushes. For someone with such talent, she's remarkably modest.

I glance at the sun, high in the sky. Not too far in. I have no inclinations to suffer Lady Celeste's fate. With this resolve, we clamber into the woods, fighting high grass and sharp twigs. This battle with nature reminds me of the untamed woodlands of Onyx.

The king's hunting forest isn't in a constant changing state like the Forest of Four. Squirrels collect nuts at a leisurely pace, not in the frenzied, frantic pattern of Onyx squirrels. Once, we see a deer raise its majestic head and stare for a long moment.

Patches of sun marble the area, whirling in intricate designs the way the flecks had in Muuth's little "kaleidoscope." A black bird caws and swoops across my path—an ominous sign, or a benevolent omen? I can't recall.

"Over there," Patience says, approaching a yellow, flowering shrub. She sets down her bow, and pulls out a bag and a rudimentary knife. "The leaves and the bark are the valuable part." She hands me the knife. Her cheeks turn pink. "Get to work, lazybones."

Under Patience's guidance, I gather what we need from the witch hazel, enjoying the soft cadence of her voice. She tells me an old folktale about two lovers who met under a full moon by a witch hazel tree and how, even long after the lovers passed away, the shrub's flowers bloomed blood-red as a sign of the intensity of their forbidden passion.

After we take what we need from the shrub, Patience changes course and steers me to a different plant, a ginger flower. Some of the herbs she mentions are not ones I'm familiar with; they aren't native to Onyx Island. There's a plant, it seems, for any type of ailment.

I allow myself to relax, slowly, and simply enjoy the company. I've never had a real friend before, someone my age, someone I actually appreciate spending time with. It isn't in my nature to waste words on pleasantries, but Patience fills the silence with meaningful words, small lessons, careful reflections. I breathe in the sweet aroma of wild flowers. A sweet-smelling bush weighed down with tiny clusters of purple fruit, catches my attention. I put one of the fruits in my mouth, then grimace and spit it out, disliking the sour taste tingling along my tongue.

"That's a barberry," Patience explains. "It's bitter, but it won't kill you." Then she smacks my arm. "Don't go around putting unknown fruits in your mouth. Some are poisonous."

Another, similar bush just ahead is more withered than the last. Drawing closer to it, I lift my leg high to avoid a dead log. The bottom of the bush appears to be burnt. Plenty of other dry objects lay nearby—thin twigs and dried leaves can easily have caught fire along with the bush. But the scar is contained within the parameters around the one area. A campfire? Remnants of the king's hunting trip?

Patience's fingers tighten around my arm. "That doesn't look right to me."

"No, it doesn't." I jerk back. My breath sticks in my throat. Heart hammering deafeningly in my ears, I retch. Patience puts a hand on my back to steady me. It takes several long moments before I can fully comprehend. It isn't a log.

"It's a burnt body." I put a hand over my mouth.

She draws her bow and nocks an arrow. "It smells fresh. We should leave."

The corpse's features are indistinguishable and blackened to ash. The arms and legs are positioned as if he spent his last moments defending himself. What do I do? I can't call for help. He or she is already dead. *Evidence*, I tell myself. *You've found evidence.* The thought doesn't console me. What if it's King Siles? What if I'm too late? If it is, Trana will fall into turmoil.

"We have to tell someone," Patience says.

"Who?"

"Ryrick." She studies the ground, chewing the corner of her lip. "He'll want me to examine it. I have case files of clinic visitors in my office. I might be able to identify the victim."

Of course. I'm grateful Patience is here to speak some common sense. If I'd been alone, I would have run. Deeper into the woods, deeper into danger. We need to identify the body. "Do you want us to carry it back to the castle? I think I could sling it over my shoulder..."

Patience tucks her arrow away and secures her bow. "I'll help. But we should move quickly. If whatever did this to him is still out here, our lives are in danger."

Together, we lift the flaking corpse and clumsily drag it back the way we came. Patience's face blanches with the exertion, and a streak of soot paints her cheek. Her hair is disheveled, and her eyes are glassy and wild. I'm sure I look no better. The body reeks with the most unbearable charred meat smell. Burnt skin and clothing erodes between my fingertips.

By the time we reach the servants' courtyard, I am gagging. Patience has somehow managed to keep a cool head, but I suppose that is her natural state in a crisis. She directs me to put the corpse down near an outdoor table. A flood of servants pour out of the castle.

"Go find Ryrick," she instructs one in her characteristically soft voice. To another, she instructs, "Get me a plank. I need the body on one to carry it to the tower. And you," she points. "Get a bucket of water, two fresh rags, and a couple of mugs of ale." The servants scatter.

I eye her with incredulity. "What do we need the ale for?"

"You're in shock," she says. "The drink will calm you. And we need the water and rags to wash off. Ryrick will help me move the corpse to my clinic, and you should lie down. I don't want you to pass out when it all finally hits you."

"I'm fine," I say even though my body is now shaking. "I've seen worse."

Patience nods. "Ryrick told me you're a survivor."

The servant tasked with bringing the water and ale returns, but he is not alone. Cydra follows close at his tail, her bony shoulders jerking and jolting with every angry step. She sees the corpse and her gait slows. Then she sees me and her mouth falls open. Rage simmers.

"I told you to leave," she says. "I'm calling the guards."

Patience steps forward. "I asked her to stay."

Cydra snaps a finger toward the corpse. "What is this?"

"We found a burned body in the forest," I explain.

Cydra whips her head toward me. "How dare you bring this into the king's home?" She turns as if she plans to storm off, probably to call the guards to arrest me.

"She was acting under my instruction," Patience says calmly. "The corpse needs to be identified, and a full report must be made to the king. Bodies and wellness are my jurisdiction. I believe it is safer for everyone if a proper inquiry is made. Elanor is my assistant."

"You can't be serious," Cydra says between a clenched jaw. "She doesn't know anything about medicine. She lied about working for Count Malandre. She's probably lying about—"

"Who I choose to hire is no business of yours, Cydra." Patience has her arms folded, but she is unflustered, a block of ice against Cydra's boulder-stare. "I need an assistant."

"She doesn't have papers!" the Housekeeper explodes.

Patience shrugs. "She doesn't need them. I believe she's capable of the job."

"She can't stay in the servants' quarters."

"She can stay with me."

Cydra's face turns beet red. "You'll regret this."

Ryrick slides between us. "That's enough, Cydra. You're embarrassing yourself."

"But your daughter—"

"Is not your business. One more word and I'll file a complaint. I'm saying this as your oldest friend: you are outside the bounds of your position. Go and take a few minutes to compose yourself. You don't want the king to hear you made a scene in the courtyard."

Cydra hangs her head. "I...apologize, Ryrick."

"It isn't me who deserves those words."

She looks up, and the defiance is plain in her eyes. Then she sighs in exasperation and walks briskly away. After she's gone, Ryrick turns to survey the corpse. He strokes his beard thoughtfully, but there is grief shining in his eyes. "It's Lord Darton. What a tragedy."

"How do you know?" I ask, aghast.

"His red beard. He's burned, but you can see some strands on his tunic." Ryrick points to the chest. "Do you see the gold buttons? They're melted, but you can still see his insignia on that one. He mentioned to me yesterday afternoon that he was going hunting. I told him to take a footman at least to assist, but he declined the offer."

"Will you help me carry him to my lab for study?" Patience asks Ryrick in a matter-of-fact tone, rolling up her sleeves.

I glance at her, surprised. She doesn't even appear to be

shaken by the older woman's visceral words or the corpse at arm's length. I thought I was strong and unmovable, but Patience is putting me to shame. Beyond the mild exterior, she is a warrior.

Ryrick nods and turns to me. "We'll take care of this."

I gulp down the remainder of ale and wipe my hands clean with one of the rags and the bucket of water. "I'll take the dishes to the kitchen."

I take the empty ale mugs and leave the remaining rag and bucket for Patience. I watch, sickened, as she and Ryrick lift the plank with the crispy body on it, and carry it toward the tower.

The cook is almost finished with the dinner preparations. Scullery maids frantically try to keep up with the dishes, while the assistant cook, Handen, pulls the spicy roasted meat off the spit. Longley wears a heavy woolen frock, a cream-colored hat, and two black gloves. She slices leafy green designs with metal cutters, and slivers red peppers. On an iron pan over the wood fire brick-and-tile stove top, one of her workers patiently grills mushrooms.

"Where can I put these two mugs?"

Longley arranges the freshly cut vegetables and spoons gravy onto each plate. The smell of the roasted meat causes my stomach to sour. She doesn't bother to look up from her arrangements. "You can wash them in that basin of soapy water. They belong in those glass cabinets over yonder." She dips the ladle into a gravy dish, refilling her supply.

"Are you making the meal for the banquet tonight? Can I help?"

"Didn't Cydra fire you?"

"Yes, but then Patience hired me. I wouldn't mind assisting, if you need extra hands."

"No, thank you. I heard where those hands have been today."

"You heard about the body in the forest? Already?"

Longley nods. "News travels quickly here. The king himself already knows, no doubt." Her lips grow tight. "Curious minds always find trouble," she lectures. "If you really want to help, go tell Donja the food will be ready to take to the king's private feast hall at a quarter to five."

Donja loiters outside the kitchen, wearing an impatient frown. In appearance and manner she reminds me of Raina, but where laugh lines crinkle the inn maid's face, a deep-set scowl mars Donja's. She sees me emerging from the kitchen and her expression darkens.

I breeze past her, quickly repeating Longley's message before padding up the staircase in a hurry, my heart racing. Time to see about this disguise Lord Berrel has for me. Hopefully it's a good one and the servants won't recognize me. I need to fill Berrel in on the corpse we found in the forest. If it really is Lord Darton, as Ryrick suspects, this could be the evidence we need against Malandre. Footsteps echoing below me cause me to falter.

Cydra stomps rapidly up the stairs. "What are you doing?" she growls. "Shouldn't you be off in the tower, assisting your mistress with that dead corpse?"

"She instructed me to take a break, ma'am." I could use some of Patience's cool right about now. Even though I hate to admit it, Cydra intimidates me almost as much as Silva used to. I wouldn't even be shocked to learn she's a changeling dragon. That would be a relief, actually.

"You shouldn't be in the main hall, anyway. Anyone could see you, and you aren't wearing a uniform." She pauses a moment and wipes a speck of dust off the landing. "I saw you leave the kitchen. You're no longer a between maid, so you have no cause to go there again."

"I thought maybe Longley could use some help. And I went to return the mugs."

"It's a security issue. We can't have unauthorized servants in the kitchen where the king's food is made. His food could easily be poisoned that way."

"Longley never mentioned it. I apologize."

Cydra grimaces. "Seems you're forever apologizing." She stares at her foot. "How long do you plan on making yourself a bother to everybody else?" She doesn't wait for my reply, but continues up the stairs and rounds the corner, out of sight.

I race quickly to Berrel's room and knock on the door. Rhydian opens it and gestures me inside without a word. As the door closes behind me, he rubs his hands together in excitement. I can't help but notice that he's dressed in his finest; a black silk overcoat atop a silver and green vest, his blond hair more controlled than usual.

"Do you have the dragon scales?"

I didn't even think about grabbing them after we found the corpse. "No. It looks like I have a place to stay in the castle for now so I don't need the money. Yet."

He nods. "I've got a dress and a wig. And I borrowed Celeste's handmaiden to help put it all together and dress your face."

"Dress my face?"

His smile almost touches his ears. "All part of the disguise. Malandre is gone, but we don't want any of the servants recognizing you. This way."

A demure servant stands in his bedroom, eyes on the floor and fingers entwined. The dress is laid out on the bed. It perfectly matches Berrel's attire, with the same shades of black, silver, and green, in lace and silk materials and black tulle underneath the skirt.

Berrel excuses himself while the handmaiden helps me to change, and then she directs me to a chair and proceeds to decorate my face with powder, kohl, and glittering mica. She holds a mirror out so I can see her handiwork as she paints my lips with red paste. I refuse the wig, so after lightly oiling the tips of my hair to force it to cooperate, she expertly twists it into a braid and fashions it into a bun on one side of my head. While she works, Rhydian wanders into the room again.

"Don't say a word," I say flatly. "This isn't exactly fun for me."

"I learned my lesson the last time I paid you a compliment," he replies.

"Good, because there are more important things to discuss." I fill him in on the body, and how Patience and Ryrick took it to her clinic to identify the victim. I tell him we think it might be Lord Darton. Lord Berrel takes it all in solemnly hands in his pockets, back against the wall.

"It could be enough to convince King Siles," he says. "Coupled with everything else."

I chew on the sides of my nails, thoughtful. "Rhydian, do you know much about Count Malandre's past? Where he comes from? When he started appearing in public?"

He nods. "His family was prominently visible when I was much younger, but then the Count, Malandre's father, became senile and reclusive and the name all but vanished from the court. The current Count reemerged when his father passed away."

"Do you remember the family?"

"I think I saw them once, when the king was crowned. There were only three of them; the father, mother, and the boy. The former Count was a business partner of my father." Rhydian touches his temple. "Now that I think on it, I do have an odd memory of my father recounting a visit to the Malandre estate. He said it was unsettling. When he arrived, a boy was chained like a dog to the gate, naked and covered in mud. And on all fours. When he got out of the carriage, a heavily pregnant woman dressed in rags peered out at him from a dilapidated cabin beside the manor. My father swore the woman was Countess Malandre and the boy was the son, but he couldn't make sense of their treatment." Rhydian laughs. "My father. Mystified by how another man treats his family. Quite like him."

So Adom chose to murder and replace a man who abused his family. Why does that make my heart blossom with relief?

Celeste's handmaiden puts the finishing touches on my hair; a sprinkle of shimmering mica powder, and dried baby's breath tucked between the loops of my braid. She steps away, admiring her artistry with a satisfied smile.

"Are you ready, Lady Elanor?"

I rise and take his extended arm. "Never more ready."

~ * ~

Blank, unimpressed stares meet my own and while people part for Lord Berrel, they scarcely move aside to let me through. I meekly follow Berrel inside the room, avoiding the hard scrutiny of the guards as the doors swing open, and we wait to be announced.

Gold threaded furniture catches my eye. It matches the gilded paintings that adorn the walls with flawless perfection. In the center of the room, a table with elaborate centerpieces of the finest gold and silver draws my attention. Statues fill every corner, and a fountain stands by the door. Its melodic trickling serves to reinforce my will and still the trembling in my knees.

There are several nobles in the room, some I recognize from around the castle while others are new to me. The banquet table is set with sizzling meat, red wine, and about twelve different platters piled with colorful vegetables. The serving man gestures for us to sit and begin eating. I look across the table but do not see anyone wearing a crown.

"Where is the king?" I ask Berrel.

"I don't see him," he replies behind a napkin. "That's unusual."

"I don't see your sister, either."

"No, she declined to come at the last minute," he says. "Although many of these families will be at her wedding, she doesn't really know them well. Not like King Siles does. Besides, her ankle is still hurting from yesterday's fall. That's why I was able to use her handmaiden."

"So, who are these others?"

"Lords Kennon, Pressley, Rilford and their wives. They're the king's private counsel."

"Are you part of his private counsel?"

"Not officially, but since my sister's engagement, I've been included in their meetings."

Rhydian introduces me to the other nobles, but once the pleasantries are finished I have nothing more to say to them. We make small talk with the other nobles, but as the hour slips by, I grow more agitated and anxious. Where is King Siles? Why isn't he here at his own banquet? We fall into a tense, sullen silence that is thankfully filled by Longley's wonderful meal.

The door to the banquet hall opens, and two men enter together. The first, I have never seen. He's a young man wearing a gray cloak and a gold crown, one crimson ruby set in the center. His hair is blacker than night, forming tight, wiry curls around his head, and his face is dark and gaunt. My eyes fall on the second man, the one speaking. Adom. My throat constricts.

Beside me, Rhydian curses.

"We're going to die," I mutter.

Everyone at the table stands. I sigh, set down my napkin, and push out of my chair as well. Rhydian grabs my hand, his fingers tightening in encouragement. I glance at him. *This is it.* I think. *This is the night Adom will finally eat me.*

"Pardon my lateness," says the king. "Please take your seats."

Adom's eyes scan the group of us. They briefly touch me, then move on to the next person. I suck in air. He *has* to know it's me. My disguise isn't *that* good. But if he notices, he doesn't say a word. He follows the king to the head of the table and takes a seat to the monarch's right. A servant sets down a heated dish in front of the king, then another in front of Malandre. They spend a few silent moments eating, as if nobody else is in the room.

Then the king dabs his mouth with a napkin and looks

across the table. "Thank you for joining me this evening. My apologies that the night didn't turn out as planned." He settles back into his seat. "Lord Darton..." He coughs, covers his chest with a pounding fist, then tries again. "Lord Darton has been murdered. Count Malandre and I have just gone to see his family. Funeral arrangements are underway. It is an unfortunate day for us all."

Murmurs of concern and expressions of grief buzz around the table. I glance at Adom and catch him staring at me. His gaze slips away smoothly, almost as though he doesn't care that I'm here. My eyes sink to the table, and I notice that Rhydian and I are still holding hands. For some reason, the exchange between Adom and Rhydian echoes through my head. I remove my hand from Rhydian's, perturbed. It doesn't matter to me that Adom is bothered by Lord Berrel's sudden interest in me. But I don't need another poker to stoke the fire.

"I've also received news that Princess Ora was delayed in her journey. We were expecting her late tonight, but it looks like she will not be arriving for a few more days."

More murmurs. This time, of disappointment. I glance at Rhydian. He will have to tell me who this Princess Ora is sometime soon. Assuming we survive the night.

The king takes a moment more to talk business with those at the table who came to discuss things like proprietary holdings and estate taxes and the plague that has infected the southern part of the country. No one mentions dragons, and it is all mostly nonsense to me, so I stir the food around my plate until Rhydian switches our plates so it looks like I have eaten everything. Even then, I still can't stay still, my knee bobbing up and down until he puts a hand on it. I glance at Adom and his nostrils are flaring, but he isn't looking at me.

"Again, I apologize for the way this evening went. I see most of you are finished with your food. The news about Lord Darton's murder has deeply affected me, so I'm afraid we will have to end our night here. Please, fill your wine glasses before you leave."

Rhydian and I exchange glances. My stomach rolls. King Siles waves us away. The nobles stand, and Rhydian moves more slowly than the others. While the others take their leave, Berrel strides toward the king.

"Didn't you hear what I said, Lord Berrel?"

"Sire, this woman has information I think you'll want to hear." He glances at Adom. "In private."

"Not now."

"But, Sire—"

"I said not now. I have other crucial matters to discuss with Count Malandre."

"He isn't who he says he is," I speak up.

King Siles turns his chin toward me. "Who are you?"

I glance at the back of the room to make sure all the nobles have left. It's now just me, Adom, Siles, and Rhydian. It's hard to breathe past the terror in my throat. I glance at Adom again. He's sitting straight in his seat, fingers steepled, eyes on me. I look away. I didn't plan for him to be here. He was supposed to be gone from the castle. I was going to tell King Siles everything I knew about the dragons, about Onyx, about the Tranar children who came and went from the island. About how "Count Malandre" kept me as his slave for twelve years. How he brought me to Trana to find more changelings. I could have helped King Siles train his army—the Scalers, Rhydian called them—in finding and defeating the changelings who were scorching Tranar villages. That was the plan. But now that Adom is here, everything is all muddled.

Then a horrible thought wheedles into my head: *Am I betraying him?*

Lodin's mercy. I'm not betraying him. He *kidnapped* me.

But Muuth has done rotten things as well, my stubborn mind argues.

Yes. Muuth did atrocious things. The stories he told me about his past life sickened me. And he spared Adom and brought him to the island. And he may have lied about the boat.

The difference was that Muuth never hurt *me*. He wasn't the one who stole *me*. He didn't bring *me* to an island full of violent dragons that used me as a slave and a toy for their wicked offspring. That wasn't Muuth's fault. It was Adom's.

I owe him nothing. Yes, he may have spared me from some of the violence. So did Muuth, by teaching me how to take care of myself. That doesn't mean what Adom did to me was in any way excusable. I take in a breath, shoving away the guilt. Adom's eyes burn, but I refuse to look his direction.

"I was his captive, Sire," my voice trembles a little, and I hate myself for feeling weak. "He kept me imprisoned for twelve years." Beside me, Rhydian gasps in disbelief. "I know things about Count Malandre that will make your blood curdle."

The king leans forward in his seat. "You didn't answer my question. You also didn't listen to me. I said I'm in the middle of important business. Kindly take your leave."

My stomach turns into a hollow, quivering pit. I take a step backward. Didn't he hear what I said? Doesn't it matter? I lock eyes with the king, willing him to change his mind, but he waves his hand again and then focuses on his plate of food. I spin on my heels and head for the door. Time to leave. I'm not waiting around for Adom to come and kill me now that I've exposed myself. And now Rhydian's in jeopardy, too. I was a fool to think the king would—

"Her name is Elanor Landis," Adom's voice cuts across the room. "And she's telling the truth."

A chill crawls across my skin. Every instinct urges me to flee. But I can't run. I have to face him. It takes every ounce of courage to meet his probing gaze

He points at Rhydian. "You, go." At last he really looks at me. "You, stay."

"Majesty, if what she says is true, I don't wish to leave her with this man," says Rhydian.

"I'm here," replies the king. "It sounds like this dispute is a private one. Unless you have any related information to share?"

"I do," says Rhydian. "Count Malandre threatened me. He found out I was working with Lord Darton to open a factory. I think he murdered Lord Darton."

"Is that all?" the king asks. "If so, you may go."

"Sire, if you think on it—"

"It doesn't match the timeframe. The physician reports that Darton died yesterday morning. Count Malandre was working for me during that time. He was across town."

"Couldn't he have hired—?"

"A what? A dragon? I thought you didn't believe in dragons, Lord Berrel."

Rhydian's voice takes on an edge of desperation. His eyes go wide, his pupils dilated. "I don't, but Malandre does. Wouldn't you suppose he'd do anything to secure his lands and prove to other nobles that building a factory is risky business in a land of dragons?"

"I don't know how killing Lord Darton would secure those lands," replies the king. "Now Darton's assets are frozen and no business transactions will be resolved until after the murderer is caught. And, it's my understanding Darton rebuffed you. If anything, it looks to me like you have motive to remove Darton from the picture. Didn't he tell Malandre you approached him?"

Rhydian's jaw works, but he can't form the words. I put a reluctant hand on his shoulder. "I'll find you later," I say softly. "You'd better go before this sours."

"It's already soured," Berrel growls. He takes my hand in his. "Are you certain you'll be fine alone with *him*? I didn't know about your history. It explains so much."

"I'm fine," I say, giving Adom my stoniest look. Rhydian

moves toward the door. As the slab thumps shut behind him, I curse under my breath. Adom will never let me leave this room alive. The king and I will die. Then what? Will Adom control the throne?

The king tips his goblet and swallows a sip of wine, never releasing my gaze. When he drinks to satisfaction, he returns the goblet to the table with calm elegance. "So," he breathes. "You're Elanor?" His look grows intense. "Why are you parading as a servant?"

I cast my eyes to the table. "Your Majesty," I blurt out, before Adom can stop me. "He brought me to Trana to spy out changeling dragons. I tried to escape and he caught me and took me back to the island, my prison. I had to get away." I take in a breath. "Your army is hunting dragons who are scorching the farmlands and—more lately—noblemen. But full blooded dragons aren't the ones you need to be concerned about. It's the changelings. I've read a communication between Count Malandre and someone who calls himself Fire Breather. I believe this person is a changeling hiding in your court."

No explosion comes from Adom, as I fear. Perhaps he isn't as confident as I first assumed. If I dive in front of King Siles and cry out for the guards before he has time to respond, he might find himself overcome and subdued, his plan foiled. I glance uneasily from one to the other. Siles doesn't appear angry. He lifts his goblet and drinks deeply.

"Changelings? I'll admit it's a compelling story. But do you have proof outside your word? Anything tangible that will convince me?"

Nothing tangible except the body in Patience's office. And I can't even link that to Adom, definitively. Exhaling, I utilize my best defense. "Count Malandre is a changeling dragon, Sire. And if you send a boat to Onyx Island, the place where he kept me you'll find a herd of wild dragons there. Malandre is their leader."

Siles' forehead furrows. He surveys Adom again. "Is this true?"

I wait with baited breath, my whole body tense. Adom will finish us off now. His secrets are out, his guise demolished. He can no longer continue this charade.

He bows his head with such timidity I almost scream. He should rip my head off for my betrayal. "I *am* a changeling, my lord," he admits, in a voice so soft I almost can't hear him.

"And are you working with another changeling, a man called Fire Breather?"

"I am, Sire."

Siles stands. He slams his fists on the table in a singular display of fury. "And do you plan to overthrow me with this Fire Breather creature so your dragon herd can decimate Trana?"

"I'm your servant, Majesty. My only wish is to honor and protect you."

"He's lying," I interrupt. "On Onyx Island, he has a cave full of gold and priceless artifacts. He scorches your lands and steals your cattle to feed the herd." I begin fumbling with the hooks on my dress. "If you want tangible proof of his villainy, I can give it to you."

Siles holds up a hand. "What are you doing?"

"I'm a slave, your Highness, but I wasn't born a slave. I was once a farmer's daughter." I've undone the dress enough to pull it down over my shoulders. I half turn, shielding my front with an arm, and yank the dress down. It rips as it falls. I hold it around my lower back, exposed enough that the king can see my burn scars. "And then one day, Adom came and burned down my village. He captured me. The dragons abused me. *He* abused me. He murdered my family. So when I say he is working to destroy you, I say it fully knowing that *he* is the one with all the power in this room and that my life is forfeit after this moment."

As I say all this, I hold the king's gaze unwaveringly. My heart is pounding— no—*exploding* in my chest because this is it, the moment I've spent my whole life dreaming of. And I'm so afraid that if I look away, blink, falter for even one small moment, the reality of it will fade and I will be back in my cave, or back in the cellar, trapped. There are people who spend their whole lives as slaves, born into a world of pain and forced to endure violence I can't even comprehend until their bodies break, and they are nothing but compliant flesh beneath a cruel whip. That isn't me. I once had freedom, and because of that privilege I can't release the king's gaze, can't allow him to deny my humanity.

"What you've shared tonight isn't news to me," says Siles sadly. "I wish I could say it was. When I see firsthand the scars on your back..." He grimaces and turns away.

"You knew?" My heart stills. "You *knew* I was his captive?"

"And I knew who you were the moment I walked into the room." He glances at Adom then and mouths something I don't catch. Then back to me. "I'm truly sorry, Elanor, for all the pain this has caused you. But you must believe me when I say that all of it was necessary, and that Adom acted under orders. Your suffering has, perhaps, saved the lives of hundreds of Tranars. And now you are here right where we need you the most."

"You knew about the other changelings?"

He nods. "I am intimately aware of the changeling problem. That's why Adom and I have been working together to discover them." The king sets aside his plate of food. His chair screeches as he slides away from the table. Slowly, he rises with carefully measured movements. His regal cloak billows out around him.

"You see, Elanor of Onyx, *I* am Fire Breather."

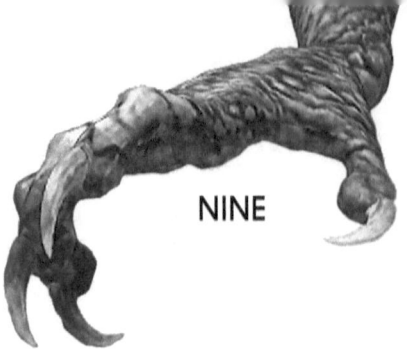

NINE

WARMTH CREEPS ALONG MY cheeks. My jaw drops while I drag my gaze back and forth from the king to Adom's sad visage.

Adom…

Damn him!

I pull the dress up around my shoulders and hook it with nimble fingers. The tear is small, and I don't think anyone will notice it, but I still feel guilty because Rhydian gave it to me.

"You're Fire Breather?"

The king's eyes narrow. "I'm not going to eat you."

A tide of sickness washes over me. "So Adom isn't trying to connect with the other dragon changelings to work against you?"

"I've worked for King Siles ever since he came into power." Adom steeples his fingers. "He ordered me to take control of the dragon herd. That's why I came back after Ona killed the dragons who protected me. That's why I challenged him."

"You acted under orders. Not revenge?" My voice sounds strange and breathy to my ears.

The haze grows thicker. Adom's words, slow and succinct, become oddly unintelligible. "We're attempting to make contact with all the changeling dragons. We have large numbers of them hiding in a changeling compound in the foothills of Skydive Peak. Mostly, they are frightened and want only to live normal lives. But some have refused our attempts to help."

"So you are certain that it's not the herd scorching Tranar lands?" He shakes his head. "Did you murder my parents?"

The king opens his mouth to interject, but Adom holds out a hand. "I didn't."

"Then why did you let me believe it?"

Concern and reluctance wars on his face. He takes in a breath, his shoulders squaring. "You told me you wanted to die. That first night on Onyx. Don't you remember? You wanted me to kill you. So, I told you what you needed to hear. Something to channel all your hopeless rage into so that you would live. I didn't think you would make it, otherwise."

There it is. So simple an answer to a question that has plagued me for weeks. I don't remember telling him that, but everything about those first days on Onyx is a blur. If Adom didn't kill my family, who did? Was it one of the changelings he was tracking? Or someone in the changeling compound he mentioned earlier? My heart quickens. "Why didn't you tell me what you were doing in Trana? And why did you bring me?"

He stands now, and the circle is complete. We are, all three of us, standing around the banquet table: me, with my dress askew; the king looking like he might pull out a sword at any moment; and Adom, now bizarrely vulnerable.

"I didn't tell the king I was bringing you to Trana," he answers. "I made that decision independently. So I couldn't tell you fully about the mission until I spoke with him." He can't seem to meet my eye. "It wasn't an easy decision. I wanted to tell you. But I didn't want to jeopardize everything we were working toward. I had to see how you'd react to being back in Trana, surrounded by humans, so that I could report to the king. We had to know we could trust you."

My mouth works. "You could have told me. I wouldn't have tried to escape."

The king's eyes narrow. "You hate Adom, correct?" He doesn't wait for my nod. "Had he revealed his association with me earlier, you would have hated me as well. You might have attempted to assemble a Tranar rebellion against me, revealing my true identity, just like you revealed Adom's. That's how deep your hatred runs."

He's right. I recall countless conversations with Muuth that revolved around the upheaval of Siles' reign, when I thought the king was a weak monarch. And I *did* betray Adom to the king. If they hadn't been working together, things could have gotten bloody tonight. Honestly, I didn't think the king could overtake Adom given our current circumstances, with no preparation and no guards in the room. But it would have shattered Adom's human identity and his ability to continue his charade as Count Malandre. Maybe there was a small part of me that secretly believed even with all his threats of murdering me he would spare me. If things had gone differently, if I'd told the truth and the king had been horrified, had Adom attacked us, that would have confirmed my worst fears. Then I could have resumed plotting his violent death.

Siles is still talking and I've ignored half his words. But now I bring my attention back into focus.

"Adom brought you to Trana so you could see the reality of the situation," King Siles says. "This, he hoped, would instill new loyalty to your native country, something we supposed was stripped from you by the dragons."

"Is it true, Adom?"

His face, downcast and lined with obvious discomfort, pales at my inquiry. "For weeks, rogue changelings have left scorched bodies in our backyard. Lord Darton isn't the first. We've tried to cover up the others so as not to cause a panic. Since the servants found Darton's body, however, the news is public now. Questions are being raised. We need to move quickly."

"What are your plans?"

"Find Lord Darton's murderer. Make contact and attempt to teach them a different way. Direct them to the compound where they can learn about their abilities."

"And you're comfortable killing them if they refuse to work with you?"

"I am not comfortable with it, no." Adom glances at me,

then looks away. "I told you I'm a murderer. I never lied to you about my past. That's why I chose the name Slayer."

"And who are the others in the message I read at the Volcourt Inn?"

Adom sighs. "What we think is that there are two dragons that use the forest as their hunting grounds. They might be from the city or the farmlands—we're not certain. Although we've found ebony and ivory scales near the charred remains, Cinderrider and Leviathan, as we call them, continue to elude us. We hunt for them almost every night. Sometimes, farmlands near the city have also been scorched but we've never been able to connect those incidences to the murders in the forest."

"How many victims total?"

"Three lords. All found in the woods."

"When did the murders start?"

"About three months ago, after we started our initial search for Cinderrider and Leviathan."

I stare at them both for a long moment. "Are you certain the victims are changelings? Maybe the murders aren't the work of the rogue dragons trying to undermine you. Maybe the murderer is somebody who knows about the changelings and is determined to kill them."

"We have considered a rebel group of humans. Like Muuth," he says, and then his eyes widen as if he is thinking twice about making that comparison in front of me. Adom's forehead furrows. "Changelings don't die so easily."

"I know dragons can be poisoned, although I'm not certain if that applies to changelings as well. They *do* burn in their human form, though." I think of the day I saw Adom covered in burns after an altercation with Ona. Realization comes to me. I frown. "You can't go back to Onyx," I say, after several moments. "Your life is in danger there. When he left me in Trana, Ona threatened to challenge you again. He...he threatened to kill Muuth. All because of the trouble I've caused."

King Siles purses his lips and stares sideways at Adom. "Trouble at home?"

"I can manage it," Adom replies quickly. "It isn't a problem."

I realize then that Adom may not have told Siles about the challenges he faces, about the attacks. Then I remember that the king ordered him to this life. I'm not the only casualty here. My heart aches, and tears suddenly prickle in my eyes. I sniff and blink rapidly, pretending that it is just the dirt in the room and not emotion that is making me so suddenly congested.

"Why did you take me back to Onyx?" I ask Adom.

He grows rigid. "I changed my mind."

"Excuse me?" I try hard to keep the ire out of my voice.

"I decided we didn't need you after all." After all the honesty and the vulnerability I've seen from him tonight, he is wearing that bored, aristocratic mask again.

"You're an idiot, Adom," I say, unsmiling.

"It doesn't matter now," he says, with a note of admiration in his voice. "You're here."

"That's right," the king says. "And where are you staying, Elanor?"

"Here in the castle," I answer.

Adom coughs. "Since Cydra fired you yesterday?"

My head swivels toward him. "How'd you know about that?"

He touches his nose. "I've been keeping tabs on you. To make sure you were safe."

"So you knew I was hiding in Lord Berrel's linen closet this morning?"

"It might have been one reason I decided not to leave for Onyx today."

"Lord Berrel is an ally. He's been helping me—" I stop short. Now that I know Adom isn't the killer I thought he was, things would have to change between me and Rhydian. Somehow, I don't think he'll understand that Adom is the *good* kind of changeling. Especially after what happened to his sister.

"You're welcome to your allies," he says, with an air of disgust and disapproval. "But I'm trusting you to keep our secret. Don't get too close."

"I didn't tell him, Adom."

"It's...Alistair here. Not Adom."

A moment of confusion fogs my brain. Who? Then I remember that all Tranars have two names. Theodore Faigen. Rhydian Berrel. Elanor Landis. "Alistair?"

"That was the name of the former Count Malandre. My birth father."

I suck air between my teeth, making a soft whistling noise. "But I thought...?"

His mouth curves. "You thought I was abandoned by my birth family. I was. By my father. He cast out my mother and me when I was seven, and even helped Muuth track us down and try to kill us. Alistair Malandre was a terrible, cruel man."

Now Rhydian's words from this evening rock me. *A boy was chained like a dog to the gate, naked and covered with mud...* Suddenly, Longley's succulent meal is in my throat and all I can think of is a terrified little boy and a man who must surely be more a monster than the dragons of Onyx. No wonder Adom never spoke about his past. No wonder he left so many things unsaid in the years I've known him. What horrible traumas must he have faced?

"I don't like to talk about it," he says, as if reading my thoughts. "My full name was Alistair Malandre, but when Muuth spared me I asked him simply to call me *Adom*. It means *new one*. My father always called me *Alistair*, so it isn't a name I cherish."

But *Adom* is? Adom, the name of the monster of Onxy Island? The one who haunted my dreams? Strange, but it sounds so backwards. "But you're using Alistair now for political gain?"

"It's a reputable name. Many of the older nobles remember

my father fondly."

King Siles, perhaps impatient with the detour our conversation has taken, abruptly takes his seat again and begins pulling apart the roasted chicken breast and leaving the bones in a neat stack beside the plate. Adom and I quickly take our seats as well.

"Elanor, I know you have much to think over," says the king. "And I know you may be tempted to run again. Don't. One reason we didn't bring you in sooner was because we worried you would try to leave. This news can't be made public. We can't afford liabilities."

His tone is pleasant, but I catch the subtle undertones. He's threatening me. If I try to leave, he'll come after me. It isn't Adom I have to fear, anymore. Adom might be the leader of the dragon herd, but Siles is a dragon king. One who is telling me that I must work with them. Or else. A cold chill starts up my back, and I lean tentatively away from the table.

"I won't run," I promise. "But I do have things to think over."

Adom nods. "I'll walk you to the east tower."

I straighten my dress. We wait for the king to dismiss us, and as soon as he does Adom jumps up and holds my chair and offers his arm to help me out of it. I take his arm and bob my head in deference to the Siles, surprised by the relief I feel that it is only Adom walking me back, not armed guards. Only the same demon-monster I have dealt with for twelve years.

~ * ~

After all the fantasies of stabbing him in the neck or ripping off his scales one by one , here I stand next to the man and for once I have no desire to see him suffer. He walks with a slight hunch, eyes sad, mouth pressed together as though there are still more secrets he must carry, more burdens he must take upon himself, even if it means my hate.

Instead of going straight to Patience's clinic, we take a

detour to the forest and sit beside a creek. For a long while, Adom is silent, eyes on the water, palms against the ground. When he speaks at last, his voice croaks and he holds a fist to his lips, clearing his throat. "Take all the time you need to think on the king's words. He'll call on you in two weeks to find out if you'll work with us." Adom turns to me. "He'll reward you for your service."

I'm not worried about anybody overhearing us—Adom has always had an exceptional sense of smell and could sniff out lurkers from miles away. "What will you do in the meantime?"

"I'll retrace Lord Darton's final steps, find out who he was with and why he entered the forest alone to begin with. I can track his scent in the forest, too. If it isn't too old."

"Can you track the scent of the murderer?"

"I'll certainly try."

"And what if something else comes up? Another scorching?"

He gives me a reassuring smile. "We'll call on you if we need you. But remember, King Siles can send the Scalers. He's already doubled the guard around the forest perimeters. He has trackers pouring through the caves searching for any signs of a changeling."

"It can't make things any easier for you." Empathy doesn't fit well in my mouth, but I suppose it's like a muscle that must be used in order to thrive. Mine has long since atrophied, but Adom deserves a little now.

"We try to work without *changing*. Or, if we do need to *change*, we do it far from Foghum. With the knights, the king's guard, and the city watchmen all on alert, it isn't safe for us, either. My fear is that, if the rogue changelings are not discovered and stopped, it won't be safe *anywhere* in Trana for dragons soon. Except for Onyx Island."

His eyes follow a flock of blackbirds bursting out of a copse of trees and sailing into the twilight. "I would like to take you to the dragon compound sometime soon. To show you what we've been working toward, Siles and I."

"Can you take me now?"

He stares at me with amusement. "What about tomorrow?"

"I can do tomorrow," I agree reluctantly.

~ * ~

When we reach the door to Patience's tower, Adom and I part ways. By the time I climb to the top, I hear voices echoing beyond the door. I fling it open to find Rhydian and Patience sitting across from each other at the table. Patience's eyes shine with relief.

"You're here," she says, and flicks a finger at Rhydian. "You have a guest."

Rhydian stands up and paces the room. "What took you so long?"

"And why are you dressed like that?" Patience inquires.

Rhydian glares at her. "We need space, physician."

Pink blooms in her cheeks. She rises slowly from the nicked, darkly stained table, her knees cracking at the joints. She takes careful, deliberate steps toward the door, then pauses and bows. "I'll take my leave, my lord." She grabs a sack off the wall and slips past me.

"Patience, you don't have to l—"

But she's already gone.

I square tight shoulders and fold my arms. "This is her home. You don't need to be rude."

"I thought they might have killed you."

"Don't be dramatic."

"Dramatic?" His voice rises in anger. "You found a body in the forest this afternoon. We just confronted the king to tell him his best man was hiding dark secrets from him. And then I find out this man held you captive for twelve years?" He slaps his palm against his forehead. "Why didn't I guess it before? It explains everything."

"We got things sorted."

"Sorted? It isn't as though you left to do laundry." He points to the window. "Then I see you returning to the tower, chatting with Malandre as if the two of you have been long friends?"

"We aren't friends, Rhydian. Nothing's changed. Malandre has an alibi for the murder, and they have other, more likely suspects."

"And what about how he treated you?"

"He had a plausible explanation for all of it."

After a moment of us defiantly glaring at one another, Rhydian finally throws his hands wide. "Well? What's the explanation?"

"I'm not at liberty to say."

Baring his teeth, he seethes. "So there are explanations, but you can't share them with me and now, after everything, you've decided to stop pursuing justice?" He regards me with disappointment and pity. "What did they do to you, Elanor?"

I rub the back of my neck. "They didn't do anything. You can't build a future on revenge."

He rolls his eyes upward, staring at the ceiling in consternation. "I assure you, you can."

My temper builds, tightening my chest. "Well, I'm ready to move on." And as soon as the words are out of my mouth, I realize they are true. I don't want to hurt Adom anymore. I don't even want to fight the herd dragons. If Muuth came back today and tried to catch my interest with schemes of dragon torture, flaying and gushing blood, I'd probably just roll my eyes and ignore him. I'm no longer Muuth's little, bloodthirsty sidekick.

Rhydian's nostrils flare. "That's rubbish. You trusted me with your secrets when you needed a friend, and now you've magically moved on you're trying to cut me out." His face turns ashen. "It's Malandre, isn't it? He's gotten to you. He's infected you with his theories."

"Now who sounds insane?"

He throws his hands into his curly hair and spits a curse that would make Muuth blush. After closing his eyes and swallowing what are surely acidic words, Rhydian sighs. "I don't want to fight, Elanor."

Of course he doesn't want to fight, I realize. He was enjoying this. He liked it when I was his secret, when he could help and protect me. Now that Adom and I are talking again, and I'm done plotting against him, Rhydian is feeling—what? What *is* he feeling? "Then what do you want, Rhydian?"

"I need you," he says, his hands coming down to the table. "I need you to be on my side."

For several long seconds, there is no sound except our breathing and the cracking of the hearth fire. "I *am* on your side. What's happening with Malandre has nothing to do with you."

He lets out an exasperated huff. "My sister once said something like that to me. Then she went crazy and my father murdered her." There's emotion on his face—pain.

Once I notice it, it's difficult to look away. My heart feels too heavy, and my chest aches. "I don't know much about people," I say softly. "But I think you need to hate Malandre because you need someone to blame for what happened to Siren. And you need me to side with you and plot revenge because you need a friend."

His back straightens and he sniffs. Furrows his eyebrows and puckers his lips. "No," he says, shaking his head. "That's not it at all. Malandre is up to something nefarious. And you…" His eyes sadden. "You won't help me anymore. It's fine. I'll deal with it on my own."

"Rhydian…" But he brushes his hands against his thighs, walks haltingly to the door, and is gone.

~ * ~

I find Patience in the back below the tower shooting arrows into a straw man. Her face is mottled and the hard line around her jaw tells me she's upset. I approach her cautiously, half-afraid she'll shoot me instead of the target. After the way Rhydian treated her, I deserve it.

"The way he spoke to you wasn't acceptable," I say.

"Lord Berrel is a stuffed pigeon," she says. "I would be wasting energy feeling put-out."

I observe her aim with admiration. "It looks like your energy is being put to good use anyway. My knees are quaking for all the actual pigeons out there. Carry on."

She strings her arrow, aims, and fires. The arrow hits the target in the heart. Three more times she nocks her bow, pulls back with the force and agility of a tiger, and releases in a smooth, swift movement. Then she tosses the weapon to the ground. "What did he want then?"

"We were collaborating together on a project, but things didn't work out. He's frustrated because I want to end it. I think he's afraid this means we won't speak anymore."

"He's a brute," Patience replies. I don't think I've ever seen her so ruffled. She didn't even bat a lash at Cydra's sneering words, but with Lord Berrel, she's become a different person. "I meant to ask you before. After we found the body. Do you know how to use a weapon?"

"Not really." Unless she counted the axe I used as a kitchen knife to hack up huge chunks of meat back on Onyx. "I don't like to think about killing." *Anything other than dragons, that is.*

"Bodies in the woods," Patience mutters. "You need to learn a skill. You can't go traipsing into the forest unless you want to be the next victim."

"They haven't killed any servants—" I stop short. I'm not supposed to know this.

Patience grimaces. "Who knows who's doing this? Or why. And with nobles like Lord Berrel stomping around, disintegrating our humanity, we can't count on *them*. We need to save ourselves." She picks up her bow and swings around, holding it out to me. "Are you ready?"

"You want me to learn how to shoot a bow?"

She shrugs. "I'll teach you."

I point to the moon. "But it's the middle of the night!"

Patience glances at the sky as if she hadn't noticed. "You think dragons are concerned about the dark?" she asks. "Besides, there's lamplight at the arena. I normally go there to train."

"All this because you're worried about me getting eaten by a dragon?"

She tugs on her ponytail, lifts her shoulders, then makes a sound that is half of a laugh. "Maybe I'm the one who's afraid. Maybe I need a sparring partner. All the men fear me."

"As they should," I say, clapping her on the shoulder proudly. "You are quite fearsome."

"Let's start tomorrow," she suggests, raising an eyebrow.

I nod, then remember Adom's promise to take me to the changeling compound. "Maybe not tomorrow," I say slowly. "I have plans." At her doubtful look, I swallow and try filling in the blanks. "I'm so sorry, but I need to leave the castle. I'll be gone all day and into the evening."

"Is everything all right?" she asks, concern creeping into her voice.

"Yes."

She nods. "Take all the time you need, then. We can do lessons later this week."

"Thank you, Patience," I say, pressing my palms together and holding my hands to my nose. "You're more than a friend to me. You're a decent human being."

She gives me a look that's something between quizzical and flattered. "I should hope so."

~ * ~

I glance over my shoulder at the clearly defined footprints on the ground, the wake of our exhausted horses as they thump heavy hooves into the white sand. The cold stiffens my joints, and the pit of my stomach gurgles with hunger. I swear my extremities are turning numb.

"How much further?" I ask Adom who is riding a horse beside me. I brush off the white flakes that are already soaking through my shawl and clothes straight into my bones. "I'm not impervious to weather like you are, remember?"

He unhooks his cloak and offers it to me. "You're more like the full blooded dragons, aren't you?" At my scowl, he laughs. "It's just beyond that peak. I won't let you freeze to death."

I snatch the cloak from his hands. It's only decorative on him, anyway. Wrapping the additional warmth around me, I hug myself tight. "Why didn't we just fly here again?"

"It's part of the code," he answers. "No dragons past that marker where we landed. It's to keep the villagers safe, so no one suspects changelings are camping out here."

"To keep the villagers safe?" I repeat, sarcastically, but the wind picks up at that moment and not even Adom with his sensitive hearing can catch my words. I sink into myself, savoring the warmth of the horse beneath me and Adom's wool cloak draped over me. I blow hot breath into the cocoon I've woven around myself. I'm beginning to believe this compound isn't worth finding. *These changelings want privacy—let them have it! I'll take the hearth at the castle, in Patience's home, with a fully belly and a dry pallet.* As soon as I think this, I realize how soft I've become. How quickly Trana's pleasures have spoiled me.

Then, just when I'm about to tell Adom that I'm no longer interested in going to the compound, I see a village ahead in the midst of the blustery flurries. I shout for Adom's attention. The horses seem to sense that food and shelter are close by. They kick hooves to the ground with more enthusiasm. As we approach, a group of people wearing long, thick fleeces that drag along the snow appears on the trail to meet us. Their heads are covered with animal pelts.

"You've come a long way," one of them comments.

Based on how much farther in front of the rest he is standing, he looks like he could be the leader. He's a bulky, squat man with huge muscles and not a great deal of height. His black eyes are deep set in a leathery, flat face, blinking up at us between gray animal fur. His gaze passes across Adom and falls on me. I stare back at him, unflinching.

Then he breaks out into a wide, toothless grin. "I'm Odeba, governor of the mountain people." His gray furs flutter in the icy wind. He bows in deference to Adom. "Count Malandre. Welcome again to the village. Will your friend fit in?"

"She's not a changeling," Adom answers. "She's here to learn about this place."

Odeba frowns. "We don't give out information. You, of all people, should know that."

"Yes, but I vouch for her," Adom says. "I thought that should mean something."

The squat man peers at him, his mouth puckering. Every breath creates puffs of hot air, like smoke rising from his mouth and nostrils. "Who is she to you? Is she family? Your lov—"

"She's family," Adom answers resolutely.

In spite of the chill, my cheeks are burning.

Odeba bobs his head. "Very well then. You know the rules." He turns to me and holds up a hand, palm facing me. "Swear the oath."

"The...oath?" I glance at Adom in confusion.

He nods. "Touch your palm with his and repeat his words."

I've never made an oath before. It sounds serious, like if I say the words I'll be bound to Odeba. Even though it gives me feelings of unease, I don't think Adom would bring me all this way to meet the changelings if there were any danger.

I dismount and step knee deep into a snow mound. *Crunch.*

Crunch. Soon, I am directly in front of Odeba. I peel off a heavy glove and press my clammy bare palm against his. In seconds, I can't feel my hand in front of me, it is that cold here on the mountain.

Odeba recites, "I am here on glass ground to greet the fire, and should the glass break or the fire be snuffed, may I burn with Kainan on the setting sun."

Somehow, I manage to contain an audible groan. It sounds like a riddle, which of course drives me mad because it makes me think of Muuth and all his nonsense. I repeat the words anyway, and it seems to satisfy Odeba. He proceeds toward the village, his solemn tribe falling into step behind him. Adom gracefully dismounts his horse, and the two of us follow Odeba in silence.

As my feet indent the snow, I notice other people standing out in the streets of the small ramshackle town, staring holes into me. There are stone-and-wood buildings, but most of the people are emerging from tents made of various animal skins dyed in blues and reds.

What was described to me as a compound I now see as a small village. We walk a short way and Odeba gestures for us to enter the largest tent. Adom holds the flap open. A wave of heat swallows me whole as I enter.

Odeba removes several layers of clothing until he is only wearing a loose, beige tunic and some tight hide pants. He sits cross-legged on the floor, long black hair coiling around his shoulders. Adom does the same, removing his outer layer but leaving on the basics. I copy him, but of course I don't remove as much clothing—I'm still frozen.

Odeba waits, his face unreadable. Another person enters the tent, and a gust of wind smacks my back, an incredible contrast to the unbearable heat from the fire in front of me. The tent smells like sweat and half-cooked partridge, odorous and stuffy. I lift my nose and try not to grimace while I avoid taking in the unpleasant smell by way of my nostrils. The newcomer glances at our party, curious, then takes parchment and ink from a table and exits quickly, letting in another blast of icy air with his departure.

Odeba is sitting on a scattering of furs on the floor while a wooden cabinet is set up just to the right. Plates and cups are piling up near the tent flap. This reminds me of my home on Onyx Island. A rush of emotion consumes me. I'm simultaneously revolted and homesick.

Beside me, Adom *ah hems*. Odeba's chin pivots toward him. "Yes?"

"A word outside?" Adom asks.

"Of course." Odeba bends and then pushes himself up off the pelts. He wraps a blanket around himself and hands Adom another. Then the two of them exit the tent.

The heat is stifling now, but I'd rather be seated here with warm furs wrapped around me and animal skins to cover the frozen ground than outside in the bitter cold. In fact, I even wonder if the sweat freezes the moment you step outside, and I have a moment of concern for Adom. Then I remember that he has that changeling blood and so does Odeba. Though I'm going from freezing to a suffocating dry heat, they don't feel much temperature fluctuation.

After a moment, the flap opens and they both return. Odeba approaches the cabinet and pours a drink, then he offers it to me. "Please," he says. "Stay here for a few days. Rest from your travel. Maybe you'll find suitable answers to your questions."

"Stay here?" I shake my head and look questioningly at Adom. "No. Ryrick and Patience will worry about me."

"I can have someone go to the castle and let them know you're safe."

I chew on my lower lip and stare at the red coals, not sure how to pinpoint the distress I feel. Or why I feel it, for that matter.

"Maybe just for the night," I say, reluctantly.

Adom nods. "We can leave first thing in the morning."

~ * ~

Odeba's second, Gizton, shows me to my own tent while Adom is taken to separate lodgings. Several girls creep around my tent, bundled and inexpressive, watching me until I close the flap. Later, they enter without warning and hand me a hot bowl of cooked meat and potatoes for lunch. My tent isn't as hot as Odeba's, but it is actually quite comfortable. The girls bring a steaming kettle to pour into my washbowl and a mug of hot water with dried flowers to sip on.

That night, Adom and I are shown to a long table in a feast hall with Odeba and what looks like the entire village. Delicious smells waft into the room from the outdoors, and my stomach growls. From somewhere beyond, I can hear the sizzling and crackling of a spit.

"Sit down and eat with us," Odeba urges as children scooch beside us on the large bench, eager to meet the newcomers. The door opens and about twenty people enter, some of them carrying porcelain dishes heaping with a brown stew. Someone passes around bowls and others set the food down in the middle of the table. The children squeal and dive for the dishes. I fill my bowl, then lift my spoon for a tentative taste. The child on my left passes a basket of goat cheese and bread, which I reach for almost greedily. The food doesn't last long.

"Adom, why are there children here?" I ask him softly.

He leans in, and for the first time I catch a whiff of his scent—cinnamon and cloves. It is quite nice, actually. I find that breathing it in releases tension in my shoulders.

"Why are there children anywhere? Before they were changelings, these people lived perfectly mundane lives. Some of them had family they just couldn't leave," he replies. "Or they suspected their children might be changelings, too. Or they came here, fell in love and started a family. They just want to live a peaceful existence."

"But you don't think the ones who are scorching Tranar lands or murdering the nobles want to live here?" I ask.

"I don't know," he answers. "They might not know what they're doing." He lets out a soft sigh. "On the other hand, there's a tremendous amount of violence in their actions. I find it difficult to believe that they are totally ignorant of their condition at this point."

His words sink in, and I realize their full weight. If the rogue changelings don't agree to live here, Adom has to…kill them. I shudder, imagining the few, bloody options he has. Whatever the method, it is grim. The task must take its toll. How many has he had to kill?

"The king makes you do this?" I ask.

He shrugs, staring at the table's surface. "He has human business to keep him occupied. I'm in charge of the dragons. Both in Trana and on Onyx."

A connection forms in my mind. "That's why you don't tell him about the challenges?"

He takes a long sip of wine before responding. "I would appreciate it if you don't share that piece of information with him. It's my responsibility, and I accept it willingly."

"But sometimes you take on *too much* responsibility," I say softly. I stare down at my empty dish. Then, "Adom, I know you took punishments for me. I didn't know until recently, but now I do. Why? Why didn't you just set me free? Wouldn't that have been easier on us both?"

"There's a longer story there," he says, glancing around the room. "But let me tell you at a different time." He smiles. "As for the punishments, don't worry about me. The betas would attack me regardless of you. And I can take care of myself." At my look of disbelieve, he crinkles his nose. "I've done just fine so far."

Both he and Muuth tried to make me feel like it had nothing to do with me. Like the challenges would happen whether or not I was involved. But it doesn't feel that way.

How much would I have sacrificed to keep the balance of peace? If my imprisonment meant something more—not only to Adom and the king, but to me—could I have endured it without becoming bitter? The king said something strange earlier along those lines...but now with all the other revelations I can't recall just what it was.

"How many betas have you had to fight?"

"Seventy-six. Are you done with the interrogation?"

"Not even close."

He chuckles. "Must we talk about the eccentricities of home life?"

Eccentricities put it politely. Abuses. Torture. Violence. I shudder thinking of that cold place again. "You think life on Onyx is eccentric? I thought you were well-adjusted to it."

Adom's eyes meander to the ceiling. "It has its moments."

"Which do you prefer? Humans or dragons?"

"Human females. Like Raina," he says, with a dreamy expression.

He's made the conversation light, and somehow this is a relief. Underneath all the layers, there is still darkness between us. Some wrongs can't be easily forgiven. I still need answers to questions I can't even begin to form. So I embrace his topic change as a shield. "Unbelievable. Even as a human, you think like an animal."

He throws back his head and laughs.

"Do you really like her?"

His eyes blank, wide and falsely innocent. "Who?"

"Raina."

A dimple I've never noticed before appears in the lower corner of his left cheek. "She's beautiful and like putty in my hands. What's not to like?"

"Then why don't you marry her?"

He smiles again, but doesn't answer.

~ * ~

By the time we return to the castle the following day, it is mid-afternoon. Patience greets me, but doesn't seem surprised that I've been away. She asks me how my time in the country was. She is under the impression that I was visiting a friend for the day. I smile and gush about the trip until she is satisfied.

Patience and I begin a daily training schedule. I discover that she is far more talented than I previously guessed. Her skill with a bow and arrow is renowned throughout the castle. When we practice, everyone, even the knights, gravitate toward the training course to watch. She is equally good with a wooden sword, although she can't afford real steel on a physician's salary. She can spar with the best of them, frequently challenging and shaming the more experienced soldiers. But she chooses me to pick on, to taunt, to push to newer heights.

"Your greatest skill is your strength," she says, flinging an axe my direction.

I duck before the blade comes down on my shoulder, then grab the handle lightning quick and rebalance my wrist so I'm holding the weapon properly. "You almost killed me!"

She laughs. "No. I've watched you on the training course for five days now. You're agile and somehow so powerful. I can't understand how your body could be so delicate and yet so strong." She points to the pile of heavy limestones arranged in the corner of the training course. "I saw you lift three of those bricks at the same time like they were nothing. How?"

"I was a farmer's daughter, remember?" I point the axe at the wooden target and warm my shoulder muscles for the throw. "It requires a certain degree of hardiness to harvest crops and lift barrels of feed for the livestock." I wind my arm, and release the handle of the axe.

It hits the wooden man directly in the forehead.

Patience gives me a crooked smile. "You have fine aim," she says. She shields her eyes and looks toward the dying sun. "And during twilight, no less."

"I often see better at night."

"Really?" she studies me. "That's odd. Most people have less acuity at night."

"Lady Malandre?" someone calls me from behind.

A shiver crawls down my back at the name. I've gotten sloppy. I should have been keeping my head down. Now that Adom knows I'm here, I don't have to avoid him any longer. But how could I have forgotten about Lord Faigen? I pivot, squinting into the dusk. Lanterns on poles to help illuminate the training course.

"Lord Faigen," I say softly. "What brings you here tonight?"

Patience eyes me with a clear *What-did-he-just-call-you* look. I consider asking her to leave, but then I think better of it. She's still holding a bow, after all.

Theodore draws closer. "You're dressed like a servant," he observes, his tone skeptical.

"When I took you back to Foghum, I considered it odd Malandre would let you walk without an escort. Then, as I left you at the castle, you said you didn't want the servants to know your name. I think I know just what is going on here."

"You've found me out," I make my voice light. My eyes scan the sandy course to see how close the nearest guard stands. There are a few straggling knights practicing their swordsmanship, and one or two beating each other with sweaty, bruised fists, but nobody is paying us any mind. They are accustomed to Patience's presence here. Mine, too, apparently.

"You're his mistress, aren't you? You've been quarreling. That day I found you, you were running away. That's why you brought a pack of clothes with you."

"Suppose I was," I say slowly, keening aware of Patience's

boring gaze against my back.

"I'm supposing." Faigen winks. "I think you've come back here because I told you about Malandre's search for you. You chose a job here in the castle so you could retain your dignity without being too far away from your lover. Am I correct?"

"On all but one account. It's over between us."

Faigen's smile grows. A curly brown lock drops into his eyes, and he brushes it away. "Then will you permit me to tell you what I truly think of him? He's a scoundrel and a lout," he confesses. Taking my hand in his own and planting quick kisses along my wrist, he purrs, "And I wish you'd forget him."

I giggle, more because his warm breath tickles my hand, but also because I'm strangely nervous. Then he straightens and grows serious. "Will you come dancing with me?"

"Tonight?" I squeak.

"Of course tonight. I *need* you, lovely Elanor."

Patience clears her throat. "Elanor, we have elderwood cream salves to produce tonight."

"That's right." I tug my hand away from Faigen. "I'm very sorry. Have you met Patience?" I gesture loosely toward her. "She's the king's physician. And she's brilliant."

A group of enthusiastic, lace-and-ribbon ladies bedecked make their way to the alcove just above the training arena. The lanterns illuminate their bright, flushed faces, Lady Celeste striding at their head, wearing an ivory robe that matches her porcelain skin.

One of the ladies, a young woman who is two inches shorter than Lady Celeste, with a pleasant face but eyes that look too tired for her years makes a soft, impatient sigh. "Celeste, really, you're about to be married to the king. These boys can't interest you."

Celeste lets out a mischievous laugh. "Oh? Can't they now?" She waves at one of the soldiers, a broad, muscular man who is busy hacking away at a wooden dummy. "It's just harmless flirting, my dear Ora. Nothing more." They wander to another corner of the alcove.

At the sound of the ladies giggling, Lord Faigen's smile falls. "Pleasure to meet you, Prudence," he says, not looking at Patience. "Elanor, maybe we could meet another night?"

"Maybe," I say, trying to sound as noncommittal as possible. I enjoy Faigen, but now isn't the time for foppery and foolishness. I couldn't care less about dancing.

Faigen seems to savor that. "Farewell," he calls before fleeing the training course.

"*Prudence?*" Patience grumbles.

"Be thankful," I say kindly. "If he knows your name, he'll probably try to woo you."

"Yes, at least I'm spared that torment. Although I seem to have this general effect on men. I think they might be afraid of me," she admits, and her gaze lingers on Lady Celeste. A thoughtful expression appears on her face. Her eyes follow the direction Lord Faigen went. "Elanor, I consider myself a fair judge of character, but that man truly baffles me." Then, more timidly she asks, "Did you mean what you said? About being Malandre's mistress?"

"Of course not," I say, setting my axe on the bench with the other weapons. "Faigen has been trying to figure me out since the day we met. I thought it would deter him if he thought Count Malandre and I were in a relationship."

"In other words, you lied to him."

Lied to him, to Lord Berrel, even to Ryrick and Patience. Goodness—I'm becoming quite talented at deceiving people. Almost as good as Adom. "It's complicated, Patience."

She sits on the bench and unties her boot straps. "Didn't Lord Faigen find you in a scorched village? I thought you told my father that when you first came looking for a job."

"Faigen and I met before that," I admit. "I'm not comfortable talking about my past."

Her eyes soften. "I can understand why you would want to reinvent yourself. Your past is your private business." She tosses the wooden sword into the weapons cache where it lands with a clatter. "You don't have to tell me your life story. Just don't lie to me, Elanor. I like to trust the people I live with."

~ * ~

"Elanor, wake up."

I groan. "Go away. It's not morning yet."

The voice persists. I lift my head and force my eyes open against the blackness, disoriented. Then I recognize it as Ryrick, and realize he shouts through the keyhole.

"Come quick," he rasps. "An injured lord is out in the courtyard. Go and get Patience."

I lurch up, instantly awake. Adom? I dress and check Patience's room and laboratory. I can't find her anywhere. I throw the door open. "She must have stepped out. What happened?"

Ryrick leads me through the winding staircase. "I'm not sure. A guard woke me up and told me someone was injured in the hallway. I took him to the courtyard, but it's clear he's in bad condition." He lifts a torch to illuminate the way.

I stifle a yawn. "What time is it?"

Ryrick stops at the bottom of the staircase. "It's late enough that Patience shouldn't be stepping out by herself." He shakes his head. "That girl imagines herself invincible, but with what happened to Lord Darton, she just isn't as safe as she thinks she is."

A crumpled form writhes on the ground outside the kitchen entrance, smearing blood and ash across the entryway. Lord Faigen. I cover the distance between us.

"Can you talk?" I feel for a pulse. It beats faintly, and Faigen's eyes flutter open. His skin is feverish, and the smell of burnt flesh sickens me. To my relief, the ash appears to be coming off his clothes and hair—not his skin. Maybe he isn't burned badly, after all.

"Attacked by dragon," he breathes. "Help me."

I look to Ryrick for help. "He's lucky he isn't dead." Sighing, I cradle Lord Faigen's sweat-soaked head in my hands. The visitors' suites on the second floor are filled with high-profile guests. It will be next to impossible to cart Faigen's body inconspicuously into one of those empty rooms without anyone noticing. "Are there any spare quarters on the main level? Some place safe I can take him?"

Faigen's eyelids close. I fear he might slip into a coma.

"He can't stay here," Ryrick reproaches, licking his lips and staring woefully at Faigen. "Cydra would order us to put him up at the Volcourt Inn, send for a local healer, and report the whole mishap after he's well on his way to recovery. That's the best treatment we can offer him." He stands several feet away, about to bolt at the first sign of trouble.

My throat burns with the acrid smell. "Ryrick, he won't make it to the Volcourt Inn in his condition. This happened on castle grounds, just like with Lord Darton. The king will want to know, and I'm sure he'd want Patience tending to him."

Ryrick hesitates. "What if the other guests find out?"

"He can sleep on the pallet Patience is letting me use. Help me to carry him."

We bear him through the open courtyard, whispering, and somehow manage not to wake anyone. At one point I swear when I almost trip. Faigen snorts once, his body limp and heavy.

"On the pallet," I breathe, opening the door to Patience's office. Ryrick heaves the lord onto the bed. I rush to find the jug and bowl I use every morning to wash my face. "Can you find me some salve? It should be in that drawer above the cabinet." I point at spot. "And I'll need a vial of nightshade to make him sleep. It's behind the dried huckleberry."

Ryrick obeys without complaint, closing the door behind him. I light a lantern. Faigen is in bad shape, his right eye bruised and swollen. Other cuts and scratches on his arms and neck indicate he was in a fight. But with whom? Some of the cuts run deep. Dragon talons made these.

Faigen opens his eyes and looks at me. "Angel." His head rolls back, onto the pillow.

I check his pulse again and breathe easier. He isn't dead yet, merely unconsciousness.

Ryrick returns with salve and the sleeping potion. "I also found this." He hands me a pouch filled with herbs. "Patience sometimes mixes this with water and pours it down the burn victim's throat. It's supposed to soothe the abused internal muscles and balance his energies."

I arch an eyebrow. "Are you certain?"

"I've watched her respond to plenty of emergencies. I'm certain this will help."

My heart swells. "You're wonderful, Ryrick. Now go back to sleep. I'll wait for Patience and we'll watch over him tonight. We can tell Cydra when we see her in the morning. He'll hopefully be in a better state then." I can handle dragon burns better than most.

"I can't help but feel like the dragons… they're plotting something unpleasant for us." Ryrick's eyes dilate as he fixes his stare on Faigen.

"Get some sleep, and we'll talk tomorrow."

He wipes his damp forehead, mutters under his breath, and leaves.

I go to work on Faigen, mashing the herbs in the pouch, adding water to them, and making Faigen swallow the concoction. Then I uncork the vial of nightshade and drip a couple of drops into his mouth. Ripping the hem of my dress, I make small rags that I wash and dip in salve. I strip off his clothes, careful to avoid the burned places. The right side of his body is whitish-pink and blistered.

"The white dragon!"

I draw a sharp intake of breath.

"The white dragon!" Faigen cries again before sinking into a restless sleep. I wash his burns with the utmost tenderness. Then I wrap the salve-drenched bandages over his wounds.

He can't be a changeling, can he? He left in a hurry today. What does he know about the white dragon? Maybe his work as a knight is a cover. Maybe *he* is the dragon who scorched Salcom village. Or maybe he came too close to one of the rogues and they tried to kill him. I can't know for sure until he recovers and I can get him to talk. Changelings can be injured by dragon fire—I know this from the times I saw Adom recovering from a battle—but they heal quickly.

The door creaks open and Patience enters. She sees me with Lord Faigen, stares at me bleakly for a moment, then heaves a sigh. She sets a knife down on the counter and comes to my side. "Rest," she says. "I'll take care of him now. You've done well."

I fall to the floor, exhausted, and curl up in a corner of the room. Perhaps I can catch a quick nap before the day begins. Tomorrow I have to find Adom and tell him about Faigen.

~ * ~

The door bursts open. I roll over, my back cracking. From the doorway, Cydra glares at me. The world spins as I rise. "There's a noblewoman going into labor and you're needed immediately." Her eyes fix on my cot. "Who's that?"

Why had I slept on the floor? Then I follow Cydra's gaze and I remember. "Lord Faigen. A dragon burned him yesterday."

"Why wasn't I informed?"

"Ryrick and I had it under control. Ryrick thought you'd want to send him elsewhere, but the lord was in no condition to be moved. We planned to tell you first thing this morning."

Cydra's face screws into a pinched frown. "Get him out of

here. Can you imagine the scandal if the king found out you had a lord in your bed last night?"

I bite my tongue. It won't do any good to correct her. Cydra wants to believe the worst about me. Where is Patience when I need her to take Cydra down a peg? I approach my washing bowl then step back. The water's tinged red with Faigen's blood. *Never mind washing my face.*

"Don't just stand there. Find Patience! She's been summoned."

I smile politely and close the door in Cydra's face. I can hear her seething on the other side as I lock the hatch. After dressing, I throw another worried look at Lord Faigen, and go about my chores. Patience left behind a list asking me to gather wild mushrooms, strip bark from certain trees, and deliver tinctures and salves to her elderly patients.

Faigen can't go anywhere in his current state. He needs rest and plenty of bedside care for the next few weeks, at least. If he turns out to be a rogue dragon, he can't pose a threat now. No one but Cydra, Ryrick, and Patience knows he's here, and I'll take careful pains to keep the door locked. If Cydra has him moved, I'll tell the king.

Longley finds me in the hallway and raises a hand to catch my attention. "You offered me your help earlier," she says. "I'm ready to accept your assistance in the kitchen."

"What if Cydra finds out?"

She rolls her eyes. "Cydra likes to think she's a queen, when really she's a dustpan. Besides, Princess Ora arrived today and with her a host of Corvan nobles. I'm short staffed. I'll pay you twice whatever Patience is paying you to help me this afternoon."

"Done," I say, hoping Longley doesn't find out that Patience isn't paying me. "But first I need to find her. Cydra says she's needed for a delivery."

"I just saw Cydra speaking to her by the stairs not five

minutes ago," Longley replies.

"In that case, let me finish my task list and I'll join you in the kitchen this afternoon?"

"Good," says Longley. She scans my attire, another dress modified into a suit by Patience. "Better roll up your sleeves. We have horrifying numbers of dishes to do."

It takes several hours to complete the tasks Patience has assigned me. I find I'm particularly good at dealing with the elderly patrons in the room visits. All they want to do is talk and fawn over me, and the only thing I need to do is shut up, listen to their stories, and give them their medicines. They all look younger than Muuth. But they are wealthy, and they are sad at how quickly life has gotten away from them, and all they want is a little bit of attention. It is easy for me to be what they want.

After I'm finished, I return to the clinic to check on Lord Faigen. He isn't there, but Patience is. She's washing blood from her hands in a bucket of water.

"Where's Faigen?" I ask.

"He was doing better, so I had him moved to his own room."

"Is that his blood?"

"No, I just returned from an early morning appointment with a patient who needed a limb removed." She places a soggy hand over her brow. "He had infection in his hand. It wasn't going away. I had to sever the whole hand to keep it from spreading."

She's trembling, so I come up behind her and set a hand on her shoulder. "I'm so sorry."

"I came back and saw Faigen here, and I just couldn't take it. Ryrick moved him."

"Did you deliver the baby, too?"

She blinks. "What baby?"

"Cydra came this morning and said you were needed. I

went looking for you, but then Longley said she saw you and Cydra talking so I assumed she told you herself."

Patience frowns. "No. She didn't say anything about a delivery. She mentioned needing more poultice for her foot, but nothing about a baby."

"That's odd. She made it sound like an emergency."

"Maybe they found a midwife?" Then she lets out a curse and shakes her head. "No, I know what this is. When she couldn't find me right away, she decided not to tell me. To make me look bad. She's done it once before." She dries her hands and begins packing her bag. "I'd better go find out about this baby. Thank you for telling me, Elanor."

"Do you need any help?"

"No, I'm fine. The chambermaids usually like to help get me hot water and rags, and really that's all I need. But thank you for offering."

I shrug. "I finished the visits and found the mushroom and bark you needed. Longley asked if I could help in the kitchen when I was done. Do you mind if I go?"

She nods, but looks a little disappointed. "We'll miss practice today."

"We could do it later tonight."

Her face brightens.

I leave for the kitchen, but on the way, Rhydian catches me by surprise, ducking around a corner and popping up just in front of me.

"Elanor."

He looms ahead of me, giving me no chance to sidestep him. I scoot back as far as I can get, until my back is against the wall.

"Elanor, I'm sorry I accused you of working with Malandre. I'm sorry I insinuated that you didn't care. It was wrong of me to put you in that position, especially after learning all you've endured." He hangs his head. "If you don't want to take vengeance out on Malandre anymore, I'll respect that. It doesn't change how I feel about him, or my goals, but I won't pressure you to join my schemes. Just please don't cut me off." He holds up his hands as if in prayer.

I bat his hands away, looking down the hall anxiously. "Fine, I won't, but if anyone catches you in the servants' quarters—"

"They'll what?" He grins. "Fire me?"

"No. Fire *me*. You shouldn't be here. It won't look proper."

He purses his lips and stares at me solemnly. "You're avoiding me."

My face flames. I can see how he would think that since I haven't seen him in days. Between the trip to the mountains, work and training, I haven't had a single moment to think about Rhydian. And after what's happened to Faigen, I don't want to put Rhydian in danger if I can help it. "I don't have time to talk. Guests are arriving today, and Longley needs me—"

"I'll do chores with you."

I glance at his hands, which are soft and refined. This man has never worked a day in his life. "You don't have a clue how to wash dishes or pluck a chicken, do you?"

"You learned."

Rhydian moves, slightly, and finally I have a window to slide around him and make my escape. He follows me like a shadow, my own personal storm cloud. "I've work to do, Lord Berrel."

He lets out a strangled gasp. "I liked it better when you called me Rhydian."

"And I liked you better when you didn't pry."

He jumps in front of me and walks backward, his eyes narrow and squinty. "Did you know that there is no island south of Cornoc?"

My heart begins to pound, and my feet go still. "Maybe you have an outdated map?"

"I looked at four made in the last three years."

"Perhaps you should plan a trip?"

"Where are you from, really?"

"South of Cornoc," I insist. "Where there's nothing on your map." I resume my walk, and without looking I know that he's still following me. Why can't he leave this alone?

"You're different from anyone I've ever met," he says, a little breathlessly. "You're not a normal noble woman looking to find a good marriage match and live an easy life. And you aren't a very good servant; you're obstinate, self-directed, and you don't listen well. You believe in the dragons, and like me you have a dark history with Malandre, but you're not one of the crazy ones who wanders from village to village shouting nonsense about the end of times. It's like you don't want to share what you know with me. And I know you know *something*. I can't shake you." He catches up to me and walks beside me now.

"Please don't shake me. I don't like to be touched."

He smiles. "It's an expression. It means I can't put you out of my mind."

"I see."

As we make our way past the stables, two children poke past Longley's guard dog, eyes fixated on the great tower high above. They aren't servants' children—this I can tell by their fine attire and wide-eyed wonder. I face the tower, but see nothing out of the ordinary.

The boy crosses his arms resolutely across his chest, shaking his head with vehemence. Tufts of reddish-copper hair jut out from his head. Every now and then he attempts to smooth a piece only to have it *sproing* out of control the moment his hand jerks away.

"I won't do it," he shouts at the girl.

She takes hold of one of his crossed arms, tugging, and with her free hand she points to the sky. "*Please*, Hivan. You've got to protect me from the dragons."

I glance at Rhydian.

"It's a game," he insists. "They're pretending."

"Of course." I smile meaningfully at him.

"Fine." He sounds surprisingly annoyed. "Let's go investigate."

The girl and boy look about six years of age, and while the girl tugs at his arm in persistence, the boy's face is fixed. "Leggo of me, Erma," he whines when he can't manage to disentangle himself from her firm grip.

We step closer to the pair.

"Can I help you?" I say.

Two sets of wide eyes fix on me.

The pudgy girl drops the boy's arm. "Nothing!" she squeaks. "We're not up to mischief."

Rhydian gives me another meaningful look.

The boy, now extricated from her clutches, he rubs his arm. He points accusatorily at the girl. "Erma's trying to make me go to the watch-tower."

"He's my knight," Erma explains defensively, pouting as if to soften me up. The effect is somewhat lost, for I find myself distracted by her many chins, potbelly swagger, round face, and thick limbs. She wears her hair cut short, and it curls around her baby face as if her parents thought to hide a few of her layers behind excessive curls. When she notices my unaffected stare, the girl continues. "'Sides," she argues. "He saw it. It's his responsibility."

"Saw what?" Rhydian asks.

Both children gape at each other as if determining how much they should tell us. Finally the boy straightens, lifts his regal chin, and points at me. "You go get it. I *order* you."

"Hivan," the girl huffs. "You can't order a woman to get you a dragon. It isn't chivalrous."

Hivan turns red, his eyes defiant. "I'm a prince. I can do whatever I wish."

"Prince Hivan and Princess Erma," Rhydian says, making

the connection. "You're here for the royal wedding, aren't you?"

"Naw, that's our parents," says Hivan. "We're here to go dragon hunting."

"Prince Hivan is from Eppax," Rhydian explains to me. "And Princess Erma comes all the way from Newaka." He bends on one knee and grins at them. "I'll bet you heard fairy tales about the Tranar dragons at bedtime and now you're hoping to see them?"

"My momma says Tranars are idiots for pretending the dragons don't exist. Everybody knows dragons are real. We don't have them in Eppax 'cuz of the position of the sun."

"That sounds *very* logical," Rhydian agrees indulgently.

"Where did you see a dragon?" I ask.

"It came from the forest," the girl whispers in excited tones. "Hivan saw it first."

The boy nods. "From that mount over there. That's where it came from."

My heart tumbles to my toes. "Where did it go?" I press.

"The watchtower," the girl says in a sing-song tone.

I look at Hivan, who offers solemn confirmation.

"You may not be able to order me around, but Lord Berrel is perfectly capable of battling dragons," I say. "Did you know he's the brother of Lady Celeste?"

Erma gasps. "Oh, you're very handsome, sir knight. Will you marry me?"

Rhydian smiles. "Ask me again when you're old enough. In the meantime, it would be my profound honor to protect m'lady from any dragon. I'll take my leave now to slay your beast, and in the meantime you both should return to your quarters and pray for my safety."

"Can I give you my kerchief?" Erma asks. "For good luck?"

Rhydian accepts the handkerchief, and bows low over it. "I'll bring you back a scale from the nasty creature," he promises her with a fond pat on the head.

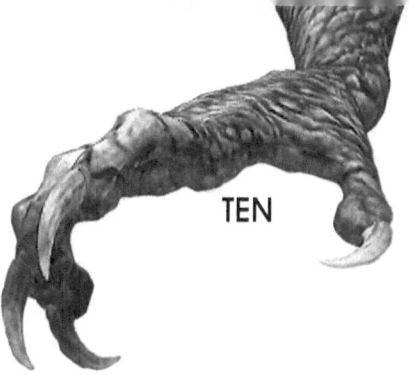

TEN

MAYBE YOU SHOULD GO and get help," I say, for the first time nervous about Rhydian's well-being. "I can go on ahead and see what's up there."

The thin-lipped response he gives me is loaded with flat disbelief. "And who would you have me go get?" he asks drily. "Malandre?"

I open my mouth and then close it again. Adom is precisely the person I want with me right now, but I know I can't ask Rhydian to fetch him. Not when he doesn't even believe.

"There's something I didn't tell you before," I say to Rhydian as we sprint toward the watch tower. "Another lord appeared on the grounds with burns on his body." My fingers feel for the pocketknife Patience gave me. It won't be much protection against a dragon, but it's better than nothing. I know how to creep, to make myself invisible. It's Rhydian I fear for.

"Who?" he asks, hand on the hilt of his sword.

A sword won't work. Dragon scales are too tough—they would split his sword in two. And by the time he draws a sword a dragon could slash him to bits. A pocket knife thrust into a jeweled eye is far more effective. Although it wouldn't do permanent damage, it'd provide a distraction to help us escape.

But Rhydian won't understand how I know all this, and there isn't any time to explain. I just have to hope this dragon has enough self-preservation to know not to draw attention with a fire blast in the king's tower. Hope that Rhydian has the sense to stay quiet, like me.

"Faigen," I answer.

His eyelids shoot open. "Lord Faigen? I just talked to him yesterday. Is he dead?"

"No. He's severely injured." The watchtower is nearer now. I slow my gait. No sign of a dragon from here. "Maybe the children were pretending after all? I pray this is the case."

"Where is Faigen now?" Rhydian whispers, a note of urgency in his tone. "I'd like to see him. If he has burns, like you say, it would help me believe you. About the dragons, I mean."

I clamp my mouth shut as a sudden rush of servants saunter by, unconcerned. Nobody else seems to have noticed a dragon landing on the watchtower. The children are either hyper-vigilant, or the dragon has a particular ability I haven't yet encountered. Some dragons can make themselves camouflage with their surroundings, but I haven't heard of a dragon who could make itself invisible. Yet. It wouldn't surprise me to discover new types of dragons in Trana.

We're almost to the watchtower when Rhydian gazes at me in disappointment. "I thought you trusted me."

"Patience had him moved," I whisper back, dismissively, surveying all the entrances, windows, and exits. We need a few escape routes planned. "I don't know his current location."

He waits to speak until a group of servants passes out of earshot. "Why would she move him if he's as injured as you say?"

"For his safety. I didn't ask for details."

Rhydian scratches his beard and unsheathes his sword. He puts a hand on the door to the watchtower. "I thought you and Lord Faigen were friends. That's what he told me when I spoke to him the other day. He seemed to think you and Lord Malandre were married. Strange."

"He was mistaken." I touch his sword hilt and shake my head. He'll only draw attention.

"About your friendship? Or about you and Malandre?" Rhydian slips his sword back in the sheath, agitated. "Who *do* you care about, Elanor? Lord Faigen? Lord Malandre?"

"Shhh." I place a fingertip against my lips. "If there's truly a dragon up there, we don't want to alert it to our presence. No swords. We can't fight it. We aren't prepared. Understand?"

Rhydian nods, and draws in a breath before opening the door. He takes his time, lifting the hinges so that they won't squeak as the door opens. Silence greets us.

"I'm going in first. Stay behind me at all times."

An amused look crosses his face. "Elanor, I don't think—"

"Promise me," I plead.

He looks like he wants to argue, but then the stubborn gleam fades and he shrugs.

I step inside. He closes the door behind us. After a few cautious steps up the spiral staircase, I pause and listen again. Tiptoeing up additional stairs, I follow the steady incline to the top of the watchtower. We approach the light that looms ahead, steadily growing more luminescent with each round we take. Rhydian stays close by my side, in the shadow of my footsteps.

Voices, cool and confrontational, reach my ear. I freeze, straining to hear the words that come from the top of the watchtower. Beside me, Rhydian draws a heavy breath, tilting his head to better hear the conversation. I put a hand on his arm, and cover my mouth with a free hand. He does the same. We don't dare to move, rooted to the spot, like statues against the wall.

At first, there is an angry growl. It could be a beast. Or, it could be a human. Then a voice speaks, and it's so low and marred that it could come from either a man or a woman. Or, it could be a dragon attempting human tongue. It's difficult to tell. "No one saw me. Quit worrying."

"You can't be so careless," says a second, female voice. Though familiar, I can't quite pin it. "The knights are crawling all over the place. If one of them had seen you—"

"No one saw me. Nobody *ever* sees me."

"You can't know for sure. Children sometimes notice."

"People don't listen to children," the voice scoffs. "And if it's a problem, I'll take care of the situation like I did with the housekeeper's son."

"We don't want to draw unnecessary attention. Remember, there are others who won't be fooled. They could identify us if we don't win them over."

"And we, in turn, could accuse them." Then the first voice sighs heavily. "All right. I take your point. I'll be more careful in the future."

"Did you contact the riddle keeper?"

"I did more than contact him. I stole him."

"You *what*?" the second voice growls.

"He's ours, now. He's going to help us."

A long, painful pause ensues. Then, "I thought you were just going to ask him the date?"

"He has more information than that," the first voice chides. "Why not use him?"

"Fine." The second voice sighs. "What about the purple thorn-shooter?"

"Hunter? I hired a vigilante to take care of her. She won't be a problem for much longer. It's the other two I'm most worried about. What if they catch on before the wedding?"

"Then we reach out to…" the voice becomes muffled for a moment, as if the speaker has leaned in to whisper a name. "He'll help us," she continues at normal volume.

"He might have the financial resources we need, but if he's like his father—"

"He's not," replies the second voice. "I'm sure of it."

"Fine," the first barks. "Have you talked to him yet?"

"No. He's still scheming against Count Malandre. He needs to be in a better state."

The first voice tuts, disapproval dripping off each offended breath. "Count Malandre is essential. You have to tell Lord Berrel before he disrupts the plan."

Rhydian lets out a low hiss at the sound of his name. Icy

panic courses through my veins. A human wouldn't hear it past the sound of the wind, but a dragon...

"What was that?"

"What?"

The voice quiets. "Someone's coming. You'd best go. Time to make myself disappear."

We fly down the remainder of the steps. I reach the door, pull, and throw myself into the open. Rhydian and I exchange terrorized glances, breathing gruffly. I lift my head, heaving for air, and spot Longley coming toward us with a wooden spoon clenched severely in her hand.

"There you are!" She freezes mid-step, eyes latched onto Rhydian. "Trouble, my lord?"

"Lord Berrel asked me to check the watchtower. He thought he saw a dragon, but he was mistaken." I rush to her side. "Need help?" I attempt to steer her in the direction of the kitchen.

"Not anymore," Longley grumbles. "Donja already did the dishes, lazybones. I worried when you disappeared. It isn't good for you to be off alone with all these strange happenings."

"I can take care of myself." I peer over my shoulder at the door to the watchtower. Rhydian is long gone. Lady Celeste emerges, her eyes darting across the courtyard. Many servants mill about the area, and though her eyes scan their faces, they never once settle on me. Celeste frowns, her face uneasy, before she locks the watchtower door and turns away.

~ * ~

With a long, flour-covered finger, Longley points out a sack of cherries. "Pit those."

As I wash the cherries in a bowl of water, I can't help but dwell on the conversation in the watchtower. One of the voices was definitely Lady Celeste's. Did Rhydian recognize it? Did he see her leave as I did? The children said they saw a dragon perched on the tower. I don't believe it's a coincidence then that Celeste emerged from the stairwell.

It adds up. Muuth said he'd sometimes had to kill whole families because he didn't know who was suspect. Berrel's mother must have been a changeling, and she passed the disease to her children. Whatever happened to his mother, anyway? How could she let Berrel's father kill Siren, knowing what she knew? Or maybe she didn't. Muuth said some of the changelings never knew they had been infected. Siren knew, and it appears that Celeste knows as well.

But what about the person Celeste was speaking to in the watchtower? The voice was so low and scratched, it was difficult to tell whether it was male or female. What date were they discussing? Why did they want to bring Rhydian into their plan? And why is Adom essential to their schemes? Riddle-keepers? Vigilantes?

I sigh loudly, aching to get away from the kitchen to see if Rhydian has any ideas.

"Something wrong?" Longley asks, arching an eyebrow.

"Just tired of riddles," I mutter, slicing another cherry and ripping the seed out of it before tossing the ruby flesh into a bowl and the gray pit in a bucket. One thing was certain; they knew about one other changeling, the one they called *Hunter* and they wanted him or her out of the picture. *Her,* I correct myself. They'd referred to it as a female.

Longley wipes her forehead and accidentally paints a long line of flour on her face. "Then maybe you should spend more time with them that tell it to you straight," she says. "I'll say what's on my mind, no matter how irritating, and you can take it or leave it." Her back straightens. "I don't like the rumors I'm hearing about you, girl. They say you've been seen with Count Malandre, with the murdered Lord Darton, and with Lord Faigen. They say you are sneaking around with Lord Berrel. It's dangerous work, what you're doing. The servants think you're bringing bad luck to the castle." She takes a breath and focuses on pounding dough.

Slice. Pit. Drop. I stare at her for a long moment. "What do *you* think?"

"I think you're a confused young woman and you don't know who to trust."

Slice. Pit. Drop. "Any pointers to help me sort through my confusion?"

"Leave the nobles to their dark affairs. They aren't interested in you. Only how they can use you to their gain." She grabs a rolling pin and begins to flatten the dusty dough. "Trust the ones who've opened their doors to you, fed you, protected you from Cydra. They're the ones who truly care about your well-being. Don't take them for granted."

The other voice had said she'd taken care of the housekeeper's son. Does that mean they killed Cydra's son? "It isn't about my well-being," I say softly. "I want to protect them, too."

"Then stay away from those who wish harm on your real friends."

I pull my lower lip inside my mouth. Does Longley even know what's really going on with the nobles? Changelings and scorchings, lies and revenge? She's warning me about people who could harm me, but does she realize that the real threats are monsters and murderers, not womanizers or classism? Their affairs are so much darker than she could imagine.

~ * ~

Three raps on Rhydian's door produces a paler-than-usual face. "Are you well?"

He pulls me into his room and slides the door shut. He presses me against the broad, mahogany door and stares into my face, wide-eyed and panting, his hand splayed against solid wood. "I have no idea who to trust or where we can go to talk privately. Do you think we're safe here?"

I push against his unyielding chest. "I think we at least have a wider berth than just these three inches?"

"Apologies." He steps away and begins pacing. "What did you make of that conversation in the watchtower earlier? I'm sorry I fled. I didn't know what else to do."

"I don't know." I stare at the ceiling for a long moment, debating on whether or not to reveal that it was his sister. "Did you recognize the voices?"

Rhydian nods. "I heard Celeste, but I didn't recognize the person she was speaking to. I hoped you might know." His fingers compulsively find their way to his mouth, and he works on the nails of his two middle fingers, distressed. "Any ideas?"

Relief blossoms in my chest when he names his sister—at least I don't have to break that news to him—but it's quickly replaced by chagrin. The more I involve him, the greater the danger to his life. "It sounded like someone she's hired to help with a problem." I leave out the part where Adom and King Siles speculate that Leviathan and Cinderrider might be a nobleman and a servant in court. Could it be a noble*woman* and a servant, instead?

Rhydian's eyes meet mine. "You think it's a dragon-related problem?"

"The children *did* say they saw a dragon land on the watchtower."

"They saw a large bird," he insists.

"Why would your sister hide in the watchtower? And whoever she was talking to made it sound like they didn't want to be seen, either." I expel a breath. "Cydra's son died. I think that's who the other person was talking about when he or she made the comment about taking care of the housekeeper's son. Why would they bring that up?"

He taps his finger against his lips. "How and when did Cydra's son die?"

"I don't know, but I can ask around."

Rhydian shakes his head. "It wasn't the only reference to murder they made. They hired someone to kill a person named Hunter. Malandre is, apparently, essential to their plans. And they want to bring me in on it at some point." He resumes pacing, until I reach out and put a hand on his shoulder. Then he looks down at me, defeated. "I thought Celeste was spared the brunt of the family scandal. She was the youngest child, and was away at school when my father..." He balls his fist. "Why would she risk her position now? What is she plotting?"

"Maybe you could ask her directly?"

He covers his eyes with a hand. "No more sneaking around. I'll ask tomorrow."

It feels a little low to play him like this, when he is already down, but I have to plant the thought in his head. "Would your mother know anything about Celeste's plan?"

"My mother?" His head snaps up. "She died after Celeste was born."

"Oh," I say, fixing my eyes to the ground.

"We were raised with wet nurses and nannies, so I can't even recall her face." He stalks over to the side bar, pours brandy from a decanter and gulps it down. "Maybe the family pool *is* tainted. My mother might have been the only normal one among us." He crooks his head. "And what about your parents?"

"They died in a dragon scorching."

He lets out a curse. "I wish I had known before I said such callous things to you."

"Don't be sorry. I know you still question my account."

"Something traumatic must have happened for you to hold fast to these convictions."

There's no point in disagreeing, so I let his insinuation slide.

~ * ~

When I return, Patience has dinner ready for me. Later we go out to spar and shoot arrows until my shoulder blades ache and my lungs hurt from gasping. She assures me I'm getting better, and in spite of the skill gap between us I *do* feel much improved. I've slept better at Patience's place than I ever have in my life, and I don't know if it's the food, the fact it feels more like a family between us than I've had in a long time, or the physical, aggressive exercise she makes me participate in that accounts for the rested nights.

Today, however, Patience doesn't let me sleep. Instead, after we take turns bathing and resettle by the hearth, she asks if I could watch Lord Faigen for her. "Just for tonight," she promises. "I can't explain it, but I don't trust he's safe on his own. With the day I've had—"

"You don't need to explain," I say, patting her knee. "Tell me where he is and I'll gladly watch over him." I omit that this could be my chance to get him to talk if he's cognizant enough.

She passes along directions to the room and before I know it I am in a different wing of the castle, sitting alongside Faigen's bed, dabbing his sweaty brow with a wet rag.

"You're safe here." I reconsider my words. "*We're* safe with you here."

Lord Faigen remains unconscious throughout the night. He moans often and thrashes in the bed with painful gasps. Does he dream of dragons and fire? His legs took the brunt of the brutal scorching. I peel back bandages and smear on more salve. He's lucky. The burns seem about as severe as intense exposure to the sun. The claw cuts on his chest are worse.

"Harminy," he moans.

My hand stills. I draw in a breath to still the quivering of my heart. Wringing out the rag with one hand, I lift Faigen's head so I can pour water into his mouth.

"Must warn… Celeste…"

What did he just say? I hold my breath. A fierce wave of trepidation falls over me. Faigen's head falls against the pillow. I let out a small gasp. Then a shadow clouds the wall and I turn my head the opposite way to greet the intruder. Adom stands at the doorway.

"How did you get in?" I ask. "The door was locked."

He disregards the question. "I went looking for you to tell you I'm going on a trip, and to ask you questions about Lord Faigen. What do you know?"

"Ryrick brought him to me last night. It's a dragon burn. I was going to tell you, but Ryrick said he sent word to the king and I figured he'd tell you about it."

"He did, but we were trapped in meetings all day. This is the first moment I've been able to check in. Did you learn anything else from him? When did it happen? Where?"

"No, I don't know anything else, but I'm hoping when he wakes I can get him to talk. Ryrick found him on the stairwell, so we don't know where he'd been."

Adom closes the door behind him. He approaches the bed and sinks beside me, his knee touching mine. "He isn't a changeling," he pronounces.

"How do you know?"

"Look at the burns. A changeling can walk through a natural fire without injury. He can survive a blast from a full grown dragon and look like he'd only spent a few hours too long in the sun. How long has he been here? Hours? He should be fully healed by now."

"So he's just a human. Another scorch victim." I drop a second rag in the basin of bloody water and set an empty pitcher on the desk. "Do you know the name Harminy?"

Adom frowns. "Not in polite society, no." He stands from the bed, casting another unhappy glance in Lord Faigen's direction. *Poor Adom.* Wherever he travels, people die. An unfortunate side effect of being a dragon changeling.

"Is anyone related to Lord Faigen with that name?"

His forehead furrows. "A cousin who's fallen on hard times. She's shunned from society because of her business endeavors.

She lives in Southside."

Her name sounds familiar, and the more I think about it the more I'm sure I've heard it before. A vague memory of my first meeting with Faigen floats into my mind. Wasn't there a woman there, at the tavern? Didn't she call herself Harminy? And she looked desperate, like she needed Faigen's help. "I'll visit her," I breathe. "She may have information."

Adom's eyelids narrow. "The south side of the city isn't safe."

My eyes dart restlessly to the door. His nearness induces borderline panic. "Then I'm the perfect person for the job." I smile weakly. "Patience is teaching me how to use a bow and arrow and how to swordfight. This will be a test of my skill."

After a moment, he nods and slides his hands into his trouser pockets. "Do you want me to come with you?" he offers in a voice that sounds just a little bit too casual.

But hadn't he just said he was going on a trip? He's suggesting putting it off to escort me through the dangerous city. What—does he think I can't do it by myself? It galls me when I remember that my last experience with the city involved being grabbed and locked up in a cellar. And Adom had to rescue me. I'm not about to let him assume I'm the same woman.

"I'm not afraid," I breathe, nostrils flaring.

His mouth quirks up. "I never suggested you were."

"And I'm more than capable on my own."

"I know you are. That doesn't mean I don't have the instinct to protect you." His eyes dilate. "I only came to tell you that it's time for me to pay a visit to Onyx. If I spend too many days away, Ona's control starts to tighten. I need to remind them of my strength."

By that, I know he means he'll need to accept challenges and battle other dragons to prove his dominance. "Please be careful. Ona made some threats—"

"Don't worry about it."

I lower my head. "Check on Muuth, too, will you? I know he's done things, but…"

"You worry about him, too?"

I turn honest eyes onto Adom. "He was my only friend for twelve years."

He runs a thoughtful finger across his cheek. "I'll tell him you're safe and you miss him."

Mixed feelings wrestle in my gut. Relief at Adom's respect—he never brought up the kidnapping incident. Pleasure at his appreciation. Deep, tumultuous terror. My eyes stray to the bed.

"It's hard to explain why I care about him," I say softly. "He told me what he did to you. He told me everything about his life before Onyx. About all the violence he committed. I am repulsed by him. But everything he did—he didn't do it to me. He took care of me when I was a child. Made me food, gave me things, and told me stories so I wasn't scared. He remembered my name day, and kept a calendar scratched on the walls of the cave so he could give me gifts. He defended me. I always thought he was half-mad. And now I know why. I was raised by a madman, Adom. But he loved me just the same."

"I don't begrudge you your love for Muuth," Adom says softly. "I'm glad you had him in your life. Somehow you turned out quite well, and that is to *his* credit, not mine."

"I don't know about that. You haven't seen the drawings on the cave wall."

~ * ~

Even though I told Adom I didn't need an escort, I can't think of a good quick alibi to leave the castle until Rhydian comes along and asks if I can help him find a present for his sister's wedding. It's such a harmless request, without any of the intrigue and sneaking around we've done so far. It's as if he wants to spend time with me regardless of what else is going on with his sister and my connection with his sworn enemy.

While we have a million things we could have talked about in the downtown marketplace—did he ask his sister about the watchtower conversation? Is he still convinced I didn't live on an island south of Cornoc?—instead we talk about idiocy like will this blanket match her rug, and does that goblet come in pairs. When we're done at the marketplace, I let him know that I'm going to take a detour to Southside. I tell him I want to go alone, but when he asks for details I fill him in on the basics: Faigen has a cousin who lives there and may know something.

I'm honestly shocked when Rhydian offers to come along—this isn't his world any more than it is Adom's. He even stops to buy clothes off a street tailor so that he doesn't look like a fancy target for thieves. After a brisk walk to Southside and a long stretch of door-to-door inquiries, we finally stumble across a shantytown on the far end of Foghum. We've been directed to an old house on the end of a cluttered street. Flecks of gray paint peel from ramshackle walls. The window has cracks, places spiders claim as web territory. I lift my hand to knock on the door, half-wanting to cover my mouth to keep from breathing the repugnant fish oil scents seeping through the door.

"Who's there?" someone screeches from within.

I withdraw my fist from the rotting door, and glance at Rhydian, flustered. He has a handkerchief to his nose, yet still offers me a weak smile. "Miss Harminy?"

A large woman with beefy hands comes to the door, swinging the hinges so wide they should have snapped. Her hair reminds me of one great rat's nest, complemented by a face and arms covered in black soot. "I'm her chimney sweep," she says in a deep, gravelly voice. She needn't have explained herself; I can guess her profession based on the smell.

"Nice to meet you," I reply taking her hand firmly in my own.

The woman gapes. "What are you touching me for?" She ogles. "Your hands are all lily-white and shouldn't be stained with my soot."

As I struggle to understand the dialect, I withdraw my arm. Dirt doesn't bother me. I share a look with Rhydian again. He's dressed down, but still we look out of place on this street, next to a pair of blind, scraggly beggars and a lunatic playing a broken instrument and cackling to himself. We didn't pick anything out from the market today, although we narrowed it down to two gifts, and I'm glad of that. A fancy package would have drawn the wrong kind of attention.

"Where are you from?" I ask the chimney sweep.

"Eppax," comes the woman's curt response. "Come from hill country."

I've heard of Eppax before. My papa mentioned it once or twice when he returned from his trips to Foghum city.

"Hear it's beautiful country." I smile. "Never been there myself." I can't think of anything more to say, and the woman just stares blankly. Rhydian rocks back on his boots, clearly uncomfortable. "Can you tell me where Miss Harminy is?"

She bobs her head. "She's in the back room. Come in."

As we step inside, a putrid rotting fish smell fills my nostrils. "Don't mind the smell," mutters the woman. "It's her sick girls." She shows us to the parlor, and I sink into a chair. Sheep wool spills out like entrails from ripped pillows. Rhydian feels the seat cushions carefully before taking a seat on the chair beside me. His mouth turned down, he appears stiff and in physical distress. I put a hand over his and squeeze gently.

"Wait here," the woman instructs us before disappearing down a dark hall.

We wait. Upstairs, I can hear a moaning sound, like an alley cat or sick dog. *One of her ailing children?* Someone enters the room, and I pull my hand away from Rhydian, suddenly self-conscious. The woman closes the door behind her and approaches us.

"Miss Harminy?" Rhydian inquires.

A stick-thin woman, Miss Harminy wears her blonde hair

braided in one long coil behind her back. For all appearances, she has the look of an aristocrat. Only heavy bags beneath her blue eyes and the fine lines around her mouth reveals she's fallen on hard times.

"Let's be frank," she says, reclining on the couch across from us. "I run a discreet business. Men come in and out of here all the time. They don't anticipate their wives' reprimands because I see to it their wives never know."

Discreet business? I weave my fingers together in distress, unsure how to respond.

"I have many connections with people in power. Prying eyes and wagging tongues are not welcome in my home. They will be dealt with harshly."

"Miss Harminy, I—"

"Tell me," she leans over and places an elbow on a satin pillow. "Which one of them sent you?" Her keen eyes wait for my response, measuring me in a way that makes my blood run cold. She wants to bribe me, or bargain with me.

"Sent me?"

"Which wife?"

Heat burns my face. "No one sent me."

Rhydian clears his throat. "You misunderstand."

She examines me anew. Chills tingle my spine. "Ah. I see." Her voice takes on a honeyed tone. "So you want work?"

"Work? No, I—"

"You have a lover who comes here?"

Red blooms on Rhydian's face. I stand. "I'm here to ask about your cousin, Lord Faigen."

At once, her cool demeanor dissipates. Two blotches color her cheeks. She fans her face with one hand; the other flutters over her dress, motions as anxious as a butterfly's wings. "How'd you know?"

I note brown stains on the dress. "Lord Faigen is a… friend of ours."

She draws her braid over her shoulder. "Are you in love with him?"

I return to my seat. "No. But he's in trouble. Can you help?"

"In trouble? How?" This revelation seems to visibly upset Miss Harminy.

"He was scorched by a dragon last night," Rhydian says.

The thin woman's face crumples. I stand again and awkwardly pat her hair. "I... always warned him... too impetuous for his own... good."

"He's not dead," I murmur.

Her head shoots up. Tears shimmer on dirty cheeks. She thumbs them away.

"He's someplace safe."

"Someplace safe? Where?"

"I can't say." I glance again at Rhydian, who is leaning forward, eagerly listening to our conversation. I hate lying to him, but with Celeste involved in changeling business I don't know if I can completely trust him. And I definitely can't trust Harminy. "But I saw him last night, and I can assure you he's much improved."

"They probably sent him to a convent," Miss Harminy mutters.

I school my face carefully so Harminy doesn't guess that I know where Faigen is being kept. "Do you know about his dealings the past few days? People he's come in contact with? Maybe he went somewhere recently that stands out in your mind?"

Harminy's back straightens. "I may."

"Please," Rhydian says. "We need the information to protect him."

"From what?" Her voice turns brittle like toffee, but bitter like rancid milk.

"People who might want to kill him in his...vulnerable state," I answer directly.

Faigen is a knight, and so it doesn't come as a shock to Harminy he'd be burned by a dragon. But as a minor lord with affluence in the community, I can easily imagine any countless number of people won't mind seeing him dead. From the gossip I overheard among the ladies who accompanied Lady Celeste last night, Faigen's interests obviously extend beyond me. I recall the insinuations made by the guard at the gate on the day Faigen brought me to the castle. Surely Harminy could believe her cousin, although well-loved by some, also maintained grave enemies.

"I think you probably understand the kind of discretion we need right now," I add.

"What people?" Harminy demands. "Who's after my cousin?"

"I'm afraid I can't tell you," I say. "We just don't know enough at this time."

"It's likely there was foul play involved in his injury, so we're retracing his steps," says Rhydian. "Anything you know could help us determine his last actions."

Miss Harminy folds her hands in her lap, her head lowered. "He was here four days ago. He had a lady friend with him. When she spoke, I could hardly tell it was a woman. She sounded as though someone had poured acid down her throat."

"Did you catch her name?" he asks.

"I did," she acknowledges, her eyes downcast. "Faigen called her Siren."

Rhydian makes a noise like he's choking. I put a hand on his knee and squeeze. He grasps me and returns the squeeze. His grip hurts—I glance at his white-knuckled fingers.

"What did she look like?" he asks.

"Tall and thin, with pointy features and a pretty manner about her." Miss Harminy shrugs. She purses her lips. "She wore all white. And I remember them talking about the dragon scorchings." At last, she meets eyes with me. "That's all I can remember."

I mask my excitement. "Can you tell me what they did here?"

She gawks. "They must have been lovers, of course. Why

else would they have come?" She straightens. "They left in the morning. Faigen left a bag of gold on his pillow—the usual amount. I haven't seen either of them since."

~ * ~

As we leave, Rhydian walks ahead of me several paces and doesn't stop to look back. I quicken my pace to catch up with him. He won't look down at me, not even when I take his hand. Something is very, very wrong with him. "I'm so sorry, Rhydian. It must be a shock."

"Obviously she's lying," he says with grim-faced determination, staring straight ahead.

"Is there a chance your sister survived?"

"I saw her body go into the ground."

"Nightshade won't kill a dragon. It will only make them sleep."

Rhydian stares at me with cold, disbelieving eyes. "What are you suggesting?"

I return the stare, setting my mouth in a tight silence.

"You really think my sister was a dragon? That she faked her death?"

"I don't know what to think. If Count Malandre thought she was—"

He takes a significant step back and throws his hands between us. His pupils dilate, and when his eyes settle on me they are unfamiliar. "Count Malandre is a lunatic, and so are you."

"Rhydian."

"Stay away from me, Elanor. You're poisoning my thoughts the same way Malandre poisoned Siren's. The same way my father poisoned her."

"You have to at least consider—"

"I trust you can find your way home from here? Yes? Good. I'll take my leave now."

He storms away, leaving me standing in the middle of the street, a funny aching feeling in the pit of my restless stomach.

I breathe deeply, in spite of the stench, and tuck my cloak around my frame so I can walk through the streets without drawing too much attention. The sun is drooping in the horizon, and I'm not exactly sure where the castle is in relation to this street, but this time I'm determined not to be a victim. I walk with sure, purposeful strides, eyes straight ahead, no hesitation in my movements. I see thieves and drunkards and make bold eye contact.

A man steps in line behind me and begins following me as I turn a corner. My heart quickens. I increase my pace. He does the same. I slow down. He follows suit.

I turn around. "Are you following me?"

He reaches for me with broad, greedy hands.

I pull out the knife Patience gave me and hold it high between us. "One step closer, and I'll cut out your eyes."

The man throws his hands in the air. "No harm intended." He takes a slow step backward. "I'm not interested in the ones who'll fight back." He spits at my feet.

"One day, someone will carve you so you aren't interested in anyone ever again."

The man slinks away without a reply.

I turn and continue my trek to the castle. I can't shake the feeling that someone is following me. I turn again, twice, but there is no one there I can see.

Finally, I reach the steps to the back entrance of the palace. The guards recognize me and let me in without fuss, and on the other side of the gate I let out a stunted breath of relief.

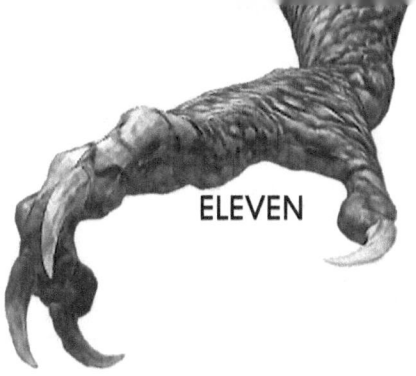

ELEVEN

PATIENCE CORNERS ME BEFORE I can swipe a dinner tray and head upstairs to Lord Faigen's sick room. She stands tapping at the ground with one foot. "And where are you off to?"

"Just to check on…" I lower my voice to a whisper, "our patient."

"Ryrick's with him," she replies. "Don't you want to come out to the arena with me?"

If Ryrick is with Faigen, I'll need to wait for a better time to get information from him. I need to find Rhydian and make sure he's…make sure he's okay. He said he wanted me to stay away from him, but he can't really mean it. Can he?

"Actually, I was thinking about heading into the forest to restock our supplies. If you have a list of things you need, I'll look for them."

Patience glances at the low ring of dying sunlight. "Not at this hour."

I smile at her, but she doesn't seem amused. "I'll be fine."

She puts her hands on her hips. "What has gotten into you? You disappeared today, and when I checked with Ryrick he said you'd gone with Lord Berrel to pick out a present for his sister's wedding." She gives me a look that tells me she thinks the response I gave Ryrick was rubbish. "I *saw* how Berrel looked at you when he showed up at the clinic. I don't believe for a minute that you two were picking out presents at the market."

"It's complicated," I say, grimacing.

Patience is silent for a long moment. "I'm still here, aren't I?"

I glance at her feeling a peculiar desperation I've never

felt before. "I want to tell you. But it's...I just don't..." My voice falters.

She holds up a hand, mercifully cutting me off. "I told you before that you didn't need to tell me anything." She sucks in a breath." But you're lying, Elanor. And not very convincingly, I might add." Her eyes stare at me, crushing me with their disappointment. "Look, if you need my help, just ask. And for goodness sake, *don't* disappear for hours on end without telling me, leaving me to hear your half-baked lies coming out of my father's mouth."

"I don't know what to say," I lower my head, ashamed. "I'm sorry."

"I thought maybe a dragon had gotten to you." Now I hear the tears in her voice.

"I'm not used to people worrying over me."

She opens her mouth to reply, but a nobleman flings open the door to the kitchen and lets out a vigorous, terrified gasp. "Help!"

"Lord Taggart? How can we assist?"

"It's Princess Ora. She's locked herself in her room and refuses to come out."

Patience frowns. "The palace guards could—"

"It's a delicate matter. It could inflame the situation to include them." He looks at me, as if skeptical of my abilities. Then he turns to Patience. "You. Do you know of anyone who could coax the Princess out? She's in a fragile state, emotionally, and it's all my fau—" He stops and abruptly covers his mouth with both hands.

"I'm the castle physician. It's my job to talk to people about what ails them."

Lord Taggart nods with enthusiasm, his hands dropping to his sides and his jowls jiggling. "Yes. That's exactly who she needs. Please come quickly."

Patience crooks a finger, indicating I should follow her.

Lord Taggart swings around. "Not you!" he says, glaring at me as if I've somehow insulted him. "We need discretion."

"She's my assistant," Patience insists. "She could help."

I shake my head. "It's fine, Patience. I have the other chores to attend to."

"Please don't go to the woods tonight," she begs.

"Why?"

"Just please," she pleads.

I realize that she has no real reason to ask. She's just worried about me going in there alone. The dragon scorchings have her all frazzled, and she actually cares about me.

I gesture to the door. "Go ahead. Fix people. I promise not to go to the woods tonight."

They leave, and I head to Rhydian's room to see if he's cooled down after our encounter at Miss Harminy's house. I knock, and wait, and knock a second time but he doesn't answer. Maybe it is more than just his shock at hearing his dead sister's name. Maybe he really doesn't want to see me ever again. Even thinking it makes my heart hurt.

Sighing, I start back toward the kitchen. Longley doesn't have any work for me, so I decide to return to Patience's clinic and wait to hear about Princess Ora. I'm sure it'll be a fascinating story. But as I cross the courtyard, a flash of color in the woods arrests my movement. It looks like a bit of metal, gleaming from between the trees. Something hanging, perhaps? A helmet or a piece of armor resting on a tree branch? It's odd enough for me to shove down the pang of guilt I feel, change course, and steer for the glinting bit of light. Patience did say she didn't want me going into the woods. But on the other hand, Adom *did* ask me to look for changelings. *I'll just take a quick look at what this light is before heading back home.*

As I move forward, it withdraws. I pause mid-step, and stare forcefully at the spot. Another flash, this time in a different spot, still high off the ground. Now my heart hammers, because there is only one thing I can think of that can move so quickly, has a sheen that refracts the light as bright as an open flame, and is agile enough to move from tree to tree without shuddering the branches.

A dragon.

Since it isn't making itself known, and since it hasn't blown me to smithereens as yet, I suspect it knows I'm watching and expects me to follow.

Adom doesn't hang on trees. It could be Fire Breather or one of the other changelings. I could be walking into a trap. But if I don't follow, I could miss the chance to confront Lord Darton's killer, the same person I suspect also attacked Lord Faigen.

I slip into the trees, eyes fixed on the moving metal that glints and flickers ahead of me. Small clues confirm my suspicions—a branch drops here, a tree sways against the wind there. As I draw nearer, moving further and further out of sight of the castle grounds, I begin to hear the slight *scritch scratch* of talons scoring the huge redwood trees as it leaps from branch to branch.

There's only one Tree Hopper in Onyx, and he isn't one of the Head Dragons so I don't interact with him much. They're a smaller variety, so he generally avoided the rest of the herd to keep from being challenged. He caught me, once, when I tried to escape. He slinks like an oversized cat, curving his body unnaturally around tree trunks and using talon-like claws to grasp thick branches and climb the high redwood trees. He was on me before I knew it.

But this is a different dragon and a different time. I know how to track them now.

My feet sink into mud and I quickly grab leaves and use them to tug myself free. There's an axe buried into the trunk of a sycamore, and I snatch the handle and pull the weapon free. The lights in the trees blink, and I make out a distinct pair of steel-gray eyes. A vine drops, and it takes me a moment to realize that it isn't a vine at all. It's a dragon's tail. The rest of its body is hidden by the dense branches and trunk of the tree it's wound around.

"I know you're here," I shout. "You might as well come out."

Branches crack, and a blackened body lands at my feet. Chills shudder up my spine. My stomach attacks my throat. I can't make out a face past the cooked helmet. It's another knight. I sink to my knees and extend trembling hands toward the dead man. Mindful of the hot metal, I tug the helmet to reveal the knight's identity. The face is nothing but blackened char, but the hair...oh God, the hair...

It's a blond man. The hair is the exact texture and color of Rhydian's.

Thump.

I raise my eyes. The dragon is standing before me now, hissing and snarling, dripping great globules of drool over the dead man's chest. I fight the urge to plunge the axe into the horrible beast. *The body isn't Rhydian*, I promise myself. *He's not a knight.* I let the axe slip.

"Stand down," I say in dragon tongue, holding a hand out. "I don't want to hurt you."

Wide, soulful eyes return my gaze, then flick to its forearm. It lets out a roar and sinks fanged teeth into the fleshy part of its limb. There's a long, bloody gash scarring the arm. My eyes stray to the dead man. Nearby, there is a broken sword strewn against a tree.

"You're injured," I say. "He struck you with a poison-tipped sword."

My words earn another roar.

"I think I can help."

In answer, the dragon swoops open its wings, sharp looking things like blades on its back. It snatches me with wide talons and bounds into the air. I am unafraid—if it wanted to kill me, it would have done it already. We travel for miles. Then, under a canopy of trees, at the base of a mountain, it drops. Into a cave maw, past the set of human-made tracks and wheelbarrows filled with stones, shovels and mounds of dirt. Into blackness illuminated only by eyes of fire.

At last the creature settles on the ground. It doesn't squeeze me, as dragons are wont to do when I'm caught in their claws, so I take it is a sign of peace and slide carefully away from the sharp, metallic edges of its talons. I back away slowly, waiting for my eyes to adjust to the gloaming. In moments, I can see the sad creature licking the wound on its arm and staring at me with frightened, suspicious eyes. It splays out beside me, letting out a soft groan.

"Let me see it," I say in dragon tongue.

"I understand you," the thing speaks back. "How?"

"I lived with dragons."

Scales clack as it shifts and stretches out the arm for me to inspect. The wound is nasty, but a cut like this won't kill it and the poison on the sword shouldn't slow it down for long.

"Who did you kill?" I ask.

"Lord Reuben," the dragon replies. "He crept up behind me."

I can't help the strangled moan of relief that escapes. "I know why you did it."

"I didn't mean to."

"Did you kill Lord Darton?"

"No."

"Did you attack Lord Faigen?"

"I wouldn't do that."

"I need light to see what's wrong," I say softly.

The dragon blasts fire near the entrance of the cave. A broken wheelbarrow catches flame. It burns quick and brilliant—the fire won't last long. I peer at the wound and see a small sliver of metal in the bloody mess. "There's a bit of the sword still in here. It broke off when he stabbed you. That's probably why it hurts so much."

"Take it out."

"It'll hurt."

"Do it."

"Will you kill me afterward?"

"I won't."

"Swear it."

"I swear on my blood."

Maybe it's because I'm back in a cave and feel compelled to obey the dragon, or maybe it's because of its sorrowful eyes. Something about the way it talks, even in the harsh dragon language, relaxes my fight instincts and moves me to help it. I touch the wound, then draw back slightly as the dragon flesh shudders. With deliberate, quick motions, I slap my fingers into the wound, grasp the sharp object, and tug it out. With a *splurt* and a gush of blood, the flesh releases the metal. The dragon lets out a bone-chilling roar. Scales around the wound drop off, delicate as flower petals against the taint of poison. I place the sword's edge on a rock and wipe my fingers, coated in black dragon's blood, off on the underside hem of my dress.

The dragon scuttles away from me until it is against the wall of the cave. It presses its back along the cave wall and slides across the rock. The sound is like knives sharpened against stone. Sparks brighten the space for a brief few seconds, and in that time I see a multitude of colorful dragon scales scattered all around the cave and buried in the rocks. The creature claws at its long neck, and scales drop like overripe fruit. It continues like this for several minutes.

"You need to stop," I say at last. "You'll damage your armor."

"I have to get it off," the dragon says. "I want it off."

"Why? Does it hurt?"

"I'm not a dragon," it replies. "This is all a horrible nightmare."

Suddenly, it all makes sense. Adom had Muuth to fill in the gaps for him. Muuth knew about the changelings, and he knew how Adom came to be. He took Adom to be with the dragons on Onyx Island so he could learn how to manage the dragon part of himself.

The other changelings were not so fortunate.

"It's not your fault," I tell it. "You don't know why this is happening to you."

"I'm a monster," the thing croons sadly. "If I had known the knight planned to kill me, I would have let him. He did not deserve to die. I do."

I crook my finger. "Come here."

The creature pads slowly toward me.

"Do you want to die?" I ask, picking up the piece of broken sword.

It stares at me with expressive, glittering eyes. "I deserve it."

"Do you want me to kill you?"

"No."

"Good." I let the metal fall. I doubt I could have killed it with the small piece of sword, and if it had said yes I would have been hard-pressed to murder the thing with that sad look in its eye, but I'm not about to tell it that. Instead, I pat the ground near my lap. "Lay your head here."

It shuffles closer and eases its head to the ground.

Silva had a tender spot around her jawline that she used to make me work on. She always kept her eyes wide open, watching, teeth glistening as my fingers moved across her snout and under her chin. This dragon does not harbor such inherent distrust. As soon as its head collapses, it lets out a halting snort and its eyes slide shut. I reach over and splay my fingers on its jaw. Very gently, I work out the tightness around the creature's face as I used to do with Silva.

"You're safe with me," I say, realizing that this may be the first time I've ever felt compassion for a dragon. But this one is so different. It's scared and confused, more like I was when I first arrived at Onyx Island, disoriented by my situation.

As it sleeps and the fire dies out, the cold chill of the cave sinks into my bones. The creature isn't like other reptiles—its body radiates heat. For the first time, I realize this is an attribute unique to the changeling dragons. Adom is hot blooded, too. The dragons on Onyx are cold, like snakes. I make a mental note of that fact; it could help me down the road.

It can help me right now, in fact, as the cold seeps into my blood and numbs my extremities. I've never cuddled with a dragon before, but in this icy, dank place that reminds me of too many terrible memories, I find myself sliding closer to the beast, pulling myself against it, gravitating toward its searing core. The dragon snorts and turns its head to the side.

Hours later, or maybe days, we awaken as one to the midnight cave.

"Where am I?" he says in Tranar tongue, his voice hitched and panicking.

I know this human voice. "We're still in the mine, Rhydian."

Skin slaps against skin, and he lets out a mortified curse. "Oh, God. I'm naked."

"I won't look," I whisper, laughing.

He rises shakily to his feet. "I can't see a damned thing. How do we get out of here?"

I push myself off the ground. "We have two options. You can change again and fly us out of here, or you can follow me. I know caves well enough to find an opening."

"I can't control it," he says. "Until now, I thought it was nothing but a horrible dream." His breath comes in gasps. "It can't be real. I can't really be—"

I reach for Rhydian's hand. "Then I'll take the lead."

We wander into the next cave, following light and the flow of air. He missteps, nearly tumbling off a jagged edge, but I pull him to safety. My feet act on their own, without thought. This isn't the world I was born into, but it is my world nonetheless. Calm envelops me as my toes plod over familiar terrain; harsh ridges, clods of dirt, and sharp stone.

"Is this a dream?" he asks me, suddenly.

"No, Rhydian. You changed and brought me here."

"And Lord Reuben?"

"He's dead, but it isn't your fault."

We squeeze through treacherous, narrow pathways. Someone dug this path out long ago, and there are remnants of human life along the walls, clues of ages long gone. Cloth sacks, and bones, and every now and again a torch hanging along the wall.

"I need to turn myself in. King Siles will see me hanged for murder."

"You can't turn yourself in without revealing you're a changeling."

"I could say I burned him in a house fire."

"They'll know."

"I could blame it on Count Malandre. He calls himself a changeling, doesn't he?"

At this I clamp my mouth shut. Rhydian might guess that Adom's claim is real, but it won't be me who gives away the information. Rhydian already thinks Adom's a monster.

He's silent for a few moments. Then, "He told Siren the truth, didn't he? She *was* a changeling and so was he. What my father saw was real. My father murdered a monster."

"If Siren really was a changeling, nightshade couldn't have killed her."

"Miss Harminy said Faigen was with a woman called Siren."

"It could have been someone else."

"Or it could have been my sister. She could still be alive." For the first time since his awakening, a note of hope creeps into his voice. "Celeste should know."

"You have to be careful, Rhydian," I say. "Not all changelings feel as you do about their abilities. Some of them may take pleasure in the power it gives them over humans."

"But she's my sister," Rhydian replies. "If she's done anything wrong, it's because she fell under Count Malandre's influence." His fingers grip mine in vise-like intensity. "I could ruin Malandre with this information. He doesn't suspect my secret, but now I know his."

"He might suspect your secret," I point out, my heart hammering in my throat. "If your sister was a changeling, he might know that you're one as well. And you can't prove that he's a dragon. It's not like he'll demonstrate before the court if you accuse him of it."

I feel Rhydian's eyes on me, thinking. "You knew that Malandre was a dragon?"

I tug him around a stalactite and suddenly my feet are walking across a set of tracks. "He's not a changeling, Rhydian."

"Then why did you come here after he kept you as a prisoner for twelve years?"

"Maybe it's because I care about him?"

"You don't. You can't."

"Suppose I do?"

Stunned silence hits me like a bag of stones. It buys me a few moments of relief. I don't really love Adom, but Rhydian can't rationalize away my emotions the way he has tried to do with my history, the dragon scorchings, and my connection to Lord Malandre.

The blackness softens to a dirty brown. We are nearing the entrance of the cave. I hasten forward, but Rhydian locks his knees. I squeeze his arm, but he doesn't move.

"What's wrong?"

"I'm naked."

"Do you want my dress?"

"I just need...a covering."

It takes a bit of concerted effort not to inform him that male genitals are nothing I haven't seen before. A family of brothers, a crazy old man, and a changeling prison-keeper have all strengthened my constitution in this regard.

When I begin to undo the laces of my bodice, Rhydian says, "You don't have to do that. Your apron will do."

In moments, Rhydian is clothed and we emerge, blinking, under the dawning sky. The moon is full, majestic above us, and the horizon wreathed with an orange glow. I glance over at his face—he's covered in dirt—and the gaping scar on his left arm looks painful. I entwine my fingers between his.

He pulls away. "I thought you didn't like to be touched," he reminds me.

I can't ignore the stab of hurt I feel over this small rejection. "Are you angry?"

"Yes. I'm angry and confused. The worst part of it is, I don't know why. How could I be this...*thing*? How did I never know? All the dragon scales in my caves, were they all mine? Is my sister really alive?" He latches eyes on mine. "How can you be in love with him?"

Of all the lies I could have told him, why did I choose *this* lie? It seemed easiest in the moment to stop him from asking pointed questions about why I'm sticking so close to Malandre. But now I realize it's only going to torment him a different way. "I don't know," I say, not sure which question I'm answering. "We'll find the answers together, Rhydian. You can trust me."

"I don't know if I can."

"I swear that I won't tell Count Malandre about you."

His eyes soften. "Thank you."

"But you have to promise you won't try to frame him for Lord Reuben's death."

"I won't frame him for Reuben's death, but I can't promise you that I won't ruin him."

My heart aches. "You have to let it go. Malandre didn't do anything wrong. If your sister is a changeling, he never lied to her. And if she's not dead, your family can be reunited."

"It isn't about any of that now," Rhydian says, avoiding my eyes.

~ * ~

We steal a horse and a set of farmer's clothes hanging out to dry, and Rhydian rides back to the castle with me, now fully clothed. The castle guards recognize Rhydian, and one of them——a bulky one with beady eyes——gives me a dubious look as though he remembers me as well. Come to think of it, he might have been on duty the day I showed up with Lord Faigen all those weeks ago.

I slink back to the servants' quarters, praying no one has noticed my long absence. When I arrive at the clinic, a message from Patience is pinned to the door. The note says that Longley has asked if she can spare my help today. The cook instructs me to the dining hall to ready the floral arrangements for breakfast. I wash, change outfits, and set to work, ignoring the aches and groans of my joints. Work goes quickly. On the way back from the dining hall, I pass the door to the parlor room. A tinkling laugh fills my ears and a masculine chuckle follows. Adom? So he's returned already? After barely a day?

"Your skills on the pianoforte are phenomenal. Your family is proud, I'd imagine." His voice sounds warm and pleasant. I've come to appreciate the deep richness of his speech.

I dodge out of eyesight and peek between the crack of the partially opened door.

Celeste laughs. "They're more impressed with my marriage match than my piano skills."

"Of course."

"And do you ever intend to marry, Count Malandre?"

I squint to better see. The sliver of light only affords me a blurry glimpse of the room.

"Never," he says. "Marriage wouldn't suit me."

"Really? Why not? I know many eligible women who would leap into action to steal your heart. Then again, perhaps you're right. Maybe you aren't actually capable of love." She says it with a smile on her lips and a playful look in her eyes, but there is a note of pain in her voice.

"I loved Siren faithfully when she lived," says Adom quietly, gazing out the window.

Lady Celeste studies him carefully. She lifts a glass of champagne and sips. Then she returns the glass to the top of the piano. "Where were you when she was dying? You never came. You never even sent a note." She clears her throat. "We never saw you again."

He looks her square in the eye. "I was on a boat, on a diplomatic mission for the king. The message didn't reach me until after she was gone. If it had, I assure you I would have defied the king, abandoned the mission, and stayed by her side until the bitter end. I *loved* her, Celeste."

"I see." She sits beside him and rests a hand over his. "Do I look like her?"

"Unbearably so," he says with throaty voice and wetness in his eyes. Then he stiffens and stands quickly from the chaise. "Forgive me, Celeste. There's business I must attend to."

Her face falls. She struggles to reassemble a composed visage. "Of course, my lord. Thank you for answering my message. I've always enjoyed our conversations."

Without thinking, I dart behind a tapestry. Adom closes the door. He passes the tapestry and I bite my tongue, knowing how foolish I'll look if I reveal my location.

"I know you're there," he says under his breath.

I step away from the tapestry. "Adom."

He approaches me in two steps, eyes narrowed. "That isn't my name."

"Forgive me... Count Malandre."

His muscles relax. "It's all right."

I lower my head, feeling inexplicably subdued. "I have news."

"So do I. Let's go." He takes my hand and pulls me along

the corridor in the direction of King Siles' private dining chamber. I wiggle away from his grip.

He rotates. "What?"

"It won't look proper," I whisper.

A muscle twitches in his jaw. He nods and turns to the stairs. I follow without a word.

~ * ~

"What did you learn from Miss Harminy?" Adom turns to me once we are both seated in front of the king. "Were you able to visit her?"

I dip my chin. "She saw Faigen the day he was scorched. A woman accompanied him." My eyes flicker to Adom's. "Her name was Siren."

Siles frowns. "That can't be right." He puts a hand on Adom's shoulder. "We don't know if it's the same woman. I'll assign a man to review the city census data for the name."

"If Siren was a changeling, she couldn't have died of nightshade poison."

"Nightshade poisoning?" Adom's eyebrows shoot up. "She died of a fever."

I shake my head. "Rhydian said the family lied to cover the truth. Her father poisoned her with nightshade because of…" I look at Adom and feel heat scorching my cheeks.

"*Rhydian?*" he asks, his face a calm mask, dissonant with the rage in his voice.

I am bungling this meeting with the king as badly as the first. "What if Siren lived?"

Adom is unusually quiet. I keep glancing his direction, waiting for his anger to boil over. He's so unlike Rhydian who, as much as he talks about logic and reason, can't contain his feelings for even a moment. In contrast, Adom is well-practiced in the art of hiding emotion.

Siles tilts his head toward Adom. "Would she harbor ill

feelings, Adom?"

"Why would she?" I blurt out. "None of it is Adom's fault. He didn't poison her. And you sent him on a voyage when it happened, so he couldn't come back."

Siles frowns. "I never—"

Adom plants his palms on the table and stands. "That's enough of this. Siren hasn't returned. Someone is masquerading as her to get under my skin." He turns resentful eyes on me. "I wouldn't be surprised if *Rhydian* is behind it. I didn't realize the two of you were so friendly."

"Rhydian isn't your enemy. He's hurt, and his anger is misplaced. If you had talked to him then, when he needed it, and if you had explained why you weren't there—"

"You don't know why I wasn't there," he cuts in.

"You told me you were on Onyx. You told Lady Celeste you were on a boat."

"You were listening to that?"

"Of course I was. It's what I do."

"Eavesdropping is rude," he comments dryly.

"And how would I know that?"

His nostrils flare. "You want to know why I didn't return when Siren was at home, dying? I received the message. Siles sent it to me the same way he sends all the messages—through homing pigeon. I could have *changed* and flown and been there in hours. I could have stood at her side and smelled the nightshade on her breath and saved her before she died."

I shrink away. "Then why didn't you?"

"Because of you."

My gut sinks. "What do you mean?"

He places his hands at his sides and is suddenly calm again. "You were in trouble that day—you'd tried running away again. The dragons were talking about disposing of you. I didn't trust that they wouldn't hurt you while I was away, and I couldn't take you with me—it would have raised too many questions. Siren had never *changed*, so I wasn't sure she was a changeling. But Muuth swore her family had taken Jetarna's treatment, so I took a risk and stayed with you."

I breathe in and out very carefully. "Are you blaming me for what happened?"

"It isn't anyone's fault that she died."

"Is this why you kept me prisoner all these years? To punish me?"

"Lodin's ashes No." His eyes widen in horror.

In my mind's eye, I hear the voices at the watchtower again. Lady Celeste speaking to someone with a broken voice. Someone who wanted to start a war. To kill off all the dragons.

"If Siren *is* alive, she wants revenge."

Adom's eyes glint, but then the light dulls. "For what?"

I tell them about the voices Rhydian and I overheard in the watchtower. About seeing Celeste leave the tower alone. About the children who swore they saw a dragon perch on the tower only moments before.

"You abandoned her. You gambled with her life. She *knew* you could be at her side in hours if you'd wanted to be there. Maybe she was testing you the same way you tested her. You thought she would live, so you didn't come."

The king lets out a soft moan. "Could there be another explanation for Celeste's involvement?" he asked, brows furrowed together in a look that strikes me as agony.

"Rhydian is going to ask her. He believes in her innocence." I hold up a hand. "We can't know anything from that conversation. Don't assume the worst."

"But shouldn't I cancel the wedding?" the king asks.

"No. If she's one of the changelings, it will only raise suspicion."

"Why wouldn't Siren contact me? Why would she wait until now to reappear?" Adom shakes his head. "No. Lord Berrel is feeding Elanor lies to unsettle me. He might have hired someone to meet with Celeste and stage the words so it sounded like Siren."

"It doesn't add up," I say. "Lord Faigen was with a woman with a mangled voice who called herself Siren. His own cousin testified to it. Then he appears on our doorstep with dragon burns. Rhydian is clever, but he can't hire the whole town to play along. There's a changeling involved."

"Berrel could have hurt Faigen himself," he argues, but doubt creeps into his voice.

"He didn't. You should have seen his face when Harminy mentioned—"

Adom rounds on me. "You took him with you? How much does Berrel know about our investigation?"

"Nothing. He wants to find out who burned Lord Faigen as much as we all do."

"So he knows about Faigen?"

"Everybody knows about Faigen. The servants talk."

"And what about Darton?"

My eyelids drop. "He knows about him, too. Remember the announcement you and Siles made to the group of lords the first night we spoke again? Berrel was there. He's my friend, Adom. I trust him."

Adom thumps into a seat stiffly, arms crossed and face avoiding my gaze. The tips of my ears burn, but I'm not sure whether it's because of Adom's angry voice or that the king can hear us bickering. My heart flutters in my chest.

"What about Muuth?" I ask gruffly as Adom cuts me a slice of cake. "What'd you learn from him?" My thoughts gather in a swirling tempest. The answer to this changeling riddle is so close. Right in front of me.

Adom hesitates. "He wasn't there. It's why I left so soon."

King Siles leans forward in his seat, his fingertips drumming against the table. "What do you mean he wasn't there?"

Adom shrugs. "I couldn't find him."

"And how is that possible?" Siles inquires.

I take a bite of the moist, spongy cake, then take a drink of water to quench a sudden thirst. The dessert has a peculiar aftertaste, like a spicy fruit I don't remember. Yet there is something potently familiar about it, as if I should be able to identify it.

"I think he escaped. He probably used the boat."

"There was no boat," I say. "Muuth told me it had been destroyed a long time ago." All at once, my tongue feels heavy and my thoughts sluggish.

Adom levels an unimpressed look my direction. "He lied. The boat was there when I left you on Onyx. I checked myself. He buried it beneath a pile of rags and ropes, intact." His eyebrows rise. "You might have noticed if you didn't blindly trust your friends."

The jab burns more than the ache in my side from all the walking this morning.

"Why now?" Siles inquires. "He could have left at any point."

"Elanor?" Adom asks. "You know him better than anyone."

"Something's changed," I whisper hoarsely. "He wouldn't leave Onyx without a reason. He feels like he has to stay in case the sun's acid comes back. To warn you and the dragons." My eyes, suddenly dry, squint against the brightness of all the flickering lamps lit in the room.

"Sun's acid," Adom breathes softly. "And what if that's the reason?"

Siles sits back in his chair. "We don't know for sure."

"We shouldn't take chances until we do," Adom says. "We can't leave the castle until we find Muuth. If that's the reason he's left Onyx, the other dragons will be equally as helpless."

The world blurs. "Don't touch the cake," I rasp.

My throat thickens. The room crinkles. I tumble off the seat, and my eyes hone in on the one thing pulling me out of the blackness: Adom's terrified face.

~ * ~

Poison! Someone tried to kill the king. Suddenly alert, I organize scattered words that are all mixed up in my pounding skull. My voice cracks, unintelligible and garbled. I groan a second time.

"Don't move," says a voice above me.

"Adom?" This time, the sound makes sense in my ears. I open my eyes, but everything is groggy and hot and black, like my head is covered by a burlap sack.

"I'm here."

I struggle up, but my head swims.

"Stay still."

At last the dark spots whirling across my vision cease to move, and I can just make out the silhouettes of Adom and the king standing over me.

"I'm not dead?" I croak.

"No," says King Siles. "You can thank Adom and Patience. He raced to her and she made an emetic. That's why your voice is so scratchy. We suspect nightshade."

I tilt my head to the blur I guess is Adom. "Thank you."

The world clears in lazy, pulsating dark spots. Adom's profile grows distinct. I sit up. My pulse beats with abnormal rapidity. Satin pillows and delicate embroidery cover the king's chaise like myriad colorful leaves. I glance at the dinner plates stacked on trays by the dinner table. The cake lay untouched. I inhale slowly. How long have I suffered? A few hours? And how much longer until the queasiness in my stomach subsides?

"Who's responsible for it?"

Adom sits on the edge of the chaise. "Lord Berrel told you his sister was poisoned. Didn't you say it was nightshade? Nobody but the family knew the details of the death."

"Rhydian didn't do this," I insist. "It has to be Celeste."

"Does he know you meet with us?"

"No. He thinks I'm avoiding you."

"Maybe he knows. Maybe he's playing you."

"He wouldn't risk my life to get revenge on you," I reply.

"How can you be so sure?"

I refuse to answer. Adom wanted me to help him track down the changelings, but the one changeling I found doesn't want Adom to know about it. How can I help them both when they hate and distrust each other?

Then I think of something. "Who delivered the food?"

Siles shares a weary look with Adom. "Cydra. We're waiting on news from the guards."

"Is she a changeling?"

"We don't know yet," Adom replies.

The queasiness intensifies. I cover my mouth in sudden panic. Adom hands me a basin. I retch.

"I feel terrible." I wipe my mouth with the back of my hand.

King Siles hands me a wet rag and a cup of water. I sip, letting the water cleanse my mouth and soothe my burning throat.

"You look terrible," Adom grunts, but his eyes twinkle. Then he grows serious. "Elanor, nightshade is potent stuff. You could have died."

"Better thank Patience with extra gold coins and maybe some new hunting equipment." I dab my forehead with the rag King Siles handed me. The king notices my efforts and pries the rag from my hand. I numbly allow him to moisten my face. "I have a long list of tasks I really need to get to."

"Are you insane as Muuth?" Adom explodes. "You need rest."

"If Patience knows, the servants will soon be talking. Ryrick will worry, too. I have to show them all there's nothing wrong. They'll wonder why you both attended to me."

Adom throws me a sidelong, unhappy gaze. "Are you sure you aren't more concerned with what Lord Berrel might think?" My silence seems to drain him. "Please, Elanor. Stay and rest. I'll explain your absence to Ryrick and the staff, and even to Lord Berrel if you want it."

My body feels as though an entire mountain fell on top of me. My stomach hasn't relieved itself entirely, and it's only a matter of time before I reach for the basin again. Attempting a weak smile, I allow Adom this small victory. "Anyone hungry for cake?"

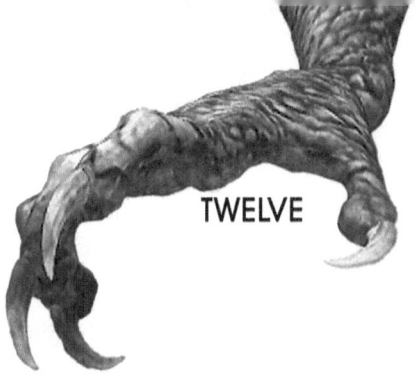

TWELVE

MY PULSE COMES IN short, erratic bursts. I breathe in the crisp night air, hoping to cool the fever in my mind, the swirling, disorienting fear that holds me captive.

"Elanor." The king calls out my name softly, his shadow appearing at the doorway between the rooms. Against my protestations, Adom and Siles moved me to the king's antechamber. They claim it's more secure, away from prying eyes. A servant leaving the king's chambers under such circumstances was sure to draw attention.

He edges closer. A ray of moonlight casts an eerie glow on his countenance. "It's time for me to leave. With Adom gone in search of Muuth, I'm the only one left to guard the countryside. I've asked Patience to watch over you tonight. She should be here momentarily."

Pain in my upper abdomen evolves into convulsions in my lower gut. The king peeks in through the canopy curtains and observes me for a moment. He thumbs a wet spot on his cheek. It catches me off guard—why would Siles cry over me?

"I've never seen Adom ruffled before," he says. "When you're with him, he comes alive."

"It's easy to come alive when you're with someone who wants to kill you," I say.

"You don't really want to kill him, do you?"

"If he doesn't stop ordering me around, I might."

Siles chuckles. "You're too hard on him. He only wants you to be happy."

"I'm not going back to Onyx."

"I don't think that's what he wants, either."

"You knew about it. Even sanctioned it. Why?"

The king pauses for a long time before replying. "Because there was a monster on Onyx who needed taming. Who needed not lose touch with their human side."

"Adom," I mumble, licking cracked lips. "But why me?"

"That's not for me to explain," the king says. "Nevertheless, I agreed to his plan. But it is his story to tell, not mine."

"I'm Tranar. I belong here. Don't let him take me away again."

The king smiles. "Yes, you're more a Tranar than others who've lived in this country all their lives. You won't return to Onyx. I'll see that it is so." He draws an object from his pocket. Its hilt gleams in the moonlight, the rest covered in leather. He tucks the dagger under my pillow, leans down, and kisses my forehead. "Sleep well."

In another moment he is gone, on his way to the forest no doubt, to *change* and hunt dragons in the frosty, mid-night sky. I lie on the bed, my heart twisting and burrowing deeper inside my shaking chest.

The door creaks open and Patience's shadowy silhouette appears in the doorframe. She approaches my bedside, holding up a yellow candlestick for light. When she sees me, her mouth forms an "O" and she shakes her head sadly. "How are you feeling?"

"Couldn't be better," I say with a growly voice.

She sets the candlestick in a holder by the bed and reaches for the water pitcher to pour me a cup. She hands me the cup with aplomb. As I gulp down the water, she sits next to me on the bed, opens her satchel and removes a dry bit of biscuit and a box of herbs. She sprinkles the herbs on the biscuit and hands it to me. "Eat this. It will help settle your stomach."

I protest—the desire to eat hasn't yet returned—but Patience gives me a look and I cave and nibble on the biscuit without any further fuss. It tastes of ginger and peppermint.

"You saved my life," I whisper after the biscuit is gone. "I owe you a debt."

Patience stares at the ceiling. "You owe me nothing, Elanor."

"Did Count Malandre explain why I took ill?"

"No," she lowers her eyes until they meet mine. "Nobody explains anything."

"I didn't want to involve you. Not like this."

"But I've always been involved." She fiddles with the corner of my blanket, suddenly thoughtful. "Elanor, I need to be honest with you."

"You've always been honest with me."

"No—that's just it. I haven't been. And I'm afraid it's put you in this situation." She stares at the balcony window and lets out a long, sad sigh. "I know you've been hunting dragons. I know that's what you and Count Malandre, the king and Lord Berrel have all been up to."

My jaw drops. "How did you—?"

"I've known about Malandre and King Siles for a long time now." She stares at the floor. "When Malandre asked my father to look out for you, I knew you were someone special. It's why I wanted you to move in with me after Cydra dismissed you."

The hair on the back of my neck stands on end. My eyebrows knit together. "Malandre asked Ryrick to look out for me? When was this?"

"Before you arrived at the castle. We were expecting you. But Elanor—"

"Malandre knew I would be coming?" Adom had said something about hoping I would escape Onyx and find my way back to Trana. But how could he know for certain that I would come to the castle unless...My heart sinks. Unless he had planned it from the beginning.

"Go to a safe place," he had instructed me after he brought me back to Onyx. *"I need to speak with Ona."* Could he have instructed Ona to bring me back to Trana when I was ready to

return? And what about Lord Faigen, who was coincidentally returning from Salcom village at the same time Ona delivered me to Trana? Could that have been a fabrication, too? Had Lord Faigen been instructed to bring me to the castle? But no—that had been my idea. Hadn't it?

Patience puts a hand on my arm. "Elanor. There's more."

"Malandre lied to me," I sound betrayed, even though I don't know why. It isn't as though he hadn't lied before. "He's trying to keep me here, to keep me close."

"I know," she says. "I tried to warn you. But there's something else."

"Why am I even involved in any of this? I should have run to Corva. Or Eppax. Why am I still with him, listening to his lies? Letting him control me." I stare at her with horror. "I've let him hand-select my friends. Berrel is the only real friend I have here."

Patience stands up. Her face looks tight with anger, and the dim shadows somehow make her look inhuman. "You aren't ready to listen." She grabs her satchel and throws open the front. Pulling out a vial, she thumps it down on the nightstand beside me so hard I think it must have broken. "I made this for you. It's dragonsbane—my own concoction. Tip your arrows in it and you can do some real damage." She points to her face. "Aim for the eye." She pulls the satchel over one shoulder, snatches the candlestick, and heads for the door.

As it closes behind her, I stare at the vial in disbelief. If Patience knew about Malandre, why would she leave me with this? Especially after what she just told me? Does she want me to hurt Malandre? But why? I reach for the vial and hold it contemplatively.

Somewhere in the room, a latch comes unhinged. I close my eyes, focusing on breathing normally. Reaching underneath my pillow, I clutch the knife Siles left. Its hilt has many carvings, and from the feel of it a dragon scale decorates its base. My other hand grasps tightly to the vial.

I crack open my eyes. Moonlight illuminates a mirror in the corner, hanging askew. Shadowy darkness replaces the spot on the wall where the mirror once rested. A secret door. Light catches the white from wide, lurking eyes.

My hand closes around the hilt of the knife. The figure appraises the room and spots my form on the bed. It stares, immobile for several seconds. Then it returns to the secret corridor. In moments, the corridor vanishes and the mirror settles into its usual place.

I count twenty heartbeats and then pull myself out of bed. My head swims. So do the contents of my stomach. On impulse, I tuck the vial of Patience's mystery concoction into my shirt. Then, I tiptoe to the mirror.

It looks perfectly ordinary. Did I imagine it all? I fumble with the edges. Using my dagger, I try to pry the mirror from its spot. It won't budge. I reach my hand along the sides of it, running down and underneath, until my fingers find a small ridge along the bottom.

Something clicks. The mirror swings open, and I grab it before it smashes into the wall. The darkness before me draws me in like a black cave. I smile. Caves are my specialty.

I hold the knife out and enter the secret hall. It's cool and damp within, much like Onyx's caves. The smell of mold clings to the air and the floor strips the callouses from the soles of my feet as effectively as pumice. My eyes adjust. I stop and listen to the padded footsteps running down the hall. I venture after the sound. It isn't long before I lose the footfalls. Does the person suspect me? Is someone waiting for me in the shadowy distance?

The hallway turns. My hand trembles. Can I kill if I have to? I doubt it. For all my jokes about murdering dragons, I never lifted a finger against them. It doesn't seem likely, then, that I can lift my finger against my own kind. I lean against the wall, stopping to listen once more. My fingers feel along the wall until they find a hinge. I stifle a gasp. Another secret door.

"No, my lady," says a voice on the other side of the wall. I recognize it as Donja. "She's in his bed. I don't know where the others have gone. If you'd like, I can ask the doorman."

"Yes, please do," answers the syrupy voice of the future queen. "And thank you for your discretion. When I heard from the guards that there was an attempt on the king's life…"

"It's fortunate it was only the servant girl who struck ill."

"Yes," Celeste replies. "It is. Now go."

Silence. I squint at the wall, which I now recognize as the backside of a mirror. Through a small crack in the curtain, I manage to see Donja's back as she exits the room. The lavish surroundings hint that I've stumbled upon Lady Celeste's chambers.

Once Donja is out of the room, the lady calls her guard in. "Grym, we have another problem," she says. "It's that servant girl, Elanor. She's sleeping in the king's quarters."

"You want me to take care of her?" asks the guttural voice I identify as the voice in the watchtower. "Or do you need me to do worse—"

"What is *wrong* with you?" Celeste snaps. "I just need you to bring her to me. The old man won't talk unless I bring her to him, and she's made things complicated with my brother. It's time to use her to Malandre's disadvantage."

"So you want me to kidnap her?" the bulky guard inquires.

I stare at him more intently and feel certain I've seen him before. He was the one at the king's chambers the night Berrel and I met the king together. He was one of the guards who not-so-secretly scorned Lord Faigen the day I came to the castle. And one of the men who nodded me into the castle when I returned from my trip to Miss Harminy's. So, who is this man—Grym—and why is he working with Celeste?

"Not kidnap. She's been poisoned, so we are just borrowing her for a short while."

"And then you want to give her back? After what she knows?"

"From everything our captive told me, I'm certain she'll want to be with us when everything falls apart. But, we need her now to get the information, and after that we can decide what to do with her." Celeste dances toward the mirror. "Take the back way."

Grym bows and struts purposefully toward the secret door. I retreat from the space. At once, a wave of nausea grabs hold of me. I hold onto the wall until the swirling passes. My hand finds the secret door, and I lean against it, panting.

As the spots fade from my vision, I hear a gut-wrenching sound. The *click* of a trapdoor releasing. The support snaps, and my weight falls forward. The world spins off-angle as I tumble onto the floor. Consciousness swirls. The blackness swells and recedes.

An icy lump slides down my throat and settles in my stomach. I open my eyes, fully aware that horrors await. Grym and Celeste crouch over me. I cast a queasy eye toward the door.

Celeste drops to one knee beside me. "Why are you spying on us, Elanor?"

I blow spit her direction. "Why are *you* spying on *me*?"

She leans away and wipes the spit off her cheek with the back of a gloved hand. "Not spying. I heard from Grym here that the king had been poisoned. No one is allowed near his chambers now, so I asked Donja to take the closed-off passageways to find out if Siles was in any danger. You just happened to be in his bed." Her eyes narrow. "*Why* were you in his bed?"

"You know exactly why I was there," I say, careful not to give away anything about the king's condition. "I heard Donja telling you I was poisoned." I point to the heavy-set man. "You were sending him to go kidnap me. What for?"

Celeste lifts her hands in a gesture of surrender. "Stand up and take a seat on the chaise over there. I worry you'll pass out here on the floor. You look like you died and just haven't had the sense to realize it."

I scrunch my face and reject her offer of help when she reaches out to assist me. "I heard you plotting with the guard about a prisoner. And I know you're planning to kill someone. You're no friend of the king, so you're no friend to me."

"You're correct. I'm no friend of the king," she says very solemnly. "I know he's a dragon changeling, same as Malandre. Same as Grym." She nods in the direction of the guard, who has been silent since my appearance in the room.

I push myself to a stand, wobble toward the chaise, and slide into a seat. "If you're no friend of the king, why are you marrying him?"

"It's a necessary sacrifice to secure his assets," Celeste replies. She must have interpreted the look on my face as one of revulsion, because she jumps quickly into an explanation. "He's stolen from the Tranar people. Don't you see? He's a dragon, Elanor. A *dragon* is ruling our country. Eating bread produced by the sweat of farm laborers, living in a castle built on the backs of human workers. Don't you realize how diabolical that is?"

I channel my inner Rhydian and put on my best doubting face. "A dragon? Ha." I clutch my elbows and shrug my shoulders. "Rhydian said everybody in his family was slightly off. I guess the king isn't marrying you for your keen wit."

She casts a resentful eye on me. "There's an army gathered in the northern mountains. We have evidence that Siles is diverting food and weapons away from the Tranar economy. Do you know about the food shortage in the south, or the refugee crisis closer to home? All due to dragon scorchings."

I study Celeste carefully. To my knowledge, Rhydian hasn't told her about his change. It isn't my secret to tell. I feign wide-eyed innocence. "But didn't you hear? Dragons aren't real. You should check in with your brother more, he's very informative on the subject."

"You don't have to pretend. I know all about you, El from Onyx."

I glare at her.

A small dimple forms on her right cheek. "We could be allies in this battle. Even though you are leading my brother around by his nose, the horrible idiot."

"Leading Rhydian around? What makes you think that?" I'm dying to ask what she means by *battle,* but I doubt she'll tell me anything she thinks I don't already know.

"Maids talk. They like extra coins, so whenever they see something out of the ordinary they bring it to my attention. Hoping for a treat." She glances at Grym. "Not him, though. He's in this for other reasons." She signals to the door. "Go and wait for Donja."

Grym moves toward the door, eyeing me up and down with suspicion. "Shout if you need my assistance," he says to Celeste before he exits the room.

She stands at the window and looks out on the forest. "The secret is out. There's a growing number of Tranars who know about the changelings. They had a sibling who changed once, like me. They're a parent to one, like my father. Or maybe they lost their home and family to a scorching. They saw a snarling dragon between the licking flames of a fire. Or the flash of wings." Her eyes sharpen knowingly. "I'm sure you understand why these haunted people come to us thirsty for justice. In any case..." She shrugs, leaving the thought unfinished.

Her words sound eerily familiar. The feel of ash against the soles of my feet as I stumbled through the burning house. The charred remains. The brother who died in my arms. Adom changing and the scattering of white ash as he flapped his wings.

"Aren't you going to say something?" Celeste asks after a minute.

"Yes, actually," I say, my mind scrambling. "I think the

physician was planning to check in on me about now. I should go before my absence arouses any suspicion."

"You aren't going anywhere," she says. "Grym is guarding the door."

"And if I scream?" I ask, my voice a little breathless.

She bats long, silver lashes at me. "Then Grym will come in here and knock your head into the wall until you are silent. He doesn't like shrill noises."

A sinking despair settles on me. *Trapped. Again! And how am I going to get out of this predicament?* Malandre and Siles are both gone, and Patience probably thinks I'm sleeping, and Rhydian doesn't want to have anything to do with me. My mind circles around Grym.

"You said your silent friend was a dragon, too?" When she nods, I cross my arms. "He doesn't look much like a dragon to me. Are you sure you aren't going the way of your sist—"

"Shut up," Celeste snaps. "My sister wasn't crazy. She was poisoned before she could fully change. Grym explained it all to me. That the changelings are like humans until they turn for the first time. All the normal things that kill humans can kill a dormant changeling."

My breath catches before I'm able to hide my reaction. I didn't know this.

Fueled by my unplanned reaction, Celeste smiles crookedly. "The Paradigm is drawing up a manifesto. Once complete, we plan to distribute it all across Trana. Even you must see how that's a good thing. The people need to know about the changelings. They need to know that the myths about dragons aren't just myths. That real danger is living among us."

"If changelings are real and Grym is one of them, why would he help you expose his own kind?" I ask, truly mystified.

"Because he's one of the good ones," she says with devotion. "He believes changelings should be revealed to the public and willingly step down from positions of power. We believe dragons should have no part in Tranar government. They're too powerful. Too manipulative. You've seen the way Count Malandre muscles his own agenda into every decision. As citizens of Trana, they can have it all. Wealth, in the form of dragon scales. Power through fear and intimidation. Special abilities they can use to control."

Only a short while ago I would have joined their cause without hesitation and even with some ferocity. Now? "You can't be serious," I say softly. "No one is going to believe you."

"There are more of us than you think. And we're everywhere." Celeste smiles with a bitter half-turn of her lips. "Grym learned about the king and Count Malandre, through friends he's made at the changeling compound they have set up in the mountains."

"Did you kill Cydra's son?"

The smile fades. "I said we have no interest in killing. I didn't say it was out of the realm of possibility. We have a duty to the crown. Not the one the king has sullied. The human crown."

"Says you and your friend."

She gives me a curious look. "It was you in the watchtower that day, wasn't it?"

"Who's Hunter?"

"She keeps interfering. Grym's been tracking a dragon who blends in with the trees, and the Hunter keeps jumping in, deliberately throwing us off the scent. We believe it's the chameleon who murdered all those lords in the forest. A serial killer. Since we don't have any justice system in place for violent changelings, Grym and I have to work by our own judgment."

"So your plan is to kill the Hunter so you can more easily kill the Tree Hopper?"

"Tree Hopper?" The smile returns. "Is that the technical term for the chameleon? Where did you learn it, Elanor? Was it on the dragon island where Malandre held you captive?"

"You didn't answer my question." Obviously, Celeste

doesn't suspect her brother is the Tree Hopper, or I doubt she'd be trying to kill him. "And while we're on the subject of breaking laws, who are you holding captive?"

"I'll tell you all about our captive in a moment. As for your question? It's called justice." She puts a hand on the foggy window. "Once we catch Hunter and this...Tree Hopper... Paradigm will judge their deeds and punish them accordingly."

"And that's what you're planning to do with the count and the king as well?"

"Precisely."

I don't completely trust Adom and the king, but Celeste strikes a sour chord with me. I can't tell if it is the placid smile on her face or the madness in her eyes, but my instincts tell me she's not being completely truthful. But before I have a chance to pry more answers out of her, the door creaks open again.

Grym steps inside and closes the door. "Donja returned. The doormen report that the king left for the country several hours ago and the count left just prior to that. The guards don't have any information on the count's whereabouts. Do you want me to track him?"

"Leave it." Celeste turns to me. "You want to know who we captured? Right this way."

~ * ~

At first, I fear Celeste and Grym may manage to forcefully escort me right out of the castle doors without raising a single eyebrow. Either the servants don't know about my near-death encounter, or they are too blinded by Celeste's radiance to even notice I'm with her. Where are Cydra or Longley to bark at me as I abandon my duties to abscond with a noble? Where's Patience?

But then, as we reach the bottom of the staircase, a regal young woman with auburn hair, a purple gown, and a face as perfect as a doll's breezes out of a side room with a nobleman

I recognize as Lord Taggart trailing behind her. I remember her from the group of ladies accompanying Celeste the other night. She glances at our party and her eyes brighten.

"Celeste," she says. "Where are you going so early this morning?"

Celeste smiles with ease, ignoring a hulking Grym behind her. It seems as if she's completely oblivious of my presence, too. "Hello, Ora. I'm taking a walk. Siles likes me to take a guard, and I brought a handmaiden for company. I twisted my ankle in the forest not long ago. It was an ordeal. I've learned not to go walking without an escort."

"That's a wonderful idea," Ora says. "The weather is perfect today. Can I come along?"

"I'm sorry," Celeste's smile slips. "I'm not feeling up to company."

"Next time, then," Ora says breezily and begins moving up the stairs.

As she passes me, she stops. Her gaze falls on me curiously. "A new handmaiden, Celeste? Whatever happened to the last one? This one looks dead on her feet."

"Yes, she has many responsibilities," Celeste interjects. She sounds slightly shrill. "If you will excuse us, Ora? Let's plan to meet for lunch later today?"

Ora nods, but her eyes narrow slightly. She glances up the stairs. So do I. Cydra is standing at the top of the stairs, arms crossed, staring at me with abject confusion on her face.

Ora's mouth opens. "Guards!" I hear her shouting and pointing. "Grab her."

Celeste half turns and so does Grym. A host of guards descend on Cydra. That's when I remember that everybody thinks Cydra tried to poison King Siles last night. I don't know for sure if she's guilty, or how Ora knows about it, but now is my chance. I make a run for it.

Grym pulls me back by my neckline. I gasp for air, but no one hears the sound. All eyes are fixed to Cydra's fighting form as the guards wrestle her toward the dungeon. Grym's solid hand presses me toward the exit. I comply, glancing once more behind me.

While everybody else is fixated on the scene with Cydra. Lord Taggart is watching us. He looks distracted, like he's not really watching even though his eyes are on us. Before I have time to signal to him, Grym pushes me forward. I turn a corner and then Taggart is out of sight.

Did Cydra really poison the king? If she did, why was she standing there in the middle of the staircase, watching me? Wouldn't she have run as far as she could—to another country, perhaps? Wouldn't that be logical? Why return looking like she wanted to scold me?

I wait to ask until we are well into the forest, traipsing along under a canopy of maples and elms. "Did you attempt to poison the king last night?"

Celeste and Grym exchange a discreet look. "Of course not. It wouldn't make sense for us to kill him now. We need him and Malandre alive until after the wedding."

"And then, once you're queen, you'll conveniently depose them?"

"Not right away. I need to have his child, first. To have a rightful heir so we aren't challenged by others. After a short while, we would have to remove the king from office, yes."

"Your child could have the disease."

"I'm aware. But as Queen Regent, I could pass laws before my child is of age to take the crown. We could establish ways to adjust to our new reality. By the time any child of mine ascended to the throne, no one will be disputing the existence of dragons. No one will be questioning the problem with changelings. My children will know that if they are changeling, they won't be eligible to serve in politics."

"And you'll be able to happily continue to *serve* in their stead?"

Celeste dips her chin incrementally. "If that's what's

required of me."

We pass the tree, the place I once found Celeste nursing a swollen ankle. Then deeper still into the forest, until the castle is far behind us, shrouded from view.

Grym gets on all fours and crouches low, like an animal.

"Stand back," says Celeste, sidestepping a root. "He's big when he's changed."

I want to tell her I know all about it, but I bite my tongue. I've never seen Adom on the ground like a dog when he changes. Something I'm learning is that the changelings have had to make their own way, alone, because one doesn't talk about being a dragon in polite society.

When he shifts, my smugness dissipates slightly, because at first he is black like midnight, and then his coloring distorts until I can't see him at all. He isn't camouflaged, like the Tree Hopper. He is a...nothing color. The shrubs move around him and dirt rises as he stamps his claws, but there is nothing to see where his body should be.

I reach out and touch him, and feel warm scales vibrating beneath my fingertips.

"Why can't I see him?"

Celeste puts a hand on his side and pats him roughly. "The changelings we know all seem to have independent traits. Grym's dragon armor is a color that can't be perceived by human or dragon eye, except for when he's shifting, he transitions to a black color first. I've heard of a dragon whose scales are literally gold, and there's a hermit who can dig deep into the ground in seconds, like a monstrous mole." She swings up on his invisible back like she's done it a thousand times, and reaches out to me. "I thought *you* were the dragon expert?" she says, and again I'm left wondering how she knows anything about me.

I accept her hand and clamber up Grym's nothingness back until I am settled in front of Celeste, holding tight to his invisible neck. He doesn't have a mane the way Adom does, so it takes greater skill and no small dose of faith the moment he leaps into the sky. All I see below me are trees and brooks and ancient rocks, not a hair or a scale in sight. It is unsettling.

"The changelings choose dragon names that are separate from their human names. Grym goes by *Zero* when he's in this form."

"Do they all choose names?" I ask her, thinking about Slayer and Firebreather. Before, I'd assumed those were code names to keep correspondences discreet.

"Yes," says Celeste. "I don't know why they do it. It is almost like instinct for them to compartmentalize their dragon and human forms. It identifies them to other changelings, too."

No wonder Adom and the king haven't added Grym—Zero—to their list of changelings to uncover. With this incredible ability, he truly is invisible.

It isn't long before we reach the mount, the same one Celeste pointed out to me on the day she injured herself. Grym lands abruptly, which sends me careening through a brambleberry bush. Celeste manages to hold on and slides off his back elegantly.

"This way," she says, flattening her already perfect hair as she rounds the corner. "Come quick. Grym needs to take a moment to assemble himself. He has clothes hidden away."

I follow her with speedy footfalls, not interested in waiting around for Grym to change back into a naked human. On the other side of the mount, ferns cover the entrance to a diminutive cave. I still don't feel like myself, and wish I had another one of Patience's biscuits to consume to keep the nausea at bay. Taking a deep breath, I plunge into the cave's darkness.

Only it is not so dark. I can already see a lantern's light glowing not too far ahead.

"I should warn you," says Celeste. "The man is completely mad. Grym found him in the middle of the sea on a sinking boat. He was escaping the dragon island. And he said he wouldn't talk until we found you and brought you to him."

I race ahead of her and enter the dwelling place. He's seated at a desk, solemnly writing on a piece of parchment, looking dignified with a white wig and fancy clothing. I throw my arms around his neck. "How I've missed you!"

"Clever girl," Muuth chirps, ruffling my hair. He rotates in the chair and smiles up at me. "Look how pretty you are with those nice clothes. You look like one of them."

"You clean up nicely yourself."

"The queen is taking marvelous care of me."

The queen? I glance at Celeste who shrugs and points to her head as if to say he's made up that title for her. "I should hope so. Has she hurt you?"

Muuth's wig goes a little lopsided as he crooks his head to look at me. "What do you mean?" He stares at me with confusion. "My lady, won't you have a seat?"

My smile fades. I can't tell if he's feigning confusion for Celeste's benefit or if his mind has degraded more rapidly in the weeks I've been gone. Is that why he tried to escape Onyx? Did he know his mind was leaving him? I put a tender hand on his knee.

"I brought you the girl you asked for," says Celeste to Muuth. "Like you said, I found her working among my staff, close to the one you call Adom. Now, give me the list."

Muuth stares at me with vacant eyes. "Be a dear and fetch me my stockings, Jamie? My feet are so cold after all this standing."

"It's Elanor," I correct him. He ignores me. Sad, I straighten and regard Celeste. "What information do you need from him?"

"We want names," she says. "Muuth lived on that island for decades. Surely he knows—surely he overheard—the names of other prominent changelings Count Malandre has working for him. Nobles, and wealthy businessmen. Anyone who could have used their abilities to gain power and riches."

Rhydian, I think, but I keep this to myself. "What will you do with the information?"

"That isn't your concern." Celeste's eyes flicker to Grym as the massive guard bends almost in half to enter the small room. "Get him to talk and we won't need to hurt either of you."

"There's another way to save Trana," Muuth coos softly. "Eliminate the dragons."

Grym silently slides his sword out of his sheath and begins inspecting the blade.

I swallow. "Can you give me some time alone with him? I might be able to coax it out of him without others in the room."

Muuth points at Grym. "They are a danger to us. Their *blood* is a danger to us. Nature has given us sun's acid as a way to cull them."

"Let's go," Celeste says to Grym curtly. To me, she says, "We'll be outside."

When it is just Muuth and I, I turn to him suspiciously. "You're riddling them, aren't you? Tell me you know what's going on. That you know who I am."

He offers me a brilliant smile. "Of course I know you, Jamie. I only wish your mother would hurry home from the McCready's house. She spends too much time in the lab these days, not that I'm complaining, but then she's out all evening visiting her pregnant patients." He lets out an ugly, hacking laugh. "It's just you and I these days isn't it, sweetheart?"

"Muuth, I'm Elanor,"

His smile sags. "But Elanor is dead."

"No, I'm not."

"Yes. I saw you die. It was such a shame, you changing like that in the middle of the field. Burning up everything in sight. You murdered that poor family. And then you turned to stone, and I took a chisel and cracked you apart until you were nothing but dust."

I lean against the wall, my breathing shallow and my body quivering. He saw *me* die? No. None of this is the truth. He's just confused. He thinks I'm his daughter. Or he thinks I'm a changeling. Or maybe…maybe his daughter was the changeling.

"What happened to Jamie?"

"She's right here," he says, pointing to me. Then his whole face sags. "No. She's in ground. The fog got her." He winces, and then rocks back and forth. "Oh, Jamie! Oh, Jamie!"

I try a different tactic. "Muuth, would you like to play a game?"

"I adore games," he says earnestly.

"Let's do a riddle."

He nods eagerly. "I love riddles." His wig slips off, revealing a hairless, speckled head.

"We are the ones who feast on fire, who spell with smoke your doom, our ire subdued by the shackles of a human wrist; human names on a hidden list."

Muuth yawns. "That one is easy. You mean the changelings."

"That's not the answer."

"Oh?"

"The names are the answer." I don't want to give Grym and Celeste a list of all the changeling families Muuth might remember. But I don't know what else to do. I don't think I can overcome Celeste and Grym. And if I don't give them *something* they'll probably kill both of us. I'm certain they won't let us go. We could warn the king if she did that.

I don't know enough legitimate names to falsify such a list. Worse, any name I toss out to Celeste could put innocent people in harm's way.

I can only hope that Muuth has sense enough to mislead them somehow while still generating a list that looks believable. There's a part of me that thinks this whole insane act is just that—an act. Muuth hasn't really lost it. He's playing to confuse our enemies.

He points to his head, knocks it like a squirrel cracking a nut. "But I have all the names. The list is right here. I see no reason to share it."

"If I told you a riddle and the answer was water, you wouldn't be satisfied if I said the answer was 'liquid'. It wouldn't count if I'm not specific."

"The twenty-third of Haymonth," he replies.

"What?"

"The dragons will die on the twenty-third of Haymonth."

That's a fortnight from now. I'm stunned to speechlessness. What does he mean *the dragons will die*?

"My turn," he says. "I am a house made of stone and blood, live inside me, keep safe from the sun; live inside me, don't open the door. With one touch I crumble, I am no more." He leans forward, at the edge of his seat. "What's the answer, El?"

I let out a small breath of relief. At least he recognizes me now. "A house of stone and blood?" He nods with gusto. "Could it be a cave?"

He frowns. "Fail."

"The mountain on Onyx Island."

"I thought you were good at this?"

"I'm out of practice. Give me some time to think about it, old man."

He groans his disappointment. "I solved your riddle without fuss."

"No you didn't. You didn't give me the names."

He picks up the parchment on his desk. "Of course I did. They're right here."

My heart slams against my chest. "May I see it?"

"You didn't answer my riddle, El."

I force my mind to focus. A house of stone. I keep thinking of the caves in the mountain on Onyx. But that does make any sense. How would the caves be made of blood? An image of Adom's blood splattered on the floor in the central cave manifests in my mind, and I shudder. What else is made of stone? *"I own a mine where the 'scales' are found in abundance,"* I hear Rhydian's voice in the back of my mind.

Gemstones.

A house of stone.

I bite at my lower lip.

All the changelings were affected during the last sun's acid event. But not all the dragons. Why?

Because the scales—Rhydian's valuable stones—could have protected them from the fog. But when they were exposed in their human skin, they turned to stone. Only the dragons with wounds from the battle died.

"It's the scales," I say thoughtfully. "The changelings could live through the sun's acid fog if they know to change into dragons before the event occurs."

Muuth grins. "Your prize, Lady Malandre." He flaps the parchment in front of me.

I glare at him and snatch the list from his hands. I'm dying to lay it out flat and read through it right here, but Celeste and Grym enter at just that moment.

She holds out a hand. "Thank you, Elanor."

I cling to the list. "I can help you."

"You already have. You're free to go."

"I have the date of the next sun's acid fog. If you'd just let me look at the list—"

"It's the twenty-third of Haymonth," says Celeste.

My shoulders droop. I glance at Grym. "He was listening in, wasn't he?"

"I enjoyed your riddle," he says, a note of humor buried beneath layers of disaffection.

Celeste slides a small letter opener out of her dress pocket. She sidles close to Muuth and lets the tip of the opener slide along his cheekbone. "If you breathe a word of this encounter to King Siles or Count Malandre, Elanor, I'm afraid we'll have to dispose of your friend."

"You'd kill an old man just to keep up this charade of doting fiancée?"

Her face becomes hard, and it is suddenly quite repugnant. "He's not an innocent old man, either. I've heard some of his stories. I know you were kept as a prisoner on that island to keep him from devolving into the dragon-killer again."

Her words spark a recent memory. Hadn't Siles said I was kept on Onyx to keep a monster in check? I'd just assumed he meant Adom. Was he really referring to Muuth?

I hold out the parchment. "I won't say anything. Just leave him be."

Celeste tucks away the letter opener and is suddenly serene and magnanimous as she removes the parchment from my fingers. My spine tingles with disgust.

"I'm sure it will be thrilling reading," I say. "Muuth never knew who specifically was affected by the changeling disorder. It's probably a list of surnames, and you'll have to track down the families and determine for yourself who is changeling and who is human."

She bobs her head. "Grym and I are prepared to do that hard work."

"You might want to pause your efforts against Hunter and the Tree Hopper—"

"—we're calling it Chameleon."

"Well, you might want to stop trying to kill changelings before you know who it is you're actually pursuing. There's one surname I know with certainty will be on that list."

"And what's that name?"

"Berrel."

Her eyes go glassy. She stares beyond me for a tense moment. "Are you implying something?"

"Yes." I cast one last look at my aging friend. "I'll see you shortly, Muuth."

"Don't go out into the sun today, Jamie," he replies, waving. And then I make my exit.

I walk along the perimeter of a whooshing brook, hoping

it will take me back to the castle. I know I'm traveling in the general direction, Still, Grym's brief flight to the mount where they are keeping Muuth could take much longer on foot.

Leaves crunch beneath my feet as I stride forward, hoping I don't stumble upon a bear. I have a knife and the vial of poison Patience left me, but I don't know what good that will do me unless a beast comes close enough to bite. Then again, if that happens, I'll be thankful to have *any* weapons.

I hesitate mid-step, wrestling with mixed emotions. If I go to Siles and Adom and tell them what I know, the king will cancel the wedding immediately and send out guards. But that could be too late to save Muuth. Rhydian could be arrested, too. I'd swear he had no involvement, but he's a changeling with a sister who's working against the king and another who could be back from the dead, seeking revenge. It doesn't look good for Rhydian.

What I know for sure is this: Grym is *not* either of the dragons they are looking for. Though Cinderrider is black, and so was Grym at first, Celeste said Grym can't be perceived by either human or dragon after he transitioned. He can't be Cinderrider. That means he's not one of the rogues burning down villages, murdering farmers and nobles in the woods.

I also know the date of the sun's acid event. The twenty-third of Haymonth. The day after the wedding. Was that one of the things I'm not supposed to tell Siles and Adom? My stomach sinks. With Grym's ability, I'll never know for sure if he's listening or not. If I'm not certain it is safe to share, I shouldn't say anything. Muuth's life hangs on the line. But Adom, Siles and Rhydian are also in danger. If I can't tell them that another sun's acid is coming in a fortnight, they won't be prepared. They could be caught up in the fog and turn to stone. My stomach rolls. No matter what I do, someone will be in jeopardy.

Can I free Muuth myself? Somehow, I doubt it. Celeste

and Grym wouldn't have brought me to him if they weren't reasonably confident they could keep him. The more I think about it, the more convinced I am that Grym will be attached to me like sap on a tree from now on. He could even be following me this moment. I glance over my shoulder. The hairs at the back of my neck prick up. There's just no way be certain he's not.

Hours later, and the castle still isn't in sight. I'm convinced I'm going the right direction, but in the dense forest there are no obvious visual cues to give me guidance or comfort. I settle into a break-neck pace, nervous about what Adom and Siles will do if they find me missing. They'll ply me for information, and I've never been wonderful at lying.

Then I hear the rustling. The branches cackle and moan, and only steps beside me something explodes from a shrub. The *something* looks large enough to be a bear; my throat sinks to my knees. No. Bigger. I reach for my knife as gnarled wings unfold high above.

"I don't want to hurt you," I say quickly, and on instinct my words are in dragon tongue.

The dragon freezes. It looms over me, three times my size, and then it cranes its neck into a sort of curly-cue and bends abnormally until it is eye level with me. Its deep purple scales click and clink like fine dishware clattering in Longley's kitchen. Cat-like eyes measure me, intense and unreadable. The stare is simultaneously bright as if pleased and…disapproving.

"Who are you?" I ask boldly.

The dragon growls, and my confidence falters. I take a step back. It bounds over me, barely missing my head with its hind claws by several inches. Then it is gone, dodging between two trees and out of sight. Why didn't it talk to me? Why didn't it scorch me? My toes itch to follow it, to warn him or her of the danger he was in, but then again I don't know if this is Lord Darton's killer, the creature who burned Lord Faigen. Some people don't deserve to be saved.

That sounds like Celeste's thinking. Like Muuth's thinking. Like Adom, Siles, and Rhydian's father. Am I going to assume the worst of this dragon, this person, before I've ever met him or her? Maybe it's a changeling like Rhydian, confused and in denial. It isn't my job to judge. I start after the dragon.

Whoosh. The dragon reemerges from the shadows and circles me. I step away. There's something in its mouth. I wish Celeste had at least equipped me with a lantern. The dragon leans forward and nuzzles me on the shoulder. The thing it carries falls into my open arms.

I accept the bag and after seconds of the dragon staring intently at me, I open it. Instead, I find four objects. A bow. A quiver and arrows. A dress altered so that it ends in pants. A tin that is no doubt filled with medicines and herbs. I look up.

"Patience."

And then she changes.

THIRTEEN

Hunter

I FELT AWFUL THE moment I left you, but then that Lord Taggart needed me again and by the time I went back to the room you were gone," says Patience, hugging her knees together as we sit by the brook and nibble on a tin of ginger mint biscuits. "I shouldn't have stomped away like that. It was not..." She lowers her head. "It was not professional."

Her words and her mournful expression are so pathetic I can't help the bubble of laughter that escapes my throat. I slap a hand over my mouth, instantly embarrassed.

She glowers at me. "What?"

"You don't have to be professional with me, Patience. We're friends. You had something...*incredible* to tell me and I wasn't listening. I'm sorry for being such a dunderhead."

"And I'm sorry for not telling you straightaway. Especially after I demanded honesty from you."

"It's not exactly easy to say, *I'm an incredible healer during the day, and an amazing swordsman in the evening, and in my spare time I'm a clever hunter and oh, also, I'm a dragon.*"

"You really think I'm all those things?" She lifts her head, laughing. Then shakes her head in wonderment. "You are taking this much better than I had imagined."

"Does Ryrick know?" I ask.

She plants her chin on her knees. "Of course he knows. Ryrick knows everything."

My cheerful mood dissolves into gloom. "It isn't the most shocking revelation of the past two days." My eyes dart nervously over my shoulder, peering into the foliage. Grym is out there, somewhere, watching. Is he with me now? Does he now know about Patience? My heart turns to ice. If Patience is in danger because of me, I have to warn her. Even if it means risking Muuth's life.

"There's no one out there," she says, as if reading my mind. "You're safe."

I turn back to her. "How do you know?"

She taps at her nose. "All dragons have a keen sense of smell but mine is better than most. I think all changelings have a unique ability, and mine is tracking." She smiles. "That's how I found you. I panicked when you weren't in the king's chambers when I went looking for you. So I followed my nose and found you'd gone through a secret entrance and came out at Lady Celeste's bedroom."

"So you use your sense of smell to track?"

"Yes. It's almost like a second vision. I can smell a single raindrop over there, on the third leaf, second branch of that tree. There's a rabbit in an underground burrow directly to your left."

"Can you smell dragons?"

"They have a scent like mildew and wet springs and clay. It is very pungent. I can smell them from a mile away." She looks at me curiously. "Is there a particular dragon you're afraid of?"

"I'm not afraid of dragons," I say. "But there's one who's threatening the life of a friend. He's working with Lady Celeste, and the two plan to unseat King Siles and Count Malandre." Saying all this aloud makes me feel like I am betraying the king and Adom, until I remind myself that I haven't said anything that gives them away as changelings. I trust Patience, but I wouldn't share their secret.

"It's Grym, isn't it?" Patience asks.

"How do you know?"

"They were together the day Lady Celeste injured herself in the forest. I can smell changelings even in their human form, so I've known about Grym for a long while. But the way he acted when she was hurt...it was like she'd been stabbed instead of just twisting an ankle. And then he keeps following around other changelings, like he intends them harm when they don't even know he's there."

"Wait—you can smell other changelings? In their human form? And you can smell Grym even though he's invisible?" Adom said it couldn't be done. That he couldn't detect a difference between changeling and human. If he knew what Patience could do, he'd be insistent on using her for his mission.

She gives me an anxious look, then takes a biscuit and nibbles on it carefully.

"You can trust me, Patience. I won't tell."

"The simple answer is 'yes.'"

"How many are there? How many have you come across?"

"In the castle or in the city?"

"Both," I say, pulse racing. If Patience knows the names of all the changelings, we could warn them before the sun's acid event happens. We could at least give them a chance to protect themselves. Then I'd have a list for Adom, too. My mission would be complete. I could go free.

"Twelve in the castle. Ninety-four in the city."

I blow out air. "That's more than I could have imagined."

"There might be more. I can't track them if they're dormant."

"Dormant? What do you mean?"

"If they haven't yet transformed, their smell is different. They smell human."

"If you know about Malandre and the king, why didn't you ever say anything?"

She rolls her eyes. "You know as well as I do why I kept silent. They're nobles. Politicians. They use everyone around them for their own gain. It isn't my business to tell the secrets of others."

"But that's why you warned me about them?"

"Yes."

"And Berrel, too?"

Her eyes widen slightly. "You know about him?"

"It's a recent discovery."

"Does *he* know about him?"

"Yes. But he's struggling."

She puts her hand over mine. "I was so worried about you. I've been tracking him for months now, and in his dragon form he can be incredibly violent. He attacked me the first time I encountered him. I was afraid that maybe he was the murderer. It wouldn't have been his fault. It can feel like a dream-state, and the denial can make a changeling more destructive in their dragon form."

"You thought he might change and kill me?"

She nods. "Hence the lessons."

I reveal the vial. "And the dragonsbane you gave me?"

Her eyes brighten. "It won't kill. I tried it on myself."

"All this time you've been trying to protect me?"

"I even followed you and Berrel when you went to see Harminy. I was so afraid something might happen, that she would trigger something in Berrel, and then he just left you in the middle of that dangerous street so I followed you back to the castle to make sure you were safe."

I don't know how it happens, but my arms stretch out on their own accord and suddenly I am hugging her. I've not hugged anyone but Muuth in years. "No one's ever gone out of their way to look out for me before. Not like this."

Patience turns pink. "I failed one friend, once, and it was devastating."

I start to ask what she means by that, but then something else she said strikes a bell in my head. "Wait. Why would Harminy trigger something in Berrel?"

She frowns. "I thought you knew."

"What?"

"Harminy's the white one. The one they're calling Leviathan."

My heart thumps wildly in my chest. "Leviathan's a

murderer," I say. "She's the one scorching villages across Trana." I cover my mouth. "She's Faigen's cousin."

Patience pales. "I didn't know they were related."

"She could be the one who scorched him," I say, voice breathless. "She could be the one scorching them all." My mind races. "She *lied* to Rhydian about his sister, Siren. She made him think Siren was alive. Why would she do that?"

A massive shadow blots out the sinking sun. Patience hops up and tilts her head toward the sky. "Cinderrider," she breathes softly. "It's headed north-east."

Toward the changeling compound. I realize, and a chill starts up my spine. "Do you know who it is?"

"No, I've never caught the scent in human company."

"Do you suppose it could be a real dragon?" I say, in hushed tones. "Not a changeling?"

"Maybe. Only Leviathan knows."

"Can we follow it? Find out where it's going?" As I ask the question, I wonder if Patience will protest. Does she think I'm not strong enough? Is she afraid of what I'll see?

She crooks her head to study me. Then she gestures to the bag. "Dip the arrows with the poison. You need to be prepared to shoot at a moment's notice. Meanwhile, I'll go and change."

Moments after I dip the arrows into the dragonsbane and return them to the quiver, Patience returns and changes into the purple-speckled, long-necked dragon again. I spring up her back and in moments we are sailing over the forest. We cut through the sky. The sun, soaking in its pink and amber brine, emerges from the clouds. I can see Cinderrider moving in spirals, flying first with wings facing the heavens and then rotating around so it's wings are pointed toward the ground. It looks like it is enjoying itself. I feel the same way, clutching tight to Patience, the wind battering my face and hair. It is chilly but I'm so exhilarated by the dips and swoops, and Hunter's warm scales beneath me keep me toasty the same way coals do. I scan the skies for Adom or Siles.

Another curving form ripples in like an *S* around Cinderrider, and the two pause to greet each other by touching tails. It is Leviathan, as crystalline as a diamond with a center as white as snow. She glitters brilliantly, and now I know why she only emerges at night. During the day, , Leviathan is magnetic, not difficult to spot in the sky. While Cinderrider moves like a shadow, Leviathan is like a gemstone. Dazzling. It's hard to believe that she is the same woman Rhydian and I met only the other day. And with her easy access to dragon scales, why was she struggling to make ends meet? Was she really the one who burned Faigen?

We soar over a mountain, and then another. The air is chillier here, and I'm not exactly dressed for the weather. I wrap my arms around Patience's purple-speckled neck.

"If we get any closer, they'll see us," she says in dragon tongue.

"What do you suppose they're doing?"

"I don't know, but that's the dragon compound over there," she crooks her head slightly to the right. "I don't know what kind of abilities those changelings might have, and I don't want to be identified."

"Okay," I agree. "Let's go back."

As Patience flips her wings to do a hard turn, Cinderrider flies over the compound. It lets out a horrific screech, like the belt of a lion and the hiss of an attacking cobra. It swoops lower, then puffs out its chest and blasts the compound with a generous spray of fire. In seconds, the entire community is engulfed in flames. Changeling dragons emerge from the blast like corn kernels over an open flame.

My jaw drops. "What did it just do?"

Patience lets out a creaky groan. "There were humans in that compound. Children."

Images of the laughing faces of Odeba's family sear my mind. "Why would it…?"

And then Adom appears from the northern mountains. The sky is thick with writhing dragon bodies and swirling, black smoke. It is chaos. The confusion, the bellowing of dragon kin, the screams of their human relatives down below. It all settles in my stomach like a greasy lump. Adom was right. Cinderrider and Leviathan are the real monsters.

Leviathan spits out a stream of smoky liquid, and moments later the screams subside. The smoke clears. The entire village is coated in a layer of ice, its inhabitants frozen in screams of pain and terror. Adom shoots toward Leviathan while Cinderrider is tackled by an army of enraged changelings. Patience dips behind a mountain for cover.

"We can't leave," I whisper. "All those people they murdered."

"Get out your bow and arrow," says Patience in dragon tongue. "We are going to end them."

I grab hold of an arrow and tug the bow from my back. Patience dives into the melee, neatly dodging knife-like teeth and the swipe of angry claws. We surge forward as one, targeting Leviathan—Harminy— who is already engaged in a fierce battle with Adom.

She digs her claws into his scales, popping them off his flesh in countless numbers. Her teeth sink into his neck, and she rips a chunk of skin and mane. He heals quickly, the scales growing rapidly to replace his broken armor. But Leviathan is fast and strong.

Adom slams her into the side of a mountain, causing a crater-like hole and an avalanche that crushes two dragons below them. She spews liquid ice into his face. He careens back and topples into a range of trees. Leviathan bounds for him, teeth out and drooling, aiming for his neck.

Patience swoops in, blasting heat at Leviathan's wings. The white dragon crashes into a rock, temporarily crippled. Patience drops and sets foot on the ground, eye level with the enemy dragon. Her long neck weaves back and forth like a cobra about to strike.

"I thought you were neutral," Leviathan roars in dragon tongue.

"Why would you do this?" Patience demands.

"He's breeding an army."

"There were children in that compound," I scream. "Human children."

"They would kill us, if they had the chance. Humans are beasts."

"Elanor," says Patience, voice trembling. "Shoot her."

I take aim, but my resolve weakens. I'm not a killer. I'm not like Muuth, or Adom. I thought I could kill without flinching. It isn't so.

Smoke billows from Leviathan's nostrils. "You think an arrow will stop me?" She growls, crawls up, looms over us. Her wings jet out, fully healed. She spits and hisses.

Patience jumps onto her hind feet, knocking me off her back. My body tumbles backward, my fall caught by the overgrowth of ferns below. The arrow and bow fly out of my hands. I leap to my feet, but it is too late. Patience swings her tail deliberately, knocking me out of the way just as Leviathan propels another stream of smoky liquid.

Patience takes the full torrent. Her body stiffens, encased with steaming crystals. She's frozen, trapped beneath layers of ice. "No!" I mouth, dragging myself up one more time.

Leviathan's snout shifts toward Adom. She slithers his direction. I grab the bow, draw another arrow and climb a large rock beside Patience. If I hadn't hesitated, she wouldn't have been hurt. The poison-dipped arrow won't kill Leviathan, so why did I wait?

I grit my teeth. I won't this time around. I can't look at Patience, too afraid she is gone, like the villagers. I take aim upward, suck in a breath, and say a quick prayer.

Zing. The arrow flies true and strikes Leviathan in her

glassy blue eye. Her responding cry is fizzling with outrage and murderous promises. She cranes her neck, searching for me. Then, when she sees me, she snaps the arrow in two with a claw. Part of the arrow is embedded, a wooden shard in her orb. She tries to move forward but suddenly seems to lose focus. Her limbs wobble like blood pudding. Every step shakes the ground around me.

Adom lumbers up and stalks toward a confused Leviathan. She stares up at him, wide-eyed and frightened, and then her pupils roll up into her head. As the poison seeps into her bloodstream, Adom takes a hard swipe at her neck. Her head snaps off with a sickening crunch. It lands at Patience's feet, tongue lolling and one half-open eye fixed unsettlingly on me.

From not far off, Cinderrider roars the sound of a hurricane screaming at the mountain of Onyx. I whip my head around to aim at it with another arrow from my quiver. Cinderrider pulls back its head and shoots forward like a deadly snake, mouth fully open, a stream of molten fire flowing directly at me. The heat wave hits me before the flame, singeing off my eyebrows. Seconds before the inferno's barrage, another figure springs out in front of me, blocking me from the explosion. A nimble dragon colored like the bark and leaves of a tree. Rhydian.

But there's no time for a reunion. Cinderrider is after him now, talons raised while the other dragons work to keep up. Some have already retreated to other mountains. Others are diving into the devastated village, attempting to pull out the frosty human statues, to try and revive them. Cinderrider has wounded a number of the changelings, who are resting along the sides of the mountain with broken tails, fried wings, and huge bloody gashes in their midsections and necks. They will recover, but Cinderrider is clearly an alpha. It's bigger than any of the other dragons on the battlefield, larger than Adom and Patience combined. Almost as tall as the castle. With that molten fire blast, the others are just no match.

Adom lands with a heavy *thunk* at my side. He *changes* into a human and whirls on me. "What are you thinking?" he demands. "Why are you here? It's not safe." His body is burned, black scorch marks and dirt over pink, healing skin. His hair is wild, and for the first time since I've known him so are his eyes.

I gesture at Leviathan's head. "I had to help. She would have killed you."

He nods toward Patience. "You came with her. Who is she?"

I point to Cinderrider, engaged in battle with Rhydian. "The more important question is who is *that* dragon? And why aren't you helping the Tree Hopper?"

"Who is he?" His mouth curves up but I can't tell if it's a smile or a look of disgust.

"He protected me. That's all you need to know. Please help him."

Adom bows. "As you wish." Then he charges and changes in one sweeping jump.

I glance up at Patience, and to my relief, she's thawing out. She blinks and filmy icicles drop like scales from her eyes. She shakes her head, and her neck winds back and forth going the opposite direction of her head, scattering slushy liquid everywhere. She sees me and drapes a wing the size of a cloak over my shoulder, a gesture of assurance. "It's fine."

"I thought she killed you." My eyes cloud over with tears.

"I knew she wouldn't." Patience withdraws her wing and steps over Leviathan's head. She sniffs at the dead dragon's eye. "A perfect shot," she rumbles.

"I had a good teacher."

"Care to try again?" she asks, nodding to Cinderrider. "She's running out of time."

"She?" I stare at the ferocious alpha, swiping Adom with quick loops and spinning circles around Rhydian. The female dragons of Onyx weren't much compared to this.

"Now that we're close, it's obvious that she's a female."

"Can you tell who it is?"

"The scent is still unfamiliar. Although, I think I caught a whiff of it on Faigen."

"Harminy said Faigen was with Siren just before he was burned."

"But she lied, didn't she? And how can you trust her?"

I climb onto Patience's back. It's a good thing we're far enough away from the castle that no one could possibly see what's happening here. I suppose this is one reason Adom and Siles selected this spot for the changeling camp. "If you don't recognize the scent, it could be her."

"Maybe," she agrees, launching into the cloudy sky.

Cinderrider smacks Rhydian aside with her tail as easily as if he were a fly. She chomps Adom's neck and hangs on, bones cracking beneath her jaws. Rhydian rams into her claw and her hold on Adom loosens, allowing him to retreat to the mountaintop to recover, his head drooping onto his chest at an awkward angle.

Rhydian tries to engage her with a slash to her left wing, but she ignores him and comes after us. My heart shudders and then stills. Cold washes over me. Patience lifts herself onto her hind legs and swipes at the incoming Cinderrider. But Cinderrider swoops over Patience in the last second. Her sharp claws stretch out and clasp me. Her talons puncture my shoulder.

She lifts me up and away from Patience's neck. Bile creeps up my throat. I fumble for my bow, but the nails in my shoulders make my arms flop lifelessly, incapable of movement. I crunch my midsection, swinging my legs up over my head to kick at the dragon's claws. She tightens her grip, ripping craters into my muscles. Excruciating pain ripples up and down my skin.

To my left, Adom is coming at me. To my right, Patience. Alongside us, Rhydian flies, hissing and swiping but not doing much damage at his angle and with his smaller size. In fact, none of them are. Where are the firestorms? The ramming heads? The swiping claws? My stomach sinks. She's using me. She's using me as her shield.

No. I am not a victim. I don't need them to protect me. *I will not be used ever again.*

I take in a breath, crunch my midsection again, and pull up my legs. Locking my ankles around the back of her claws, I pull. Pain lances through me, but my groan is drowned out by the wind. I pull again, pressing against a pressure point I know is there. Reflexively, her talons loosen. I yank myself free and flip, then wrap my body around her talon. I'm trembling, my shoulders shredded and bleeding profusely. But as Cinderrider screams and kicks and twists to knock me loose, I hang on tight.

I still have my bow, draped around my shoulder, but when I open the quiver one arrow remains. The rest must have tumbled out when I flipped. I clench it with my teeth, cross my knees, and lock them around her leg. Then I begin to climb up Cinderrider's body.

She's clearly distracted and bothered by my presence, but Patience, Adom, and Rhydian have her cornered. She's headed toward another mountain range, the centermost mountain steaming and rumbling. I know what kind of mountain this one is. A volcano.

As I crawl up her back, using loose and damaged scales as footholds to balance myself, I see a dragon emerge from behind the volcano, headed straight for us. Then another. And another. I recognize one of them. My heart stills. It's Ona. And at the front, there is a dragon with great horns on its head, like antlers, and its body is black but somehow transparent so I can see glowing red every time it breathes, every time the scales split away just enough to reveal the cavern of lava within.

Its eyes are red and monstrous, and black curls of smoke pour out if its nose and mouth. His wings are coated in steel, like knives, glinting against the afternoon sun. A gold rope is tied to its hind foot, and a green satin bag swings on in, tightly secured.

Even Cinderrider stops when she sees him—maybe not just him alone, but the vast number of dragons following behind him. She flaps frantically, looking for a way out. But if she goes forward, she'll have to battle the horned dragon and all the ones behind him. If she turns, she has Patience, Adom, and Rhydian to contend with. I glance over my shoulder. The changelings from the compound are behind us, snorting and growling and itching for a chance to swipe.

I pull myself up her neck and point the poisoned arrow at her eye. "Surrender now, and they'll show you mercy. Fight, and they will kill you like they killed Leviathan."

Her eye swivels, then focuses in on me. On the arrow aimed at her eye.

Slowly, we begin to lose altitude. In moments, we drop below the tree line. Then, her claws crash against the ground. Dust rises. I sneeze, nearly catching her eye with my arrow.

I slide down her neck and hop off, racing away quickly. Every movement induces pain in my shoulders, but I am used to pain and it will lessen with time. It always does.

Patience lands, and I go over to stand beside her. Adom hits the ground, then Rhydian. The others soon arrive and surround us, changelings to the south, dragons to the north. And the big horned dragon breaks free from the others and joins our inner circle. He changes first.

King Siles. He is as regal in his nakedness as he is with all the royal adornments. In moments, he reaches into then bag that had been tied around his leg when he was a dragon and withdraws a purple robe, the kind that he drops over his head and billows out like a fabric balloon around him. A gold insignia of an open-mouthed dragon is stitched into the front.

So. That was Fire Breather. I let out a small noise of appreciation. No wonder Adom listens to him.

Slayer changes into Adom next. The king hands him a

similar robe, only this one is black with an orange house crest on it. Adom dresses quickly. Hunter and Chameleon, who only I know are really Patience and Rhydian, don't change. They must still have fears about Malandre and Siles using the knowledge to their advantage.

"Show yourself," King Siles orders Cinderrider. "You're trapped."

"I'd rather die," Cinderrider snaps, flecks of spit flying from her snout.

"This could have ended differently," Adom says, his voice sad. "We want to *help* changelings. To help *you*. But you destroyed their compound. They'll demand blood for blood."

"Then my debt is paid," answers Cinderrider. Her eyes glitter. "Blood for blood."

Adom frowns. "What debt?"

In response, Cinderrider looks to Rhydian. "You side with *him*? After all he's done to us? Left your sister for dead, stolen your seat at the king's table?" Her nails click together. "You and the king. This was how it was orchestrated. How the queen—and her lady in waiting designed it. You were meant to be so much more than the estranged son of a murderer."

King Siles squints at the ground, puzzling it out. "My mother...?"

"Made you who you are," Cinderrider replies. "She lived a normal life, died a normal death. Except for the day when she thought she would lose you. That's when she called on my mother to find Jetarna. To make her perform her magic over your mother's swollen belly so that you would live."

"Let's talk as humans," Adom says.

Rhydian growls deep in the back of his throat. Something about it causes the hairs on the back of my neck to rise. He knows something. I'm sure of it.

"And when Jetarna performed her spell, she was paid well. And my mother was paid with a promise. That my family would forever be bound to yours. That her children would be protected."

Rhydian creeps forward, head bent, tail slithering like a snake behind him. "Change."

"I can't," she says, and there is a sad note to her voice. "I have lost my human."

"If you can't change, then you're only a dragon," says Adom. He nods to the stony beasts flanking King Siles. "The dragons of Onyx have come to take you."

"There must be blood," snarls one of the changelings. "She must be punished for the murders."

"She will be," answers Adom. He glances at me. "But not here. Not in this moment."

"I won't be taken prisoner," she hisses, backing away. "I'll fight."

Patience lowers her head to my ear. "Elanor," she breathes. "The arrow."

"I can't," I whisper. "She damaged my shoulders. I don't think I have enough strength." Gingerly, I unhook the bow from my aching shoulder and nock my last arrow. I pull back with tentative movements, but it is not enough. Despair swirls in my gut.

"I was made for you, King Siles," Cinderrider says. "My love for a traitor ruined it, ruined our family." She lurches forward, attacking Adom in his vulnerable human form.

In seconds, he changes and raises his claws to block her blow. Rhydian leaps between them, and Adom's talons sink into his side. Rhydian throws back his head and howls.

Human hands grab the arrow and bow from my hands. I stare, astonished, as Patience nocks the arrow, draws back the bow until the shaft of the arrow touches her ear. She's human. She risked everything—her freedom—to help me end this. Disbelief and admiration alight in my chest.

Patience lets the arrow fly. Cinderrider moves, and for a

second I don't think it will hit her. But then she moves again to push Rhydian out of the way, and the arrow lands in her pupil, sinking in all the way up to the shaft. A river of blood pours down her cheekbone.

Rhydian's head swivels my direction. He changes and stares at me, long and hard. "It's Siren," he says. "And with that arrow, you've chosen your side."

Patience and I exchange glances. She shot the arrow, but he was obviously talking to me. He blames me. My stomach drops, and I can't help the tears that spring to my eyes.

Rhydian clambers up Cinderrider's back as she thrashes and snarls. He hobbles across her neck and reaches for the shaft poking out of her eye. Inch by agonizing inch, he pulls it from her. The whole time, he coos and whispers words of comfort, rubbing his free hand along her jawline.

By the time the arrow is out, Cinderrider is on the ground, collapsed. As Rhydian slides away from her, she begins to change. Underneath the hideous form, the scales like black coals, the golden eyes and talons like swords, there is only a woman. A small, jet-haired woman with a frame so delicate I'm certain I could break her in half by accidentally stepping on her. Her hair is so long it hangs to her knees, and it shrouds her body like silk mourning garb. She lifts her head and I see now what Patience's arrow has done—gouged out the eye of that ethereal being. Siren lets out a soft whimper.

Rhydian rotates around, staring unfocused at the dragons in our midst. "Clothes. She needs clothes." To Adom he says, "Avert your eyes."

Patience tugs on the bag I'm still carrying. "I have an extra dress she can wear." I untangle the bag from my shoulder and we both approach the Berrel siblings cautiously.

Rhydian's accusatory eye settles on me. "Not you."

Patience holds out a hand. "I can help heal her eye, my lord."

A muscle moves in his jaw. "She's a damned dragon. She

doesn't need your help."

At the word *dragon*, Siren begins ferociously scratching her skin, leaving long red marks across the pale white. She screams and beats herself with dirty fists, convulsing wildly. Her black hair collects leaves and twigs as she crawls across the ground, moving toward Siles and Adom.

"No," she moans. "No, I'm not a human. I'm not a human. I'm not."

My gaze shifts to Adom. I can't help but wonder how he feels seeing Siren, the woman he loved—maybe still loves—like this. But I see nothing on his face except the same, unreadable expression.

"I'm a dragon," she insists. "Not this weak thing. Tell me Siles. Tell me it's true."

When the king doesn't answer, she wails. The dragons of Onyx close in on her. Rhydian changes, but he is no match for the entire dragon herd. It takes only a matter of moments. Then they leave, each one trailing after the other like a flock of geese. At the head, Ona flies into the dawn. In his talons, he clutches Siren's defeated form, blowing back and forth as it surrenders to the wind. Rhydian flies limply, severely wounded, behind them.

~ * ~

After it is all over, Patience stays behind to help the changeling dragons with their injuries and assist as many human survivors as she can. Adom patches me up with stitches and splints to keep my shoulders straight. He carries me near to the castle in his claws while the King stays on to communicate a new plan with the remaining changelings. When we're a safe distance away, Adom changes again and we walk the rest of the way back.

When we arrive at the castle, there's a commotion at the front gates. Ryrick is there, and so is Princess Ora. The guards are standing close by, waiting. The captain of the guards takes Adom and I aside so we aren't overheard by the others.

"Count Malandre," says the captain of the guards. "Where is King Siles? We need to speak with him immediately. We thought you were with him?" His eyes fall on me, and I'm sure I look a sight covered in blood and bandages and the splint. He looks away, quickly.

"What's wrong?" Adom asks, not answering the question about Siles' whereabouts.

"We apprehended the individual responsible for poisoning your food."

Adom sighs. "You found Cydra. That's a relief."

The guard frowns. "No, my lord. It wasn't Cydra."

"Then who—?" Adom freezes. Understanding dawns on his face. "It was Lady Celeste."

"She swears she didn't do it, but we found this in her chambers." The guard pulls out a bag and hands it to Adom. He takes it, opens it, and sniffs it. "Princess Ora has more information. She's the one who reported the strange activities Lady Celeste was involved in."

Adom raises an eyebrow. "Such as?"

Even though we are far enough away from the crowd that we can't be overheard, the guard lowers his voice. "The princess noticed Lady Celeste acting oddly this morning. She followed the lady into the woods. She was with one of the guards and…" he glances at me again. "When they didn't return after lunch, Princess Ora reported it and I ordered a search of the woods. We found a cave." The guard shakes his head. "She was torturing an old man there, sir."

I glance at Adom and see him nodding, eyes wide with disbelief.

"We apprehended her, but we couldn't find the guard or the handmaiden she was with. Then, when we searched her room, we found this vial of poison among her things."

"The old man?" I ask, breathless. "Is he all right?"

The guard bobs his head. "We paid him a large sum to keep quiet and then we sent him along his way. There are guards with the lady now, trying to get information from her."

Adom moves forward as if he's forgotten me and the guards lead him toward the dungeon, speaking to the guards in low, urgent whispers. I hesitate and then decide that I don't want to follow them, that I'd much rather fill Ryrick in on the details of my day and let him know that Patience is safe and will be back home soon.

Ryrick makes eye contact with me and the two of us start toward each other. But moments before I reach him, Princess Ora steps between us.

"I knew something was wrong this morning," she says. "I thought when I heard the news about the old man that maybe she had killed you." She stares at my shoulders. "Did she do that to you? Why? Was it for pleasure?" She grimaces. "Celeste liked pain, even in Academy."

I can't help but wonder what dark memories Princess Ora must be harboring to merit that comment. Instead of answering her question directly, I say, "Thank you for following us."

She takes a moment to respond. "I do have a request to make of you."

"What's that?"

She reaches into a satchel and removes a piece of parchment. She holds it out, but doesn't let go of it when I reach for it. "I suspect this list of names is valuable to you? The old man said it would be. He asked me to give it to you before he left."

My breath hitches. "Yes. Yes, it is."

Ora smiles slowly. "Under one condition."

"Anything," I gasp.

She steps forward as if embracing me in a hug. "Celeste didn't put poison into the king's cake. The evidence was planted in her room. Someone wanted her away for good."

Suddenly, I can't breathe. "Excuse me?" I rasp.

Princess Ora releases the parchment. "You take that list and give it to the right person," she says softly. "We'll speak more about this at a different time."

I take the list and give it to Adom as soon as I find him, but I'm not sure what to make of my conversation with Princess Ora. Maybe she's a dragon changeling. Maybe she's a member of Paradigm. Then again, maybe she's just in love with King Siles and is relieved that Celeste is out of the picture.

When the king returns, we lock ourselves away to begin the long debriefing process. I tell them about Celeste's duplicity and how she and Grym had been holding Muuth inside a cave near the castle. I fill them in on Muuth's warning, that there may be a sun's acid fog on the twenty-third of Haymonth. And of course, we discuss the list of names at length. It isn't complete, and most of the names we already know about. But there are one or two leads that Adom and Siles plan to follow up on, a few potential changelings.

Some days after the scorching, with my shoulders beginning to heal thanks to the salve Ryrick helps me apply and the stretches that Longley insists I do every day before coming to work, I find a gift box on my bed. When I open it, there is a chainmail vest, only instead of metal it is made of purple-speckled dragon scales. My heart swells. It is the same vest Patience was working on all those weeks ago. I'd presumed she found the scales in the forest and had been making the vest for her hunting trips. Now I know the scales are hers and that she never needed a vest like this anyhow. It was always meant for me. When I thank her for it later, she smiles fondly and doesn't say a word.

Faigen wakes up after days in a comatose state. He clasps my hand, elated to find me by his bedside at last. As if caring for his broken body is a sign of my undying affection for him.

"Marry me," he rasps through cracked lips.

"Not in a million winters," I say, as kindly as I can manage, applying oil to his lips and squeezing his hand. "Though I *am* delighted to see you awake again, my lord."

The twinkle in his eyes dulls slightly. "Did the knights catch her?"

I feel like I shouldn't have to ask what *her* he referred to. But I need to understand Harminy's motives. What would make her harm so many people? She was human, even related to Faigen. Why would she do such terrible things? "You showed her kindness, Theodore. Why did she do it?"

"Resentment and disappointment," he says with care. "The world was a cruel place, and Harminy's world was crueler than most. People cheated her constantly. Lords who wouldn't pay after using—and abusing—her girls. Family who cursed her name and spat on her misfortune. Then she changed and discovered Cinderrider and the thrill of her new powers."

I think of Salcom village, Faigen's home town. Did Leviathan burn that town along with Cinderrider for revenge, to devastate her family for betraying her? What about the lords in the forest? Could those have been nobles who hired her or her girls but then refused to pay? But Leviathan couldn't have done it, not alone. Her ability was ice liquid and the nobles were burned. I lean forward, hesitant to ask more questions when Faigen was still recovering but needing answers.

"Is she responsible for the deaths of Lord Darton and the other nobles? Is she the one who burned you?" I ask.

Faigen shook his head. "Once she met Cinderrider, she was like a slave. She did everything Cinderrider instructed her to do. Cinderrider wanted to burn villages. Harminy helped. She wanted to murder noblemen. Harminy picked the ones she knew from work and brought them to Cinderrider's lair. She hid them in the king's forest so they were noticed."

Not a slave, I realize. *A beta.* Alphas can have that affect. "Why did she do it?"

"Cinderrider promised Harminy that if she helped, she would be elevated from her circumstances. She said Harminy would one day be the handmaiden to the queen. But first, they had to kill Count Malandre, ruin his plans, and allow Lady Celeste to marry the king." His eyes swim with tears. "Harminy came to me for help. She tried to tell me about Cinderrider. Tried to tell me she was a changeling. But I didn't listen. I only realized her involvement the day I saw a dragon in the king's forest. I followed her and watched her change. Then she told me everything. And then Cinderrider appeared, and tried to kill me, but Harminy must have stopped her. I think she brought me back to the castle."

He asks me what happened to her, and I have to tell him that Leviathan is dead and Cinderrider is gone. The look in his eyes is haunted, the sparkle is all gone. He closes his eyes and slips his hand away from mine and is quiet for so long I think he is asleep. Then he asks, "Why Count Malandre?"

"What do you mean?"

"Why is he so important?"

I fumble for the words. "Cinderrider clearly had a political agenda. She wanted to control the throne. But we won't know how she planned to do that for a long while."

"Do you know who she is? Is she a human like Harminy was?"

"The sister of Rhydian and Celeste Berrel. They thought she was dead."

"Berrel was my friend. So was Malandre. When he asked me to wait for you by the brook in the country, I did so without question. For days. Do you know why?"

"Why?"

"Because I believe in human goodness. And I believe that my friends are good. Even when they keep to themselves. Even when they clearly have secrets."

"You could write a poem about it," I joke.

"I think I will."

EPILOGUE

WIDE BROWN EYES STARE solemnly at the world. And as the little boy gazes at a toy horse, the ghost of a smile creeps on his face. He rolls it along the edge of the porch. His ruddy cheeks and brown hair make him look almost angelic. The front door opens. An old woman hobbles out, gripping a cane in one hand. She leans to pat his head. Without warning, Nathaniel drops the toy and throws himself at the old woman's feet. The woman releases the cane and stoops to enfold him. Her gnarled body seems withered next to his stout, flushed form.

Perched on the tree beside me, Adom watches with a somber veneer.

"So, this is what happened to him." My voice breaks.

He says nothing for a moment. "Don't tell the dragons."

"Is that what you did for all the survivors? You found their families?"

He avoids my eyes. "There are two classes of survivor, Elanor. The human ones that survived the scorching when a rogue dragon burned their lands. I put those children up in my country homes where they are cared for until relatives are found who will take them in."

"What's the other group of survivors, Adom?"

"Children who, like Lord Berrel, can't acknowledge that they have a terrible and dangerous secret. Changeling children."

Every muscle in my body tightens. "And which am I, Adom? You brought me to Onyx, but I've never changed before." The blood begins to pound in my temple. "I don't think I've ever changed before."

His silence perturbs me.

"Adom, please tell me that I'm not a changeling."

"I don't know, Elanor."

"Then why would you bring me to Onyx? And why am I the only one you kept there?"

Adom looks to the east. The haunted look in his face sears my soul. Gently, he places a hand over mine. I flinch, instinctively expecting pain. He catches the look and draws back, his eyes reflecting both horror and self-loathing. "To answer that, I have to go back. Do you have time for a story?"

"As long as you don't speak riddles, like Muuth, I'll listen."

"There was once a wealthy man who had a despondent son and lovely wife. The man was dark and cruel. He beat his wife and starved his son. He made them live in squalor and only showed kindness to them when they were in public. The man began to believe that there was something wrong about them, something evil. He hurt them more and more until it became unbearable for the wife. She took the boy and they left."

"You're telling me your story."

"Yes."

"But how does it connect to me?"

"For a while, my mother and I lived peacefully, away from the abuse. But he was merciless, and he couldn't leave us alone. He heard of a dragon-killer roaming the land, murdering changelings. He hired the killer to help him track us. At last we were found, one frigid winter's night, hiding in a cabin at the edge of a woods. The killer made quick work of my mother. He beheaded her in front of me."

"Was your father there?"

"He was. But he only stayed for a few moments. To stare at the face of the woman he had married and to gloat that this was her punishment for leaving him. Then he left the killer to finish the job. I submitted. I fell over Mother and wept, but I didn't fight back. I knew I was going to die."

"So the killer spared you."

"Not quite. The killer gave me a terrible task and said if I fulfilled it, I would live."

"What was the task?"

"Mother was pregnant. The killer told me to take the baby out of the womb, go into the woods, and bury it under the permafrost. He wanted me to murder my own sibling."

"And did you?" I ask, on a breath.

Returning once again to the safety of a narrative, Adom continues, "The boy turned his hand into a claw, and ripped open the mother's womb. He took the baby out and cut the cord. There was blood everywhere, and the boy wanted to be sick. But when he heard the baby cry, when he looked into his little sister's eyes for the first time, he loved her." Adom turns hollow eyes onto mine. "He took the baby into the woods, but he didn't bury her. He walked through the forest, to a neighboring farm. He took off his cloak and wrapped the baby up tight. He knocked on the door, fled to a nearby tree, and waited for someone to answer."

"And someone did."

He nods. "Someone did. The boy didn't stay to see what happened next. He knew the killer would be waiting, and if he didn't appear soon, he would be hunted. That they would both be hunted. So he went back, and told the killer he'd completed the task. He swore his allegiance to the killer, and vowed to do whatever the killer asked of him. The man took the boy to Onyx, where he was enslaved by the dragons and worked as their servant for many years until two dragons took pity on him and taught him the dragon way. They made him strong, yet still showed him kindness. When they were murdered, the boy left and went back to Trana, and that's when he met the dragon king. I think you know most of the rest by now."

"That's a horrible story, Adom." I put a hand over his. "I'm so ashamed. I shouldn't have wasted so much energy hating you." I bend my head so he can't see the emotion in my eyes.

Adom says nothing. Nathaniel and his Grannie finish their loving embrace and enter the small house. Adom grabs the tree branch below us, folds his legs so his feet rests on the branch, and swings backward. For a moment, he hangs suspended over the ground. Then he lets go of the branch and lands on the ground with a thud. I follow his example, my mind overwhelmed.

So many questions had at last been answered these past few weeks. I don't have to creep in order to avoid Adom's wrath. I don't fear him anymore. "I'm so sorry."

Adom watches with deep, pain-filled eyes. "You must know, Elanor. I've always admired your courage, your resilience, your uncanny ability to cut right to the heart of every matter." He shudders and lets out a breath. "I wish I had an ounce of your bravery."

My whole life revolved around the prospect of revenge. I had planned to kill Adom, to avenge my family, to destroy the dragon herd. And what will that accomplish now? Absolutely nothing. I want so badly to hate someone. But not Adom. Not anymore.

We walk in silence. The world dims with the coming of twilight. Vibrant rays of orange fill the sky. A beautiful white dove rises out of the trees and soars toward the sun. "You didn't answer my question," I realize out loud. "Do you suspect I'm a changeling?"

He stops walking, his entire body tense and radiating shame. I hug my arms against the slight chill. "It's past," he says. "Please—let's not discuss it. I can't think..."

"But I have to talk about it." I step closer. He shifts away, and his face hardens. "Adom, we have all these unresolved... *things*." I search for the right words. "You hurt me. And you let me hate you. Why did you keep me on Onyx? And why didn't you tell me about your past?"

"Don't," he rasps, his voice breaking.

I sense untapped emotion boiling beneath the surface—a whole well of it he never once revealed. My heart dances in my chest. My freedom is secure. "Tell me."

"Fine. But you won't like it. The home I found you in after the dragon scorched your farmlands? It was the same home I'd left her at. The place I abandoned my infant sister."

My mouth gapes open. "You think I'm…"

He nods. "You emerged from a pile of ashes. Unscathed. Your only memories of the event were of your parents screaming at you in terror and then shoving you into a cellar."

"You think I did it. I changed and burned down my own home. Killed my own family."

"I think…it's very possible…that you have Malandre in your blood. I also think it's possible you have dragon in your blood. Between those two things, I couldn't let you go. I've tried interviewing people in your home town to see if anybody knew anything specific about the fire or your family, but so far I haven't had any luck."

I can't wrap my mind around anything else he's said. "You think I'm your sister?"

"Does that upset you?"

"Maybe." I swallow several times and draw patterns in the dirt with the toe of my boot. "Could we go back to the compound? Talk to Odeba's people again? One of them might know, might remember, something about that day. Some of them would have been around then."

He nods. "That's a good idea. Yes, once the compound is together again, I'll take you there. We'll talk to them, see if anybody knows about the fire at Avery village."

Suddenly my throat is thick and everything around me blurs.

A hand falls on mine. "Elanor?" he asks. "Are you well?"

I swallow several times. "I didn't know that was what it was called."

"I'm…so sorry." And his voice sounds broken, like he really means it.

A dark figure darts across the sky. Adom hasn't noticed it yet. I look past him, my attention fixed, fascinated with its graceful loops and twirls. It paints the sky with its tail.

"Adom." I jab at air.

He spins. "Go get the horse and return to the castle," he orders. "I'm going after her."

"I don't think so," I reply, reaching for the arrows in my sack. "I'm going with you."

He stares at me, incredulous.

"You think I'm a changeling, don't you?"

"But I've never seen you change. Believe me, I've tried my best to provoke it out of you. And you're not trained for combat. Please, Elanor. Reconsider."

"These arrows are tipped in dragonsbane, a little concoction Patience made up when she thought my life might be in danger. She's training me in shooting and on the sword as well."

"Even if you are a changeling, you haven't learned to control the change as yet."

"I don't need to change, brother." At that, he winces. "All I need is a compliant dragon who will let me catch a ride. I'll do the rest with my flaming arrows." I'm lucky to be currently wearing the dragon armor that Patience made for me underneath my servant's clothes.

After a moment, he sighs and runs past the hill, out of sight. In moments, a greenish gray figure emerges from the shadows of the mound. I race across the plains toward the serpent. The dragon bellows, its eyes transfixed on the figure in the sky. I clamber on its back, and after I'm securely clutching the folds of its neck, Adom bounds into the clouds in fast pursuit of the rogue.

I don't know if Adom is truly my brother. I can't even process how I feel about it right now. I don't know if I'm a changeling, as he suspects. After we confront this rogue, we'll go and see this Odeba again. If Adom's suspicions are correct, I'll need time to think about what it means. To be Adom's sister. To be a changeling dragon. My head reels even thinking about it.

So, instead of worrying about the *what ifs*, I say a prayer for Nathaniel and his Grannie. The new dragon doesn't appear to be heading this direction, and so far I don't smell smoke or see any charred lands. It's a good sign, but one can never be too sure when dealing with dragons.

www.ingramcontent.com/pod-product-compliance
Lightning Source LLC
Chambersburg PA
CBHW031101260626
47172CB00001B/159